A Note on the Author

JAMES RUNCIE is an award-winning film-maker and the author of seven novels. *Sidney Chambers and The Shadow of Death*, the first in 'The Grantchester Mysteries' series, was published in 2012, soon followed by *Sidney Chambers and The Perils of the Night*, and *Sidney Chambers and The Problem of Evil*. In October 2014, ITV launched *Grantchester*, a prime-time, six-part series starring James Norton as Sidney Chambers. James Runcie lives in Edinburgh.

www.jamesruncie.com
www.grantchestermysteries.com
@james_runcie

The
GRANTCHESTER MYSTERIES
SIDNEY CHAMBERS
AND
The
Forgiveness
of Sins

JAMES RUNCIE

BLOOMSBURY
LONDON · OXFORD · NEW YORK · NEW DELHI · SYDNEY

BLOOMSBURY PAPERBACKS
Bloomsbury Publishing Plc
50 Bedford Square, London, WC1B 3DP, UK
29 Earlsfort Terrace, Dublin 2, Ireland

BLOOMSBURY, BLOOMSBURY PAPERBACKS and the Diana logo
are trademarks of Bloomsbury Publishing Plc

First published in Great Britain 2015
This paperback edition first published in 2016

British Library Cataloguing-in-Publication Data
A catalogue record for this book is available from the British Library.

ISBN: HB: 978-1-4088-6220-9
PB: 978-1-4088-6227-8
ePub: 978-1-4088-6221-6

8 10 9

Typeset by Newgen Knowledge Works (P) Ltd., Chennai, India
Printed and bound in Great Britain by CPI Group (UK) Ltd, Croydon CR0 4YY

To find out more about our authors and books visit www.bloomsbury.
com. Here you will find extracts, author interviews, details of
forthcoming events and the option to sign up for our newsletters.

For Marilyn

'To love means loving the unlovable. To forgive means pardoning the unpardonable. Faith means believing the unbelievable. Hope means hoping when everything seems hopeless.'

G. K. Chesterton

Contents

The Forgiveness of Sins

ONE COLD THURSDAY MORNING, in February 1964, a man walked into the church in Grantchester and would not leave. He had fled from his Cambridge hotel after waking to discover that his wife had been stabbed to death. He had been sleeping beside her, the door and windows were locked on the inside and a knife was on the bedside table. The man could remember nothing. Now he was claiming sanctuary.

The skies were a sombre grey but the day was filled with light after three days of snow. The vicar, Canon Sidney Chambers, had just returned from walking his Labrador, his baby daughter had croup and a new curate had only recently been installed. The last thing he needed was a crisis.

The stranger had dressed in a hurry, using the clothes he had left on a chair from the previous night: an evening suit, a bow-tie that was loose and draped around the collar, and a dress-shirt. Despite the cold of that Lenten morning he was in a feverish sweat. Beads of perspiration formed beneath eyes that had still not completely woken to the day.

Sidney was sure that the ancient law of sanctuary, in which those accused of murder could be given forty days' protection from revenge and the law, had been abolished in the

1

seventeenth century. But perhaps there were exceptions, he told himself. He knew it was his Christian duty to speak to strangers and offer compassion.

'My name is Josef Madara,' the man began. He spoke with an Eastern European accent and his gaze was fixed on the middle distance, as if he was speaking to someone dead or far away. 'I am the principal violinist in the Holst Quartet. My wife, Sophie, plays the cello. We were performing last night: Tchaikovsky, Schoenberg, late Beethoven. All was good. We had some dinner afterwards and then a nightcap at the hotel. That is all I remember.'

'Were any other people with you?' Sidney asked, troubled by the intensity of the man's eyes. They appeared caught between colours.

'Only Dmitri and Natasha Zhirkov, the two other members of the quartet.'

'And they play the violin and the viola?'

'We are two couples. Five years we play together.'

'And there was nothing unusual last night?'

'Nothing. It is like a dream. Am I here now, in this church? Is this place sacred? Who are you?'

As a clergyman and now, almost officially, a part-time detective, Sidney was used to unexpected arrivals, unfortunate departures, accident, surprise and the apparently inexplicable. The key thing, he told himself, was not to rush. 'You are safe here,' he replied.

'Can I stay? I am not free from fear.'

'You are welcome to remain for this morning; but there will be evensong this afternoon. You will have to leave the chancel.'

2

'But this is sanctuary. I cannot move.'

It was too soon to press a point. 'We will come on to that,' Sidney said calmly.

'If I am here, I am safe.'

'Perhaps you would like to tell me what happened?'

Josef Madara pulled a pouch of tobacco from his pocket and began to roll a cigarette.

'Please . . .' Sidney asked. 'Not in church.'

'I know, I know. I am Catholic. It is something to do with my hands.'

'You were going to tell me . . .'

'All I remember,' the stranger continued, 'is waking up and thinking that something was wrong. I was lying on my side. Then I saw blood. At first I thought I had cut myself. Perhaps the glass by my bed had fallen. I moved but I felt something sharp and looked down . . .'

'Was it light?'

'It was grey. I could see darkness against the white of the sheet. A knife. I turned on the light. I saw Sophie and the blood. Her face was in the pillow. I sat on the bed staring. The blood was everywhere. I looked across at the knife. Then I went to the door. I was going to get help but the door was locked and I couldn't remember where we had put the key. I washed my face. I thought I might still be asleep. The water was cold. I wanted to wake up. But I couldn't. Or I was already awake. I couldn't remember anything. I got dressed. The key to the room was in the pocket of my trousers. I drew the curtains to see what the day was like. I don't know why I did that. I saw a bus. It said it was going to Grantchester. I decided to go there. I would follow its direction. Then I could be free.'

'Were the windows closed?' Sidney asked.

'There was a door on to the balcony. We never went out. There was snow. I unbolted the window and threw the knife outside. My hands were frozen and there was the blood. I closed the window. I put on my coat and saw Sophie. She had a white silk nightdress. It was red. The heart. I think an artery. I could not look any more. I turned out the light. Then I opened the door to the room. I locked it from the outside. I left the key at the reception. I did not say anything. Then I started to walk and I came to this church.'

'Why here? There are others.'

Madara's response was puzzled. Had Sidney not been listening? 'Because of the bus.'

'And you have told no one?'

The man had little left to say. 'I like the colour of the stone here; and the glass. When was the church built?'

Sidney needed more information. 'As far as you know, your wife is still in your room?'

'She must be.'

'The hotel maid will discover her body.'

'Unless Dmitri and Natasha . . . they will knock. Perhaps they will find her.'

'When were you due to leave?'

'Today.'

It was after eleven o'clock, and Josef Madara had the settled look of a man who had decided that his day's work was done. Sidney needed help and he thought of Inspector Keating. 'I must tell a friend of mine what has happened.'

'I stay here.'

'For the time being, yes.' Someone was at the North Door.

4

'It is good of you to come to my church,' Sidney concluded, trying to be as honest as he could. 'And I can assure you that we will look after you. I will have to lock the building. It is not something I like doing, but at least it is the middle of the week, and it will be for your protection. What was your room number at the hotel?'

'It was on the second floor.'

'Your name again?' Sidney checked.

'Madara. My family are originally from Latvia.'

'And I can trust you to wait here, Mr Madara?'

'The Church is my hope,' the musician replied. 'I see the cross of Jesus before me and I know that he is coming down to greet me. Against the light, he comes.'

The figure that emerged from the darkness was not, however, the Lord and Saviour of Mankind, but Malcolm Mitchell, the new curate. Having previously challenged his parishioners with Leonard Graham's intellectual demands (one of his sermons on Kierkegaard had been entirely incomprehensible), Sidney had chosen, as his replacement, a larger-than-life, cake-loving, model-railway enthusiast.

Malcolm Mitchell had a ready smile and a boyish excitement, prepared at any time for the opportunities God gave. He sat down next to Josef Madara and asked, quietly and patiently, if there was anything the man needed. Would he like a cup of tea or a glass of water? Was he warm enough? Perhaps he required a blanket? Even when the church heating was on, he said, it was hard to feel any warmth.

Sidney explained the situation, made his farewells and bicycled across the frozen meadows to his friend, Inspector Geordie Keating, at the police station. He could already hear the exasperated reaction in his head. 'Sanctuary! Murder! Why didn't you telephone? It would have been a hell of a lot quicker.'

Keating's response would have been justified but the unusual nature of the situation made Sidney want to discuss it in person. The gritters were out on the roads, the first snowmen had begun to appear across the town and Geordie was on his third cup of tea of the morning. 'This is trouble, isn't it?' he asked.

'I am afraid so. I think you will want to come with me to the Garden House Hotel.'

'I have had my breakfast, Sidney – an inadvisable kipper – and it's too early for lunch. What has happened?'

'I am not sure.'

'Even when you're not sure, you worry me.'

'Then please help me find out what's happened. You have time?'

'Sometimes I think you take advantage of our friendship.'

The hotel was a modern building on the River Cam and its distance from the police station allowed Sidney enough time to brief his friend as they walked down Mill Lane. It was a bitter morning, without birdsong, the traffic sparse and subdued as people made their way fearfully through the streets. An old man fell, a child cried, a young girl slipped, screamed and laughed. Inspector Keating asked the hotel manager if he wouldn't mind showing them up to Josef and Sophie Madara's room on the second floor. A coach party huddled at reception, reluctant to step out into the world.

As they climbed the stairs, Sidney dreaded opening the door. He imagined the sheets awry and covered in blood, a female body eviscerated: a chaos of hatred.

And so it came as something of a surprise to find a perfectly ordered room with the bed made, suitcases packed and clean towels left out. There was nothing amiss.

'Are you sure we've got the right room?' Keating asked.

'This is 211,' said the manager.

'Look. Here is Madara's violin,' Sidney noted. 'And a suit-case. Their name is on the luggage label.'

'Any sign of the wife's clothes?'

'I'll open it.'

Inside was a skirt, blouse, underwear and a make-up bag. There was, however, no sign of Sophie Madara's cello. 'Perhaps she left it at the concert hall?' Sidney suggested.

'I can't believe you are wasting my time with a nutter's cock and bull story.'

'I believed him, Geordie.'

'Sometimes I think you accept things too readily.'

Sidney had a sudden thought about Easter: the discovery of the empty tomb, the linen left unfolded like a napkin in the middle of a meal, the symbol that Jesus would return.

Keating turned to the manager. 'Has the room been cleaned?'

'I can't be sure. The covers aren't arranged in the usual way. The toiletries have yet to be replaced. Perhaps it's the new girl. I'll make some enquiries.'

'Is it possible the couple never slept here at all?'

'Someone has been in the room.'

'Then either Madara, or his dead wife, must have tidied up.'

Sidney wondered if he had been tricked. He had always thought himself a good judge of character. In fact, he prided himself on his ability to distinguish between truth and falsehood. But if Madara was not a fantasist, who would have come into a locked room and how could they have tidied up the scene of the crime without anyone noticing? More importantly, where was the victim?

The manager explained that it was a busy hotel. There had been a fiftieth birthday party the previous night. It would have been almost impossible to remove a dead body.

'I have never known anything like it,' Sidney fretted.

Keating tried to be generous. 'It's unlike you to make a mistake.'

'I would never claim to be perfect. But I felt sure Madara was telling me the truth.'

'Where's the wife then?'

'I don't know. Perhaps it didn't happen here but in his home?'

'It's more likely she's left him,' Keating continued. 'They had a row and your man dreamed that he killed her without doing anything of the sort. Did you ask if he was taking any medicine?'

'No . . .'

'And could he have been drunk, or not himself?'

'I can only judge what was put in front me: a man in distress, convinced that he had unwittingly stabbed his wife to death.'

'I don't suppose he had the knife with him.'

'He said he threw it out of the window . . .'

'Talk about a wild-goose chase . . .'

'I *believed* him, Geordie.'

'Perhaps his wife wasn't staying with him at all.' Keating turned to the hotel manager. 'Did anyone see her?'

'I can ask . . . I wasn't on duty yesterday.'

'We need to speak to whoever was. You say he slept in the room?'

The manager checked the bed. 'Someone did.'

Sidney confirmed, 'Madara told me.'

'And if his story is true then perhaps he was the one that tidied up afterwards; and he was too shocked to remember anything he was doing?'

'He told me he just left.'

'But we can't be sure of anything he has said.'

'So why make all this up, Geordie?'

'I don't know. Perhaps it's because he wanted a bit of drama, or someone to talk to. Either that or he wanted you out of the way. Perhaps he's going to rob your church?'

'It's quite an elaborate way of doing things.'

'Nothing surprises me, Sidney. Do you want me to come and talk some sense into him?'

'I don't think there's much we can do here.'

They were about to return to the staircase when a couple emerged from the room next door. They appeared furtive, as if they had been caught in the act of leaving without paying their bill. Sidney noticed that they carried musical instruments along with their luggage.

'Are you, by any chance, members of the Holst Quartet?'

'How do you know?'

'You seem to be leaving in a hurry.'

'Who are you?' the woman asked.

'Never you mind who he is,' Keating interrupted. 'I am a police officer.'

'Are you departing?' the hotel manager asked.

'Our friends seem to have left already,' Dmitri Zhirkov said.

9

'We thought that we would wait for them as we normally travel together but I suppose they've decided to go on ahead.'

He was taller and thinner than Josef Madara, with receding hair, a slight stoop and round silver-framed glasses. Sidney remembered a friend telling him that just as couples sometimes grow to look like each other, so musicians matched their instruments. You never saw a fat flautist, she said, or a thin tuba player, or even an introverted percussionist. Looking at the couple, he wondered how much this was true, and if the missing woman was as shapely as a cello.

'I think we need a bit of a chat,' said Keating.

The manager took everyone down to one of the hotel's hospitality rooms. There was more space there than in his office, he said, and they would not be disturbed for a good half hour.

The room contained the remains of the celebration from the previous evening. Deflated balloons were still tied to the chairs. Smeared plates, half-empty wine glasses and overflowing ashtrays were scattered across the tables. It needed an airing but someone had probably decided that it was too cold to do so. Sidney thought they should check how many of the guests had spent the night in the hotel and if it was worth keeping them in. He mentioned the idea to Keating but the inspector reminded him that there was no sign of any crime.

'We'll just ask some questions and then check if Sophie Madara has gone home or back to her mother's. I don't suppose you offered your man the use of a telephone?'

'Madara thinks his wife is dead and that he killed her. Why would I suggest that he telephone her?'

While coffee was poured and biscuits offered, the Zhirkov

couple repeated that they had assumed the Madaras had gone back to London. They were anxious to return themselves as they were due at an orchestra rehearsal on Monday.

'Is that the only thing you are worried about?'

'At the moment, yes.'

'Then let me give you a little more to concern you,' Keating warned.

Natasha Zhirkov leaned forward as she listened to the inspector, her dark hair cut in a bob that had been sharply styled to break up the roundness of her face. 'Josef is very highly strung, Inspector,' she explained with unusual calmness. 'I am sure he is making all this up.'

'He's . . . he's what you might call eccentric,' her husband continued.

Neither asked how their colleague was, or how he could have got himself into such a state.

As the conversation went on, Dmitri Zhirkov kept repeating that he wanted to get back to London. His wife tried to bring the interrogation to a close. 'I'm sure you don't need very much from us, Inspector. Being a police officer, you must have been able to work out what's happened?'

'Were there tensions in the quartet?' Keating persisted. 'What is Mrs Madara like? Why would her husband say that he had killed her or why might she disappear?'

'Shouldn't you organise a search before asking these questions?'

'I have already made a telephone call,' Keating assured them. Sidney knew that this was not true. They had not been apart since the discovery of the empty bedroom.

Sidney asked if the couple would come to the church and

talk to Madara. Perhaps the fugitive would tell his colleagues a little more than he had said already?

'I very much doubt it,' said Natasha.

'But he is your friend.'

'You wouldn't have thought so if you had seen us all last night.'

Dmitri Zhirkov stopped his wife. 'I hope you are not going to start on that.'

'Why not?'

Sidney checked. 'I thought you were playing in a concert?'

'We were; and it went perfectly well. It was what happened afterwards . . .'

Keating interrupted. 'You had an argument.'

Natasha Zhirkov was looking out through the steaming windows to the snow on the grass, the parked cars. It was a day that had already seen the best of the light.

'What was it about?' Sidney asked.

'It's awkward,' said Natasha Zhirkov, as the hotel maids entered the room and began to take down the balloons, clear away the plates and empty the ashtrays. One of them turned on the Hoover to clean the carpet.

'I never imagined it was going to be easy,' Keating replied. 'If it was simple we would have finished by now.'

'You might as well tell him,' Dmitri Zhirkov cut in. 'He'll find out soon enough. This bloody vicar probably knows already.'

'I have an idea,' Sidney began, without quite being able to decide if he did or not. It always happened when he was tired. He would begin sentences and then hope that the sense would come to him halfway through what he was saying.

'Josef thought that we should break up the quartet . . .' Natasha began, perhaps hoping that the noise of the hoovering would drown out her words.

'And why was that?' Sidney asked.

'He blamed our playing; even when it was Sophie making the mistakes.'

'And you told him so.'

'We hinted . . .' her husband added.

'But he didn't understand . . .'

'So we spelt it out . . .'

'And then we all started talking at the same time. It wasn't very edifying.'

'You can't unsay things after an argument, can you?' Dmitri Zhirkov concluded.

Keating aimed for clarity. 'But you don't think this dispute could have led to murder?'

'I don't know, Inspector. You can't always predict these things, I imagine. And if Josef did what he said he did . . .'

'He hasn't actually confessed,' said Sidney, surprised that their colleague's alleged death should have such little effect on the couple.

'Then what has he said?' Natasha Zhirkov asked. 'How much has he told you?'

Sidney offered to go ahead and check that the fugitive was still in the church and that Malcolm was coping. He didn't want to repeat the hotel experience by leading Inspector Keating to a second venue where someone had vanished; although he did half hope that his sanctuary-seeking guest might have gone back to London. Perhaps the eccentric musical couple had reunited after an unusual tiff, a terrible night and a hopeless fantasy?

No more snow had fallen but, with a further drop in temperature, any slush had frozen. It was too risky to bicycle home. It was safer for Sidney to walk with his head against the wind across the meadows. His hands were cold, his feet were damp, his cheeks red and his ears so frosted that he was not sure he could hear properly. He had forgotten his hat and he remembered his father telling him how much body heat escaped through the head. There was no such thing as bad weather, only the wrong clothes.

'As soon as you feel the cold, it's too late,' he had told his son. Well, it was certainly too late now.

Sidney tried to think of the sermon he had to prepare for the first Sunday in Lent. He wondered if he could utilise the surprise he had felt at seeing the empty hotel room and imagine the shock Mary Magdalene experienced on finding the empty tomb of Jesus.

It must have been astonishing to have expectations so subverted; to be so bereaved, confused, lost and then finally exhilarated to discover the resurrection. How could that shock of faith be re-created today, Sidney thought, in, say, an anonymous hotel room, a home, a school or a factory? What would it mean to tell Josef Madara that the wife he thought had been dead was not lying in their room but alive again, however miraculous that might seem; that hope could remain even in the most desperate of situations?

His momentary optimism was dispelled by the familiar sight of Helena Randall talking to the churchwarden. An ambitious journalist from the *Cambridge Evening News*, she at least had prepared for the weather and was dressed in a duffel coat, wellington boots, fur mittens, what looked like a Russian fur hat, and a long scarf.

'Since when did you start locking your church?' she asked. 'I thought it was supposed to be open for prayer at all times. Your lovely new curate won't let me in. He's very diligent.'

'How did you hear about this?' Sidney replied, determined not to let her get the upper hand.

'I am an investigative journalist. Have you forgotten?'

'Did Geordie tell you?' (Helena had been flirtatious with the inspector for years and Keating still had a soft spot for her.)

'I never reveal my sources.'

'What do you want?'

'Access, if you don't mind.'

'You are not normally so keen to enter a place of worship.'

'Well you don't *normally* provide anything so intriguing.'

'I am not sure it is our role to entertain,' Sidney replied. 'There are other venues that await your pleasure . . .'

'We have spoken about this before, Canon Chambers. The public has a limited appetite for religion, particularly when the atmosphere in your church is so drearily Victorian.'

'Matters of morality, eternal life and the certainty of death are hardly dreary.' Sidney looked for his keys and began to unlock the door.

'You can't take the public's interest for granted,' Helena continued. 'They have so much more to do with their leisure time these days. They're also less afraid of eternal damnation. The old frighteners don't work any more. Are you going to let me come in or not?'

The police joined them before Sidney could answer. On

seeing Helena, Keating muttered an 'I might have known' before announcing that Dmitri and Natasha Zhirkov had asked to talk to their colleague at the station. They wanted time to collect their thoughts. In the meantime he had telephoned Inspector Williams in London, who had agreed to send a couple of men round to the Madara flat to see if there was any sign of the missing wife.

'Is our man still inside?' he asked.

'I haven't been able to ascertain,' Sidney replied.

'What's kept you?'

'I have been speaking to Miss Randall.'

'I suppose it's simpler to have her working with us rather than against us.'

'I've always proved my worth in the past,' Helena smiled. 'And you both love me really. You're just reluctant to admit it.'

'Don't count on it.'

'You'll miss me when I'm gone.'

'Where are you off to?' Sidney asked.

'I can't stay in this backwater much longer.'

'Cambridge isn't a backwater.'

'It's hardly London.'

'You want the big city and the bright lights?' Sidney asked.

'One big scoop and I'm there,' Helena replied. 'And this could be it.'

'I wouldn't be so hasty,' Keating snapped back. 'All we've got so far is an empty room, a mad fantasist and an unlikely story. You can wait here while we talk to him and then we'll decide what to do.' He turned to Sidney and gestured to the open doorway. 'Shall we?'

They walked into the nave. The soft winter light took away

16

all sense of modernity. It could have been a hundred years ago. Malcolm Mitchell was reading quietly in a pew, pretending that the situation was perfectly normal. He had fetched a blanket and given the fugitive a cup of tea and a slice of cake. Josef Madara was praying.

Sidney wondered if the stranger had heard their approach and deliberately positioned himself in a state of penitence. Tears had fallen over his cheeks and his eyes (viridian) now appeared large and sorrowful. He looked like a cross between an El Greco painting and Alan Bates in *Whistle Down the Wind*.

'Did you find her?' he asked, without looking at his visitors. 'Is she still there?'

'She is not,' Sidney replied.

'Then God must have taken her.'

Inspector Keating stepped forward to introduce himself. 'I think we have to find a more plausible explanation.'

'I left her in the hotel room.'

'And was her cello still there?' Keating asked.

'It was. She never leaves it anywhere.'

'Well it's gone now.'

Keating was about to ask the man to describe the crime scene when Sidney jumped ahead of him. He wondered how Madara had met Sophie, how long they had been married and had she loved anyone before him? Did she have fans and admirers? Were there things that she never told him about? Did she have secrets? How much time did they spend apart? Did she ever go missing and did he always know where she was?

Madara kept to his story. His wife was the sweetest woman. She was a Madonna and he was the sinner.

17

'In killing her?'

'No,' the man corrected himself. 'Before then.'

'What do you mean?'

'It is too much to explain. Many terrible things.'

'An affair?'

'You know?'

'With Natasha Zhirkov?' Sidney asked.

'Yes.'

'And your wife knew?' Keating checked, impressed by Sidney's intuition.

'I'm not sure.'

'Did Dmitri Zhirkov?'

'Definitely not.'

'Well, whether he does or not, at least three out of four of you knew,' said Keating. 'And if your wife really is dead, then every surviving member of the quartet has a motive for killing her. I think you'd better come with me to the station.'

'But here is sanctuary.'

Keating spared Sidney the trouble of answering. 'We are no longer in the Middle Ages, Mr Madara. Other people need to come to church too. You can't have it all to yourself.'

'There can be no forgiveness. I am a miserable sinner.'

'Then we can talk about your sin at the station.'

Helena was waiting in the church porch. She was writing in a pair of fingerless gloves that must have been under her mittens and she looked up from a shorthand notebook that was filling up fast. Sidney wondered how much, if anything, she had overheard. 'Can I come too?' she asked.

'Of course not,' Keating answered, all too testily. 'We'll brief you when we can. Don't get your hopes up.'

'Charming. Have you anything to go on?'

'I am sure you can make it up.'

'I'd rather have the facts.'

'And so, Miss Randall, would we.'

Once they reached St Andrew's Street, Keating told Sidney what was on his mind. 'How much is this wish fulfilment? If Sophie Madara really is dead, then why is your man telling us this? And if he didn't kill her, then how did one of the others, or anyone else for that matter, get into a locked room? Why didn't Madara wake up during the attack; and why wasn't he killed at the same time?'

'Whatever his story,' Sidney replied, 'we have to find the wife. If she is dead then it's a full-scale murder investigation. And if she's alive . . .'

'Perhaps she can tell us what the hell everyone is playing at,' Keating completed the sentence. 'Have you ever known the like?'

It was mid-afternoon by the time Sidney returned to the vicarage for a baked potato and some cold ham. His mood was not improved by the fact that they had run out of chutney. What he really wanted was a warming stew and a hot toddy but it was Lent, he was not drinking, and he was in no position to make demands.

Hildegard had abandoned all hope that they might eat together and was settling their daughter for an afternoon nap. Anna was recovering from croup. Neither parent had been getting very much sleep, walking the floor in the night, holding their child close. (She was not yet three months old; a baby who was only just beginning to respond to feelings other than hunger and pain, contentment and sleep.) What was Sidney doing involving himself in this latest incident?

'I don't have any choice, my darling. Josef Madara just walked into church.'

'Can't Inspector Keating deal with it?'

'He needs my help.'

'I need it too. I am tired.'

'Is something the matter?'

'I don't think so. I was worried. It's nothing; only the lack of sleep perhaps.'

'Nothing?'

'Sidney . . . do you think we will ever leave this place?'

'We can't stay for ever.'

'And where will we go?'

'Wherever the Lord takes us.'

'He moves in a mysterious way?' Hildegard asked.

'Although not as mysteriously as some of his subjects. I wish there wasn't so much to do. It all gets in the way of being with you.'

'I should say I am used to it. But I don't want to get to a stage where I don't mind.'

'Neither do I.'

'I don't mean to worry you,' Hildegard continued. 'And I'm sorry. I don't like complaining. At least we are tolerant of each other's faults.'

'We are.'

She smiled. 'Even if one of us does have more than the other.'

'Life, God willing, is long, Hildegard. These things even up over time. I hope you're not keeping score?'

'I am. One day there will be a great reckoning. One that will be even more frightening for you than the Last Judgement.'

'I look forward to it, then.'

'Why, Sidney?'

'Because when it is all over the subsequent peace will be wonderful.'

He kissed his wife and made for the study. He was behind on his Easter preparation and this new case had only made the situation worse. He thought of Harold Macmillan's explanation of the precariousness of political life and the unpredictable nature of events that could destabilise the most organised routine. No matter how diligent he was as a vicar there was no end to the amount of time he could spend on the spiritual care of his congregation. Unlike a builder or a decorator who could stop in the hours of darkness or when a project was over, the labour of being a priest was never complete.

He cleared out the grate and began to lay a fire. As he did so, he could hear Hildegard singing Anna a lullaby.

> *'Guten Abend, gut' Nacht*
> *Mit Rosen bedacht*
> *Mit Näglein besteckt*
> *Schlüpf unter die Deck.'*

His wife had such a beautiful voice. What was he doing, sitting at his desk worrying about a case in which he had already become involved when he could have been enjoying the company of his wife and daughter? What had happened to his priorities?

*   *   *

At teatime the following afternoon, as they were keeping warm by the kitchen stove, Sidney realised that his workload could be lightened if he asked his curate to preach that Sunday. Malcolm was covered in cake crumbs and had been hoping that his life at that moment consisted of little more than the acquisition of a second slice of Victoria sponge. Discombobulated by the lurch back into work, he tried to find an excuse.

'I've only just arrived.'

'We need to let the congregation have a good look at you,' Sidney encouraged.

'It's rather soon, don't you think?'

'All the more reason to get on with it. You can make an impact . . .'

The telephone rang.

'I'm not making much headway with the lunatic,' Keating began. 'Technically we have to release him but the man doesn't want to go. He keeps saying he is a sinner. If we can just find the wife. I've asked Dr Robinson to come over and have a look. We might need a psychiatrist. Everything about this case is the exact opposite of how things normally are. Most people shut up. This man's telling us everything. But nothing makes sense. What the devil do you think is going on? Has he done in his wife and hidden her, or has she run away?'

'The London boys are sure she's not at home?'

'Of course she's not. A neighbour told Williams's men there's been no sign of her since last Wednesday.'

'The day of the concert. But when were they last seen in the hotel together?'

'Around ten at night. A barmaid did notice the row, but they went outside. She didn't know much about it because the party was a bit of a riot. The birthday boy was a rugby player.'

'So what about Sophie Madara? Did anyone see her on the first morning trains?' Sidney asked. 'And where is her cello? If she was murdered then why is the instrument not in the hotel room?'

On the Sunday morning Malcolm Mitchell gave his first sermon. Appropriately for Lent, it was a meditation on Christ's words 'Father forgive them for they know not what they do': an investigation of the tension between sin and conscience.

'Was Jesus correct?' Malcolm asked. 'Perhaps he was being overgenerous? Are we to take his words at face value?'

Steady, Sidney thought.

'We *do* know what we do,' Malcolm assured his listeners. 'We must be responsible for our actions. A baby is not born in sin; people are not murderers from birth. We have all been given a conscience. We know that it is wrong to torture a cat . . .'

It was old-fashioned good-and-evil preaching. Men and women should instinctively know, the new curate argued, right from wrong, and if they did not, then they could be taught.

Malcolm's predecessor Leonard Graham, who was now vicar of St Luke's, Holloway, had come to pay a visit. At the parish breakfast he congratulated the new man while Sidney stayed on to discuss a few pressing issues with the church-warden. (There was a problem with the church guttering, complaints had been made about the Sunday School teacher, and they were behind on the Easter garden because of the snow.)

'It appeared to go down quite well,' Malcolm answered

before taking a large bite out of a buttered roll. 'Your former housekeeper said she enjoyed it very much.'

'Mrs Maguire? She's never been that keen on sermons.'

'I told her that I had heard reports of her baking skills.'

'Ah . . .'

'And she offered to make me her "walnut special".'

'That normally takes years. Well done, Malcolm. And especially on the sermon.'

'I've preached it before . . .'

'I know a vicar who has a two-year cycle: one hundred and four little homilies with a few extra for high days and holidays. It leaves him free to get on with his hobbies. Do you have one?'

'I am something of a model-railway enthusiast. I think it is because I was an only child. I had to learn to amuse myself.'

Leonard smiled. 'I expect you get rather carried away.'

Hildegard joined them. 'What are you men talking about now?'

'Trains, Mrs Chambers. Malcolm has plans to run his tracks all over the house.'

'I never said any such thing . . .'

'Before you know it there'll be a branch line from the kitchen through to the dining–room. Where Beeching cuts, Mitchell reinstalls . . .'

The curate was shocked by the teasing. 'I don't think the family are ready for anything like that . . .'

Hildegard was conciliatory. 'Anna might like the trains when she gets a bit older. Although you will probably have moved on by then, Malcolm.'

'I've only just arrived.'

Leonard picked up a biscuit and checked its snap before asking, almost casually, 'Any criminal investigations yet?'

'It's funny you should ask that . . .'

'Home at last,' called Sidney, stamping the snow off his feet before hearing that his new curate had made a conquest of Mrs Maguire. He had noticed Malcolm's appetite and wondered whether he would offer up the walnut cake for everyone in the vicarage or keep it in his room for secret scoffing in times of need.

Hildegard prepared the lunch and Leonard asked about the Madara case. He extemporised on the obsessions of married murderers with reference to Shakespeare's *Othello*, Tolstoy's *Kreutzer Sonata* and the complete works of Dostoevsky. Then he began to expand on the theme of imaginary death as wish fulfilment, the replacement of fatality with fantasy as psychological protection and the possibility that Madara might be suffering from Munchausen syndrome.

'Please,' Hildegard interrupted on returning to the room. 'Don't start giving my husband any more ideas. Sidney, there is a lady waiting to see you. I've shown her into your study. She said it was urgent.'

'Who?'

'A Mrs Zhirkov.'

'From the Holst Quartet?'

'Yes,' Hildegard answered. 'It's an unusual name.'

'Why?' Sidney asked.

'Gustav Holst is not known for his string quartets . . .'

Natasha Zhirkov told them that the first music they had all played together was an arrangement of the Jupiter suite from *The Planets*, and that Josef Madara, like Holst, had Latvian ancestors.

'He says that it is a recognition of his past. Holst's music always reminds him of the first time he met his wife. It would be romantic if not for the present circumstances . . .'

Once priest and musician were alone, Natasha Zhirkov confessed to her affair with Madara and said that she had always been scared of his wife. In fact she was more worried that Sophie was alive rather than dead.

If that was the case, Sidney asked, why would a woman make her husband think that he had murdered her?

'To get him out of the way.'

'For what purpose?'

'To give him an alibi. To make sure he isn't blamed for what she's about to do.'

'And what is that?'

From the drawing-room came the sound of Hildegard playing the Mozart Rondo in A minor, a piece of such plangent grace that it seemed to reach beyond the cares of the world.

'I think Sophie's going to kill me.'

'What?'

'That is why I have come to see you, Canon Chambers. I'm scared. I need your protection.'

'Unbelievable' was the first word Keating offered in response to Sidney's account of events. They had met for their usual Thursday-night backgammon game in the RAF bar of the Eagle. 'As I said to you, most of the time people keep things to themselves. This lot are telling us too much.'

'Do you think it's deliberate?'

'They are certainly confusing us. But we have no evidence

that any crime has been committed and we can't act on fantasy.'

'Except that a woman is missing.'

'And another thinks she's for the chop. That could be a lie too. Perhaps Josef Madara and Natasha Zhirkov are still having the affair and they are planning to get rid of Dmitri Zhirkov as well. It's definitely some kind of smokescreen, even though nothing at all may have happened. It's all right for you; you're used to mystery. That's part of your faith . . .'

'And your job.'

'Not that I'm getting very far. It's ironic, isn't it? Normally people can't wait to get out of a police station. I've got a man here who is desperate to stay in. Do you think it's the weather?'

The next day, Sidney returned to the police station and asked Josef Madara about his affair with Natasha Zhirkov.

'Have you ever done such a thing, Canon Chambers?'

'I am asking you.'

'In my country, priests do not even marry.'

'I am aware of that. It doesn't mean that those who do have a roving eye.'

'And you don't?'

'I admit to liking women,' Sidney replied carefully. 'That is part of my job. Loving people.'

'That is simple.'

'But it must be the right kind of love. Would you like to tell me, Josef?'

'About my sin?'

'I am a priest. It seems right.'

'A confessional.'

'If you like.'

Madara looked away, not wanting to make eye contact. 'It was after a rehearsal. Natasha wanted to practise a particular section.'

'Without the others? In a string quartet?'

'She had been asked to play in a chamber concert as a guest with some friends. It was the Holst lyric movement for viola and small orchestra. I offered to go over it with her.'

'Is it difficult?'

'It was the last work the composer finished before his death. When you play you feel he knows this. It would make a good ballet. We talked about how to release emotion while controlling technique. It is sometimes difficult; when you try too hard the right playing doesn't always come.'

'So you told Natasha she should be calm . . .'

'I did. The need to be relaxed and in control. And then, of course . . .'

'Did your wife find out what happened?'

'She suspected. Perhaps that is worse. It was a mistake. We both knew. I am ashamed.'

Sidney tried a different tack. 'Where is your wife now, Josef?'

'Why do you ask? You must understand that I do not know. I thought she was dead. I saw her. She was beside me. The blood . . .'

'You have told us.'

'And you don't believe me?'

'I believe it was what you *thought* you saw. What you *actually* saw may be different.'

'You think I imagined it?'

'I don't "think" anything at this stage, apart from the need to

28

discover your wife's whereabouts. Have you ever imagined an alternative, that she might not be dead?'

'I know what I saw.'

'Did Sophie ever want to end her life?'

'You should not ask these things.'

'When were you happiest?'

'It was when we were first married. We lived in the country-side, on the edge of a small town, not far from London. It has a church with a medieval spire and a windmill. The countryside is very close. You can walk out into the fields. Sophie and I, we had a little almshouse near the windmill. Now you can rent it. When we return we like to remember how we once were.'

'It is good to be grateful.'

Josef smiled. 'When we were young we were only worried about money, but we had each other and no one knew where to find us. Music was our refuge from the noise of the world. We were good when we were alone. Some marriages are like that, don't you think? When you have no need for anyone else, you can protect yourself from pain.'

'But you can't live like that all the time.'

'Some people do. It is only when you meet other people that there's trouble.'

'As you found.'

'And who knows the price I am paying now?' Madara asked. 'Help me, Canon Chambers. I have told you everything.'

When Sidney returned home, he found that Hildegard was not that interested in his news. She was clearing out the fire, Anna was in her Moses basket, and there was no sign of any food. When he enquired, his wife stood up and suggested that they employ an au pair girl. The current situation was not working. 'I know you have your work, Sidney, and I have mine and many people think it might be easier if I was only a house-wife . . .'

'Not me . . .'

'. . . but we cannot go on like this. You are not able to provide the time that Anna needs and I cannot do everything on my own. Even the dog is neglected.'

'I don't know about that. I take Byron everywhere. It's only that it's been very cold recently.'

'And so he has been at home as well. I cannot work only when Anna sleeps. And at night I am so tired. I've written to my sister. She will be able to find someone. If we can find a girl who needs to perfect her English then it need not cost so much and Anna will speak German too.'

'Then it will be two of you against one of me.'

'It is not a fight, Sidney. And you are forgetting Malcolm.'

'He is out most of the time.'

'Not if there is any cake to be had.'

'I will have a word with him about that.'

'It's not his fault. And most of the time it's his cake. The ladies in the village like him. They say that at last they have found a priest who has time for them.'

'They mean that I don't?'

Hildegard gave her husband one of her looks. 'They say you have more urgent things to do.'

'It is for *their* benefit. I am helping to keep the peace. It's hardly my fault if they insist on murdering each other.'

'Perhaps if you struck the fear of God into them they would stop?'

'I don't know if that's the sort of thing for this day and age. It feels medieval.' Sidney mused for a moment. 'God's mighty thunderbolt has had its day; struck into the long grass by the cricket bat of destiny.'

'You can change Anna, *mein Lieber*. That will cheer you up. I don't want you forgetting all about her . . .'

Sidney picked up his daughter and took her into the bathroom. Something was different. He realised that it was the loo paper. Now he remembered. Malcolm had suggested that they should use appropriate liturgical colours: green for the season of Trinity, purple for Lent and Advent, and pink for saints' days.

Had Hildegard agreed to this? Or was it Mrs Maguire? What was Sidney going to do about his curate's plans to alter his life, step by step? He had started with cake, loo rolls and model railways. Where was it all going to end?

He began to change his daughter's nappy. This was something he *did* do, even if it wasn't very often. He sang quietly as he did so. It was a hymn rather than a lullaby. He didn't know quite why. Perhaps it didn't matter.

> 'A safe stronghold our God is still
> A trusty shield and weapon.'

He wondered how soon Anna would start to crawl and discover a world for herself, moving away from him, even when she was still a baby.

> 'He'll help us clear from all the ill
> That hath us now o'ertaken.

The ancient prince of hell
Hath risen with purpose fell;
Strong mail of craft and power
He weareth in this hour;
On earth is not his fellow.'

He had just reached the end of the hymn and picked up his daughter once more, clean and fresh and smelling of baby powder, when the doorbell rang.

It was Helena Randall.

'Don't look like that,' she said, on seeing Sidney's face.

'I think we are about to eat.'

'It's very good of me to visit. I could have telephoned.'

'Would you like some supper?'

'That's kind of you but there's no time.'

'What do you mean?'

'Josef Madara has escaped from the police station.'

'Then I imagine Geordie is pleased. I thought he wanted him to leave.'

'On his terms rather than those of the suspect,' Helena replied.

'Perhaps Madara will lead us to his wife?'

'You think he knows where she is and that all of this has been some kind of hoax?'

Sidney never found it easy to think on the doorstep, especially when holding a baby. The conversation, like the location, was neither one thing nor the other. 'I am not sure Madara knows what he knows . . .'

'Why do you think he's gone now, when he could have left earlier?' Helena asked.

'Because he needed the police station as an alibi?'

'But they have discovered no crime.'

'So far. Remember that we have also failed to discover a wife. We need to speak to Geordie.'

'That's why I've come to collect you.' Helena checked her notebook. 'Do you think it's possible that the wife, if she is still alive, could be in danger?'

'You mean Madara might plan to kill her now, *after* he has confessed?' Sidney replied.

'Either that or he could be after Dmitri Zhirkov. Then he could be with Natasha at last.'

'But if that is the case, why kill his wife first, or come up with such a story?'

'Your supper is ready,' Hildegard called out.

'Perhaps Madara is not entirely in control of his destiny?' Helena asked.

'You mean he is being used?'

'By his wife, or Natasha Zhirkov, or by persons unknown.'

'It seems a very complicated way of doing things,' Sidney answered. 'Isn't it just simpler to think that Josef Madara killed his wife but has blotted out everything that happened afterwards?'

'I suppose so.'

'Do you happen to know if he ever got to see a psychiatrist?' Sidney asked.

'SUPPER,' Hildegard repeated.

'I would like to see the notes if he did.'

'IT WILL BE COLD.'

'Can you come with me then?'

'Do you think I could have my supper first?'

'I will wait outside,' Helena replied. 'I've brought my car. You've got ten minutes . . .'

'Ten minutes?' Hildegard asked when Sidney finally arrived in the kitchen. 'Is that all the time you're prepared to spare your wife and daughter?'

Inspector Keating confessed that he had made it easy for Madara to leave. The suspect had stayed long enough, there was nothing to charge him with, and no evidence of any wrongdoing apart from his story. Now he was hoping that Madara would lead the police to his missing wife.

'And has he?'

'Not so far.'

'Why not?' Helena asked.

'We lost him.'

Sidney could not quite believe the incompetence. 'Surely he has no money and no form of transport? It can't be that hard to keep track of him.'

'Are you doing this to throw us off the case?' Helena challenged.

'We know where he lives. If he has to earn money he will play with that Zhirkov couple. Musicians have to advertise, don't they? All we have to do is keep a watch on his flat and a close eye on the papers. You can both help me do that, can't you? After all, it's your job, Miss Randall.'

'I write for the papers. I don't necessarily read them.'

'Perhaps you might learn something. See what your rivals are up to.'

'Did Madara have an accomplice?' Sidney asked, thinking of Natasha Zhirkov, and heading off an irrelevant spat.

'We think he hitched a lift.'

'Where to?'

'London probably. But then when we stopped the car we thought he was travelling in, the driver denied all knowledge.'

'A decoy?'

'Nothing as complicated.'

'So what are we going to do?'

'Wait.'

On the second Sunday of Lent, and while he was obeying Keating's instructions to do nothing until there was further news, Sidney preached a sermon on the nature of penitence.

'What is true contrition?' he asked as he thought about Madara's confession ten days previously. Could a man be *too* contrite, making a confession that was so out of proportion to the crime that it became a form of attention-seeking? Sometimes the admission of sin could almost be a kind of vanity.

The congregation looked confused. What had this got to do either with their sins or the message of Easter?

Sidney knew, from complaints about Leonard's sermons, that his parishioners did not like moral ambiguity. Stan Headley, the local blacksmith, had even requested: 'Don't make it too hard for us, Reverend. We just want to know where we stand. It's like knowing how much money you've got in the bank. We're just coming for a check-up.'

However, once he had started off, it was hard to backtrack. 'I want to talk to you this morning about proportional penitence,' he announced, only to see Mrs Maguire casting her eyes heavenwards in despair.

'Any request for forgiveness is not the property of the perpetrator alone . . .' he continued. 'It must be freely given *and freely received*. The confession and the appeal must allow room for the victim – if he or she were still alive – *to forgive with a whole heart*.' Sidney immediately regretted that he had brought the idea of murder into his sermon.

He had begun to emphasise his phrases in order to make it clear but worried that he might be sounding patronising. Malcolm Mitchell didn't seem to have this problem, producing culinary metaphors to aid understanding. He would look at all the women and explain divine spirituality as being like air in the cake mix. You had to let it breathe before it rose. (God, in his eyes, was clearly some kind of divine baker.)

'There has to be a mutual understanding of what has taken place . . .' Sidney went on. 'A time for recognition and a place for silence: reflection on events in all humility. Forgiveness may be absolute but it cannot be taken for granted. It must be re-acknowledged each time we sin. But this is vital. Without forgiveness, we are condemned to the past. Forgiveness gives us our future.'

'You got there in the end,' his curate teased in the vestry afterwards.

Mike Standing, the treasurer, was sorting through the collection. 'Your words went over my head like migrating geese.' He began to wheeze when he bent over to count the money.

'I don't suppose I need to declare my own offering?' the curate asked.

'What is it?'

'Walnut cake from Mrs Maguire.'

Sidney stopped as he took off his surplice. 'So it's true?'

Mike Standing was impressed. 'You've got them all eating out of your hand.'

36

'Or rather, he's eating out of theirs.'

'How is your investigation coming along?' Malcolm asked. 'I was worried you were sounding a bit distracted.'

'I wasn't distracted *at all*,' Sidney said fiercely. 'But it is frustrating.'

'Anything I can do to help?'

Sidney could not think of a single thing his curate could do that might bring light to the darkness. He missed Leonard Graham.

Later that day, while walking Byron, he was surprised by Inspector Keating pulling over in his car.

'Get in. Both of you.'

'What?'

'Now.'

'But . . .'

'There's been a murder after all.'

'Sophie Madara?'

'No. She's still missing. It's the other one.'

'Natasha Zhirkov?'

'That's right. God knows what's going on.'

Sidney took in the news. 'She was frightened that something was going to happen to her.'

'Well it has.'

'Where and when?' Sidney asked.

'London. Her flat. Looks like the husband did it.'

'How?'

'Stabbed. Not unlike the way Sophie Madara is supposed to have died.'

'Could Madara have done it?'

'I don't think so. It seems he was still in police custody at the time of the murder.'

'He has his alibi then . . .'

'He does.'

'But he left as soon as the deed was done?'

'A coincidence.'

'I'm not so sure,' said Sidney.

Keating sighed. 'You mean someone got a message to him telling him that he didn't need his alibi any more?'

'Possibly.'

'It sounds far-fetched. It also would have had to be some kind of inside job. Who else would have known about the Zhirkov murder?'

'Perhaps he overheard a telephone call?'

'To the police station? From his cell? I don't think that's likely.'

'Or a young journalist told him . . .'

'Helena doesn't know anything.'

'She soon will.'

'Even she doesn't find out about events before they happen.'

'Then perhaps it is a coincidence. Any pointers?'

'It's the husband. Dmitri Zhirkov. There's a knife with his fingerprints all over it. The victim was stabbed in the neck from behind and then in the throat. No sign of a forced entry. Natasha Zhirkov knew her killer. Nothing was stolen. But keep a lid on it. Williams is not saying anything publicly. And tell Helena that she can't report any of this . . .'

'She's already asked if she can have an exclusive.'

'You have to admire her tenacity. Can you come down to London with me, Sidney?'

'When are you going?'

'First thing in the morning.'

'It's my day off.'

'Perfect. You've got no excuse. I'll drop you back home. Think of the time I've saved you.'

Dmitri Zhirkov was all over the place. He confessed to the murder of his wife, then retracted his story claiming manslaughter, before changing his mind one more time and saying that he was innocent. In his anger and panic he asserted that his wife had attacked him and he was acting in self-defence. Natasha had railed at him, provoked him, told him things about an affair with Madara that he hadn't thought possible. He was also furious the police had let that bastard Josef Madara escape from custody. Everyone was conspiring against him.

Natasha had been of unsound mind when she slept with Madara, he shouted, and now he was going mad; driven to insanity by his colleagues. He could not be expected to work with any of them any more. But it didn't matter what he had done because he would always be a musician. He had talent. It was God-given. Nothing could take it away. Genius, he shouted, excused all sin.

Sidney wondered how Dmitri Zhirkov had worked himself up into such a state. He had probably confronted his wife about her affair with Josef Madara and the row had escalated in the kitchen, where a block of carving knives was unhelpfully at the ready.

Only one thought troubled Sidney. When Natasha Zhirkov had first come to see him she had been scared of the missing

Sophie Madara rather than her husband. Might Sophie still be involved? Could she have committed the murder on behalf of Dmitri Zhirkov or even have framed him?

Sidney was in the midst of speculation when a police officer told him that he was wanted on the telephone. He hoped it was not news from home because he was already late and he didn't want Hildegard to tell him off again.

'Sidney?'

It was Malcolm, his curate, on the line. His voice sounded distant, almost strangulated.

'Is something the matter?'

'I'm not sure.'

'Is Hildegard all right? Anna?'

Malcolm Mitchell coughed. He appeared to be choking.

'For God's sake, man, what is it?'

'You know that man seeking sanctuary?'

'Madara? What about him?' Sidney asked, realising that his curate was not in the process of being garrotted but his mouth was full of cake.

'He's back.'

Josef had gone first to the church and then to the police station as he had 'many things' he wanted to confess. The police officers had told him of the death of his former lover, Natasha Zhirkov, at which point he had wanted to run away. He had been prevented from doing so by the quick thinking of one of the more experienced sergeants who did not want to witness another of Keating's tantrums.

After they had ordered in their mugs of tea and bacon sandwiches, Sidney and the inspector took it in turns to ask Josef about his whereabouts. Had he been to the Zhirkov home? How had Dmitri found out about his wife's affair?

Sidney tried to be clear. 'I think we need to know if either you or your missing wife could have murdered Natasha Zhirkov.'

'How could I have killed her? I was at the police station.'

'Could you wife have done so?'

'She is dead. It must be Dmitri.'

'And do you think your colleague is the angry, murdering type?'

'No. But any man can be made to sin. That is his tragedy.'

'And you are not surprised?'

'If you live with a knowledge of human suffering then you learn to accept fate.'

'But we can take steps . . .' Sidney said, not wanting to get into a discussion of the nature of human responsibility and the problem of free will.

Keating tried to be specific. 'We are fairly sure Dmitri Zhirkov killed his wife. Probably because he found out that she had an affair with you. Were you still involved with her?'

'No.'

'You don't appear very upset by your lover's death.'

'I am still grieving for the loss of my wife.'

'But we do not know she is dead.'

'I know what I saw.'

'Tell me about Natasha Zhirkov,' Sidney continued. 'Why do you think she might have been afraid of your wife?'

'My wife was a very strong woman. Like Dmitri, she had a temper.'

'Natasha Zhirkov was more frightened of your wife than her own husband?'

'I was more frightened of her too.'

'How did Sophie react when she found out about your affair?'

'It doesn't matter. She is dead.'

'Did your wife threaten you?' Sidney asked.

'Not me . . . no . . . not me . . . we loved each other.'

'But about Mrs Zhirkov: what did she say about her?'

'She said that if I didn't stop it she would finish it all for ever.'

'She did?' Keating cut back in. 'And did she say how?'

'She said she would stab Natasha through the heart.'

There was no peace at the vicarage. Anna had had a bad night, Byron needed walking, Mrs Maguire was cleaning the bathroom with intimidating vigour, and Malcolm appeared to be busy with a new section of railway line. He had got it on the cheap from one of the parishioners whose son had left for university.

The only quiet to be found was in Sidney's study. He retreated to think through events and to listen to a new recording of *The Black Saint and the Sinner Lady* by Charles Mingus. He had bought it as a little treat from Dobell's in Charing Cross Road on his last trip to London. Impressed with the clergyman's taste, the manager had ordered it in from America.

During the second track, Malcolm interrupted to ask for some advice about his next sermon. He stood in the doorway with a slice of poppyseed cake on a plate and explained that he was going to develop the theme of nature versus nurture. Was it possible, he mused, to nurture ourselves away from sin? How could we make the most of the spiritual nourishment Christ had to offer?

Sidney wondered, having seen his curate's prodigious cake-eating in action, if all of Malcolm's homilies were to contain gastronomic metaphors. There were certainly plenty of biblical references to manna from heaven, the bread of life and thirsting for righteousness. At least there were few mentions of cake itself (Sidney dimly remembered a passage in the Book of Ezekiel about barley cake, and a fig concoction in 1 Samuel). But when had it been invented, he asked himself, and what was the moment when a biscuit became a cake? Was it the presence of sponge that allowed McVitie's, for example, to refer to their produce as Jaffa *cakes* rather than biscuits?

'Sidney,' his wife interrupted as she gave him a goodbye kiss before popping out to the shops, 'you are dreaming again.'

The doorbell rang.

'What? Sorry?'

'Malcolm was asking if you had made any progress on the case.'

'Sorry. I thought he said *cake*.'

'I said nothing of the kind. But if there is any more going . . .'

It had been Helena Randall at the door. She walked straight in and announced: 'Sophie Madara is due to appear at a concert in York. I have my car.'

'Good heavens . . .'

'How far away is that?' Hildegard asked.

'A few hours. Geordie says Sidney's to come. We can be back tonight. I'm a very fast driver.'

Sidney looked to his wife. 'I remember. I don't find that reassuring.'

'Go if you must,' Hildegard replied. 'Your curfew is midnight.'

43

'I'll hold the fort,' said Malcolm.

'What is the concert?' Hildegard asked.

'The Holst Invocation for Cello and Orchestra.'

'An early version of one of *The Planets*.'

Sidney was less interested in the musical programme, and more concerned about the case. 'What about Geordie?'

'He's bringing Madara to verify that it really is his wife.'

'It could be quite a reunion.'

'I think that's the point.'

The concert was held on the campus of the recently established university at Heslington. It took over three hours to drive up the A1 to York in heavy rain and, after a brief stop for petrol in Stamford, Sidney knew they would have difficulty being home by midnight.

A simple poster had been placed outside the hall offering a mixed programme culminating in what was clearly intended to be the university orchestra's *pièce de résistance*, Haydn's Symphony no. 35 in B flat major. There was even a photograph of a smiling Sophie Madara with her left hand holding the bow of her cello. Sidney noticed both an engagement and a wedding ring. He presumed she took them off to perform.

Her husband had spruced up for the occasion. Sidney thought of a recent production of *A Winter's Tale* in which the dead king's wife had come back to him as a living statue. With the dramatic music of Holst in the background, this reunion could have proved equally dramatic but Inspector Keating's thoughts were more prosaic. 'Let's get to Sophie Madara's dressing-room. We don't want to do this in front of the whole orchestra.'

The unlikely foursome were let in at the stage door and shown up a flight of stairs.

'This is a dream,' said Madara.

'It won't take long.'

'I know she is dead.'

Keating knocked on the door. It was opened by a small dark-haired woman who had not yet put on her make-up. She did not look very like Sophie Madara at all. Perhaps they had come to the wrong place? Could this be yet another wild-goose chase and, if it was, would Sidney be able to face a further explosion of frustration from his colleague?

'Sorry, I was expecting the conductor. Josef! What are you doing here?'

'Angela . . .'

The woman kissed Madara on the cheeks. This was not the response of a wife who had been presumed dead. 'Is Sophie coming? She told me that she was going away . . .'

'Are you aware that you are talking about a missing woman?' Keating asked.

'Who are you?'

'A police officer. Where is Sophie Madara?'

'I've no idea.'

'But she's alive?'

'I hope so. I spoke to her on the telephone a few days ago.'

'She told you she was going away. She didn't say where?'

'I can't remember.'

'You haven't been reading the papers?'

'Is that a legal requirement?'

'Who are you?' Helena asked.

'I might ask the same question about you. I have a concert to perform. Josef, who are all these people? What are they doing here? Can't you get them out of my dressing-room?'

Keating tried to restore order. 'Please answer the question, madam.'

'I don't see why I should. But if you must know, I'm Angela Jones. Sophie's dep. I think she's helping me out in Yarmouth next week. I try to keep Easter free.' She noticed Sidney. 'My husband's a priest. What are you doing here? Anyone would think I had died. Shouldn't you be making your Easter garden?'

'My wife's a musician too . . .'

'It's more common than people think. God and music tend to go together.'

Helena had her notebook at the ready. 'But on the poster . . .'

'We don't bother with out-of-town concerts. We're always covering for each other. Josef knows that, don't you, Josef? Sophie did tell you about this, didn't she?'

Madara could hardly speak. 'Sophie is alive? I didn't kill her?'

'What are you talking about?'

'I think I'd better take over,' said Keating. 'There's a lot to sort out. Bloody *hell*.'

It was well after midnight when Sidney got home but he was too restless to go to bed.

He took off his shoes, put on the thick pair of comforting bedsocks his mother had knitted him for Christmas, and made himself some baked beans on toast. He needed a good think.

He was just about to make a list of all the things he still had to do when he heard Anna cry. He would have to see to her quickly, before Hildegard woke, and he padded up the stairs in order to lift his daughter out of her cot.

She was still so tiny, half awake and half asleep. She cradled into his shoulder. He gave her a little milk and walked the hall downstairs talking to her, as he spoke to Byron, about all his cares and worries. He asked her if she was looking forward to her christening (they still hadn't arranged it and were thinking about Easter Day) and whether she thought all the stars had come out in the sky or were there more still to come?

He told his daughter how he imagined that one of the stars was looking down on her. It was her star. Could she tell which one it was? Anna's heavy eyelids closed once more, and he kept talking, as gently as he could, as he laid her down to sleep. When he turned to leave the room he saw that Hildegard had been watching from the doorway. She was wearing a nightdress that Sidney did not think he had seen before.

'Thank you,' she said quietly. 'You're very good at that when you want to be.'

Josef Madara had been taken back into custody and a psychiatric visit was arranged for the Monday. Angela Jones was convinced that Sophie Madara was still in Britain but had been unable to provide any clues as to her whereabouts. In London, Inspector Williams had charged Dmitri Zhirkov with the murder of his wife.

Sidney had to concentrate on his duties and it wasn't until the middle of the week that he could catch up with Keating. If he really thought that Dmitri Zhirkov had been framed in some way then he had no time to prove it, and little hope, as the weapon, the motive and the evidence all pointed to the man's guilt.

It was also possible that Dmitri was involved in the staged scene of Sophie Madara's death (if this had indeed occurred) and that he was working with either her or her husband, who could have been feigning his insanity.

The only relatively innocent party in the whole quartet, as far as Sidney could see, was Natasha Zhirkov, and she was dead; just as she had feared she might be.

It was one big mess and he was not sure that he was in a position to do anything about it. Was it even his responsibility any more? Madara had turned up in his church, it was true, but now 'the experts' had taken over there was little he could do. He had failed to protect Natasha Zhirkov, they had not yet found Josef's wife, and the man himself was still in an advanced state of psychiatric delusion. If anything, his visit to the church in Grantchester, and the subsequent investigation, had only made matters worse. What would have happened if Sidney had simply sent him on his way after a cup of tea and a sandwich as many of his colleagues might have done? Could the situation have been any poorer?

He tried to concentrate on his parish tasks once more: Easter preparation, confirmation classes and the requirement to lead a Lenten meditation on sin and suffering. These were the absolute bare minimum, let alone his need to visit the sick and interview potential candidates to run the village school.

Malcolm was unconcerned by such travails (what freedom Sidney would have if he were simply a curate again!) and was installing another section of railway track in his room. Hildegard joked that there were probably train delays owing to cake crumbs on the line. As they sat on the sofa, she asked her husband how his thoughts were progressing.

'Not that well. In musical terms it's more Stockhausen than Bach.'

'It's the end of the quartet, I imagine. They can hardly go on after this, even if they find a new member.'

'It's surprising that they survived so long,' said Sidney. 'Perhaps it's not a good idea for married couples to work together . . .'

'We might see more of each other if we did . . .'

'I think couples need external stimulation, otherwise love becomes insular and claustrophobic. You have to keep bringing things back from the outside world.'

'Is that why you keep going away? You think it refreshes our marriage?'

'I don't think it would be a good idea to stay cooped up here all day.'

'Some of us have no choice, *mein Lieber.*'

Sidney recognised the possibility of an argument and tried to stick to the subject. 'But a quartet? It must have been hard to know when work stopped; if they were ever off duty.'

'Just like you.'

'I do draw the line at infidelity and murder, Hildegard.'

'I'm glad to hear it.'

'And I miss you every minute I'm away.'

'Then that is why you leave? In order to miss me?'

'It is one of the consequences of love.'

'You are fortunate to have such freedom.' Hildegard thought about the case once more. 'From what I know of quartets they either love each other or hate each other. There was one group where the only woman married each of the three men in turn . . .'

'You'd think she could have looked further afield . . .'

'Perhaps she didn't need to. It's the same with your investigation, Sidney. The solution must lie in the quartet itself. But I must see to Anna.'

'I'll go.'

'No, it's all right. I'll leave you to your thoughts. You have a quiet minute to yourself.'

Hildegard gave her husband a kiss on the cheek, and began to leave the room, humming as she did so.

Sidney called after her. 'That music's unlike you, Hildegard. Very English.'

'What do you mean?'

'"I vow to thee my country".'

'No it's not. It's Holst, the "Jupiter" movement from *The Planets* suite. I was still thinking about the quartet.'

'But it's the same tune.' Sidney began to sing:

'I vow to thee, my country, all earthly things above,
Entire and whole and perfect, the service of my love;
The love that asks no question, the love that stands the test,
That lays upon the altar the dearest and the best . . .'

'It's Holst, I promise you,' Hildegard answered. 'He wrote it first.'

And then it came to Sidney. 'But it's a hymn tune. Thaxted.'

'What about it?'

He was cold with fear. Why had he not realised sooner? 'My goodness. That's where Sophie Madara could have been all this time. Her husband talked about a place they went to when they were first married; in the countryside, on the edge of a small town, not far from London; a church with a medieval spire, some old almshouses, and a windmill. Thaxted: Holst. I may be wrong, but I must tell Keating . . .'

On the afternoon of Wednesday 11th March, after a lengthy conversation with Josef Madara in which it was firmly suggested that he remain in police custody to avoid further distress, Geordie Keating, Sidney and Helena made their way to Thaxted in Essex. They had discovered that Sophie Madara had been brought up in the small market town and that her parents still lived in a timber-framed Tudor house just beyond the famous windmill. It was easy enough to track down.

'You know what I'm going to say if we don't find anything,' the inspector warned.

'Please don't take the name of the Lord in vain,' Sidney asked.

'I think he's probably used to it by now.'

'That doesn't make it any more forgivable.'

They came in two cars, with a police officer in attendance, and parked some way away in order to avoid suspicion. It was a crisp spring day, the first time in four months Sidney had been optimistic that it might actually get warm, and the church bells rang in celebration at the news of Prince Edward's birth. Listening to them, he wished he could have been there to take a wedding rather than conduct an inquiry.

They were greeted by a handsome woman in her early sixties. After Keating had told her the purpose of their visit, she admitted that she was Mrs Rimkus, Sophie's mother. The door to the sitting-room was open and inside sat a frailer man with a rug over his legs by an open fire. He was sorting through a butterfly collection. The sound of a cello came from upstairs.

'She still has her room,' Sophie's mother explained. 'She comes back to us when she is unhappy.'

'And how often is that?' Sidney asked.

'Every other year or two. Have you come to help her?'

'I hope so.'

'Is Josef with you?' she asked.

'Not at the moment.'

'Good. He upsets her father. He thinks she should have done better with her marriage. But Josef is very musical. We admit that.'

'If we could see her . . .' Inspector Keating took a step forward.

'SHUT THE DOOR. THERE'S A DRAUGHT. HOW MANY TIMES DO I HAVE TO TELL YOU, WOMAN . . .'

'That's Gordon. He gets in such a state. It's where Sophie gets her moodiness from. Mind you, musicians can be very temperamental. I don't play myself.'

'If we could . . .' Sidney began.

'I'll show you upstairs. It's nice to see a vicar. We don't go to church very much any more. It's such an effort and the new one, well . . .'

'I understand.'

'He keeps changing things when most of us would like everything to stay the same. We like to know where we are. That's why people go to church, don't they? Sophie's room is at the end on the left. Just give a little knock. She could do with a visitor.' Mrs Rimkus stooped to pick up a breakfast tray that had been left outside the room. 'She doesn't come out much.'

The cello music stopped.

Keating knocked on the door and opened it without waiting for a reply. A pale woman was sitting at the window wearing a long-sleeved evening dress so worn it looked like a housecoat. The bow in her left hand was half raised.

Once they had explained themselves, Sophie Madara said: 'I wondered when someone would come. It's been a long time.'

'You were reported as missing.'

'But I wasn't.'

'Nobody knew where you were.'

'I knew where I was. So did my parents. I have made no secret. Where is my husband?'

Keating was not prepared to provide an easy answer. 'Why didn't he come and find you?'

'Have you asked him?'

'He thought you were dead.'

'You can tell that I am not. Is that all you want to see me about?'

'You had an argument.'

'You could say so.'

'The quartet?' Sidney asked.

'Oh, them.'

'Do you know where your husband is now?' Keating asked.

'I am not his keeper.'

'But you are his wife.'

'That is true.'

She picked up her instrument and began to play one of

53

Bach's cello suites. It had a simple, sparse serenity and Sidney wondered how there could be such grace and peace after the chaos of recent events. How could a woman who had provoked such violence be in so different a world?

Helena continued to write in her notebook, describing the scene rather than taking it in. There were times when Sidney wished she would wait and see how things developed rather than rushing to judge and jot down.

When the music stopped, Sophie Madara looked up. 'You are still here? I hope you liked that. Would you like me to play some more?'

Keating repeated his question. 'I just want to know why your husband thought you were dead?'

'He imagines things. Sometimes I think he would believe anything. For a man with such gifts, he can be very naive.'

Sidney could still hear the music in his head. 'Perhaps that is what you were able to do, Mrs Madara. Make him believe anything.'

'I didn't have to try very hard.'

'But why go to all that trouble?'

'And what trouble would that be?'

'Disappearing. Faking your own death.'

'I will admit to leaving him, if that's what you want me to say. I wanted him to miss me; to realise what it might be like if I were dead.'

'But there was another reason . . .'

'Which was?'

'You wanted him out of the way.'

'Tell me, Inspector, where did you find this clergyman? I don't think I like him.'

'Many people think the same way when they have a guilty conscience,' Sidney observed.

'I have no guilt. My husband does.'

'And why would that be?'

'I am sure you know. That must be why you are here. A policeman and a clergyman.' She looked at Helena. 'Are you a doctor? That would make everything complete.'

Sidney did not let the journalist answer. 'Your husband was in police custody at the time of Natasha Zhirkov's death.'

'Natasha dead? I didn't know.'

'I think you do.'

'I have been here. Who would have told me?'

'Did you kill Natasha Zhirkov?' Keating asked.

'I haven't seen her for a long time.'

'Since you left Cambridge?'

'I suppose so.'

'And do you have an alibi for her death?'

'When did it occur?'

'February the twenty-first.'

'I was here. My parents will confirm that.'

Helena interrupted. 'Natasha Zhirkov had an affair with your husband.'

'Does everyone know that?'

'They soon will.'

Sidney took over. 'It must have made you angry.'

Sophie Madara put her cello down. 'Do you know what it is like to hate, Canon Chambers? To be so full of fury that you cannot think of anything else?'

'No, I try not to think like that.'

'But that's what I felt for Natasha Zhirkov. Every time she

looked at me I could see her thinking: "I have made love to your husband and you can do nothing about it."'

'So you wanted to prove that you could?'

'Without committing a crime.'

'But . . .'

'What? I have done nothing. I have been here, Josef was in safe custody. Now Natasha is dead and Dmitri will take the blame. All's fair in love and war, don't you think?'

'No,' said Sidney. 'I don't. Morality is absolute.'

'Is it really?' Sophie Madara asked. 'I thought there were certain circumstances. Killing for the greater good: the lesser of two evils. Did you fight in the war, Canon Chambers? If you did, then you must have killing on your conscience.'

'That has nothing to do with it,' Keating shot back. 'Does your husband know you are here? Has he been part of this all along? Is he just pretending to be mad? I don't understand you people.'

'I am sure he will come soon enough. He has nowhere else to go. And he will guess I am here.'

'He hasn't done that so far. He is distraught.'

'Then he might learn something,' Sophie continued. 'Penitence is good. A man can't be pardoned unless he is penitent.'

'And do you think he will forgive you?' Keating asked.

'For what? I haven't done anything wrong. I'm the one who needs to do the forgiving.'

'You faked your own death. You may have murdered Natasha Zhirkov.'

'I think you will find the evidence points to her husband.'

'How do you know that?'

'You told me.'

'I don't think I did. Perhaps you *arranged* the evidence to make it look like Dmitri Zhirkov killed his wife.'

'I did no such thing.'

'Or you persuaded him to do it?'

Sidney took over the questioning. 'Did you tell Dmitri Zhirkov about his wife's affair with your husband?'

'I might have done.'

'He didn't know? He hadn't guessed?'

Sophie Madara smiled. 'Men are easily persuadable. It's not hard to make a man think the worst of his wife.'

'When did you do this?'

'The night of the last concert. I wanted him to know what his wife had done; seducing Josef.'

'It may have been the other way round.'

'Never. I know my husband. Nobody understands him as well as I do.'

'Which meant that you knew he would believe you were dead,' Sidney checked, 'when you staged your own death.'

'I know how he panics, yes. And I wanted to frighten him. It wasn't hard.'

'And what did you say to Dmitri Zhirkov to make him kill his wife?' Inspector Keating resumed.

'Perhaps you shouldn't worry about me and concentrate on bringing him to justice. After all, he killed Natasha. What have I done? Nothing. Only a little stagecraft. I am the wronged woman, remember? You ought to be sympathetic. You should celebrate the fact that, owing to my ingenuity, a couple who made their vows before God and who have been so estranged are about to be reunited.'

'There's nothing to celebrate,' Keating replied. 'Nothing at all.'

And he was right. There was little joy when the couple met once more. Josef Madara was confused and angry. He could not believe what his wife had done. 'Why did you do this to me?' he asked. 'You have made me mad.'

Sophie put her hands on her husband's shoulders but he was not a man who wanted to be touched. 'You see how I have loved you, Josef. Natasha is dead, her husband is to blame, and neither of them need trouble us any more.'

'But they do. Our memories. It has all been wrong.'

'And now it is right. We can forgive each other.'

'I know I did the wrong thing . . . but when I was with Natasha . . . it was an accident . . . it wasn't any danger . . . It was nothing . . . and it was over . . . I didn't mean to hurt you.'

'But you did. And you had to understand that.'

'I did.'

'Not enough.'

'What is enough?'

'I wanted to make you suffer. I wanted you to feel grief. How can we learn without suffering?'

'And so you punished me.'

'Of course. *Crime and Punishment.* Isn't that your favourite novel? It is a pity you did not learn from that.'

'I have not killed anyone.'

'You killed my heart.'

'I used to wonder how I ever found and married you,' her husband replied. 'What a miracle it was, how lucky I was to be with such a beautiful, talented, creative woman.'

'You are.'

'Now I almost wish I had continued with Natasha. Even though we deceived you it was more honest than this. Do you have no guilt?'

'None.'

'You have become so cold. Natasha is dead. Dmitri is in prison. They were our friends.'

'Forgive me, Josef, just as I have pardoned you.'

'How can I? You have no shame. How can I forgive without penitence? We can never be the same.'

'We can start all over again.'

'No, Sophie, it is ruined. Everything is finished.'

On Easter Day Sidney preached on guilt, conscience and the forgiveness of sins. His argument was to build the rationale for Christ's death and the necessary fact of the resurrection. He thought once more about the Madaras' empty hotel room, and planned an impromptu peroration on the literary tradition of abandoned graves and people faking their own deaths: Juliet in *Romeo and Juliet*, the false execution of Claudio in *Measure for Measure*, Troy's drowning in *Far from the Madding Crowd*. But in the unique case of Jesus Christ, Sidney affirmed, there was no trickery. The truth of the resurrection was not fiction.

He referred back to Christmas. Once the child had been born, there was no going back to the womb. Now there was no return to the grave. It was as empty as the womb had once been. It could not be reoccupied. This was the nature of Christ's triumph over death. It was a rebirth that could not be unborn.

Sidney acknowledged that there were perhaps doubts about appearance and reality. Could the disciples be sure that they had seen what they said they had seen? Could it have been a mirage or a delusion, a neurotic fantasy?

Not when so many were witnesses, at different times and in different places; not when they felt the presence of the Living Christ, in the garden, on the road to Emmaus, in an empty room. The disciples saw, they knew, and they trusted. Some things remain in mystery, Sidney concluded. Others are utterly and abundantly clear.

Christ is risen!

As he spoke, he saw Josef Madara sitting quietly in the third row. A shaft of morning sunlight, coloured by stained glass, angled across his face. A tear fell down his cheek. Sidney paused briefly to consider it: and, as he did so, he realised that he would never be able to know if that tear was caused by the sudden brightness of the light, by contemplating everything that had happened, or the power of the story he was telling. For some people, it was true, there could be no redemption.

The following day, Sidney met his two colleagues in the Eagle. Lent had passed and he was allowed to return to his regulation two pints of bitter; although now Helena had joined them there was a question over whether the men were allowed a third drink.

Sophie and Josef Madara were estranged; their marriage unable to recover from the trauma of events. Dmitri Zhirkov had made his confession. His was a crime of passion and he was prepared to take the consequences.

'There's no way he can get off', Keating explained. 'But he might manage manslaughter.'

'And Sophie Madara goes scot-free?' Sidney asked.

'Despite faking her own death . . .' Helena added.

'We can't even prove that. The room was tidied. We only have Madara's word. I don't think that will stand up against his wife in court. She knows how to manipulate a conversation. She will have no trouble convincing the jury that her supposed death was one of her husband's nightmares.'

'And what about her persuading Dmitri Zhirkov to kill his wife?'

'It's hard to prove.'

'Isn't it odd,' Sidney asked, 'how so much crime stems from an inability to forgive?'

Inspector Keating reached for his pint. 'Will Madara ever take her back, do you know?'

'I don't think so.'

'So his wife's plan was in vain?' Helena asked.

'Perhaps they should have talked sooner,' Sidney replied. 'Then they might have been able to forgive. Perhaps it's easier when you are honest straight away.'

Geordie was in a ruminative mood. 'We should take this as a lesson. Cathy can get a bit funny if I see too much of one woman or another . . .'

Sidney was surprised his friend was being so open in front of Helena. Perhaps he was either trying to tell her something or turning over a new leaf? 'I don't think either of us are murderers, Geordie.'

'No, but you never know: our wives might be.'

Helena Randall felt the discomfort and asked the men if they would like another round. She normally drank vermouth but switched to pints when she was with them.

'I am sure it's my turn,' said Sidney. 'Besides, you're a lady . . .'

'I'm glad you think so. But a modern woman can buy her own drinks. I've just got a pay rise.'

'Really?'

'The *Evening News* are worried they're going to lose me to one of the nationals.'

'And are they?'

Helena smiled. 'I don't know yet. I think they're going to see how this story develops. I'm after syndication. There might be quite a few bob in it.'

'Perhaps we should get a cut?' Keating asked.

'That is corruption, Inspector.'

'I was *joking*.'

'It might even be a book,' said Sidney.

'Or a film.' Keating brightened. 'Basil Rathbone could play the priestly detective. Or Richard Attenborough.'

'Aren't they a bit old for the part?'

'I shouldn't worry,' Keating replied. 'Knowing my luck Sid James would probably be me.'

'No, they'll ask someone more handsome,' Helena cut in, quickly enough to sound gallant. 'Richard Burton would be good. Have you seen *The Longest Day*?'

Geordie was appalled. 'Since when was I Welsh?'

Helena laughed. 'And Kenneth More for Sidney. This story could make my name. I'm very grateful to you both. I've been so lucky.'

Despite the jocular nature of the conversation, Sidney had a quiet moment of melancholy. 'Wouldn't you rather that none of this had happened?' he asked.

'Of course,' Helena replied, without sounding entirely convincing. There was still something uneasy about the atmosphere.

'Oh look,' she said. 'There's Malcolm.'

'What does he want?' Sidney asked.

Keating became anxious. 'I hope there's not another fugitive in your church.'

'You've no need to worry,' Helena said breezily. 'He's taking me out to dinner.'

'Malcolm?' Sidney asked.

'Him?' spluttered Keating.

'Is there anything wrong with that?'

The eager curate was all smiles. 'I must say, Helena, you look absolutely divine.'

'Why, thank you, Malcolm. You always give me such a warm welcome. Where shall we go?'

'There's a rather nice place off Market Square. French. Just opened. I hear very good reports . . .'

'Then lead on . . .'

'I can't wait. This is so exciting. They have a special chocolate soufflé. Once you start it's almost impossible to stop. Your mouth just *explodes* with the sheer puddingness of it all.'

Helena giggled and put her arm through Malcolm's. 'We can feed each other.'

After they had gone, Keating exploded. 'Him? What on earth . . .'

'I know, Geordie, I know. Ours not to reason why.'

'*I must say, Helena, you look absolutely divine.* What's he got that I haven't? *I hear very good reports . . .*'

'It's more a case of what you've got.'

'And what is that, Sidney?'

'A wife, Geordie. Drink up.'

63

'The case of the exploding mouth. The soufflé murders. It has a certain ring, I suppose.'

Sidney bicycled back to Grantchester and took Byron out for his evening constitutional across the meadows and down to the river. The fritillaries would be out soon and, even though it was far too early, he could have sworn he heard the first cuckoo of spring. Should he write to *The Times* and tell them? he asked himself. No. He had better things to do, not least the enjoyment of his Labrador's comforting companionship.

Was to understand all to forgive all? he wondered. How dependent was mercy on penitence and were some sins so great that, despite any amount of contrition, they were beyond redemption? He would think and preach about this, he decided. Perhaps he could even write a book: *Responsibility and the Moral Imagination.* But when would he ever have the time?

He arrived home, closed the door quietly in case Anna was asleep and saw the sausages resting under tin foil, the mashed potatoes keeping warm, red cabbage by its side.

Then he stopped in the hallway and listened to Hildegard singing a last lullaby to their daughter:

> *'Der Mond ist aufgegangen,*
> *Die goldnen Sternlein prangen*
> *Am Himmel hell und klar;*
> *Der Wald steht schwarz und schweiget,*
> *Und aus den Wiesen steiget*
> *Der weiße Nebel wunderbar?'*

He stayed still, while Byron hovered around his ankles, plaintively but hopelessly, waiting for his dinner.

'Wie ist die Welt so stille,
Und in der Dämmrung Hülle
So traulich und so hold!'

Sidney translated the words to himself as he walked back into the kitchen. He waited silently beside the sink until his wife had finished singing. He wanted no other sound.

How the world stands still
In twilight's veil
So sweet and sung . . .

'Als eine stille Kammer,
Wo ihr des Tages Jammer
Verschlafen und vergessen sollt.'

As a still room,
Where the day's misery
You will sleep off and forget.

He turned on the tap, poured himself a glass of water and thanked God amid the stillness of the night for the gift of his wife and daughter: the sanctuary of home.

Nothing to Worry About

BY NOVEMBER 1964, SIDNEY and Hildegard had reached the stage of parenthood when they could leave their baby daughter overnight, in the care of others, for the first time. Sir Mark Kirby-Grey and his wife Elizabeth had invited them to a shooting party at Witchford Hall. It promised to be a formidable gathering, including Sidney's oldest friend, Amanda Kendall, together with her new potential paramour, a rich widower on the lookout for a second wife.

Amanda had begged them to come, saying that she was concerned she had lost her touch with men and that she wanted both Sidney and Hildegard to take a good look at Henry Richmond and make sure he was up to scratch. She was all too aware of the irony that she seemed unable to deploy the skills she displayed so effortlessly in her work as a curator at the National Gallery (judgement, taste and the ability to spot a fake) in the world of romance. She was also worried that their hostess, Elizabeth Kirby-Grey, had been behaving strangely of late. She wouldn't mind if Sidney had one of his 'annoying intuitions'.

'What on earth do you mean, Amanda?'

'I'm not going to say any more. Something's not right.'

'With the marriage? Her health? Money?'

'I'm not sure. But you often notice things before anyone else.'

'I don't know about that.'

'It's because you're so nosy.'

'I am not nosy, Amanda. I hope people don't think . . .'

'They're too polite to say anything.'

'I am curious, concerned, and ready for all things.'

'In other words: nosy. Just come, Sidney. Not for Elizabeth, but for me. I don't want to make another ghastly mistake. You know how hopeless I am with men.'

'You're not hopeless.'

'Hildegard has to stay too. She's just as clever as you.'

'I'm not going to argue with that. It's only . . .'

'I'll see you on the twenty-seventh. Make sure you arrive in time for drinks.'

When the day came, Hildegard worried about leaving Anna for not one but two nights, even though Sidney's mother had welcomed the chance to spend some time with her only grand-daughter. (Sidney's sister and her husband, the jazz promoter Johnny Johnson, had provided a couple of boys; his brother Matt had not yet settled but was down to what was surely his last wild oat.)

Although Iris Chambers was due to arrive well before supper, Mrs Maguire had kindly offered to baby-sit for the hour or two beforehand. Malcolm Mitchell would also take the service on Advent Sunday morning. They were little more than an hour away and Sidney's driving was now sufficiently accomplished to ensure a speedy return should there be any emergency.

He did, however, acknowledge that weekending with the

aristocracy was not one of his favourite pastimes. Grand houses were seldom heated properly, the beds were uncomfortable and the food predictable: the game from the estate, riddled with shot. Conversation could also be hard-going, filled with solipsistic indifference to those who had not been born to similar advantage (despite occasional bouts of ostentatious charity towards 'the deserving poor'), and a hovering air of indolent entitlement made the company of the privileged a test of endurance.

Sidney tried to tell himself that this weekend stay would be good for his patience; that Sir Mark was an influential local figure whom it might be good to cultivate for parish funds, and that he might, at least, enjoy a bit of shooting. (It was years since he had last taken part in such a venture and he had borrowed some of the requisite clobber and a couple of Purdeys from a friend in the village.) He also told himself that both he and Hildegard could do with a weekend off before the mania of Christmas.

A manor house that had once been used as a vicarage, Witchford Hall was built in the seventeenth century in brown brick with red sandstone dressings. It had a symmetrical five-bay Jacobean façade, rusticated Doric pilasters, two floors of sash windows and an attic level that contained four blind oval windows. It would be impossible, Sidney imagined, for a Church of England clergyman ranked lower than a bishop to occupy such a residence nowadays.

He refused to be intimidated by the grandeur of the approach and remembered his mother once telling him 'it's not all jam at the big house'. A Labrador and two Dalmatians ran out into the drive to meet them. Sidney and Hildegard were shown into a cream entrance hall panelled with fluted columns, and their

68

luggage was carried up an imposing staircase with twisted balusters by a lugubrious butler called Muir. Above hung a series of family portraits most of which, Amanda would almost certainly point out as soon as she arrived, were in need of restoration.

The house had somehow managed to make itself colder than the exterior temperature. Once they had unpacked, they were shown into the drawing-room and asked to wait. Sir Mark would be in shortly for a welcoming drink. The room took up the central part of the rear of the house and looked out on to a large lawn, a formal garden, and a ha-ha that divided the cultivated ground from the fields and farmland beyond. Mature oaks and elms framed the edge of the garden, and the last autumn leaves blew across the grass as the sky darkened into night.

Sir Mark Kirby-Grey had the air of a preoccupied man who was doing his best and was not prepared to take criticism. Prematurely bald, and smaller than he wanted to be, he wore a bespoke navy suit with one cuff button undone, and he spoke to everyone as if they were employees who fell short. Unused to relaxation or sitting still, he preferred to 'get on with things', and his quick, attentive movements were either a sign of shyness and social discomfort or a deliberate attempt to remind people of his influence and importance.

His wife, Elizabeth, was a watchful woman who wore a high-collared full-sleeved evening dress in black with white lace appliqué over a mesh bodice. Her conversation was filled with self-deprecation ('I am sure no one would notice if I just disappeared') despite the fact that her days were filled with running the house and the estate, ordering delicacies from Harrods, typing her husband's letters and helping out with various charities. She didn't see too many of her friends because she was so busy and so it was 'absolute bliss' that Amanda had agreed to come and stay. Elizabeth had high hopes of her friend 'making a go of it' with Henry Richmond 'despite the recent difficulties'.

When Sidney enquired as to what had happened to the first Mrs Richmond she replied that it had all been 'too ghastly to explain' but that Amanda's potential beau was a free man and her friend was an independent woman. Although it was unrealistic to hope for children it certainly wasn't 'too late for happiness'.

Asked about her other friends, Elizabeth was equally reticent. She seldom travelled away from home. 'Mark doesn't want me to. He says it's because he needs me so much; and he does like to take care of everything, especially the money side of things. It makes life so much easier. And it isn't too much of a sacrifice. I love my home.'

She had a quick smile that soon faded, perhaps worried about being caught out, and Sidney could see that her attentiveness as a hostess included keeping a close eye on her husband's alcohol consumption. Sir Mark had enjoyed two large whiskies in company before dinner and they were probably not his first of the evening. It was likely that he would be well oiled before the port and cigars.

Amanda was wearing an evening dress in midnight-blue silk and wondered whether she should change between cocktails and dinner. 'I am worried this is all a bit too revealing but I suppose a shawl covers a multitude of sins.'

'Hildegard's noticed that there's no heating.'

'There never is, darling.'

She looked magnificent with her hair pinned back to reveal pearl earrings that matched her necklace. She smelled of jasmine, violet and vetiver. It was Je Reviens.

Henry Richmond was an inoffensively handsome man in his early forties, with thick dark brown hair parted cleanly and, Sidney suspected, held in place with a touch of pomade. His olive skin gave him a continental air, a demeanour enhanced by an over-liberal use of Trumper's aftershave, but his deep clear voice, confident jawbone and firm handshake were enough to reassure any doubter that he was distinctly English.

Dr Michael Robinson, with his wife Isabel, had also been invited, together with Major Tom Meynell, of the Royal Artillery, an ebullient widower who was known as 'Shouty' to his friends, and Serena Stein, a psychologist with a surprisingly fruity laugh. She began by telling Sidney that she was writing a history of contraception; a conversation-stopper if ever there was one.

After all the introductions had been made and the drinks poured, the guests began to share news of acquaintances of whom Sidney and Hildegard had never heard. (Giles Cox-Slaughter was going to be a judge, so at least they could all be guaranteed a sympathetic hearing if they ever got into trouble; Marcus Treeves was leaving to start a salmon farm in Scotland despite there being 'plenty of fish in the sea already'; and Shouty Meynell's daughter Wistful (named after one of his favourite hounds) had become engaged to a second cousin who had a bit of 'a lack' but she was fortunate to find anyone on account of her being so plain.) Sidney and Hildegard felt they were spending a first night at a school that they had been reluctant ever to attend.

Amanda was all ears as Henry Richmond regaled the

company with a series of well-rehearsed anecdotes concerning the pranks he had played on his friends. He had once managed to convince a naive colleague that if you put a pigeon next to a magnet it would always face north due to high levels of iron in the blood; that chickens fly south for the winter; and that kilts were originally made from the tartan pelt of a wildcat.

They partook of a winter consommé before settling down to lean pheasant, on which Sidney made little purchase. This was served with overcooked vegetables and underdone roast potatoes. Sidney wondered if the glacial room temperature and the indifferent cooking were a deliberate attempt to make the Kirby-Greys' guests drink more of the welcoming burgundy that had been laid down by the host's father in the early 1950s. Such thoughts he knew were ungrateful, and he told himself that he really should be less judgemental, especially when a rather decent bread-and-butter pudding was produced for dessert.

The butler poured a too-sweet wine as an accompaniment while two maids, Kay and Nancy, circled the table. Sidney saw that Sir Mark was particularly watchful of Nancy, the smaller and darker of the two; a girl in her early twenties who was at pains to avoid eye contact. Her service was one of indifferent, even sullen, efficiency.

Serena Stein noticed Sidney observing the maid in action and gave him a nudge. 'It's rude to stare.'

'I didn't think I was.'

'Your reputation precedes you.'

'I was unaware I had one.'

Miss Stein's voice was deep, and she clearly knew that it was one of her most seductive features, with her head held back in a mixture of interest and amusement. 'Tell me, Canon Chambers,' she asked confidentially, 'with all your experience, can you ascertain, perhaps even just by looking, if a couple are happy or not?'

'Not always.'

'And when they first come to you and say they want to get married, do you have a good idea whether it's going to be a lasting union?'

'I haven't had a failure yet.'

'You mean you haven't had a divorce. That's not quite the same thing.'

'Some couples think that the initial stages of being "in love" will see them through any difficulty ahead . . .'

'And you don't believe it will?'

'I think friendship is often as important as love.'

'That may not be enough.'

'I am not saying it is. You need both. Love has to be supported by care, patience, tolerance and understanding. Kindness too . . .'

'But when the passion goes,' Serena continued, glancing at the maid, 'then all of those things might not be enough. One or other of the partners could start to look elsewhere.'

'And that's when friendship should protect that passion,' Sidney replied. 'You have to put each other first.'

'Is that what you do in your marriage?'

'I try. It's different every day.'

'I thought that love was "an ever-fixed mark", as Shakespeare has it?'

'The love should be fixed but its workings are not. Like a

watch, perhaps. It is always the same entity but the parts keep moving . . .'

'Until the watch stops.'

'Then you have to keep winding it up.' Sidney reached for his wine. 'This is not a very good analogy. I'm sorry.'

Serena Stein was conciliatory, leaning in with almost a whisper. 'I think your wife must be a very fortunate woman.'

'I rather think I am a very lucky man.'

'I heard you were going to marry Miss Kendall.'

Sidney put down his wine glass and hoped for a speedy refill even though he didn't actually like dessert wine. 'That was never a possibility.'

'I think it was. She told me.'

Sidney checked that his friend was fully engaged in a conversation elsewhere before continuing to speak about her at the table. 'Amanda could never have married a vicar. And besides, I am happy . . .'

'I am glad to hear it.'

'As soon as I found Hildegard, I knew.'

'You did, did you?'

'*Yes*,' Sidney snapped. '*I did*.'

He wished he could sit next to his wife instead. He wanted them both to be on a sofa back in Grantchester with Byron asleep at their feet and their baby daughter beside them. What was he doing at this hopeless dinner party, seeking justification and approval from a ghastly woman who kept asking him impertinent questions? He tried to catch the butler's eye for another drink.

Serena Stein was still speaking to him when Sidney realised that he had not been listening. He regained his awareness as

74

she repeated a question. 'Do you not want to answer? Plenty of people have made a go of a second marriage.'

'You know that Hildegard had a previous husband?'

'I have done my homework, Canon Chambers. It could be that you benefit from the experience of someone who has been through it all before.'

'Perhaps I do.'

'The vicarious experience of failure. Are you here to approve of Amanda's new man?'

'I wasn't sure he was.'

'He will be by Sunday.'

Sidney tried to deflect the questions back on his interlocutor. She was bloody rude, he decided. 'You're not married yourself?'

'No. I am not.'

Sidney then wondered if Miss Stein was a lesbian. That might, at least, make the conversation more interesting; talking to someone who, in his father's words, 'batted for the other side'.

'I don't really believe in that kind of thing,' Serena continued. 'I don't think a woman needs a man to be happy.'

'I am sure she doesn't. But perhaps we all need someone to help us feel a little less lonely.'

'Are you lonely, Canon Chambers?'

'Sometimes.'

'Really?'

He had walked into Serena Stein's trap. Why had he made himself vulnerable? 'It's not always easy,' he confessed.

'Being married or being a priest?'

This woman was clearly good at her job. 'Both . . .'

'Would you care to explain?'

'Not really. I think we all have moments when we don't quite know who we are or if what we are doing is the right thing.'

'You have doubts?'

'Not about my marriage. Or my faith. I think.'

'You sound as if you're trying to convince yourself.'

Sidney was even more irritated. How dare this woman make assumptions? It didn't matter how attractive she was. It didn't give her licence to talk about his marriage. 'I don't think this is an appropriate subject for the dinner table,' he answered. 'Perhaps we should listen to the general conversation? People will think we are being rude.'

'Do you find intimacy impolite?'

'When it is at the expense of others. I am not afraid of intimacy *per se*.'

Serena Stein smiled. 'Then I look forward to being better acquainted.'

Henry Richmond was beginning another of his anecdotes, explaining away his volubility by saying that he had an extraordinarily taciturn older brother and had therefore grown up speaking for both of them. 'The strange thing is that he's become an ambassador, which means that he is forever in the public eye.'

'Has he got a good wife?' Sir Mark asked.

'Not as fine as yours, of course.'

'That goes without saying.'

'I went to see him in Paris earlier this month and he told me that the only day he really enjoyed was Remembrance Day because he didn't have to speak to anyone. All he had to do was lay a few wreaths.'

Shouty Meynell turned to Sidney. 'I imagine in Grantchester you lost a few good men?'

'Sixteen in the Great War, six in the last. Even in a small village . . .'

'Did you take part yourself? Or were you a conchie?'

'No, I fought.'

'Unusual for a clergyman.'

'I wasn't one at the time.'

'I would have thought it might put you off.'

'Most people say that, but once you have seen such darkness and despair perhaps you reach out for hope.'

Sidney could hardly contain himself. Why was he being put on his mettle like this?

There then followed a discussion of how war affected faith and Serena Stein asked Hildegard 'what it felt like' to be a German, before Amanda changed the subject by asking Henry Richmond about his plans for Christmas. No one dared mention his dead wife.

Just before the women left and the port and cigars were brought in, Sir Mark drew the dinner to a close by looking forward to the shoot on the morrow. He said that the weather was set fair and he hoped that he would outdo his previous record provided there was no poaching of his air space. Did everyone know the rules? 'The main one being that I have to bag the most.'

'I am sure no one needs to worry about that,' Shouty Meynell laughed. 'You always do.' Then, perhaps thinking that this was a joke everyone had missed, he repeated the phrase: 'I say, YOU ALWAYS DO.'

'Now we have a doctor and a priest with us we should be well catered for should we have any mishaps,' Sir Mark added.

'We also have a detective,' Amanda pointed out.

'Oh I don't know about that . . .' said Sidney quickly.

'Ah yes, I have been hearing about your exploits, Canon Chambers,' Sir Mark replied. 'It appears that the clergy are just as capable of murdering each other as everyone else.'

Sidney knew he was referring to a rejected ordinand who had taken revenge on his former tutors. 'I think that was an exceptional case.'

'I should hope it was.'

Dr Robinson intervened quickly. 'Canon Chambers has something of a reputation for his powers of observation. We shall have to be on our toes . . .'

Serena Stein reclaimed her previous intimacy. 'I've just been privy to his acute sensibility.'

Sidney smiled. 'A clear conscience is the safest way to a happy life.'

'BUT WHO'S GOT ONE OF THEM, CANON CHAMBERS?' Shouty Meynell asked. 'We're all guilty of some misdeed or other.'

'That's why people go to church,' said Elizabeth quietly, rising from her chair in order to take the ladies out of the room. She made a slight adjustment to her hair as she did so, revealing a large red burn at the back of her neck.

'Oh, gosh . . .' said Amanda.

'What is it?'

'I'm sorry. I didn't mean . . .'

'What?'

'Your neck.'

Sir Mark cut in swiftly. 'That's a very personal remark, Amanda.'

78

'I do apologise. I shouldn't have said anything.'

Lady Elizabeth was flustered. 'I think I must have sat under a dryer at the hairdresser's for too long.' Everyone was staring at her. 'It's nothing to worry about.'

'Elizabeth's always having little accidents', Sir Mark explained. 'Aren't you, darling? She has to learn to take better care of herself.'

'I try my best, but it's not always easy.'

'Then perhaps you just have to try a little harder. Port, chaps?'

It was well after eleven before Sidney and Hildegard were alone. They had been given a spacious bedroom that included a sofa and a couple of armchairs on either side of an occasional table stacked with back issues of *Country Life* and three or four contemporary novels that had never been read. Hildegard had brought a copy of *Jane Eyre*. She had made it her mission to get to grips with some of the English classics and was already wondering if Witchford Hall was similar to Mr Rochester's Thornfield. So far, however, there had been no sign of any Grace Poole, no hidden flight of stairs and no dark laughter from the attic.

As they prepared for bed (grateful that the maid had provided them with a hot-water bottle) and worried about Anna (would she really be all right without them?), Hildegard teased her husband about his dining companion. 'Serena Stein was very attentive. Had you met her before?'

Sidney knew that any questioning on the subject of how much he had enjoyed the company of a woman who had asked so directly about the nature of his marriage would not end well.

'I heard her tell you that she looked forward to being better acquainted. Were you flirting, Sidney?'

'Of course not.'

'I don't mind if you were.'

'I was not. And you do.'

'Would you care if I behaved in a similar way with a man?'

'Of course not.'

'Liar.'

Sidney decided to change the subject as quickly as he could and was aided by a knock on the door. It was Amanda.

'Let me in, darlings. I've forgotten my toothpaste.'

'You could have asked the maid,' said Sidney, rather ungraciously.

'It's *an excuse*, you stupid man.'

Sidney opened the door. 'Are you coming for a midnight feast?'

Amanda flopped on to one of the chairs. 'We could do with one after that dinner. Those pheasant had no meat on them at all. And as for the potatoes . . .'

'Stone cold.'

'I liked the pudding,' Hildegard remarked, sitting down on the edge of the bed. 'But not what happened afterwards.'

'Have you come for a debrief on Henry?' Sidney asked. 'He seems a very agreeable chap.'

'He certainly knows how to tell a story. He likes being popular. A bit like you, Sidney . . .'

'I don't court popularity.'

'But you don't mind it when it comes.'

'I was just teasing him about that,' said Hildegard.

'I think I can make up my own mind about Henry,'

Amanda continued. 'He's a bit too eager to please but there are worse faults. Did either of you get another look at Elizabeth's burn?'

'I did,' said Hildegard.

'And what do you think?'

'It was not an accident at the hairdresser's.'

'Exactly. I think Mark's responsible. And not for the first time.'

Sidney could see that his friend was about to embark on a theory. 'But do you have any other evidence?'

'There was another one a few months ago, on her forearm. She explained it away by saying that women with an Aga often burn themselves. You can also tell from their children's jumpers. They always have scorch marks when they've been left too long to dry. The only thing is . . .'

'She doesn't do the cooking,' Hildegard replied.

'And they lost their child.' Amanda turned to Sidney. 'I don't know if I ever told you about that.'

'I would have remembered if you had.'

'A little boy. Peter. He drowned. I don't think either of them have ever recovered.'

'Do they blame each other?' Hildegard asked.

'Of course. And themselves. They don't talk about it. But Elizabeth's become very withdrawn in the last few years. And you saw how scared she was of her husband? It's horrible.'

'Has she said anything about this?'

'No.'

'Nothing at all?'

'I can tell she's hiding something.'

'But she hasn't said anything specific?' Sidney checked.

'Sometimes women don't need to tell each other things . . .' Amanda continued.

Hildegard agreed. 'We just *know.*'

'And she couldn't be harming herself?'

'I hadn't thought of that.'

'She doesn't seem happy at all . . .' said Hildegard. 'But perhaps it is grief. That would be enough.'

'Grief doesn't make you burn yourself on purpose.'

'Have you ever seen Sir Mark lose his temper?' Sidney enquired.

'No.'

'Have you asked Henry about this?'

'I know he's Mark's oldest friend but he's not the type of man to rock the boat. I don't think I can put a dampener on things at this stage. That's why I'm so glad you're here.'

'What have you actually said to Elizabeth?'

'I tried to ask but she stopped me. She doesn't want anyone to think there's anything wrong.'

'How long have they been married?' Hildegard asked.

'About fifteen years. She was very young when they became engaged; it was just after her twenty-first birthday . . .'

'Many people think that's a good time . . .'

'You can tell she's terrified of her husband. I am not imagining it.'

'It's always hard to know what goes on in a marriage,' Sidney replied. 'There's never a single story. People tell you different things. They leave out what they don't want you to know; anything that might make you less compassionate.'

'But what could be more sympathetic than to tell a friend that your husband is hitting you?'

'Unless you fear that, by doing so, he will find out that other people know and punish you for the revelation.'

Sidney thought for a moment about the nature of intervention in friendship; whether it was advising someone to leave his or her job, avoid an affair, give up alcohol or escape an abusive marriage. A friend had to be sure of his or her facts. The timing had to be right.

'Whatever's going on', Amanda continued, 'Elizabeth is desperately unhappy. It's more than grief.'

'She *was* nervous tonight,' Hildegard agreed. 'But if her husband is hitting her why do you think he's doing it?'

'Blame, perhaps. Frustration. Lack of success. Failure to keep a son and heir. It could be all these things.'

'Did you notice the maid?' Sidney asked.

'Which one?'

'The small girl with the bob. Big dark eyes. Looked a bit sullen.'

'Like the act of service was beneath her?'

'That's the one. I think she's called Nancy.'

'What about her?'

'She was avoiding Sir Mark all evening.'

'What do you think is going on?' Hildegard asked.

Amanda stood up. 'I'll try and get something more out of Elizabeth. For once we could stop something before it starts . . .'

'I fear it's already begun.'

Hildegard turned to her husband. 'Perhaps you could talk with the doctor tomorrow. He may be able to help you. He has done so before.'

'You would like me to ask some unofficial questions?'

83

'I would like you to ask as many questions as you can,' said Amanda.

There was a light frost in the night and the Saturday morning was dark, threatening snow without ever producing a flurry. The sky looked as if it had been shaded in charcoal, given a light wash of pale blue and left for the day. Sidney stood at the bedroom window and wondered what on earth he was doing in this gloomy country house when he could have been back in Grantchester with his beloved daughter, his parishioners and his enthusiastic Labrador. He had thought of bringing Byron but he had only just reached his first birthday and he would have proved too unreliable a companion, intimidated by the other dogs, possibly to the same degree that Sidney was by the other guests.

He went down for a breakfast of lukewarm hard-boiled eggs and cold toast. At least the tea was hot. Despite an obvious hangover, Sir Mark read out the news he felt might be of interest from that morning's copy of *The Times*. Decca had released a twelve-disc recording of Winston Churchill's speeches in honour of his ninetieth birthday. Someone had complained that the Oxford and Cambridge boat race was a waste of money; and the four-year-old granddaughter of the Canadian prime minister had discovered a hotline to the White House and pretended that war had been declared.

'We've come to a pretty pass if the next world war is started by a four-year-old girl,' Shouty remarked to everyone in earshot.

Hildegard asked if she could use the telephone in order to check that all was well with Anna at home. Sidney went upstairs to complete his ablutions and change into his Norfolk jacket for the shoot.

His wife was impressed by his easy style. 'I sometimes think you can wear anything, Sidney.'

'That is one of the benefits of being a clergyman, my darling. We are so used to dressing up in all manner of clothing that we learn not to be self-conscious.'

'You will be careful?'

'I will try my best.'

'With the guns, I mean. You know how I hate them. We don't want an accident.'

It was not often that Hildegard, even obliquely, reminded Sidney of the death of her first husband (murdered by gunshot) and he realised it was perhaps insensitive to bring her to such an occasion. Perhaps she would have been better off at home? 'Will *you* be all right?' he asked.

'I like Amanda very much, as you know. And we can keep an eye on Elizabeth. I might even ask her one of your questions.'

'What do you mean by that?'

'The innocent enquiry that isn't what it seems. I know what you're like.'

Through the high windows Sidney watched his shooting companions assembling for the morning briefing. 'I should go.'

His wife kissed him goodbye. 'Be very careful. I'd rather have a husband than a hare. I'll see you at lunch.'

Sir Mark called the party together, checking that there were no stragglers and calling, 'Anyone not here, speak out!'

'ALL PRESENT AND CORRECT,' Shouty Meynell responded.

Musket, Sir Mark's black Labrador, circled round him as his master explained that there would be two drives followed by elevenses and a quick sharpener; then two more drives before lunch at Denny Abbey; followed by a fifth and possible sixth drive after lunch. The day would end just before four o'clock. He was hoping for over a hundred birds: mainly pheasant, partridge, mallard and duck.

'Please,' Elizabeth said quietly to her husband before kissing him goodbye, 'don't shoot the woodcock. You know how I love them.'

'Very well,' her husband replied and resumed his instructions. 'NO WOODCOCK. Don't bother with the pigeons and no ground game. You need to see the sky behind your barrels at all times.'

Sleet had begun to fall: not fiercely but enough to lower the mood and make everything seem more of an effort. The gamekeeper set off to marshal the beaters, and the shoot divided into three Land Rovers and drove to the furthest copse from Witchford Hall. Sidney sat in the same vehicle as Sir Mark. 'It's a wonder how you manage it all,' he said.

'We do have staff. Although the cost is getting prohibitive. A Labour government doesn't help. Wilson thinks the aristocracy is richer than it is. All the capital's in the land. We've no cash for tax. Fortunately Elizabeth has quite a bit of money so we won't run dry.'

'I presume you have to be careful.'

'She's given over her finances to me. That gives us a bit of a buffer. There are also advantages in having a wife who's a Roman Catholic. To some extent I can do what I like, knowing that she's never going to divorce me.'

'I am sure she could; in a civil capacity.'

'But she won't. She hates any kind of fuss and she's made a vow before God. You, of all people, know how serious that is.'

'Marriage vows are taken by both parties, are they not?' Sidney asked mildly.

'Don't worry. I'm not planning on doing anything *mad*.'

Sir Mark turned his concentration back to the road ahead. The frost had melted, and the sleet gave the tarmac a light gleam. A pheasant flew out from the nearby hedgerow. Rooks perched in the skeletal trees.

Sidney pressed his point. 'It still does not give either of you licence to do what you like.' He tried to smile as he spoke in order to make his words sound less judgemental but Sir Mark either failed to notice his censure or ignored it, preferring to tell the other people in the Land Rover how he planned to sell off some of the land they were passing 'to house a few plebs'.

Shouty Meynell made a loud observation from the back seat. 'Builders will pay anything these days and there's good money in property.'

'Don't you want to preserve the estate as it is?' Henry Richmond asked. 'Leave it for future generations?'

'There's plenty of land left for my nephew. Besides, what does it matter? If you only live once then you've got to live well. I've little hope of heaven.'

They arrived at the copse and before unloading the guns Sir Mark offered Sidney his hip flask. 'Whisky Mac?'

'Bit early for me.'

'Nonsense. It's a cold day . . .'

'I wouldn't like to see you run dry.'

'Rita will come and replenish it soon enough – she sees to most of my needs . . .'

'Rita?'

'Her real name's Nancy but her surname's Hayworth, so I call her Rita. Makes her feel like a film star.'

'I'm sure it does.' Sidney knew that this might be the moment to ask more about Sir Mark's marriage but Shouty Meynell was close. He didn't want to make any questioning look obvious.

'*Entre nous* I'm hoping she'll soon be seeing to a lot more of them, if you know what I mean . . .'

Had Sir Mark forgotten that Sidney was a clergyman or did he not care? He was being addressed as if he was still in the army.

Shouty Meynell rejoined them. 'We get your drift all right.'

'It's my house, my staff. One has to have the odd perk even if it does take a bit of time to scale the battlements. Let's get going.'

Sir Mark strode ahead, assuming that everyone would follow. He was not the type of man to look back. 'I normally start on the fourth. Then we take it in turns. The gamekeeper will sort you out. Make sure your gun is loaded and ready by the time you reach your stand. The beaters will let us know when the birds are on their way.'

The sleet eased, and the first drive was conducted in customary silence apart from the usual cries of 'Yours' when a gun was leaving a shot for the next man, or 'Mine'. There was a goodly stock of birds and plenty of beaters to do the work, and the game was easy prey; somewhat too easy, Sidney thought as he fired at will. By the time they had reached the third drive there were murmurs of approval at his prowess.

'Who'd have thought a clergyman would be so good with a gun?' Sir Mark observed as Musket arrived at his feet with a pheasant. 'Not sure if that's one of mine. Could be yours. I'm not going to argue now I've seen the way you shoot.'

'Army training . . .' Sidney explained.

'One wonders why you ever became a clergyman.'

'Like the war itself, there wasn't much choice.'

'You could have been a padre.'

'It was on my conscience to fight; just as now it is my duty to be a priest. To fail to do so would be to deny God. He has knocked and I have answered.'

'Well I only hope he doesn't come banging on my door.'

'It is considered a blessing,' Sidney replied.

'I'm happy with my life as it is.'

'Really?' Sidney asked. 'Most people feel that there's always room for improvement.'

'That may be true,' Sir Mark replied, 'but, as you can probably see, I'm more body than soul.'

Sidney was tempted to talk about the corruptibility of the flesh and the incorruptibility of the spirit but this was not the time. He unloaded his gun, slid it into its sleeve and joined Dr Robinson for the next drive.

Lunch had been arranged in a makeshift gazebo in the grounds of Denny Abbey. There was a sit-down meal for the guns and the women who had joined them for lunch while the beaters and the pickers-up had soup and sandwiches outside.

On the way over in the Land Rover, Hildegard had sat in the back and inspected the reddening around Elizabeth's neck. A scarf could not quite conceal it. Perhaps something more had happened in the night? She decided to be Sidney's eyes and ears, and would pay particular attention to the maid on whom her employer appeared so keen.

At lunch Amanda continued her flirtation with Henry Richmond. He talked about his estate, and how it had been in the family for over three hundred years, and that it was a heavy burden of responsibility to carry on his own, but he had good people around him and he had learned to manage even if it was a bit lonely at times.

There were two more drives in the afternoon before the mist drifted in from the east and the sun dropped below the tree line. Sidney remembered how quickly autumn days fell away into darkness. He used the pause between drives to replenish his stock of cartridges and have a quick word with Dr Robinson about Elizabeth.

'What did you make of that wound on her neck? Did you think it was an accident?'

'I have my doubts; and I think you do too.'

At the end of the last drive, the keeper blew his horn and told the guns to unload and re-sleeve their weapons. Sidney and his companions did as they were told, picked up any spent cartridges and stricken birds and took them to the game cart where they were matched into braces. The keeper counted the bag and made his tally: sixty-three pheasant, eighteen partridge and twelve geese. Each member of the party was given a brace and Sidney tipped with a half-crown as he had been told, only to notice that his fellow guns were handing over ten-bob notes.

'Oh I'm so sorry . . .'

'Don't worry,' the gamekeeper smiled. 'I know you're not made of money. We don't often have people like you with us. To be honest, I didn't expect a clergyman to be such a good shot.'

'Did Sir Mark tell you I was a priest?'

'Didn't need to. You're getting quite a reputation in the county. But I won't tell anyone what you're really here for.'

'There's nothing untoward, I can assure you. I have come for the shoot.'

'Of course. Mum's the word.'

'Excuse me,' Sidney asked as the man was leaving. 'Actually, what *do* you think I'm here for?'

'Lady Kirby-Grey.'

'I'm not sure I understand?'

'We all know what's been going on, Canon Chambers. I, for one, am glad you're here to see it. It's got to stop.'

By the time Sidney arrived back at Witchford Hall he was wet, tired and longing for a cup of tea and a toasted teacake followed by a long hot bath and a whisky. So far, the day had passed without any incident other than the gamekeeper's inscrutable warning. Did he mean what Sidney thought he meant or was there more? Perhaps Elizabeth was hiding something else that accounted for her nervousness; something other than grief after the loss of her son.

Sidney tried to concentrate on matters in hand, not least his need to change out of his muddy clothes and to see whether Hildegard had enjoyed a pleasant afternoon. Sir Mark called over to his butler. 'Get Rita to run me a bath, will you? See to it that she makes it nice and hot. Now where's that bloody wife of mine? I want a drink.'

The post-shoot dinner was an improvement on the previous evening: a robust French onion soup, boeuf bourguignon with passable mashed potato and a reassuring apple crumble. There was an air of tired satisfaction after the exertions of the day.

Before Sir Mark dwindled into drunkenness he regaled the company with the story of a distant relative who had been duped into marriage and squandered his estate.

'Let this be a warning to you, Richmond, now that you are back on the marriage market.'

'I have no immediate plans.'

'Even with our clergyman here to do the deed?'

'I'm afraid so.'

'Then it can be a cautionary fable for you, Miss Kendall.'

'I am aware of the need to be on my guard against fortune hunters,' Amanda replied. 'But this is hardly the right place to combine a discussion of marital prospects with money.'

'What happened to your relative?' Sidney asked, anxious to change the subject away from a public debate about his friend's private future.

Sir Mark continued, enjoying the attention. 'It was more than a hundred years ago, over in Norfolk. I think that everyone knew there was something wrong with Freddie from the start. From an early age he never could tell when he had had enough to eat, and there are stories of him screeching, howling, slavering, carpet-biting, gorging on food, vomiting at the table, and even, on one occasion, ordering seventeen eggs for breakfast.'

'Extraordinary,' Amanda commented.

'He also loved dressing up. In that respect, he was like a little boy even when he became an adult. One night he was nearly arrested after impersonating a policeman and rounding up fallen women in the Haymarket.

'How did he ever marry?'

'He was taken in by a family in St James's. That was

supposed to sort things out, but it didn't go entirely to plan. One night he scalded himself in the bath and ran through the corridors naked. His landlady mistook his horrified ranting as a chance to expose himself.'

'She complained?'

'Volubly. Although it's easy enough to scald yourself.' Sir Mark looked down the table to his wife at the opposite end. 'You've done that yourself, haven't you, my darling?'

'It was a silly mistake. I wasn't thinking . . .'

'So what happened?' Shouty interrupted. 'To your relative?'

'A beautiful woman called Agnes Willoughby is "what happened"; together with an Italian opera singer and a confidence trickster. She seduced Freddie, even though she had two lovers already, and persuaded him to make over his entire estate to her on marriage. His uncle then had to save the family fortune and annul the marriage by saying that Freddie was a lunatic.'

'Did he succeed?'

'No. The case, *De Lunatico Inquirendo*, took place in the winter of 1861–2. It lasted thirty-four days at a cost of £20,000. There were a hundred and forty witnesses called, fifty for the petitioners and ninety for Frederick Windham, who was proud of his marriage and his sanity. The case collapsed, Freddie was ruined and he ended up living with his nanny. He died at the age of twenty-five after a fourteen-hour drinking session with a group of Ipswich post-boys.'

'A lesson to avoid excess,' Dr Robinson observed.

'I once knew a priest who was prone to depression,' said Sidney, hoping that no one in the company had heard his story before. 'When he felt the horrors approaching, he would hole up in the grimmest boarding house in the most depressing town he could find, in order to plumb the very depths of his slough of despond. The idea was, that after hitting rock bottom, he would emerge into a world in which everything would look so much better than his most recent dismal experience. The town he chose for this misery, curiously enough, was Ipswich.'

'My grandmother is from round there,' Serena Stein added airily. 'Not that it matters. I only hope the lunacy doesn't run in the family.'

'I should think not.' Sir Mark turned to his wife. 'You got off lightly with me, my darling.'

'I'm very grateful.'

'You don't sound convinced,' Serena observed.

Elizabeth made to move and the men around the table began to stand up. 'I'm rather tired, will you excuse me?'

Her husband was having none of it. 'Sit down, everyone.' He turned on his wife. 'How can you be tired? We've been the people who've been out in the cold all day. What have you been doing, woman?'

'I'm sorry, Mark. I just feel very weak all of a sudden.'

'You're leaving?'

'I don't feel well. We have finished the pudding.'

Dr Robinson started towards her. 'Is there anything I can do?'

'Sit down, Michael. She's often like this.'

'Please, Mark, let me go . . .'

'What about our guests; the ladies retiring?'

'I can look after them,' said Amanda.

'You're not the hostess.'

Elizabeth turned in the doorway. 'Please, Mark, don't make

a fuss. It's nothing to worry about. I may be able to come down again in a minute or two. I just need some air . . .'

Amanda stood up. 'I'll help you to your room.'

'Hayworth can do that.'

Elizabeth was agitated. 'I'd like Amanda.'

'Rather defeats the purpose of the weekend if she goes off too.'

'The purpose?' Amanda asked.

'To find you a rich husband, you silly woman. That was my wife's plan.'

Elizabeth was too tired to argue. 'Mark, this isn't the time. I'm going upstairs.'

'I don't think that can be right,' said Henry as gallantly as he could. 'I'm sure Miss Kendall has plenty of admirers. She doesn't need to come here to find any more.'

'There are millions,' Amanda replied. 'I don't know why I haven't chosen anyone yet. I must be a "silly woman". Please excuse me. I should see to Elizabeth.'

Rather than confront an embarrassed silence Sir Mark pretended that nothing had happened. 'It's just as well it's time for port and cigars. At the rate we're going we won't have any women left. Where's Muir?' (The butler was already hovering, having seen the ladies to the staircase.) 'Tell Hayworth to come in and clear the plates.'

'That was a little harsh,' said Shouty Meynell.

Henry Richmond kept his counsel.

'Don't you think you should see to your wife?' Sidney asked.

'It's not me she needs. Besides, Amanda is with her; unless you'd like to go too. Not that you'd be much help . . .'

'I'm sorry?'

95

'Her being a Roman Catholic.'

'I don't think that makes much difference in a situation like this.'

'I think we should leave them to their own devices. Muir! Where's the bloody port?'

Serena Stein withdrew with the doctor's wife while the remaining men stayed at the table. Just after the women had left the room a plate was dropped.

'FOR GOD'S SAKE!' Sir Mark shouted but immediately relented on seeing that the culprit was Nancy Hayworth. 'That's all right, Rita, just clear it up.'

The conversation resumed, with more thoughts about shooting, estate management and the forthcoming balls, before the men finally rejoined the ladies in order to play a few rounds of bridge. Lady Kirby-Grey was 'resting' and Amanda tried not to look piqued in front of Henry Richmond. The row had left a stain on the proceedings, the resulting congenial atmosphere was unconvincing and the party broke up well before midnight.

Once they had retired to their room and exchanged a few eyebrow-raising observations on the course of the evening, Hildegard said that she was thirsty. She wasn't sure how well she was going to sleep and wondered if there was any chance of a bedtime cup of cocoa. Sidney offered to find out.

As he descended the back stairs to the kitchen he saw Sir Mark leaning down in a distant doorway.

He heard a woman's voice: 'Get off me. I've told you. No hanky-panky. Someone will see.'

'You know what I want.'

'Then you have to bring me the money.'

It was Nancy Hayworth.

Sidney retreated quietly back up the stairs. Hildegard would have to survive without cocoa.

The next morning was Advent Sunday and, because the living at the local church of St Magnus the Martyr was vacant, Sidney had to sing for his supper. He preached on the subject of fragility and vulnerability, thinking not only of the Christ child but of Elizabeth, his hostess. He wanted to make sure that even Sir Mark understood what he was saying, and so he spoke slowly, without his customary friendliness, about how it was our responsibility to console those who mourn, support the weak and comfort the afflicted be they near to us or far. Sometimes, Sidney argued, the need for moral decency was closer to home than we thought. We might not necessarily, for example, behave as well with our loved ones as we did with friends or even colleagues and strangers. It was our Christian duty, therefore, to examine our consciences and understand that our greatest strength might be to show our weaknesses; to confess our failings, and acknowledge our helplessness; to become as open and defenceless as the Christ child who came amongst us.

(As soon as Sidney started talking about the infant wrapped in swaddling clothes he missed Anna all over again. In three weeks' time she would be one year old. He was desperate to return home and see her.)

Amanda walked with him on the way back from church. After praising him for his sermon, she said that she was still concerned about Elizabeth. Sidney had brought their anxieties into focus. But how much should she confront a woman who kept saying that there was nothing to worry about when so clearly there was quite a lot going on, most obviously that Sir

Mark was taking out his frustration on being unable to have an affair, and possibly on being blackmailed, by hitting his wife?

As they gathered for drinks before lunch, both Sidney and Hildegard spotted that Elizabeth appeared to have a new bruise on the back of her calf. It showed underneath her stockings. It was discreet, as if she had been kicked in order to make her fall down, and then, perhaps, struck again, but visible.

Dr Robinson had already noticed it and, at Sidney's prompting, offered to take a closer look but their hostess refused. 'Please don't tell anyone. Especially Mark. It's such a silly thing. I banged it on the car door. It's my pale skin. I bruise very easily. I wouldn't want anyone making a fuss. It happens all the time. I'm perfectly all right. I promise.'

'Do you have any other bruises?' Dr Robinson asked.

'No. Not a scratch. We're home now. I must check if everything is in order for the lunch. Mark hates it if the food is late. I'll ask Nancy.'

'Is that the maid your husband calls "Rita"?' Sidney asked.

'Yes, it's his little joke; after Rita Hayworth. *Gilda* is his favourite film.'

'Has she been with you long?'

'A few months. Her mother is an old friend of Mark's.'

'Is it working out well?'

'Mark likes her and that's generally what matters. Now if you'll excuse me . . .'

There was roast lamb for lunch, a good-enough claret and a treacle sponge with custard for pudding. Sidney was patronised about his sermon and Hildegard was asked once more about the war, explaining yet again that, no, her father had not been a Nazi but a Communist, and that she had settled very well in England and considered it to be her home. It was clear that they had exhausted all their conversational opportunities and that they really should get home before dark.

As with all country-house parties, and despite the help of Muir and the two maids, it took a further half an hour for everyone to make sure they had all their possessions, get into the right cars, and say their goodbyes. Dr Robinson and his wife, like Sidney and Hildegard, were driving back to Cambridge. Amanda was catching a train to London with Shouty Meynell, Serena Stein and Henry Richmond.

Sidney noticed that Elizabeth was anxious with Amanda before she departed, saying quickly, 'I wish you didn't have to go.'

'Come with me then.'

'I can't. You know how he is.'

'You must stand up for yourself, Elizabeth.'

'I do.'

'Come to London as soon as you can. We could go shopping. You could get a few bargains in the New Year sales. Or sooner.'

'I need a new coat.'

'What's wrong with the one you've got?' Sir Mark approached unnoticed.

Elizabeth clasped her friend's arm and then kissed her goodbye. 'I'll try.'

'Don't try,' Amanda replied. 'Just come.'

As Sidney got into his car there was one more thing he noticed. It was not simply that Sir Mark had joined them. Nancy Hayworth had been dealing with luggage and heard every word. Had she tipped off her employer so that he could interrupt the conversation?

Although Hildegard was tired and anxious to get home to their daughter, she was keen to talk over what they had witnessed. She reminded Sidney of Sir Mark's discussion of the case of his relative. How much had he followed Agnes Willoughby's example in persuading a spouse to make over their fortune on marriage?

'Tell me one thing,' Hildegard began, asking a question that Sidney had dared not voice aloud himself. 'Do you think Elizabeth's life is in danger?'

They arrived in Grantchester just after four, and were thrown back into the routine of family and parish life. Iris Chambers told them that Anna was in fine fettle and she had enjoyed looking after her granddaughter. The dear little thing was going to be talking soon and she must come and see her cousins in London. Jennifer's boys were only a year or two older and they could help her advance. Their grandfather would enjoy seeing them all together.

Sidney was not sure how much patience or enthusiasm his father could extend to three children under the age of four but expressed his gratitude, gave his mother tea and drove her to the train station. He was back just in time to ready himself for the first carol service of the season. Hildegard had asked if she could be excused, wanting a moment on her own with Anna. She had already been to church that day. It was therefore well into the evening when Malcolm Mitchell handed Sidney a letter from the Church Commissioners that had arrived in Saturday's post.

Sidney retired to his study and discovered that he had been offered the archdeaconry of Ely. It was a promotion at last, and to somewhere not at all far – less than twenty miles – but it would mean leaving the parish he knew and loved, giving Hildegard and Anna a new start and being more involved in the running of the Church of England. No conditions were attached but he was pretty sure that he would be expected to steer clear of any criminal investigations in the future.

Being an archdeacon was like being the area manager of a bank, he decided, responsible for the upkeep of buildings, the filling of vacancies, and the settling of disputes. It was a step on the career ladder, a natural progression towards what many considered to be the ultimate goal: a bishopric. But did Sidney want that? In his current post he was given considerable freedom to do what he liked. How constrained would he be by greater responsbility? He was hardly in a position to turn the invitation down (or, if he did, he would be unlikely to be offered any other promotion in the near future) but he was worried about the upheaval. Archdeacons always got a bad press, he recalled. They were considered schemers and power players, manipulating careers and reputations. His predecessor, Chantry Vine, who had left to become Dean of Bristol, had been prone to fits of fury and frustration when priests refused to obey his orders. Perhaps there were unreasonable levels of stress involved that changed a priest's personality? Sidney thought of Trollope's Archdeacon Grantly, and the smoke rising from his head every time he lifted his hat 'preventing positive explosion and probable apoplexy'. Would he, too, discover new reservoirs of fury of which he had previously been unaware?

He wanted to discuss the matter with Hildegard but she was singing to their daughter. He stood outside the door to Anna's room and listened, not wanting to interrupt.

'Weißt du, wieviel Mücklein spielen
in der heißen Sonnenglut,
wieviel Fischlein auch sich kühlen
in der hellen Wasserflut?'

Do you know how many little gnats
Play in the sun's intense heat,
How many little fish like to cool
In the clear high tide?

He had just decided that he couldn't wait any longer when Amanda telephoned to say that she had arrived back in London. That was not, however, the reason for her call. 'What on earth are we going to do about Elizabeth?' she began. 'I've been thinking about her all the way home. She's my best friend and she's not telling me the truth. I feel so helpless.'

Sidney tried to be practical. 'I think we should ask Michael Robinson to pay her a visit when her husband is out. We probably have to get rid of the maid too.'

'Why?'

'I think she's a spy.'

'You think that she and Mark are having an affair?'

'On the brink.'

'Then we must help Elizabeth before anything dreadful happens. Prevention, if there's still time, is better than cure. Perhaps you should talk to Keating?'

'There's not much to tell him.'

'Come on, Sidney . . .'

'I know; but proving it . . .'

Amanda sounded desperate. 'Do you think Elizabeth will tell the doctor anything?'

'I doubt it. But it's a start.'

'It's not enough.'

'What else are you proposing, Amanda?'

'I have spoken to Henry. I have told him that he has to have it out with Mark.'

'I'm not sure that's the kind of thing men do.'

'What on earth do you mean?'

'Henry will consider a man's marriage to be his own business. He will want to respect Sir Mark's privacy. It's considered poor form to intrude . . .'

'Well it's certainly bad manners to hit your wife.'

'We don't know he's doing that, Amanda.'

'We have a fairly good idea.'

'There is still the notion of privacy. Henry Richmond won't want to risk his friendship with Sir Mark by asking impertinent questions or making insinuations . . .'

'He won't be as direct as that.'

'If he wants Sir Mark to listen to anything he says then he may have to be.'

'Henry's already told me that he doesn't like confrontation.'

'Then goodness knows what he is doing with you.'

Amanda did not always appreciate Sidney's wry asides and was humourless in her response. 'He's not "doing" anything with me. Besides, a man can always be trained up.'

'I'm not so sure. Hildegard thinks that men are remarkably resilient to change.'

'Your wife lets you get away with murder . . .'

'I think she'd stop at that.'

'I'm sorry.' Amanda was contrite. 'That wasn't necessary. I'm sorry. I'm upset. I am trying my best.'

'I think our friendship can forgive any inappropriate remarks.'

'That's what I've told Henry about Mark. He has to risk their friendship. Truth is more important than misplaced loyalty.'

'Then it will be up to him to decide. I am sure he won't find it easy.'

'Perhaps you could give him a few tips?'

'What do you mean?'

'Well, Sidney, you do know how to get information out of people.'

'Sometimes people just tell me things.'

'And that never interests you? You can't fool me, Chambers. You love knowing stuff that no one else does.'

'Sometimes it's a heavy burden.'

'You can always lighten your load by talking to Hildegard. That's one of the points of marriage, is it not?'

'So I believe.'

'And that's why I'm testing out Henry. Do you see what I'm doing, Sidney? Two birds, one very large stone. Goodbye, my darling.'

Amanda rang off. Sidney had no intention of giving his friend's potential partner a few 'tips'. In fact he was not sure that the relationship was a good idea at all but at least Amanda was not rushing as she had done before.

He returned to matters in hand. He had to tell Hildegard both about the phone call and the letter from the Church

Commissioners. He could hear that she was still singing to their daughter and he would start with the good news. He hoped that she would be pleased.

> *'Gott der Herr rief sie mit Namen,*
> *daß sie all ins Leben kamen,*
> *daß sie nun so fröhlich sind,*
> *daß sie nun so fröhlich sind.'*

> The Lord God called them by name,
> So that they all came to life,
> And now they are all so happy,
> And now they are all so happy.

*   *   *

Hildegard was first up with Anna the following morning and brought Sidney a cup of tea and a copy of *The Times* while he was still in bed. 'Perhaps one day we will have a butler as they have at Witchford Hall. When you are a bishop . . .'

'I don't think I want to be a bishop.'

'And a maid. You could have your own little Rita Hayworth. Would you like that?'

'Of course not, Hildegard. All I want is to be with you.'

'That is good because it is all you have got. I will get Anna dressed now and buy a map of Ely.'

'It's not a very big place.'

'It will be an adventure.' She stopped for a moment. 'Sometimes I thought we would never leave.'

'We can always come back.'

'It is time, my darling. I will let Byron out but you must walk him. You remember it is Malcolm's day off?'

'Have we got any food in the house?'

'I will go to the shops.'

Sidney took his Labrador out on to the meadows. Byron was a more unpredictable dog than his predecessor, Dickens, and Sidney had yet to get the measure of him. Although he lived in the moment, without any anxiety about the future, he appeared to anticipate what human beings around him were going to do, even if he wasn't actually able to act on that intuition. So what would Byron do if he was a human being at Witchford Hall? Would he, like Musket, be steady, 'free from chase', and unwaveringly loyal to his master? Could you teach a dog loyalty or was it instinctive? Were there parallels between the loyalty of a dog and the friendship between human beings and, if so, was Henry Richmond's reluctance to intervene a proof of his fidelity to friendship?

A few days later, on a similar outing, Sidney bumped into Michael Robinson. After a shaky start to their relationship, in which both he and Keating had suspected the medical practitioner of helping his elderly patients book an earlier passage to the next world than they had, perhaps, anticipated, Sidney had grown to like and trust the doctor's ability to bend the rules, not least in the previous year when he had dropped very strong hints as to which one of his patients might have been responsible for the theft of a baby.

Dr Robinson revealed that he had paid a call on Lady Elizabeth Kirby-Grey while her husband was staying at his club in London. She had scalded a foot while getting into a bath that was too hot for her, and was prepared to show the doctor her injury only to reveal that her back hurt too. On a cursory inspection this too was red, and her subsequent excuse (that she must have lain back without appreciating the high temperature of the water) had been unconvincing.

'You think she has been scalded deliberately?'

'Do I think, Sidney, that someone, the husband or even the maid, threw boiling water at her? Yes, I do. But until she tells me or anyone else exactly what has happened it's going to be hard to intervene. The burns are not that bad, and if this is a case of domestic violence then those responsible are being careful to make sure that any marks are on parts of the body that are regularly hidden from view: behind the hairline, on the foot, and now the back. In winter you wouldn't know that anything was amiss . . .'

'Apart from her leg . . .'

'Which may, ironically, have been caused by the incident she described. If there's a plausible explanation for that then she might be persuaded there's a reason for everything.'

'You think the maid and husband are in it together?'

'I think you do, Canon Chambers.'

'I am afraid so. Amanda detailed Henry Richmond to ferret out the truth but I don't hold out much hope.'

'Did you know we were all at Millingham together?' the doctor asked.

'The school? No, I didn't.'

'Dreadful place. Mark was bullied. We used to call him Marina Kirby-Grip. His father was a terrible man. Drank, as you might expect. Hopeless after nine in the evening. When Mark wrote to his mother saying he was unhappy at school his father intercepted the message and replied by sending the letter straight back to his son with the spelling and punctuation corrected. It's hard to know how to love when you've been brought up like that. Mark had to learn how to make friends and he did most of that by spending money and being a buffoon. After his father died, his mother ran off with another man within a month. At least Mark was left with the estate. But that's probably why he married so young. He needed someone to help him . . .'

'And someone who won't "run off" like his mother.'

'Exactly. It's often the case that the bullied becomes the bully. I'm worried this could get out of hand. It also tends to get worse with age; not to mention drink. Do you think you should alert Inspector Keating? I thought you two met regularly.'

'Thursday nights.'

'Tomorrow then?'

'Yes, Michael. Tomorrow.'

Sidney would rather have discussed his potential move to Ely with Geordie Keating but recognised that he did not really need his friend's advice. He was going to have to take the job and so the next time they met for their customary two pints in the RAF bar of the Eagle he decided that he would not mention it quite yet. He asked his friend about domestic violence instead.

Keating explained how the odds were stacked against abused women. 'There often isn't any concrete evidence that the husband is the one doing the beating. It could be a lover or another family member.'

'I don't think that's likely in this case. At least there are no children.'

'If the wife won't tell us there is anything wrong . . .'

'She won't.'

'Because she is so afraid of her husband?'

'I think so. What can be done?'

'We have to construct a case on the basis of evidence other than that of the victim. That means you, Sidney, and Amanda, and any witnesses. Her maid, for example.'

'I think she's having an affair with the husband.'

'He's made her his accomplice. What about the doctor? He's crucial. We can investigate on medical evidence. Would he testify?'

'I am sure of it.'

'Then that's a start. The best thing, however, would be to sort all this out before it gets to court. The publicity never helps and the husband often nurses even more of a grievance.'

'Even though he's the one at fault?'

'They don't always see it that way. First they deny it altogether; then they say it is just between them and the wife. Finally they complain that they have been provoked. And, in a case like this, the accused probably knows the judge, however remotely. It's always harder to convict a toff. They never think they've done anything wrong.'

'Never?'

'Hardly ever.'

'They don't even apologise?'

'Repentance is your job; and while the legal situation is tricky, my official advice is to persuade both parties to sort it out amongst themselves.'

'And your unofficial advice?'

'Is to get Lady Kirby-Grey out of her house and away from her husband as quickly as possible. These things hardly ever die down. In fact, they get worse.'

*   *   *

The next morning Hildegard brought Anna into their bed from her cot. She had discovered a new game; holding on to the bedstead to balance, facing the door with her back towards them, before bouncing up and down, then stopping and looking back at her parents to check that they were watching.

'I think she might turn out to be very musical,' said Sidney as he got out of bed to perform his first duty of the day: making the morning tea.

'Why do you think that?'

'Billie Holiday said that jazz is all in the bounce. Anna's got plenty of that. How young can she start to learn the piano?'

'She needs to be able to read first. We don't want to push her. Do you think she's progressing all right?'

'She isn't yet one. She hasn't even started to speak.'

'She has. I am convinced she said "Dada". '

'I think it's sweet that all fathers assume their daughters' first words will be about them.'

'Do they?'

'So I'm told.'

'She hasn't said "*Mutti*" yet?'

'I will tell you when she does . . . but in the meantime, she needs a feed. You will let Byron out . . .'

'It is part of my morning routine, as well you know.'

Sidney put on slippers that had seen better days (perhaps Hildegard would give him a new pair for Christmas?) and padded downstairs. Life was so much simpler when it was like this. All he had to do was make the tea and look after the people he loved. Soon Anna would be walking and speaking and

110

expressing her opinions. Would she be more like her father or her mother? How could he protect her against the disappointments, perils and dangers of the world?

It was half past seven. Sidney thought of Elizabeth Kirby-Grey. Would she still be asleep? He tried to imagine what it must be like to wake up having been hit or burned in the night; to be the subject or both subtle and explicit abuse. Why did her husband torture her in this way, and how much did Nancy Hayworth know?

He had just given Hildegard her tea and was about to shave when Amanda telephoned. As soon as she had ascertained that she was speaking to Sidney she launched into a diatribe about 'that pathetic fool of a man I've been seeing'.

'You mean Henry?'

'He didn't mention it to Mark at all. When I started to speak to him *very firmly indeed* he apologised and said "the situation never arose". Well, *of course* it didn't. I don't know much about gentleman's clubs but I am pretty sure they don't stand around the billiard table discussing the best way to beat up their wives.'

'They don't.'

'So I am having lunch with Elizabeth.'

'Good.'

'And you're coming too.'

'Really, Amanda, wouldn't it be better if you were alone together?'

'No it would not. You are not wriggling out of this one. It's in Cambridge next Tuesday.'

'I'm sure I've got something on.'

'Well, cancel it. Bleu Blanc Rouge, twelve thirty. Mark will be out. I got Henry to check. That's one thing my wholly inadequate suitor managed to do for me. Now it's up to us.'

Christmas was not the best time of year to be arranging assignations. Aside from seeing his family and sending out Christmas cards (a task that would, inevitably, fall to Hildegard), Sidney was about to embark on a run of carol services at Corpus, in church, and around local schools. He had also made a vow that he would call in on every parishioner personally to bestow the compliments of the season. Despite Malcolm's diligence, he wanted to make it clear that this was his primary duty and that he was able to fulfil his obligations as a priest without distraction. As a result, he hoped that no one would see him when he bicycled across the meadows on a cold winter morning to meet Amanda at Cambridge station. The decorations were up and a banner had been hung across the entrance: *Peace on Earth, Goodwill to all Men.*

'I see women don't get much of a look-in,' Amanda observed.

'Is Elizabeth meeting us there? I hope she turns up.'

'I think she's desperate to tell someone what's really going on.'

The Bleu Blanc Rouge had been decked with festive cheer and offered a menu that was a French version of the kind of food that might be served at Witchford Hall: a chicken chasseur, brandied roasted goose, turkey with chestnut stuffing and a *Bûche de Noël.*

'At least we know it will be properly cooked this time,' Amanda smiled before ordering a glass of champagne.

'Do you think that's appropriate?' Sidney asked.

'It'll be gone by the time Elizabeth arrives, don't worry.'

'Shouldn't we wait?'

'She said she might be held up. We're early. I didn't want her to have to be stuck here on her own.'

'I can think of worse places to be stranded.'

Elizabeth arrived fifteen minutes later and was unusually poised, dressed in a camel coat and scarf, dark woollen skirt, stockings and sensible shoes. Every part of her was covered but, Sidney supposed, it was winter. Amanda asked if her husband knew she was with them.

'He has allowed me an hour and a half.'

'Is that all?'

'I think it will give him time to see his mistress.'

'You know about that?'

'He's had one for years. Have you ordered?'

'Not Nancy Hayworth?' Sidney asked.

'Her mother.' Elizabeth spoke as if this was a natural state of affairs. 'Why do you think Nancy works for us?'

'Why would she want to?'

'Because he pays her well. And she acts as her mother's spy.' She put down her menu. 'I think I'll have the goose.'

'Does your husband know that you are aware of the situation?'

'He thinks I'm not, but I am. And even if he knew that I knew, he can be confident that I wouldn't make a fuss about it.'

'You don't mind?'

'I don't have much choice.'

'Because he frightens you . . .' Amanda began.

'Do we have to talk about this?'

'Please . . .' Amanda touched her friend's hand.

'I suppose he thinks it helps him get over Peter. Consolation I can't give because I am part of the grief.'

The waiter came to take their order and Sidney tried to assess the situation. This was a very different Elizabeth from the woman who had been his hostess. He asked again about Nancy Hayworth. 'Sir Mark seems very fond of her.'

'He's attentive to most women, Canon Chambers.'

'Doesn't that worry you?'

'They are a distraction. And they put him in a good mood. It means he's kinder to me.'

Amanda came to the point. 'Not all the time.'

'Please, Amanda, I didn't come here to be lectured.'

'Mark hits you, darling. We know. Please tell us.'

'What good would it do?'

'Perhaps we can help stop it.'

'It's too late for that.' Elizabeth looked out of the window, perhaps hoping that by doing so her fellow diners would disappear. 'Besides, I'm used to it. It's not something anyone else should be concerned about.'

'But we worry.'

'That's kind. I don't think Mark knows the pain he causes. He says he hates himself afterwards, and he needs consoling. That's hard sometimes, comforting a husband who has been violent. But he doesn't mean it.'

'Then why does he do it?' Amanda asked.

'Because he is lost. Because we don't know who we are any more. Ever since Peter . . . I don't know. He buys me presents to apologise.'

'With your money,' Amanda interrupted.

'Our money. What's mine is his.' She held out her hand.

'Look. He bought me an eternity ring. He knows that whatever happens we will always be together.'

'Are you frightened of him?' Sidney asked.

'Not all the time.'

'Most of the time,' Amanda suggested.

'Some of the time. Mainly in the evenings; and when he's been drinking.'

'That's most of the time.'

'It's been getting better. He's very sweet to me in the mornings – if he doesn't have a hangover. And he says he's trying to do better. He promises me it will stop.'

'And do you believe him?'

'He's very sincere when he makes his promises.'

The food arrived and there was a temporary respite. Elizabeth asked Sidney about his Christmas preparations, Anna's birthday (it was the following week) and if Amanda had seen any more of Henry Richmond. She thought he was coming for dinner in the next few days. How were they getting on?

'Very well. But I am taking it as slowly as I can. I need to be able to look Sidney in the face when I tell him about these things.'

'You don't need my approval.'

'You know perfectly well that I do.'

'Dear, oh dear,' said Elizabeth. 'To think if you'd married each other we would have had hours of banter.'

'Then it's just as well we didn't,' Amanda replied, refusing to meet Sidney's eye. 'But, in any case, we're not here to talk about my relationship but yours. When did your husband last hit you?'

'Really, Amanda . . .'

'Tell us.'

'It wasn't much of a blow . . .'

'What was it?'

Elizabeth picked up a glass of water, looked at it, and then put it down again. 'Sometimes I think it's my fault. After Peter . . .'

'That wasn't your fault.'

'Mark thinks it was.'

'He was with his nanny,' Amanda reminded.

'Then we should have chosen a different one. Someone more reliable.'

'You can't blame yourself.'

'I think Mark blames me for everything. He says I provoke him. I ask too many questions. I'm too nervous. I am not a good enough hostess.'

'You're a brilliant hostess,' Sidney chipped in.

'I'm not. I never know how to put people at their ease.'

Sidney put his hand on hers, and realised that he was covering the eternity ring. 'Perhaps that's because you are never at ease yourself.'

Amanda gave him a look that Sidney read as a form of punctuation: his gesture was too intimate, he had gone far enough. He withdrew his hand.

'I can't leave him, if that's what you want me to do.' Elizabeth pushed her food around her plate. She had hardly eaten.

'I think you must.'

'I made a vow on my wedding day. I cannot break it.'

'Perhaps your husband has already done so . . .' Sidney observed.

'I thought you always spoke in favour of reconciliation?' Elizabeth asked.

'Not if there is the danger of something worse.'

'There is nothing wrong.'

'We all know there is,' Amanda said gently.

And then the mask fell and the tears came. 'He says he can't help himself. It's because he is unhappy. He feels a failure.'

Sidney handed her a handkerchief. 'He doesn't look a failure.'

'It's an act. Some days he's happy and excitable; at other times he's unutterably depressed. That's when he drinks. Although he drinks when he's happy too. He says he doesn't know who he is. He can never be the man he was expected to be, the man he says his father wanted him to become. He misses his mother. He doesn't even know where she is or if she's alive or dead. She abandoned him. And he thinks I might do the same. He says he can never hold on to things – not even a son. Everything flies away. He feels utterly alone. I suppose that's why he has his affairs. He's desperate. He wants to escape his fate but he can't. He needs my money. And he says he can't live without me even though sometimes he hates me for it. I should be more of a wife.'

'Leave him,' said Amanda.

'I can't. He needs help. There's even a man in Harley Street but Mark won't do anything about it. He's too proud. He told me that he'd kill himself if I ever left him.'

'That's cruel,' said Sidney.

'I can't put it to the test, can I?'

Amanda changed tack. 'Henry's going to talk to him.'

Elizabeth gave Sidney back his handkerchief and looked at her watch. 'I don't think that will do much good.'

'He promised.'

'Mark won't listen to anyone. Serena tried again only recently . . .'

'When?'

Elizabeth picked up her handbag. 'Just before you all left. Now Mark says he never wants her in his house again. I don't know what to do. Would you like me to pay for this?'

'Not at all. We will help you,' said Sidney.

'Come and stay with me in London,' Amanda offered. 'Come now. Until things blow over. We can send for your things.'

Elizabeth stood up. 'I have to go.'

'He might kill you.'

'Then I am at God's mercy.'

'That's not enough,' Amanda observed before Sidney could say anything.

'All I can do is try to look after him. I want to make things right. If I leave he will follow me. That is what he has threatened. He will follow me to the ends of the earth and he will murder me. Then he'll shoot himself. That's what he says.'

Police cautions, Keating told Sidney, were rarely appropriate in cases of domestic violence. If something needed to be done then Sidney and Amanda would have to gather more evidence from potential witnesses. 'The morality and practice of intervention in domestic affairs is incredibly difficult.'

They were in Keating's car and had stopped before the final approach to Witchford Hall. Sidney had telephoned to ask whether he had left any of his shooting paraphernalia on his previous visit and the butler had told him that he was fairly sure this was unlikely, but if sir would like to call then he would be welcome at any time apart from Tuesday afternoon, when both Sir Mark and Lady Kirby-Grey would be out at a Rotary Club luncheon. Sidney and Keating had therefore picked this exact time for a visit in order to speak to the staff; and to Nancy Hayworth in particular.

The maid was not in uniform but wore a geometrically patterned black and white mini-dress, with dark tights and patent-leather ankle boots. A friend was coming to pick her up and take her Christmas shopping. 'I can't think what you want with me,' she said. 'I haven't done anything wrong.'

Keating assured Nancy that he was not accusing her of anything. He only wanted to ask a few questions about her employers.

'They don't like me talking.'

'Have they warned you not to?'

'I shouldn't be saying anything. You'd best speak to the butler.'

'Do you like your job?' Sidney asked.

'What's it got to do with you?'

'It seems strange. You don't seem to be a girl who would want to be in service.'

'Some of us don't have much choice.'

'Did your mother get you the job?'

'She put in a word. It's not meant to be for long. It's so I can save up a bit. I'm planning to go abroad. I quite fancy Switzerland. A friend of mine was a chalet girl. Managed to pick up a rich husband who ran his own perfume business. I like the sound of that.'

Sidney asked if there was somewhere private they could talk. It wouldn't take long.

Nancy Hayworth went on the attack. 'You should have asked when you were here last. I saw you on the back stairs. Snooping.'

'I was trying to get some cocoa.'

'No you weren't. You were *snooping*. I've heard about you.'

'Then you won't mind telling me what was going on.'

'I'm sure you could see well enough. That man gives me the creeps.'

'Sir Mark?' Keating checked.

'Who else? All he's interested in is drink, shooting and a bit of the other.'

'I was going to ask you about that . . .'

'Don't. He's my mother's *boyfriend*. What do you think I am: mad?'

'Listen,' Keating pressed, 'we don't have much time. Has he ever hit either you or your mother?'

'Neither, as far as I am aware. His wife's probably enough for him.'

'You've seen it?'

'Not exactly.'

'What have you seen?'

'Sir Mark'll go berserk if he finds out I've been speaking to you. I bet Muir will tell him and then we'll all be in trouble. I'll lose my job. You can't prove anything and his wife will deny it.'

Sidney was desperate now. 'Would you mind giving me your mother's address?'

Nancy Hayworth held Sidney's gaze. 'Why?'

'Because I don't like seeing women who have been abused and I don't want you to be next.'

'I can look after myself. It hasn't got that bad yet.'

'But it might. That man is dangerous, Nancy. He could hurt you.'

Nancy lost her defiance. 'Are you sure?'

'Positive.'

She looked at Keating. 'I don't like talking to the police.'

'Then speak to me,' Sidney suggested.

'I won't say anything,' Geordie agreed. 'I can leave if you like. He's a clergyman. A good man. You can trust him.'

'I hope you know what you're doing.'

'We're just trying to look after you.'

'And Lady Kirby-Grey.'

'Both of you. If we do nothing, things will only get worse,' Sidney replied. 'You have to help us, Nancy.'

He was in a sombre mood on the journey home, and he began to think about his next move before remembering that his actual 'next move' was to join the preparations for his daughter's first birthday party. His parents were coming, together with his sister and the boys, and even Uncle Matt had promised to put in an appearance. He knew that he had to make an extra effort because in an unguarded moment a few days earlier he had told his wife that he had a lot on and might not be able to stay for the whole thing. Failing to recognise this fundamental error (*It's your family, Sidney*), he had then made matters worse by saying that it probably didn't matter because his daughter was only a year old and wasn't going to remember much about it when she was older.

The icy reception to this remark gave Sidney notice that he would have to be a proper host to family and friends; a warning that was raised to red alert after he had tried to joke his way out of the situation by suggesting that they hide the cake to prevent Malcolm Mitchell eating it in advance of the big day. This was not considered amusing.

Amanda and Leonard Graham also came up from London, armed as godparents with the requisite soft toys, mobiles and building bricks. On arrival, Leonard was keen to know all the details of the latest case, and was intrigued by the fact that it had first come to their attention at a shooting party when so much else might have gone wrong. He was reminded, he said, of Turgenev's *Sketches from a Hunter's Album*, and looked forward to the day when he could introduce Anna to the joys of Russian literature.

Once the main party had broken up, Sidney made a surprise bid for domestic popularity by offering to do all the washing-up. Amanda said that she would stay behind and help while Leonard gave the new curate a few extra tips. Such was the intellectual terror of Leonard's presence that Malcolm had confined himself to three or four fairy cakes, a couple of dainties, and a single slice of the birthday sponge.

As Amanda washed and Sidney dried, she informed her friend that she had just had another row with Henry Richmond and had given him an ultimatum. He either had to confront Mark Kirby-Grey or they would have no future together.

'And what did your prospective beau say to that?'

'He thought it an unreasonable demand.'

'To make your love conditional?'

'Oh, I'm not sure it's love, Sidney. At the moment we haven't really got past expedience. That's why I'm so cross. As long as Elizabeth is in that house she is in danger. Have you any news yourself?'

Sidney reported on his recent visit to Witchford Hall and said that he planned to go and see Mrs Frances Hayworth that very evening.

'You mean you're slipping out? Is that why you offered to do the washing-up?'

'I thought I'd put some money in the bank.'

'You sly old dog.'

'I'll be taking Byron and combine it with a walk. She lives off the Trumpington Road. Works as a hairdresser.'

'I can't see Sir Mark stooping to the level of a hairdresser.'

'I imagine she's rather glamorous, if her daughter is anything to go by.'

'Is there a husband?'

'I'm not sure there ever was one.'

'How very risqué. You will be careful, won't you, Sidney?'

'The conversation could be a little tricky.'

'That's not what I mean, Chambers. I know your penchant for damsels in distress.'

'I have no idea what you are talking about, Amanda. I am a happily married man and, as far as I know, this woman is not in distress.'

'But she might be after one of your "conversations"?'

'I will stick to the point and be home in time for supper.'

'Then I look forward to hearing all about it. Hildegard has asked me to stay. It's a long time since she and I had a proper chat.'

'I hope you don't talk too much about me when I'm gone.'

'Don't worry, Sidney. It's possible that we might not talk about you at all.'

*   *   *

Sidney hoped that Nancy's mother was a dog-lover since he had found that people were seldom put out when in the presence of a Labrador.

Frances Hayworth was not as spellbindingly sensual as Sidney had been expecting. However, as he had often found in the past few years, it was always foolish to assume that a man's mistress was more attractive than his wife.

She was a woman of medium height with a high neck and a head that was almost too large to balance on top of it. She walked barefoot (following the example of singer Sandie Shaw), greeting Sidney in a simple low-cut dark-green dress with an accompanying silver necklace, earrings, and bangles that clanked together every time she moved; particularly when she raised her right arm, either to take a drag of her cigarette or a sip of her Cinzano.

'Could you leave your dog outside?' she asked. 'I can't stand the creatures.'

'Of course.'

'I don't want any dirt on my new white carpet.'

Sidney took off his shoes. He explained that he had recently spent the weekend at Witchford Hall and that he had met her daughter.

'She's not in trouble, is she?' Frances Hayworth asked.

'Not that I know of.'

'What did she tell you?'

'Only good things,' Sidney exaggerated. 'I gather you helped her get the job.'

'I did, but I can't see where this is leading.'

'Sir Mark has become something of a friend recently . . .'

'It's unlike him to welcome a vicar. He hasn't said anything to me.'

'And as a result I have worried about him.'

'Have you indeed?'

Sidney surprised even himself by this confident opening. Still, he might as well keep going. 'In fact, I rather wanted your advice; as a fellow friend, you understand.'

Frances Hayworth poured herself another Cinzano without offering any to her guest. 'Is it about his marriage, his money or his drinking? I'm not sure you can help in any of those cases.'

'If it's not too impertinent, I just wanted to know how often you saw him. It's just that I don't think he's been very happy recently.'

'No one would ever think he was content, despite the big house and the lavish lifestyle. It's because he never had a proper mother and he married a child. He comes to me so that he can be himself.'

'And what does that involve?'

'I'm sure you don't need me to spell it out.'

'I'm also worried about his wife.'

'As you can imagine, I don't see very much of *her*.'

'Indeed. Tell me, have you ever seen him lose his temper?'

'Of course.'

'And have you seen him lash out?'

'He tried to hit me once but I could see it coming and gave him a good slap. He never tried that again. In fact he started crying . . .'

'Did you feel sorry for him, Mrs Hayworth?'

'Not really.'

'And how long have you had your arrangement?'

'I'm not sure I'd call it that. A few years. Not that it's anything to do with you.'

'After his son died, I suppose.'

'What son? He doesn't have any children.'

Sidney backtracked. 'Then I must be mistaken. I wondered if either of you have ever wanted anything more.'

'Do you mean have I asked him to leave his wife? You're very nosy for a priest.'

'Curiosity is part of my concern.'

'And are you "concerned" about me?'

'I am, Mrs Hayworth. Perhaps you could answer my question?'

'I can't complain. He bought me this flat. I've got my freedom.'

'So you're happy just to carry on?'

'What else am I supposed to do? At my age there's only the married men and the rejects to choose from. At least Mark's got a bit of vim in him. And he makes me laugh. I don't ask for much.'

'And he gives your daughter money too?'

'Well, she does work for him.'

'As a maid . . .'

'Yes. What's wrong with that?'

At first Sidney had not been sure whether or not to tell Mrs Hayworth about Sir Mark's attentions to her daughter but, after her forthright responses to his questioning, he decided to do so. He introduced the information into the conversation ambiguously, so that Nancy's mother might fill in the gaps and conclude that the situation was worse than it was. The impact was immediate.

'He's WHAT? How do you know this?'

'I've seen them.'

'Together?'

'On the back stairs at Witchford Hall.'

'I don't believe it.'

'They were making some kind of arrangement. I couldn't tell what it was but I'm sure the other members of staff are aware of the situation. Even Lady Kirby-Grey suspects that something is up.'

'But my daughter would have told me about this. What on earth is she doing?'

'Perhaps it's a kind of blackmail?'

'Nancy?'

'Or maybe it's something else . . .' Sidney let the silence fall. This was almost evil. 'She told me she wants money. And like you, Mrs Hayworth, she seems to be getting it. It's not a very edifying situation, is it?'

'If that man's seduced my daughter . . .'

'Of course, it may not be that at all. A misunderstanding on my part . . .'

'It doesn't sound like it. I'll bloody kill him. I don't care if I've confessed before I've done it . . .'

'I wouldn't do that if I were you.'

'But you're not me. I tell you, I'll bloody kill him.'

The following evening Sidney recognised that the case was getting to him. He felt guilty about 'leading the witness' and was worried that he might have miscalculated. What was he doing involving himself in all this?

He was so on edge that he snapped at his curate for helping himself to a mince pie before one of the carol services. 'WILL YOU JUST STOP EATING?'

'I was hungry,' Malcolm spluttered. 'I didn't have any lunch.'

'That's nonsense. You just can't remember it.'

'I can, Sidney, I assure you. It was nibbles in Newnham.'

'Followed by canapés in Corpus, finger food in Fitzwilliam, starters at Selwyn and entrées at Emmanuel no doubt.'

'Really. There's no need to be cruel.'

Sidney stopped. What was becoming of him? This was not the behaviour of a prospective archdeacon.

'It's Christmas,' Malcolm continued. 'There's no need to be such a bully.'

Sidney worried that his curate was going to cry. 'I'm very sorry.'

'You should be. It's so unkind of you.'

Sidney did not know whether to touch him or not. A hand on the arm or the shoulder? A hug would be too much. He might even be rebuffed. 'I find this time of year rather stressful.'

'It might be because you think that everything is your responsibility. You won't let other people do things for you.'

'Yes, I suppose it might be that. Once again, I can only say I'm sorry.'

'Your apology is accepted. I am having dinner with Helena tonight. I will try not to eat too much.'

'I'm sure it doesn't matter.'

'It does. We're getting on very well.'

'I'm glad.'

'I hope you approve?'

'I don't think you need that.'

'I'd *like* it.'

'Then you have it.'

'You don't sound very convincing.'

'It's early days, isn't it, Malcolm? Besides, I'm worried about the nature of relationships at the moment, as you know.'

'You can't judge everyone by the standards of the Kirby-Greys.'

'I know.'

'You have to start from your own marriage.'

'That's what I'm trying to do . . .'

The telephone rang. 'What fresh hell is this?' he asked, almost into the receiver.

Sidney was still in his particularly bolshie mood, utterly failing to count the multiple blessings of a helpful curate, a tolerant wife, a beautiful daughter and an ever-eager Labrador. He had also been neglectful and distracted with his parishioners.

'This is Dr Robinson. Can you come to the hospital?'

Such calls normally came when someone was on the point of death. 'What is it?'

'Lady Kirby-Grey . . .'

'What's wrong?'

'Please come now.'

'Is she in danger?'

'She's been beaten. Badly. But she'll live. Her maid telephoned in hysterics.'

'Nancy Hayworth?'

'She's with the police. The situation has come to a head. Miss Kendall is on her way.'

'Is Elizabeth all right?'

'Stable. But she's very weak. Her husband didn't bother to avoid her face this time.'

* * *

It was worse than Sidney had imagined. Elizabeth's skin was so pale it was almost translucent. Now her head was bandaged. She had a black eye, her lip had been split, and her arm was in a sling after it had fractured in falling. She must have been hit at least twice and then kicked whilst on the ground.

'I'm sorry,' she began.

'What on earth are you apologising for?' Amanda asked. 'Did Mark do all this?'

'I should have listened to you.'

Elizabeth explained that the butler had told Sir Mark about Sidney's visit with Keating and that he had then gone to Nancy Hayworth for verification. He was in the process of having it out with her, in public and in the hall, and he would probably have hit her too but for the arrival of Henry Richmond. The two men retired to Mark's study and the whisky bottle was produced. The butler was told not to interrupt but an hour later there was the sound of shouting and furniture being thrown around the room. The door opened and Henry left, saying that unless Mark changed his behaviour he would go to the police.

'"With what?" I heard Mark shout. "You can't prove anything. Elizabeth will never betray me." He went back to his study and continued to drink. I knew there would be no point in having supper but I couldn't think what to do. It took me a while to have the courage to face him, but the longer I left it the worse it would be for me and so I knocked on the door just as he was finishing a telephone call with the word "bitch". I asked him who it was and he said, more spitefully than I had ever heard him before: "That *was* my lover. No thanks to you and your meddling friends."

'I said that I would come back and ask about supper later but he stood in my way so I couldn't get to the door. The only way out was through the French windows but they had been locked for the winter. Mark started to rant, and because I was too terrified to answer any of his questions, or take any of the blame for what had happened, he started to hit me. It was the mouth first. He shouted that I had no use for it as I hardly ate anything and never said anything useful. I staggered back. Then he hit me again, and I fell. That was when I must have hurt my arm. He started kicking me when I was on the ground, and Nancy Hayworth came in. I heard a scream but I didn't know what was happening apart from the pain. I fainted. I only woke up when I was here. Is there any tea?'

'I'll get some,' said Sidney.

Amanda stroked her friend's hand and touched her face, as gently as she could, saying that she loved her.

'I'm so thirsty. My whole body aches,' Elizabeth continued. 'What will happen, do you know? It's kind of you to come.'

Sidney came back with the tea, and Elizabeth took a few sips before saying that she wanted to sleep. She was so tired.

'What can we do?' Amanda asked.

'We're going to tell Keating,' Sidney replied. 'I can't remember ever being this angry. We have to make sure that Sir Mark is arrested. We don't want him bolting.'

When they reached the police station they discovered that Henry Richmond was already there. He was making a statement. Nancy Hayworth had been taken to a separate interview room. She was crying.

'What's happened?' Sidney asked the duty sergeant.

'Inspector Keating said you'd be here soon enough. He's out.'

'Where is he?'

'You don't know?'

'We've just come from the hospital. Is he at Witchford Hall?'

'You'd better let your friend explain.'

Henry Richmond buttoned up his coat. 'I've given my statement. There's a tea-room over the road. Perhaps we could go there? I can't stop shivering.'

They crossed St Andrew's Street as a bus full of Christmas shoppers was pulling away into the wet night. Sidney went ahead. Amanda took Henry's arm. 'You did it, then?'

'I confronted my friend. Not that it's done any good.'

'Have you seen Elizabeth? It could hardly be worse. She could have died.'

'She might have wanted to, living with that man. At least it's over now.'

'You think so?'

They sat in a steamed-up window, feeling both the warmth of the room and the cold from outside. They could only see passers-by on the pavement when they were close, looking in at the three friends grouped around a table as if they were on display. Henry kept his voice low. 'I went to see him, Amanda. Please don't ask me to do anything like that again.'

'Did Mark admit to anything?'

'He told me that his marriage was none of anyone else's business. He and his wife often had tiffs, just as I had done with my own wife when she was alive and he hadn't thought to say anything. Furthermore, Elizabeth was perfectly capable of looking after herself. I told him it didn't look that way and that my marriage was completely different. Connie never appeared in public with burns or bruises. Mark said the injuries were minor and that anyone pointing them out was just making an unnecessary fuss.'

'Some fuss . . .'

'I told him that it wasn't acceptable to have a frightened wife. Then Mark asked me what I really knew about wives, and suggested that Connie's illness could have been my fault. I could have made her ill. I said I had never heard anything so revolting in my life. He told me I had asked for it and what was I going to do about it?'

Sidney poured out the tea. 'He thought you wouldn't dare break the code of friendship, however bad the situation had become.'

'I said I was never going to see him again, and that I would be going to the police. They had enough evidence and I would make sure he was finished. He told me that I wouldn't dare. "Watch me," I said. Then he mentioned my wife, Connie, again. I am sorry to keep mentioning her name, Amanda . . .'

'It's all right . . .'

'He said that I'd never known how to handle a woman. I was so angry. I went to the police and told them that I was sure I could get enough evidence together and that Amanda could persuade Elizabeth to give them enough information to make a charge. Hayworth and Muir too. I came here straight away. I knew I should have taken Elizabeth with me. But I was too angry. That man was a complete shit.'

'Was?' Sidney checked.

'You mean he's dead?' Amanda asked.

'Haven't they told you?' Henry replied. 'That's why I'm in this state. He shot himself: just as he said he would.'

The funeral was in early January. The new vicar took the ceremony and although Elizabeth was sufficiently recovered to attend there was little that was noble about the day. Mourners silently cursed the deceased, blamed themselves, and inwardly accused each other as Sir Mark was buried next to his son.

'To think that lives can change so radically in so short a time,' Amanda said to Sidney as they sat on a sofa in the drawing-room afterwards, cradling glasses of mulled wine against the cold. 'Even though it already seems long ago. I still worry that I haven't been a good enough friend to Elizabeth; that even by doing the right thing we were wrong. Perhaps, by intervening, we only made things worse. This wasn't meant to end in death.'

'You acted for what you thought was the best.'

Sidney imagined Sir Mark leaving his stately home for the last time, taking his shotgun and leaving his dog behind, heading out into the woodland, unable either to forgive himself or face up to reality. He remembered the Russian proverb: 'We are born in a clear field and die in a dark forest.'

They were joined by the other members of the shooting party. No matter how much they thought about the sequence of events, only Elizabeth felt any sorrow for the dead man. 'I can't help feeling that we might have been able to sort things out between us. Without the help of others.'

'You should have left him the first time he hit you,' said Serena Stein. 'That is a line in the sand.'

Amanda took some more mulled wine. 'I'd have left as soon as I knew he was being unfaithful.'

Elizabeth answered two women who had never been in a situation such as hers. 'You never quite know. That's the problem. Everyone else may have an opinion. But they never tell you. Perhaps people only intervene when it's too late.'

'He might have killed you,' Amanda said.

'It was never that serious.'

'It was.'

'I could deal with it.'

'You couldn't.'

'It was my life. We had lost a child. That changes everything.'

Serena Stein spoke without pity. 'It can't be used as an excuse for what follows.'

'Perhaps it was simply that I should have been a better wife . . .'

'No,' said Sidney at last. 'Mark should have been a better husband.'

'How can you miss a man that hurt you so badly?' Amanda asked.

'It was all I knew. And we had Peter.'

'We have to help you lead a new and better life.'

'How will I live?' Elizabeth thought out loud. 'There's no money. It's all tied up in the house. Mark's nephew will take over.'

Serena Stein was horrified. 'You mean you didn't keep any of your own money?'

'I gave it all to Mark.'

'What a beast,' said Amanda.

'Don't . . .'

'I'm sure we can find a way of managing,' said Sidney. 'We don't have to decide everything today.'

Elizabeth was not convinced. 'Perhaps I was the one who was supposed to kill myself.'

'You can't think like that.'

'I can't escape my thoughts.'

'We won't leave you,' Amanda replied.

'Tell me,' Elizabeth turned to Sidney, 'how does a woman of forty-seven with no money, no employable talent, no children and a dead husband begin her life again?'

What would have happened if they had left everything alone? Sidney thought. How much should a priest or a detective force out the truth, whatever the consequence? Does the fear of an unpredictable outcome excuse inaction; or does the more immediate need for justice overrule any concern about the consequences? Had they, in fact, made the situation worse?

He was still convinced that, however hard it might be, the pursuit of goodness should never be compromised by fear. He recalled the vows made at his ordination, that there be no place left in him for error in religion or for viciousness in life. He remembered an elderly clergyman once telling him that 'a Christian life will always be a failure' and thought about what the man must have meant; perhaps that one could never live up to the example of Christ; that inevitably a priest must fall short.

Most lives ended in disappointment of some sort. It was impossible to go on, to finish strongly or defeat death. Acknowledging that we cannot be greater than our own limited humanity was perhaps the first step towards becoming a Christian. He decided to preach on the subject of fragility and failure; although he would have to do something to make it sound a little more enticing. He would have to include the need for compassion, and celebrate our shared humanity. He could even, perhaps, quote from one of the last lines of that great Christmas film *It's a Wonderful Life*: 'No man can count himself a failure if he has friends.'

Contemplating the idea of friendship, Sidney knew that he still hadn't had a proper debrief with Inspector Keating, either about the case or his new role as Archdeacon of Ely, and he was looking forward to resuming their regular meetings in the Eagle now that they were well into the New Year. As he walked across the icy meadows, Sidney recognised that they would have to find a new pub and different excuses to meet each other once he had settled into his next job.

Inspector Keating decided the time had come to dole out some advice. 'You cannot feel responsible for everything that happens, Sidney. All these people were grown adults. In many ways they brought it on themselves.'

'But I am supposed to help them. It is my duty as a priest.'

'You cannot bear the burden for all of us. I know that's what Jesus did, but you, Sidney, despite your popularity, will never be Jesus. That's one thing I do know; and it's where my theology stops. We are all human beings, and we're all buggered.'

'I'm not sure that's true.'

'It's a good enough place to start. What are you drinking?'

'The usual.'

'Good. Keep things clear. Routine is good for you.'

'I'm not sure about that. I get bored very easily.'

'I have noticed.'

When Keating returned with the pints he began to improvise on the benefits of playing it straight. 'But you wouldn't think it if you read any detective fiction. That's what drives me crackers. Every Christmas someone thinks it might be a good idea to give me a story by Agatha Christie or Dorothy L. Sayers or some hard-boiled American thriller, and I lose my temper before I am even halfway through. The police are always slow and stupid and can't do anything right and then a maverick detective who doesn't play by the book comes along and sorts it all out . . .'

'It isn't always like that.'

'It *is*,' Keating insisted. '"The book" is there for a reason. Most of the time it works.'

'But not all the time. Hence the detective novel . . .'

'The doctor's always the murderer . . .'

'Not always . . .'

'Or the person you least suspect. Or most suspect.'

'Make up your mind . . .'

'And the copper ends up being grateful. I think it's a class thing. The gentleman amateur telling the working-class policeman how it's all done. It's snobbery, really.'

'I hope you don't think . . .'

'With you and me? Of course not. Anyway, clergymen are supposed to be classless, aren't they? Jesus was hardly a toff. And I know how uncomfortable you feel around the aristocracy. You hate going to places like Witchford Hall, don't you?'

'I wouldn't go as far as "hate", but you're right. I don't feel comfortable in those environments. And I certainly didn't enjoy any part of what we've just been through.'

'You mustn't blame yourself. That man was a right bastard.'

'He was still a human being.'

'You can't love everyone, Sidney.'

'I think I am supposed to.'

'But that's impossible.'

'Perhaps being a clergyman, Geordie, like being a policeman or a doctor, involves facing up to the impossible. We have to learn to live without favourites. We belong to everyone and therefore no one. We must serve everyone equally . . .'

Keating was thinking of something else. 'I do let you off sometimes . . .'

Sidney abandoned his peroration. 'What do you mean?'

'Well, I don't bother you with the really nasty stuff.'

'You mean you protect me?'

'Of course I do. You lead a very sheltered life, Canon Chambers.'

'Sheltered? But I've been exposed to some of the most horrific crimes in Cambridgeshire for nearly ten years . . .'

'Well, all I can say is that you've probably got about another twenty-five to go.'

'What?'

'And those will be the straightforward cases: the ones where we let the amateurs in to make them feel good.'

'Are you teasing me, Geordie?'

'I wouldn't dream of it.'

Sidney downed his drink. 'I am sure it will all be much calmer by the time I get to Ely. We'll be living in a cathedral cloister. How much danger can there be in a place like that?'

Geordie stood up to order another round. 'Let's see in a year or two. All I can tell you is that if there's no peace for the wicked then there's no rest for the good. Either way, man, you're doomed.'

Fugue

ORLANDO RICHARDS HAD NEVER imagined that he would be killed by a piano falling on to his head.

It was just after midday in late July. The Cambridge students were away on their long vacation, it was early closing, and a summer laziness eased its way across a town whose inhabitants sensed that it was far too hot to do any serious work. They should have been on the river, by the seaside, or enjoying one of the new package holidays abroad.

Sidney had walked Byron across the meadows and popped into Corpus for a brief meeting with the bursar. He needed to talk about payment for the tutorials he had taken in the academic year that had just passed and discuss his future. Now that he was going to be an archdeacon he didn't think he was going to be able to continue with his small amount of teaching. He would no longer have the time to listen to essays on metaphysical poetry, the theology of St Augustine and the influence of the Bible on English literature. Walter Collins said he understood. At least the college could make a small, but much-needed, saving.

Sidney was somewhat surprised. 'I didn't know we had any worries about money.'

'That's because I make provision for the unexpected.'

The bursar was a man who compensated for any inadequacies in charm with practicality and swiftness. In fact he conducted his business at such speed he managed to convince any gathering that he was the busiest man in the room, that the presence of others was tolerated at best, and that he had far more important things on his mind.

Byron, too, was getting restless, but Sidney was sufficiently interested to continue with the conversation. 'I did hear that you've put up the rents.'

'Not by much.'

'Sufficient to cause anxiety.'

He was worried that the poorer members of his congregation who occupied college livings weren't going to able to afford the increase. Walter Collins assured his colleague that there were discretionary funds for those in need, and that tenants were only evicted as a last resort or when they wilfully refused to pay. It would be better if the archdeacon (elect) concentrated on God and left matters of Mammon to the college.

The meeting was at an end. Sidney knew he had to get home, not least because Hildegard was preparing for her first concert in Cambridge: a serious, almost austere, idea to play the fourteen contrapuncti and four canons of Bach's *The Art of Fugue*. She had been encouraged to perform, even bullied, she almost complained, by the director of music, Orlando Richards. He had told her that it was about time she brought her light out from under a bushel.

Appropriately, given the fact that the piece was apparently left unfinished when the composer died, Anna had interrupted Hildegard's playing that morning so that she had had to break off in the middle. This had not gone down well as Sidney had, supposedly, been in charge of childcare at the time and his duty was meant to prevent such an interruption. Consequently he had promised to return early from town so that his wife could make up for her lost practice. He also said that he would not play any jazz while Hildegard was preparing for the concert. Even though she liked jazz, he did not want to put her off. This meant that he had to delay his enjoyment of what he knew was a particularly fine recording that Amanda had found for him in London: Chet Baker's *The Most Important Jazz Album of 1964/65*.

He was leaving Front Court when he stopped to take in an unusual sight: the removal of one piano and the delivery of another to Orlando Richards's rooms on the second floor. An old Bösendorfer upright was being lowered from the window and a glorious new Steinway B was about to be raised and installed in its place.

Sidney decided to study how it was done because he remembered that they would have to move Hildegard's piano to Ely soon enough and he needed a reliable firm to take charge of the operation. It was a precarious business, conducted outside, since the internal staircases of the college did not allow sufficient room for turning.

Orlando was waiting nervously below the high windows. He wore a navy suit that was on the baggy side, and a white shirt with an enlarged collar that gave him a little more neck room than normal. He was a man who hated to be either too hot or too cold, plunging his arms into hot water in the winter and cold in the summer, determined to be at room temperature wherever possible. While the bursar was a man of cool efficiency, Orlando was a living advertisement for the artistic temperament: nervous, flamboyant and prone to hysteria.

The movement of a piano was, therefore, a highly charged affair.

'Make sure your dog's out of the way,' he shouted before bidding Sidney a tense good morning. 'Byron must NOT distract the men. I don't want them tripping on a Labrador.'

A crowd had gathered in Trumpington Street to watch, perhaps remembering Laurel and Hardy's shenanigans in *The Music Box*, as a foreman shouted out instructions.

'This new acquisition is very exciting,' Orlando confided quickly. 'I've never had such a powerful piano. It's got such a big, bright sound. My touch is going to have to change. I am going to play more orchestrally: Beethoven. Liszt. I can't wait.'

There was even a photographer present, Colin Larkin, who told Sidney that he was working on a series of images of the British at work and at play. The previous year he had embedded himself in a Bank Holiday fight between mods and rockers at the 'second battle of Hastings'. He was now planning a suite of photographs that chronicled the construction of a piano from the seasoning of the wood right up to a first performance. He hoped it might find its way into the pages of *Life* magazine.

Six men were involved in the actual removal: a crane operator and handler outside, three at a second-floor window where the glass had been taken out, and Dennis Gaunt, the foreman. The Bösendorfer upright was wrapped in blankets beside the removal lorry, and the boudoir grand was carried to the crane and slid on to a platform.

Three of the men returned to the college and went back upstairs to receive the piano. The head porter came out to check that all was well. Gaunt explained that it was a simple lift on a crane that needed to be as close to the window as possible.

The legs and pedals had been removed and the piano was wrapped and on its side. The crane operator began the lift and one man, Lennie Gaunt, the foreman's nephew, travelled with the instrument on the platform, holding it close, issuing instructions about the speed of the rise, checking that the three men inside the college were ready.

Just before Lennie reached the second floor, he asked the crane operator to stop. At the same time, the bursar left the Porters' Lodge and appeared to say something to the foreman before passing dangerously close underneath, muttering that it was 'probably easier to raise the *Titanic* than move one of your keyboard instruments. Cheaper too.'

Orlando Richards rushed under the piano to tell the bursar to get out of the way. As he did so, Byron trotted over to greet him and Sidney called him back. Dennis Gaunt shouted, 'Level off and untie.'

His nephew pulled at the ropes holding the piano to the crane.

Then he slipped.

He fell away to the left and down to the ground, scattering some of the crowd. The crane operator made a sudden movement in order to try and correct the balance but miscalculated. The platform tilted and the piano slid away and dropped, hideously, on to the head of Orlando Richards.

There was a scream just before the final crash, a series of loud discordant sounds and then silence.

'Mary, Mother and Joseph,' said the head porter.

After the shock of the moment there was a panic of shouting and a babel of instructions as members of the crowd tried to lift the piano away.

Under ten minutes later, the ambulance and the fire brigade arrived. Lennie Gaunt was taken to hospital with a broken leg, the piano was lifted, and the body of Orlando Richards was revealed, as broken as a jointed doll.

There was only one thought in Sidney's mind. Someone was going to have to tell the victim's wife.

He had been a clergyman for over fifteen years but he had not become used to bringing news of a death. Perhaps if he had, he told himself, he would be a lesser priest. All that he had learned was to sit the person down and speak calmly, acknowledging that clarity and sympathy were the most important qualities he could offer.

Sidney had been a friend of Cecilia Richards ever since he had arrived in Grantchester. She was a doctor, an unusually tall, poised woman, with ash-blonde hair, a shy smile and a scar that had been on her forehead since childhood. The couple had a six-year-old son, Charlie. He was playing cricket with two friends in the garden, running in and out of the house, asking if they could have more orange squash, and when was Daddy coming home?

'He's so like his father,' Cecilia smiled. 'Where is he, by the way?'

They were about to go on holiday to the Norfolk Broads and then up to the coast at Cromer. They had friends there and Charlie was the right age for the sea. His mother was going to teach him to sail.

Once Sidney had sat her down and told her what had happened, they did not speak. He prayed but did not suggest that his friend join him. He placed his hand on hers and let the silence take its course.

After a while he offered to take her to the hospital.

Cecilia Richards was reluctant to leave her home. 'If I see him I know it will be true.'

'You do not have to come.'

'What about our boy? How will I tell him?'

Cecilia stood up and moved a few objects around on a side table. There was a book about Melanie Klein and the psychoanalysis of children, a smoked-glass ashtray, a pair of reading glasses that were not in their case. She put Charlie's catapult in a drawer. 'Orlando was never very aware of his surroundings. He was always thinking of something else. I was frightened he might be run over in the street. No one could have imagined this.'

'It was a freak accident.'

'It's weird, isn't it? You telling me this; and me still not quite believing it all. I think if Orlando heard it told he might even enjoy the story of a man killed by his own piano. He would think it amusing, or even fitting, if it had happened to one of his rivals.'

'Musical rather than poetic justice? I don't think he had any rivals. Everyone loved Orlando.'

'He liked to be loved but he never quite believed the affection people showed him. I don't know what it was. He thought it didn't count. I know he felt vulnerable when people regarded him as more of a harpsichord player than a pianist. He wanted to show everyone that he could play both. So he made quite a fuss about the Steinway. We couldn't really afford it but the company said that we could pay by instalments. At least that's what Orlando told me. And the college chipped in too. Do you suppose we'll still have to pay?'

'I don't think so.'

'The removal men will claim on their insurance?'

'I imagine so; not that any of this should concern you.'

'No, I suppose not.'

Sidney hesitated. It was far too soon to be saying what he had to say but the subject had come up. 'You could probably take some kind of legal action against them. They were negligent.'

'Yes . . .'

'And I am sure I could find someone to help with that. Hildegard's first husband was a solicitor. She still knows people if you don't have anyone.'

'I don't think we have a lawyer. There's no will or anything like that. We're still young.'

'It might help if you are short of money. Not that this is the time to discuss these things. There's no need to rush into anything. The college . . .'

'Oh. I hadn't thought. They'll want to throw us out of our home, won't they?'

'I wasn't going to suggest any such thing. I was going to say that I am sure they will do anything possible . . .'

'But this is their property.'

'Your house is a Corpus living, I believe . . .'

'I haven't been thinking. There will be a successor. They'll make us leave. Where will I go? How will we live? What about Charlie?'

148

Her son was running up and down the stairs, trying on different moustaches to go with his pirate costume. He wanted to go to his party.

Sidney had missed lunch altogether and had not been able to get a message to Hildegard. He had specifically promised to come home early and yet he had returned later than ever. He could already imagine her thinking there was nothing she could do or say to make her husband keep his domestic promises and return home on time. Were wife and daughter of such little importance?

'I'm not speaking to you,' he heard as he walked through the door. 'I don't know what you think I'm like or how you expect me to . . . oh . . . what's wrong?'

The grief burst over him. 'Too terrible,' he said, collapsing.

They sat in the garden. Hildegard remembered Orlando; how, when she had first visited Sidney on her return from Germany, he had let her use his rooms and his piano; how he had provided the music for their wedding by playing Pachelbel's *Canon* on the organ. He had laid on a special choir, filled with choral scholars and third-year students, and they had prepared some of Hildegard's favourite music: *'Also heilig ist der Tag'*, *'Bist du bei Mir'*, and Mozart's *Exsultate, Jubilate*. He had been the musical accompaniment to their married life. 'I cannot think of Cambridge without him.'

'Such a lovely man.'

'You remember his favourite anecdote . . .'

They shared the story of the hopeless visiting conductor who had come for a concert of Beethoven's Ninth and blamed a disappointing performance on the size of his baton. If it had only been smaller, he had said. And so, on his next visit, just before the first rehearsal . . .

'Orlando left a matchstick on his music stand . . .' Hildegard laughed.

'No one else would have dared.'

'I can't believe he's gone.'

'A terrible accident.'

Hildegard was hesitant, and then suggested that piano movers didn't normally make that kind of mistake. It was hard to believe that everything had come together in a single moment: for the piano to be so loosely tied, for it to fall when someone was underneath; for a man to slip and the removers not to have cordoned off the area. It was crazy that they had not taken every precaution because such a disaster meant that they would never work again. 'Why would they do such a thing?'

'I don't think they meant to "do" it at all.'

'Perhaps the man on the crane?' Hildegard asked. 'Are they different companies? It could be a form of sabotage.'

'Now you are beginning to sound like me.'

'Pianos don't fall. You have to be so careful. If it was for Orlando then it would have been special and they would have taken extra care.'

'It was a Steinway.'

'He has a Bösendorfer and a harpsichord already.'

'He wanted something with a bit more body.'

'So they took away the upright?' Hildegard checked.

'Yes.'

'And it was the Steinway that was destroyed? I wonder if there were other reasons.'

'Are you thinking about the insurance? I am not sure how the removers would profit from such a scheme. Why would they do that?'

'I don't know. But it's unlike a removal company to have such a catastrophe. You should go and see them. At least you have an excuse.'

'Because of our moving to Ely?'

'You could ask a few questions.'

'I thought you wanted me to give up on detection?'

'Not in this case.'

'I have your permission?'

'Sidney, you would have gone to see them whether you had my permission or not.'

The next morning, Sidney combined Byron's exercise with taking the ever-energetic Anna to play with a group of like-minded toddlers. The accident was the talk of all the mothers; particularly when they discovered that Sidney had been present at the scene. After enquiring if Mrs Chambers was ill (no, she was practising her piano), they wanted all the news. One of them even asked if Sidney would be conducting an investigation. He assured the young mothers that it had been nothing more than a terrible piece of misfortune.

He returned home and tried to take his mind off events as Hildegard worked through a particularly tricky four-part fugue. The music would have been relaxing if his wife had played each piece fluently, but she kept stopping, patiently separating and practising each voice to check that she was in full control, adjusting her fingering or her speed. Sidney wished he had her determined concentration.

He looked over his post and flicked through his copy of *The Times*. After a while he told himself that sitting down reading the newspaper was hardly going to buy the baby a new bonnet (one of his mother's phrases) and that he should get on, visit his former housekeeper (Mrs Maguire hadn't been out for a few days), see to the arrangements for the village fête, and write his sermon for Sunday. At least it was a Thursday, and so there was his regular meeting with Geordie to look forward to in the Eagle that evening.

'Who among those removal men would want Orlando Richards dead?' Geordie asked as soon as the subject of the accident was raised. 'These are ordinary working people.'

'I know.'

'And I don't think your friend will have been killed to order, if that's what you are thinking.'

'But it was such a new and great grand piano. And Orlando stepped underneath it at exactly the wrong time. It is more than a coincidence, don't you think?'

'That's what accidents are: unfortunate turns of events. Even if this was not, you still have to ask the question: who benefits? Richards is dead and the piano is ruined. What would be the point of murder?'

'I don't know. But surely we should try and find out?'

'I don't mind making a few simple enquiries, but really, Sidney, let's talk about something else.'

That something else turned out to be Keating's troublesome daughters. His eldest was seeing a boyfriend who looked like one of Herman's Hermits, the middle one spent so much time doing her hair that she never finished any homework, and his youngest was desperate for a pony and threw a tantrum every time her parents said they couldn't afford one. All her friends had one, she said. (When pressed on the subject it turned out that only one of them did, but this was not, Katie Keating had insisted, the point.)

'You're lucky you've just got the one daughter, Sidney. How's Malcolm?'

'As popular as ever. In fact he's such a good curate I sometimes think that my parishioners don't have much need for me.'

'That could be why you're suspicious about the accident. Is it because you need something to get your teeth into?'

'I don't think it's that.'

'Still, you'll be all right with Malcolm. Is he still pursuing Helena Randall? I don't know what she sees in him.'

'Kindness probably,' Sidney answered. 'She'll want the inside story on the piano. By the way, she told me that Dennis Gaunt, the owner of the removal firm, seems to have disappeared. Do you think that's odd?'

'He's probably keeping a low profile. I don't think he will have done a runner, if that's what you mean.'

'It's all very unusual, Geordie.'

'Well, death can be like that.'

'Hildegard was telling me about how some musicians have met their maker: Ernest Chausson lost control of his bicycle and crashed into a brick wall; Jean-Baptiste Lully stabbed himself in the foot with the pointed staff he used to keep time and Charles-Henri-Valentin Alkan . . .'

'That's quite a mouthful . . .'

'. . . was thought to have died when reaching for a copy of the Talmud on a high shelf. The bookcase fell on top of him.'

'Really? I suppose it's not dissimilar to being crushed by a grand piano. It's my round, Sidney. Are you having another?'

Keating went to the bar. After he had put in his order he was momentarily distracted by the sight of a man taking out his false teeth and popping them into his pint of cider. He wanted to stop people drinking out of it while he went to the gents.

'He does that all the time,' said the barmaid. 'Are you discussing the accident?'

'There's not much to talk about.'

'I never know with you two.'

'We're a bit too far away for anyone to eavesdrop on our conversation. Don't tell me you've got some thoughts.'

'Not really, Geordie. I just hope the college looks after the widow. They've been upping the rents and not everyone can afford them.'

'Prices are going up everywhere.'

'Especially the heating. Last year a couple I heard about got carried away with their insulation: they sealed themselves in so well that a gas leak poisoned them.'

'There's a cheery thought.'

'Money makes people desperate.'

'I don't know whether that's got anything to do with this case, Sally.'

'The poor old choirmaster. At least the music will be better in heaven now that he's there.'

Keating returned with two pints of IPA to find that Sidney had been ruminating. 'I think I might go and visit Lennie Gaunt in hospital.'

'And who, pray, is he?'

'The man from the removal firm who fell and broke his leg when Orlando was killed. The owner's nephew.'

'One of your pastoral visits?'

'It can't do any harm, can it?'

Before he did so Sidney had to get through the small matter of the village fête. He had been hoping that Malcolm would be able to look after most of the proceedings, but his curate was in a curiously vulnerable mood. Always sensitive to criticism, he had reacted badly to Leonard Graham giving him a copy of Chekhov's *Short Stories*. One of the tales, 'Oysters', featured a feverish boy who becomes so hungry that he imagines eating not just a pile of oysters, but their shells, his place setting, his napkin, his father's galoshes, and everything in the restaurant. There was nothing that the boy didn't want to eat.

'I don't think Leonard gave you that story deliberately, Malcolm . . .'

'I'm a little touchy about these matters as you know, Sidney. Sometimes I don't know if I eat too much because I am unhappy or I am unhappy because I eat too much.'

'Other people have the same problem with alcohol, Malcolm. But this is not the day to worry about these things. Everyone loves you: especially Helena Randall, I've noticed.'

'We're just friends.'

'You are a very popular man.'

'I'm not sure that good Christianity is about popularity.'

'It's certainly a start. Unpopular vicars can kill a congregation.' Sidney hesitated. 'Not literally of course.'

'No. That *would* be unpopular. So, do you think it was an accident?'

'What do you mean?'

'The *book*. Leonard's present. Were you thinking of something else?'

'Not at all.'

'You were, I can tell. It's that business with the piano . . .'

'It's a terrible tragedy. Orlando was well liked. As you are, Malcolm . . .'

'It's not a competition.'

'No, of course it isn't,' Sidney said quickly, while inwardly acknowledging that there were certain times when he behaved as if it *was*. It was ridiculous to feel even slightly aggrieved that his curate was proving such a success.

His unease was, however, made worse when he couldn't find his wallet. This was doubly irritating. There was the loss and inconvenience itself, but his generosity at the fête would be compromised. He was unable to show largesse and he didn't want people assuming he had deliberately left his wallet behind as a calculated act of meanness in order not to spend any money. If his parishioners started to think that then it would be a long way back to regain their affection.

He tried to blame Byron. Perhaps his Labrador had run off with it and chewed it to smithereens? Or was it his own negligence? He just needed to take more time over things, Sidney said to himself.

At least the weather was clement. The home produce and gift stalls were packed with the WI's best efforts, and Sidney didn't have to do too much other than wave a wand of non-specific geniality across proceedings. As long as his parishioners didn't start murdering each other (hiding dead bodies in the sandpit, battering each other with coconuts from the shy, concealing razor blades in the lucky dip – *that* kind of thing) then everything would pass without any significant incident.

The only crisis came when Mrs Maguire's sister approached to tell them that the Beautiful Baby competition had been beset by controversy. A couple had come all the way from Chepstow, goodness knows how they had ended up in Grantchester, and had entered their new daughter Joanne, ruffling a few local feathers and provoking a considerable debate about whether the contest was open only to local families or not.

'Is she likely to win?' Sidney asked.

'I'm afraid so. She's a very beautiful baby.'

'Who's the judge?'

'I think you are, Canon Chambers.'

'We'd better disqualify her then. I don't want to upset a parishioner by giving the prize to a stranger.'

As he wandered through the stalls, trying to look busy without spending money, Sidney thought about the case of the fallen piano. He was beginning to make a little deductive progress when he was interrupted by a man who wanted to ask him about the parish boundary fencing and who ended his question with the statement: 'I know you think I am boring.'

Unfortunately, this was true. Sidney had indeed thought that and was embarrassed about being caught. The man was dull, but that did not mean he wasn't decent, that he didn't have any emotions, or that perhaps he was too frightened by life to take any risks and be entertaining. Perhaps his very timidity made him more interesting.

Sidney tried to pay attention to what the man was saying. It soon emerged that he was Dennis Gaunt's brother, the father of the crane operator at the time of the accident. Now Sidney really would have to concentrate, he told himself. Perhaps he had missed something already?

It was a small world, Vic Gaunt was explaining, but at least people acknowledged what a blow this latest event had been to his family. But then, he continued, Sidney probably knew this. His curate was a family friend.

Sidney did not know this.

It turned out that Malcolm Mitchell had shared holidays with the Gaunts from the age of seven. His dad had been a pal of Dennis and they had gone with Maureen and the girls to Southsea in the mid-fifties.

Why hadn't Malcolm said anything? Perhaps, Sidney thought, it was because he had not been asked; or was it because Sidney himself had been too preoccupied, superior even, and that his colleague had never felt that the time was right to tell him?

'I suppose you'll be going to see my son in hospital?' Victor Gaunt wondered.

'I was hoping to do so, yes.'

'You'll probably get more sense out of him than you would with my brother.'

'I wasn't planning on talking to everyone; only those in need.'

'Oh, Dennis is in need all right.'

'What do you mean?'

'Lets things get to him. Some people say it's since our mother died, others blame the adult-education classes he's been taking; but he's always been a worrier. He went to the doctor and got some pills for depression but they haven't done any good.'

'Who's his doctor?'

'Robinson. Your friend.'

'You seem to know a lot about me.'

'You have a reputation, Canon Chambers.'

'I wouldn't call it that.'

'It doesn't matter what you call it, does it? It's what other people say that matters.'

'And what do "other people say", if that doesn't sound too vain?'

'Well it's funny you should use that word, Canon Chambers.' (Sidney did not like it when people repeated his name. It was a sign that they were about to tell him something unpleasant.) 'Some people say that you are a bit of a show-off.'

Sidney wished he hadn't asked.

'They say that if it wasn't for the crime business you'd be quite a decent priest. But you get distracted. That's why everyone goes to see your curate.'

Sidney considered the question of popular appeal once more. He was forty-four years old, he told himself. Was it too late to change his ways?

It was true that he was bored by administrative duties, that his handling of the parish accounts would not be what a bank manager would ever describe as 'detailed', or even accurate, and that he probably did spend more time with women than with men, but at least church numbers were up rather than down, he had baptised more children and married more couples than he had taken funerals, and he liked to think that he always offered comfort and consolation to those parishioners who had asked in hours of need. For most of the time, he had put church before crime.

He thought back to his first involvement in an investigation. It was how he had met Hildegard. Then he remembered all the subsequent cases that had followed: of burnt barns, stolen paintings, and murdered priests, jazz musicians, actors and even some of his much-loved and elderly parishioners.

This business of the fallen piano would be his last case, he told himself. He could hardly continue after he had become an archdeacon. He could already imagine being told that there were plenty of other people, better qualified than he, who would be able to investigate crime and miscarriages of justice. He would have more important things to do: meetings with the Diocesan Board of Finance, the appointment of clergy and even judging a Most Beautiful Baby competition.

On the Monday after the fête, Hildegard had arranged to have her piano tuned. Sidney seized the opportunity to ask their visitor a few discreet questions about the technicalities involved in moving large musical instruments.

The tuner, Alfred Delbern, was a thin, precise man with tousled brown hair to match his corduroy trousers and camel-toned brogues. He was a man with unrestricted clothing and precisely cut fingernails. Everything about him was drawn towards hands which were long and exposed at the end of a light-brown cardigan and a shirt worn without a tie. There was nothing to constrict their movement.

Mr Delbern spoke of how the piano was an object of transformation; how it could take on different colour and character, suggesting at any one time the singing voice or even a full orchestra. Its action should be well measured in key depth and resistance, and it should, ideally, be suited for a concerto no less than for a lieder recital.

This was more than Sidney needed to know but, as he took

in the lengthy process involved, he couldn't help but question if it bore any resemblance to the art of detection.

He sat for a moment and listened as the tuner hit each note hard to see how long each string stayed in tune and how long it took for the sound to die away. It was longer than the piano had taken to fall, but not as long as the echo of the metal frame, soundboard, ribs, bridges, strings, hammers, dampers and keys.

He wondered if the length of the echo was determined by the duration of the fall. Was there a limit to the volume involved and how much did the height of the drop matter? If the piano had fallen from a first-floor rather than a second-floor window, would Orlando still be alive? Did it matter which part of the instrument had hit him and where it was at its heaviest? Would a removal man have been able to calculate the nature of the drop and how difficult would it be to time it?

The piano tuner responded briefly to Sidney's questions. He didn't like to be disturbed in his duties and suggested that they stop for a cup of tea if the matter required further discussion. Once they had done so (to Hildegard's considerable irritation – why couldn't Sidney just let the man get on with his work?), Alfred Delbern put forward the idea that there was no such thing as the death of sound; that it never died but diminished in amplitude. He had a friend who believed, for example, that Stonehenge was a repository of dormant sound, and that if you invented the right device you could uncover lost music. What would the music in the stones of a Gothic cathedral sound like?

As the man was talking, Sidney shifted position on the sofa and spied his wallet. It had fallen down the side. Although he had not sat there for ages he was convinced that he had turned over the cushions eight times on the day of the fête, hunting in vain. What was his wallet doing there? He couldn't help but feel that there was some kind of conspiracy.

He tried to concentrate. A man was being exceptionally interesting but all he was doing was worrying about his wallet. Had the piano tuner noticed that Sidney had been distracted?

No. He was still talking. Hildegard had come in to listen. They were speaking about silence.

It was the basis of music, Alfred Delbern continued. 'We find it before, after, in, underneath and behind the sound. Some pieces emerge out of silence or lead back into it. But silence ought also to be the core of each concert. The word "silent" is an anagram of "listen".'

Sidney thought he could preach well about this. It was amazing how ideas came to him when he stopped and appreciated what people were telling him. The nature of silence and the opportunity it gave for prayer and contemplation might lead, he thought, to what he could call a 'music of the mind'.

He would work on that, just as he would think about the possibility that sounds, like ideas, never died. They were waiting to be found. If he could apply that logic to the case on which he was working and find clues that were always there, ready to be discovered, then perhaps he might make some progress.

He knew his way round Addenbrooke's Hospital from his duties as a priest but his ongoing investigations gave that familiarity added depth. It meant that he had to be particularly tactful with a hospital chaplain who had become wary of these increasing incursions on to his patch. He complained that Sidney's visits always made him feel that the cavalry had arrived.

Lennie Gaunt lay with his upraised leg in a bed by the far window. 'This is the only way I'm ever going to get plastered in this bloody place,' he told his visitor. 'Still, it could have been worse – for me, at least.'

'It could indeed.'

'You knew the man with the piano?'

'He was one of my friends.'

'I'm sorry about that.'

'It wasn't your fault.'

'Plenty of people think it was.'

Lennie was in his late twenties. He had twelve years of experience with the family firm. He had never made a mistake like this before.

Sidney asked if there was anything unusual about the lift, the arrangement of people, the calling out of instructions. 'It was unfortunate you slipped. It wasn't a wet day.'

'No, your dog put me off.'

'I think it might have been rather more than my dog. Was the piano properly secured?'

'It was at the bottom. Then we had to untie it to get it in. I lost my balance. My left leg's a bit weak, I broke it playing football a few years ago, and it just gave way. Bloody useless now, and it'll never get strong again. Just hope I can still work. They won't put me on the crane again. That is, if we get any more business and my uncle doesn't go off his trolley.'

'You mean he might?'

'He disappears. Just goes off.'

'I didn't know that.'

'We're not sure where he goes. He doesn't like to talk about it. It makes him jumpy if we ask.'

'Orlando was a nervous man too. Did any of you know him well?'

'We just did the job. We don't spend much time with college types. Town and gown. You know how it is.'

Sidney checked. 'So there were no problems?'

'What do you mean?'

'No arguments about money; or about the way to do things?'

'What are you getting at?'

Sidney needed to backtrack and yet secure information at the same time. 'I know Orlando didn't have very much money. I was surprised he could afford the piano in the first place.'

'I think the bursar paid for the move. Uncle Dennis heard that he took Wednesday afternoons off and didn't want him to slip out without paying. Money's a bit tight in our family. The secret, Dad says, is to be quick to invoice and slow to pay; but Uncle Dennis says we're always on the edge of bankruptcy. It gets to him sometimes.'

'But he wasn't desperate, was he?'

'It's a family firm, Canon Chambers. It's like a ship. If it sinks we all go down with it. That's why I've got to get back to work.'

'I imagine it'll be a while yet.'

'Then I'll have to hope that something comes up. A bit of luck on the horses to make up for my leg.'

'Did your firm have insurance?'

'For the piano, yes. Not for my leg. In any case, those bastards never pay up.'

'You've tried before?'

'Dad has. Says you can't trust them. You have to find other ways to cover yourself.'

'And what do you think he meant by that?'

'I haven't the foggiest, Canon Chambers.'

The funeral took place on Thursday 5th August. As he robed for the service, Sidney remembered, once more, how Orlando had first welcomed his wife to Cambridge and made an arrangement of Hildegard of Bingen's music in her honour. His bright, thoughtful, attractive personality was so far from the silence of death, he couldn't imagine anyone wanting to kill him. Surely this was all a horrible accident and he should just speak about fate and beauty, time and chance?

Hildegard played the opening aria of *The Goldberg Variations* in memory and tribute, and then the choir of Corpus Christi was joined by professional singers from across the country to perform the most glorious Early English church music: the Magnificat and Nunc Dimittis from *The Eton Choirbook*; the arrangements by Thomas Tallis of the Ordinal from Archbishop Parker's Psalter (the manuscript of which was held in Corpus) and the perfect seven-part miniature: *Miserere nostri.*

Sidney preached a sermon based on the late-fifteenth-century anthem *'Jesus autem transiens'* by Robert Wylkynson. Scored for thirteen male singers, representing the twelve apostles and Christ, the work was a canon in twelve sections. One by one the apostles said their name when their turn came, proclaiming the *cantus firmus* – 'Jesus passed through their midst' – and a line from the Apostles' Creed. The anthem moved from left to right across a line of singers, like light across a hillside, building to a moment when all thirteen voices were sounding: Christ surrounded by his disciples, before each one fell away until only one man was left singing on the extreme right before the piece ended.

Sidney began by affirming that 'Jesus passed through their midst' and then developed his theme: that Jesus is not static but moving. He passes through, as he must through all our lives, and as we must travel through life itself. His revelation will always be for a limited time, just as our lives have their allotted span: and even though that span might be cut short, the passing moment of revelation through faith, beauty or music was no less bright, no less defining. They were moments of definition; Orlando's decision to become a musician, to concentrate on early music, to come to Corpus and, perhaps most importantly, to marry his wife Cecilia. We carry the memory of those events as they pass among us, Sidney concluded, hoping we notice what matters and that we take the opportunity, however fleeting, of appreciating life in all its fullness.

The service ended with Mozart's '*Soave Sia il Vento*' from *Così fan Tutte*. It was the celebratory piece that had been sung at Orlando and Cecilia's wedding. This was as good as funerals got, Sidney thought, the music enhancing the structure and beauty of the language of the prayer book; a grateful ending to a life.

Sidney walked forward to give the blessing. As he did so, he noticed a man standing at the back. He was sure that he had not been there for long. It was Dennis Gaunt, the foreman, muttering and crying. He left before Sidney could speak to him.

At the wake, Cecilia Richards was appreciative of all that Sidney had said. She repeated that she couldn't believe what had happened. Sometimes she thought it was so unusual, so freakish an occurrence, that there must be an explanation. It couldn't have been a random accident. Had Sidney thought that too? Was he doing any investigating?

Rather than lie, Sidney evaded the question. He talked about the exemplary nature of her marriage.

She smiled sadly. 'No one really believes two people could be as happy as we were but there was no pretence about anything we did. We loved each other. I remember laughing that we were young enough to get up to a golden wedding anniversary and that I couldn't imagine ever being with anyone else. Perhaps I've been punished for expecting too much, for ignoring fate, for being happy.'

Her son was running around wearing a stick-on moustache and holding up a silver-framed photo of his father. Cecilia called to him, and held him close.

Sidney noticed Helena Randall and expressed his surprise that she was there. 'You're not a family friend?'

'But the funeral was a public event. Orlando Richards was a well-known and much-loved figure in Cambridge. I expressed my condolences. The widow asked me back to the wake.'

'She was being polite. These things are supposed to be private.'

'Don't worry, Sidney, I won't do anything to embarrass you.'

'Are you going to write any more about what happened?'

'As you say, it was "an accident". I am just getting a bit of colour for my report on the funeral. "When the music had to stop", that kind of thing. It's good that his wife's named after the patron saint of music. I've even found a poem by Alexander Pope: the *Ode on St Cecilia's Day*. I think I might use it at the end; although it might sound like one of your show-off sermons. What do you think?

'In broken air, trembling, the wild music floats;
Till, by degrees, remote and small,
The strains decay,
And melt away,
In a dying, dying fall.'

'I'm not sure that would be a good idea, Helena. Too close to the bone, perhaps.'

'Or even the ivory? Did you see the piano remover crying at the back of the church?'

'Dennis Gaunt? Only briefly.'

'Aha, Sidney, I knew you'd spotted him. He was blubbing.'

'You spoke to him as well?'

'I did, as a matter of fact.'

'I thought you told me he had disappeared?'

'There's a special house he goes to when it all gets too much. Didn't they tell you?'

'Not exactly.'

'Used to belong to his mum,' Helena explained. 'She died last year. He had it all cleaned out and redecorated ready to sell but now he won't put it on the market. He likes to go and sit there. Says he feels safer.'

'He told you all this?'

'I have other sources.'

'And you're not going to reveal them?'

'You never do, Sidney.'

'That's nonsense. But I'm impressed that you've found out so much so soon.'

'It's either my sharp investigative skills, my astonishing charm or my incredible beauty.'

'Probably a combination of all three. So it's a kind of safe house?'

'I don't think it's illegal or anything. But Dennis Gaunt doesn't want to let it go; which is a problem as his brothers and sisters want the money from the sale. They're accusing Dennis of dragging his feet.'

'And there's nothing else that's odd about his wanting to be there on his own? No secret assignations?'

'That's what I'm trying to find out.'

'And what would this have to do with the death of the husband of our hostess?' (Sidney did not say his name for fear of being overheard.)

'Perhaps nothing at all. I hardly think they could be having an affair. But if they're not connected then I can file two stories for the price of one.'

'And if your investigations prove fruitless?'

'There's always a story somewhere, Sidney.'

'Even if you have to make one up?'

'I never do that. I might engage in a bit of embroidery but I need a piece of cloth in the first place.'

'No matter how small?'

'The merest handkerchief will do.'

'That was enough for Iago. Can you tell me where the mother's house is?'

'It's completely empty, by the way. It looks like the removal men have just been, which is appropriate when you think about it.'

'Does Geordie know?'

'Why does he need to? The man has done nothing wrong. Dennis was only a spectator at the time of the accident . . .'

'It's his firm.'

'And he's not breaking the law. At least as far as I can see. All he is doing is sitting in an empty house and talking to himself. When he talks, that is. Otherwise he speaks to me.'

'What does he say?'

'You'll have to read the paper.'

'Are you keeping evidence from the police?'

'Nothing criminal. It's a human-interest story. Dennis Gaunt wants to get away from it all. He's Cambridge's answer to Robinson Crusoe, living without possessions, a man who says no to the madness of our modern world. It's almost religious, his desire for solitude and silence. In fact he's thinking of becoming a secular hermit.'

'Which, presumably, is rather difficult given the fact that he has a wife and family and a business to run?'

'Then you see why this is a story?'

'The next thing you'll be telling me is that he listens to Orlando Richards's recordings.'

'Now that would be something.'

'I was being facetious.'

They were interrupted by Cecilia Richards. She wanted a word with Sidney. She was relieved, she said. The bursar had told her that she could stay on in her house for as long as she needed. Her husband had been a wonderful man and the college would put no pressure on her to leave. He knew how difficult it all must be.

'It was kind of him. I should be glad. And, in a way, I am.'

Sidney put his arm around her shoulder. 'It must be hard to take anything in.'

Cecilia Richards took her time to reply. 'Grief is like an endless fugue,' she said.

Sidney decided that the most straightforward excuse for seeing Dennis Gaunt was to ask for a quotation for his removal to Ely, including Hildegard's piano.

His brother, Vic, was surprised by the visit. 'We could have spoken about all this at the fête.'

'This seemed more businesslike. And I was hoping that I might be able to help your company in what must be a time of need.'

Sidney thought ruefully that he wasn't lying exactly. What he was saying was partly true, even if there were what might be termed other considerations.

'I heard you'd been to see our Lennie in hospital. I hope you weren't stirring anything up?'

'Not at all, I can assure you . . .' (But why would Victor Gaunt be so suspicious if he had a clear conscience? Sidney thought.)

'Just ask us to do the job and we'll do it, vicar. Best price. Cheaper if you can pay in cash.'

'I thought a cheque might suit . . .'

'No. Cash is better. Dennis is the one that gives out the estimates. Do it verbally. Gentlemen's agreement. That's the best way.'

'I gather he's not here at the moment.'

'He's taken a few days off to try and recover.'

'And when will he be back?'

'No way of telling.'

'He's in your mother's house?'

'You must have been talking to that journalist. Is she a friend of yours?'

'Not exactly.'

'Dennis says she understands him.'

'I'm sure she does.'

'Nonsense. We both know she's just getting a story. Dennis is too soft.'

'Does he like to have visitors?'

'Do you want to see him as well? I can give you the address but he won't let you in. Normally you have to chat on the doorstep.'

'I think I can manage that.'

'Try not to upset him, that's all I ask. Thoughts keep going round and round in his head. The firm's never had an accident like it and no one will go near us. We're finished. You'll probably be our last ever job.'

That evening Sidney was due to dine in college. It was a far more informal affair in the long vacation as most of the fellows were away. Those that remained would need to start talking about a replacement for Orlando, if it was not considered too unseemly to do so.

Over drinks, the bursar wondered if they could get someone young and up and coming (in other words, cheaper). With his mutton-chop whiskers, Walter Collins was something of a historical throwback. He wore three-piece suits, kept a pocket watch, and was prone to perspiration, especially in the summer. His pockets were stuffed with a series of red polka-dot handkerchiefs that were produced to stem the flow from his forehead, cheeks and neck. He never took his jacket off and one of the fellows had suggested that this was because his armpits would be too horrible to contemplate. His body odour was, however, only occasionally unpleasant and he meant well; content if everyone stuck to the rules and procedures that the college had laid down in the fourteenth century and which, he felt, were still relevant today.

Sidney asked Walter how well he knew the Gaunts, how they had come to be chosen as the removal firm and why he had agreed to pay for the removal.

'It was one of my more charitable gestures, Canon Chambers; a way of supporting tenants who were behind on their rent – I was offsetting their payment against debt, much to Mr Gaunt's consternation – and I was helping Orlando flourish as a musician by encouraging his late progression from the harpsichord to the piano. As you know, he was determined to master all keyboards, even if it meant changing technique; rather like Wanda Landowska.'

'Hildegard has mentioned her. Doesn't she play *The Goldberg Variations* twice in a single concert; once on the harpsichord and then on the piano?'

'I believe so. I think Orlando was going to do the same. Such a fine musician. I don't know how we'll replace him.'

'Did he know the Gaunt firm before the move?'

'I doubt it. They are not people who have anything in common. You're not coming up with one of your wild surmises, are you, Sidney? It was an accident. I can't believe anyone would want to kill Orlando. And even you can hardly think it was an elaborate act of suicide.'

'I wouldn't go as far as that.'

'Shall we go in?' the Master of Corpus interrupted, keen that dinner should commence and the subject should change.

Sidney said grace. '*Benedic, Domine, nobis et donis tuis, quae de tua largitate sumus sumpturi, et concede ut illis salubriter nutriti, tibi debitum obsequium praestare valeamus, per Christum Dominum nostrum. Amen.*'

They sat down to watercress soup. The Director of English Literature, Magnus Mortimer, told Sidney that he hoped he might come back from Ely and teach for a term or two. 'You know how much better you are on the metaphysical poets. I'm afraid I rather stop at the *physical*. Other colleagues may be keen on complexity and ambiguity but sometimes things are as they are, and I prefer to spend my life as Milton advised, "beholding the bright countenance of truth in the quiet and still air of delightful studies".'

Perhaps that was the case, thought Sidney. The greatest literature, like life itself, might open itself up to multiple interpretation, but there was also plain fact and simple truth.

A man was dead. A piano had fallen. There was, perhaps, no special providence.

The original Gaunt family home was a modest terraced house in The Kite with white window frames and a newly painted matching door. The front garden had been paved over. Even in the height of summer, there were no flowers.

Dennis Gaunt was a large round man with a face that was never still, his expressions constantly on the turn. He was either about to smile, or he was in pain, or on the point of being annoyed. Just as some people have a naturally sulky face, Sidney thought, or others looked bored, or angry or unhappy even if they were thinking of nothing at all, Dennis Gaunt was somehow the opposite. He had the permanent unpredictability of a man who was either about to lose his temper or laugh out loud.

174

After some gentle negotiation, Sidney was allowed inside. There were no pictures on the walls, no comfortable chairs, and there were cotton blinds across the windows so that the light was soft, even and disorientating. There was a jug of water on the table and a single glass. Dennis Gaunt was not sure that he had got another, but managed to find one in a kitchen cupboard that was otherwise empty.

The house could either be taken as a brilliant piece of modernist design or an individual lunatic asylum. 'This is where I come,' the host began as he returned with the glass. 'It's like a chapel just for me.' He was dressed entirely in white.

'And very congenial it is too, Mr Gaunt. I imagine when life gets too much . . .'

'If I come here then I can try and make my thoughts the same. It's ordered. I like living with as few possessions as possible. As the philosphers advise. I've been doing a course at the Workers' Educational Association. But you can't live on nothing, despite what they tell you. Vic said you probably want to ask me about his son: the boy on the crane.'

'No, it was more about the piano.'

'Steinway.'

'So I gather.'

'It's a three- or four-man job to move. Iron frame, you see. But there's a brighter sound. More for the concert hall. Although this was Steinway B, not D. D is a right bugger. B is smaller. Some people call it the perfect piano. Have to be careful choosing the right one. Change when they travel, too. A bit like people. They need careful handling. What did you want to ask?'

'I have heard you don't like talking too much.'

'I don't mind now you're here, as long as you don't stay for too long. I've got all day. Well, I haven't, of course. Some of it's gone already. Sometimes it's hard to know how much of the day you *have got*, don't you think? How much of the day is left. What is lost now that half of it is gone? What you have to get back tomorrow. If it comes. Better to wait than to mourn, though, don't you think?'

'I'm not sure what you mean.'

'Mourn the day that's lost. There's no point. You have to look forward. Tomorrow. Not today or yesterday. If you dwell too much you go mad. That's not what you want to do. That's a bad idea. Not that it's always just an idea. Sometimes it's something else. Inside you. Is that like God, do you think? Something that's there all the time? You just have to find it?'

'Something like that.'

'So your job is to teach us how? I don't think I've ever found him. I just have ideas. Not that they do much good. Although I try to stop bad ideas. Bad people.'

'Do you mean like Orlando Richards?'

'No. No. Not at all. He was a good man. He shouldn't be dead.'

'It was a terrible accident, Mr Gaunt. No one's fault, I think, although you might be blaming yourself. Is that why you're here?'

'To blame? Perhaps yes. Accident yes. To blame yes. But not intentional. Not *with intent*. There's a Latin phrase for that, isn't there? *Actus reus*. I heard it on *Round Britain Quiz*.'

'I am sure it wasn't your fault, Mr Gaunt. When are you hoping to go back home?'

'Lennie and the boys will be worried about me. Lennie and

the boys. The boys and Lennie. It doesn't matter which way round, does it? It's just words.'

'But language defines who we are and what we think and do.'

Dennis Gaunt wasn't so sure. 'Anything could be anything, don't you think? That's what I've been reading about. It's all about perception. We could be here and not here. Life could be a dream and death could be when we wake up. Birth is when we fall asleep; death is when we wake. I often wonder what it would be like if everything was the opposite of what we think it is.'

He stopped abruptly, stood up as if he was going somewhere, and then returned to his chair. 'It's been nice meeting you, Canon Chambers. It's important to think things through. Look at life another way. Sometimes look away altogether. Especially if a piano is falling. You don't want to see that.'

'So you didn't see what happened?'

'There was a man taking photographs. What's he doing? I thought at the time. What does he want photographs for? We move pianos every day. What's unusual about that? What makes it worthy of a photograph? The *decisive moment*. Isn't that what it's called? What do you think that moment was, Canon Chambers? The *decisive moment*? Was it when the foot slipped or the piano fell? Was it when it hit the man, or when it crushed him, or when his heart stopped beating? Or was it when the man came to see us the very first time and he asked us to help move his piano and we said "yes"? Was our "yes" the decisive moment, or was it his first question, or was it the time when Mr Richards decided he wanted a new piano? Do we need a decisive moment in order to decide what we think? Perhaps all our lives are decisive moments? And there is no such thing as a *moment* anyway. A *moment*. What is that? A second, a minute, a few minutes? It wouldn't be five minutes, or three? Perhaps it wouldn't even be one? Perhaps it doesn't exist at all? Where are the photographs? Can I see them?'

'Perhaps you can help?' Sidney asked, recognising that they were getting somewhere.

'Maybe I can.'

'You could explain what is happening in each of them. You might even be able to pinpoint when it all went wrong.'

'The *decisive moment*, you mean? That would be hard.'

'I'm not sure that it would be,' Sidney replied. 'There must have been a time from which everything that followed became irreversible and unstoppable; the moment when nothing afterwards could be changed, just before the piano started to fall.'

'But what about the moment when Mr Richards started walking? Was that more important than the piano falling? If the man hadn't walked then the piano would not have killed him. You can't talk about the moment without the ifs. If your dog hadn't barked, if our Lennie hadn't slipped, if the man hadn't walked, if the piano hadn't fallen? You can't really talk about that time at all. We only have what's left; never the time itself. The ruins of a moment.'

'Then please take me through those ruins,' Sidney asked.

Hildegard was depressed by Orlando's death, not only because she had lost a good friend but also because she no longer had a champion. There was no one left in Cambridge who really understood her musicianship and so, when she discovered that her old professor, Leopold Klein, was visiting London from Leipzig, she asked him if he wouldn't mind coming to spend a day with her. She would show him round the university in exchange for a lesson.

It was some time since she had been able to talk so freely, and in such depth, about music. Professor Klein was a Mozart man who had just played a series of the composer's rare piano works on a concert tour of Europe. The pieces were so underrated, he said, perhaps because they were too easy for children and too difficult for artists.

Hildegard agreed. 'The A minor Rondo K511 and the B minor Adagio K540 are the musical equivalent of Hamlet's soliloquies.' Professor Klein smiled at her, nodded and said, 'I wish you had never left Germany. But at least, and perhaps at last, you are happy with your husband.'

'I am almost afraid to say that I am. If it is acknowledged that it is so then perhaps it will be taken away from me.'

'You have lived with enough fear, Hildegard. Do not ruin every day.'

'I try not to.'

'It is a wonder that a woman so committed to the keyboard should be so apprehensive with the rest of her life.'

'We all have insecurities. If we did not, we would be monsters.'

'Pretending to be what we are not.'

'And doing so for so long that we then forget what we are really like. But those days have gone. There is a new Germany now.'

'You could come back home . . .'

'I think the GDR is even worse.'

'But you will be pleased to be leaving Grantchester . . .'

'I am not sure Ely will be very different.'

'There will be no memories . . .'

'I think they will come with us.'

Sidney returned after taking Anna to the swimming pool. He offered to feed her, bath her and put her to bed.

'You have trained your husband well,' Leopold smiled.

'I haven't trained him at all. He is showing off in front of you; making up for all the times he has been absent.'

The professor turned to Sidney. 'You must be busy, Canon Chambers.'

'I am easily distracted.'

'Distraction is the enemy. In music, at least. You have to practise; to concentrate. Perhaps you even have to be selfish.'

'Please don't tell my wife that.'

'I will tell her everything she needs to know in order to be a better musician. Nothing must stand in its way.'

'No,' Sidney hesitated. 'I suppose not.'

He *did* have too many distractions, he acknowledged. Instead of the single-minded dedication of a musician he was part priest, part detective, part husband and part father. He was hardly a son, as he hadn't seen his parents, or his brother and sister, for months.

'O Lord,' he prayed over his sleeping daughter later that night. 'Make me a better man. Let me think less about myself, and more about others, saving my greatest gratitude for the gift of life that you have given us all. Look after my daughter, protect her from the wiles of the world, and let me always be near when she needs me. Help me to become a more loving husband, a better priest, and a kinder man. Let me understand my failings and rid myself of them as best I can, remembering that my greatest responsibility, and my greatest love, should be reserved for you, acknowledging that this world is temporary, that all things must pass, and my hope remains in the life ever-lasting.'

Sidney's desire to do some good in the world was compromised the following afternoon by an article in the *Cambridge Evening News*. As well as her detailed account of the accident, Helena Randall had written an opinion piece, aiming to provide a little background colour, in which she made a number of sly insinu-ations; not least that Orlando Richards was being given, or loaned, a magnificent piano by the college when, at the same time, Corpus Christi was threatening to evict tenants who could not pay their increased rent. Was there one financial rule for the rich and another for the poor? Did the college use the money paid by hard-working people, such as Dennis Gaunt, to subsidise the purchase of extra pianos, fine wine (she had man-aged to access the college's buttery bills) and the eccentric hobbies of its fellows? Wasn't modern Britain supposed to have thrown off the shackles of the Victorian class system and become more egalitarian since the war; building a society on merit and effort rather than privilege and heredity? How many pianos did a college need?

When this article was brought to his attention, the Master was apoplectic. The first person he telephoned was Sidney. 'This is intolerable,' he shouted. 'That journalist was at the funeral and the wake, was she not? I saw you talking to her. Did you invite the woman?'

'Certainly not.'

'But she is a friend of yours?'

'I wouldn't say "friend".'

'Accomplice, then. How can she write such a thing at a time

like this? It is perfectly normal for an employer to provide loans to employees at preferential rates. There is nothing suspicious or illegal about it.'

'I think she considers it an unearned perk at a time when other people can't pay their rent.'

'I can't take any responsibility for people who live beyond their means. This whole article is in appalling taste and you know it. She even goes on to say that Gaunts' Removals had to cut corners and use fewer men because they couldn't afford any more as a result of our recent rent increases. She also says that the bursar beat them down on the quote so that it was hardly worth them doing the job. Well they didn't have to do it, did they? If it was economically unsustainable then they could have turned us down.'

'I imagine they didn't have that luxury.'

'The fact is that they killed Orlando. Now your journalist friend is trying to turn them into victims and blaming us.'

'She doesn't go as far as that, Master.'

'Anyone can read between the lines. Does she think we're stupid? She hints that we brought the thing on ourselves and that an accident was bound to happen. It's unacceptable. I am going to demand an apology and make sure she never reports on a story about the college again.'

'I'm afraid that I don't have much control over Helena Randall.'

'Who is she anyway?'

'She was a student at Newnham. Went to Wycombe Abbey before that.'

'So she's someone who has used the benefits of privilege to become a socialist?'

Sidney's response was as dry as he could make it. 'She does have something of a conscience.'

'I don't want you extending her any sympathy. It's Cecilia Richards you need to pacify. She's incredibly upset.'

'She has seen the article?'

'Of course she's seen it. About fifteen people have "kindly" pointed it out to her. I said you would pay her a visit immediately.'

'I . . .'

'You are her *friend*, Sidney. For goodness sake. And a better friend than that bloody journalist will ever be.'

Before he acted on the Master's demands, Sidney remembered the photographer, Colin Larkin, and went to his studio in Mill Road. If he could just look at all the images taken during the removal and attempted installation of the piano then he might find clues that had previously gone unnoticed. Helena Randall's article had tactfully shown only the flattened piano after the body had been removed and the high window from which it had fallen.

Colin Larkin was aware of Sidney's reputation. 'I think I was taught by someone you know.'

'I very much doubt that.'

'Daniel Morden. He said I should look out for you if I ever found myself in this part of the world. In fact "look out" were his exact words. He says you don't miss a trick.'

'It pays to be vigilant.'

Daniel Morden had been a handsome man in his late fifties who had once worked in Hollywood during the silent era, taken to drink and become a glamour photographer, gradually working his way down the ladder before dropping out to the south of France. Sidney had met him after he had sabotaged his own studio in order to obtain the insurance money. 'Are you still in touch with him?' he asked.

'He's rather a good painter these days. Mostly abstract. Black, white and a hint of pink or grey.'

'Dawn and dusk?'

'He's obsessed with the first and last sightings of the sun. A metaphor, I think.'

'He was a charming old rogue and a great drinker.'

'Not any more. He's very monastic these days.'

'I can't imagine that. But I am grateful to him. He made me look at images in a different way . . .'

'Into the shadows . . .'

'Exactly.'

'Is that why you're here? It's very strange having two people ask.'

'You mean Helena Randall, for her story?'

'She thinks there's something fishy too . . .'

'I didn't say I thought there was anything suspicious, Mr Larkin.'

'You didn't need to, Canon Chambers. Your very presence gives your feelings away.'

'Then you don't mind if I have a look?'

'I'd be glad to show you. I imagine you will need a loupe? I should really get on . . .'

'Don't let me stop you. I'll ask if I need your help with the details.'

'I've only made a few prints; but the contact sheets are here. It's easy enough to blow up anything you want but it would take me a few hours. I assume you don't have any money . . .'

'Unfortunately not.'

'Then all I would ask is that if you do see something that might help sell the images to a national newspaper then you tell me first. I could do with a break.'

Sidney sat on a high stool, picked up at the loupe, and examined the three contact sheets and a few low-angle shots of the piano on its way up. There were several close-ups of the men's faces (Colin Larkin had clearly been influenced by photographs following the construction of Brooklyn Bridge), a lot of details of piano, rope and crane, and a few general wide shots showing the crowd, the Porters' Lodge, various comings and goings, a small child with an ice cream, the bursar on his way out for lunch, the head porter, Orlando fussing, Sidney himself looking rather too fat and too hot, and then several wide-angle shots of the piano falling and the final collapse. Sidney sifted through the images of the actual drop and its aftermath, comparing the arrangement of the crowd before and after the event.

'Good heavens,' Sidney cried. 'That's it . . .'

'What's "it"?'

'A start. An idea. A breakthrough. Thank you, Colin.'

'Aren't you going to tell me what it is?'

'I'm not sure if I'm right. It just might be a bit of serendipity. Fate correcting itself. I'll be back very soon.'

'Is there anything you need?'

'Those five images, eight by ten inches if you please.'

'They're not very dramatic. This is all before the fall.'

'I know. It *was* an accident after all,' Sidney muttered as he left.

* * *

He knew he should head back to Grantchester. His visit had taken far longer than he had anticipated but it had borne greater fruit and Sidney was determined to seize the advantage by calling in at Corpus on his way home. It would hardly take a moment, he tried to convince himself, and if his theory proved plausible then it would also save a lot of time in the long run. He might have a bit of trouble explaining all this to Hildegard but it would surely be worth it if Orlando's killer (for that is what he now thought) was brought to justice.

He went straight to the bursary. Could he possibly examine the Gaunt accounts?

'I don't see why, Sidney. You are hardly an accountant. But then again, I don't see why not.' Walter Collins asked his secretary to extract the necessary paperwork from the files. 'Will you need any help?'

'I assume the debts are obvious.'

'They will stare you in the face; as boldly, perhaps, as the good Lord on Judgement Day.'

'I didn't think they'd be as drastic as that.'

'I am afraid they are, Sidney.'

After half an hour at the secretary's desk (she had been encouraged to take a tea break in town) Sidney was both perplexed and encouraged. 'I am not sure that you have been entirely truthful with me, Walter.'

'I haven't lied.'

'The Gaunts were about to lose their home and probably their business.'

'Losing their business is nothing to do with me; as for their home, it appears Dennis Gaunt does have another place to live. I asked for their company accounts and the figures are presented in a deliberately bleak light. They hardly earn any income at all.'

'Poor souls.'

'Not at all. The figures are so absurd that they must be hiding cash away. Undeclared income. Did they ask if you could pay for your removal in cash?'

'I think they did.'

'I don't imagine the Exchequer would ever know of such a thing.'

'They don't strike me as rich.'

'They won't starve.'

'Did you challenge them on this at all?'

'Of course I did.'

'And did you threaten them in any way?'

'I did not. Although I did say that their accounts might make interesting reading for the tax man.'

'But they don't seem to be those type of people; or, if they are, they aren't very good at it. Dennis Gaunt is clearly going round the bend with worry.'

'Perhaps he should be more cautious; or honest.'

'Do you have no sympathy for him, Walter?'

'You can't expect people to live in college property for free.'

'And was there no means of reducing their repayments?'

'One of the women came to see me: Susan Gaunt. She's his sister-in-law, I think.'

'Lennie's mum?'

'Does the accounts. Tried on the charm. But it didn't work.'

'What do you mean?'

'I'd rather not go into details, Sidney. You can picture the kind of thing . . .'

'Unless you were mistaken.'

'I can assure you I was not. They seem to think that the college doesn't need the money. We can write off their debts and start again. I explained that this was not how it worked. Then they implied that this was a form of class persecution; that we did offer credit to students who didn't pay their buttery bills, or for fellows who were, shall we say, absent-minded about their finances.'

'Which is true . . .'

'Up to a point. However, this is not a matter of credit. It is, arguably, deliberate non-payment.'

'Arguably.'

'Sidney, I don't know why you are defending them. They have no respect. They think we wouldn't dare ask them to leave.'

'So what *did* you say to Dennis Gaunt?'

'I told him that we were considering legal action if they didn't pay three hundred pounds by the end of the month and that they would be evicted if no monies were forthcoming.'

'That doesn't sound very charitable.'

'I wasn't aware that we are a charity.'

'I thought we were.'

'You know what I mean.'

'Was there anything else?' Sidney asked. 'I would be interested to know how seriously you threatened them.'

'Why, Sidney, really, this is none of your business.'

'It may appear not to be so, but I think that it is.'

'And why do you think that?'

Sidney realised that the only way of shutting up his colleague or making him change tack was to tell him the truth. 'Because

I believe the piano that fell on Orlando Richards wasn't meant to fall on him at all.'

'Of course not. The whole thing was an accident.'

'It was . . . and also it wasn't.'

'What on earth do you mean?'

'It was meant to kill *you*.'

After he had returned home, walked the dog, played with Anna, pacified his wife, and checked that there were no urgent messages, Sidney decided to enlist support. Since Malcolm Mitchell knew the family, Sidney asked his curate to call in at Vic Gaunt's house and ask when their son Lennie was coming home from hospital; as he did so, his curate might also like to ask how the young man first broke his leg (was it really during a football match?) and find out, as tactfully as he could, whether there was any ambiguity in Susan Gaunt's relations with the bursar.

'I can hardly ask that in front of her husband.'

'I am sure you will find a way of waiting for the right moment.'

'I don't know her that well,' Malcolm replied. 'Maureen is my friend really. But Susan does bake an exceptional cake. You are always guaranteed a good slice of sponge when you're with her.'

Helena Randall was by his side. 'Perhaps that was what the bursar was after. A nice bit of sponge?' She managed to make the idea sound almost obscene.

'I don't think this case has anything to do with cakes.'

'I don't know,' Malcolm attempted a bit of banter. 'Perhaps you could make an arrest for "crimes against baking". The murder of a meringue, the lacing of a lemon meringue pie, the d . . . d . . . d . . . drowning of a drizzle cake . . .'

'Don't get him started,' Helena warned. 'What do you want from me, Sidney?'

Sidney looked to Malcolm. He had not noticed him stutter in excitement before. He turned to Helena. 'I don't know if this is up your street at all and it does involve a little chat with Geordie.'

'That depends what mood he's in.'

'We all know he's got a soft spot for you,' said Malcolm.

'I only flirt with him to make you jealous.'

'I don't believe that at all.'

'It works, doesn't it?'

'Every time, unfortunately.'

Sidney tried to stick to the point. 'I was wondering, Helena, if you could find out if Lennie Gaunt has a criminal record?'

'Can't you ask Geordie yourself?'

'I promised Hildegard I would be on domestic duties while she prepares for her concert. Also, I need to make things up with Cecilia Richards.'

'I don't know why,' Helena answered. 'I was the one that wrote the article.'

'She thinks we are in cahoots.'

'And aren't we?'

'Yes we are, Helena, but it is not what you might call a popular move. You have a habit of rubbing people up the wrong way.'

'Unlike you, Mr Perfect.'

'I know very well that I am not.'

'You need a bit of friction if you want to generate electricity, Sidney. You can't go round being nice to people all the time.'

'I think that's what you're supposed to do if you are a clergyman.'

'But not if you are a journalist.'

'I think we should go,' said Malcolm, excited by the challenges ahead.

Sidney picked up his briefcase. 'I'm sure you've got plenty of volts left in you, Helena. Only I wouldn't like to see you short-circuit.'

'I'm like a battery, Sidney. Ever ready.'

Malcolm was at the door. 'Shall we get on with it, Helena, or are we just going to stand swapping electric metaphors?'

'*Lead* on, my friend,' Helena smiled. 'It will be good to have an excuse to see more of each other.'

Sidney was on the point of making some kind of joke about the electric charge between them but by the time he had thought of it the couple had left.

His eventual meeting with Cecilia Richards was more difficult than he had anticipated. The association with Helena Randall appeared to have eradicated all that they had shared in the past and disqualified him from future friendship. It was a mistake, he realised within five minutes of coming to the house, not to have brought Hildegard with him. She always made everything calmer. It was even getting to the stage when he had to start acknowledging that some people really did prefer to spend time with his wife.

'That journalist . . .' Cecilia began.

'You read it?'

'Such filth. I know she is a friend of yours.'

'I don't think I'd put it like that. We bump into each other now and then.'

'I didn't know priests spent time with people who are so insensitive.'

'It is a complicated situation.'

'I don't think honesty or integrity are complicated, Sidney. Do you?'

'No.'

'Then do you think you could see your way to never working with her again?'

'I'm not sure . . .'

'Because it's very simple, Sidney: you can't be both my friend and hers. You're going to have to choose: between a widow who has always loved and supported you and whose recently deceased husband was the first person to welcome your wife into Cambridge, and a guttersnipe journalist. That shouldn't be too hard, should it?'

Sidney decided to revisit Dennis Gaunt in his mother's empty house. 'The last time I was here,' he began, 'you were struggling with a Latin phrase about intention. You mentioned *actus reus* but what I think you meant was *aberratio ictus* . . .'

'It's all an aberration, Canon Chambers.'

'It refers to the accidental harm to a person; when the perpetrator aims at X, but by chance or lack of skills hits Y instead. Sometimes it is considered an immaterial mistake; it doesn't matter who is killed, the killing has still taken place . . .'

'Death, not killing. Accident.'

'In some cases this can lead to a double charge – murder (of the *unintended* victim) and attempted murder (of the *intended* victim) – and so it is doubly serious. Do you see what I am saying?'

'An act does not make a person guilty unless their mind is also guilty. No one meant to kill the music man.'

'No. You meant to kill the bursar.'

'Why would that be? My nephew's a good boy. He broke his leg. He's not likely to do that on purpose. He's already broken it once before.'

'Perhaps that was the accident you mean then? Lennie would know all about your debts. And your financial situation.'

'He knows everything about everything. We have no secrets from each other; only from the world. None with the family.'

'And was your nephew good at his job?'

'Always on time.'

'He knew how to use a crane?'

'He was excellent.'

'And he was unlikely to make a mistake?'

'Very.'

'But according to everyone, he did?'

'I don't know how to explain.'

'I think I can, Mr Gaunt. Your nephew did it deliberately. When did you last see the bursar? It was that morning, wasn't it? Did you tell Lennie about the situation?'

'The boy knows everything. He's going to run the company one day.'

'And what company would that be, Mr Gaunt? Would it be the removal firm or something different? Even in another country? Using the money from the sale of this house? Before you have to pay your debts?'

A week later, on 20th August, Helena Randall and Malcolm Mitchell presented Sidney with their findings. Helena had investigated the finances of Gaunts' Removals and looked into their annual reports. It was true that the firm was about to go under and that the Corpus bursar had served them with an eviction notice after persistent non-payment of arrears.

In the meantime, Malcolm had been to see Maureen Gaunt. She told him that her husband's mental condition had deteriorated through the stress of the situation and that their sister-in-law Susan had indeed met the bursar but that any compensatory payment in kind had been at his suggestion rather than hers.

'She told you all that?'

'It took a while to dig it out.'

Helena put her hand on the curate's knee. 'Malcolm's got all the gory details. People tell him anything.'

'I'm sure they do.'

'Do you want to know more, Sidney?' Helena continued. 'Lennie Gaunt has a criminal record. I got Geordie to check: armed robbery, assault and battery. He's had a fair few warnings, getting lenient sentences when he was a juvenile, but now they would have to be more serious. Also, he broke his leg in a street fight; hooliganism, to be precise. It may have been football-related but he wasn't playing at the time. It was after a West Ham v Millwall game.'

'And they moved out of London . . .'

'Ten years ago. It's not clear whether they still have dealings in the capital but it looks like they've been laundering money all over the place. There are plenty of reasons why Lennie Gaunt, at least, might want the bursar dead: debt, the ruin of the family business, his mother's reputation and the fear of never working again. That's four motives, before we start thinking about the threat of an investigation by the tax man. Remove one man and most of their troubles disappear; at least temporarily.'

'And so the idea,' Malcolm summed up, 'was to stage an accident during which Lennie Gaunt breaks his own leg as a kind of alibi; like those murderers who poison themselves before killing in order to show that they too are victims.'

'That's right.'

'Only this time they got the wrong victim.'

'So do you think the bursar is safe?' Helena asked. 'Shouldn't we warn him? They might try something again.'

'I don't think so. They must have guessed we're on to them.'

'If so then you need to watch it, Sidney.'

'I know. That's why I'm due to meet Geordie in the next half hour.'

Inspector Keating made an arrest that very day. At first, Lennie Gaunt denied everything and was so resistant to questioning that the inspector resorted to all-out attack. 'You broke your leg to make it appear that you couldn't be responsible, didn't you, Lennie-boy? That was a clever move. A bit foolhardy, though, and it doesn't cover up the fact that you're guilty of murder.'

'Manslaughter. That's the best you can get me for. Accidental death. Two years in prison – if that.'

'How much did your uncle pay you to do this?'

'He didn't.'

'Dennis Gaunt may have had debts but there's plenty of money floating about. His safe house, for a start. Don't tell me he just keeps that for his nerves. What did he offer you? Five hundred pounds? A thousand? Or maybe even ten grand?'

'Don't be daft. Who has got that kind of money?'

'Your family. Stashed away. The removal business is just a front.'

'I don't think . . .' Sidney interrupted.

'Leave this to me, Chambers. I know what I'm doing.'

Lennie Gaunt lit a cigarette. 'This is stupid.'

'You're the one that's been stupid, matey. Who is going to believe your story?'

'It's the truth. Why would I deliberately break my leg when I've wrecked it before?'

'And not how you say you broke it.'

'It's not something you shout about. Street fighting.'

'Perhaps you got the wrong leg this time?'

'I didn't mean to do anything.'

'Let's be clear about this, sonny boy. We are accusing you of deliberately creating your own distraction. You knew the debts the firm had and that your uncle would have to leave his house . . . and come and live with you . . . and that would be too much for your mum.'

'That's not true.'

'If you could get rid of the bursar . . .'

'Why would I do that? The debts would still be there.'

'But a new man might look more kindly upon you. At the very least it would buy you a bit more time to sort things out. It could be six months before a replacement was found. By then you could have made other plans.'

'I broke my leg!'

'You meant to murder the bursar.'

'I didn't . . .'

'Instead, because of the timings, or because you were distracted, or because you hadn't worked out how long it would take that particular piano to drop, and because Orlando Richards walked underneath at exactly the wrong moment, he was killed, or rather murdered.'

'No one will believe I made that kind of mistake. The musician was killed in an accident.'

'Yours,' Inspector Keating insisted. 'You cocked it all up, didn't you, Lennie-boy? Perhaps you didn't plan it all. It may have been a spur-of-the-moment thing. Everything built up inside you. I know you've got a history of anger and violence. You saw the bursar earlier that morning. You talked to your uncle. He told you that Walter Collins had issued an ultimatum: pay up or get out. Uncle Dennis may even have said something about your mum. And then, when you saw the bursar coming out of the Porters' Lodge, you decided to act. It was an instinctive decision. You untied the piano too soon, gave it a push too late and lost your balance. You didn't mean to fall with it and you didn't mean to kill Orlando Richards. That's why you can keep calling the whole thing an accident. Because it was. But it was also murder. The fact that you got the wrong man and broke your leg at the same time doesn't make any difference.'

'No one's going to believe all that.'

'It will be for a court to decide.'

'It was an accident. I didn't know what I was doing. I lost control . . .'

'There's no need to say anything now, Lennie. You got the wrong man. That's all.'

'I did the right thing.'

The inquisition was at an end. Now Sidney spoke. 'What you did would never have been the "right thing", no matter how much you loved your uncle or wanted to protect him, or save his house and his business. No excuse justifies murder.'

'Except in wartime.'

'This was not a war.'

'I was fighting for my family, Canon Chambers.'

After the arrest had been made Sidney paid the bursar a visit and negotiated an extension on the Gaunt family's credit. It would at least give Dennis the time to sell his mother's house if he could be persuaded to do so. The case would come to court by the end of the year. In the meantime, Inspector Keating had launched an inquiry into whether the Gaunts were involved in any shadow companies, how much of their income was undeclared, and if they were guilty of money laundering. While the murder investigation might come to a swift conclusion, it was clear that the outstanding matters might not.

Sidney knew that he would have to give evidence at the trial, Keating would force a fuller confession, and the sentence, if Lennie was found guilty, was likely to be long after a third and more serious offence. Twenty years, possibly.

On 27th August Helena Randall joined Sidney and Geordie for their regular Thursday evening drink at the Eagle. The two men had been discussing how ironic it was that Lennie Gaunt had done more financial damage to his uncle's company by staging the accident than if he had done nothing; an example, Sidney was suggesting, that you can never anticipate the conse-quences of your actions. It would have been better to talk to all those involved, to have come to a resolution with the bursar rather than act violently.

'Although the end result has turned out well for me,' said Helena.

'What do you mean?'

'I've got a new job.'

'Where?'

'On the *Daily Mirror*. I'm going to be their crime correspondent.'

'Blimey . . .' said Keating.

'And nearly all on the strength of this investigation and my attitude to class and privilege. They said I was "spiky".'

'We could have told them that,' Keating answered. 'So now you are profiting from this too. Making money out of it.'

'That's different.'

'Is it?'

Sidney asked how she had got the job.

'Two weeks ago. I went to London. Malcolm knows. Hasn't he told you?'

Keating leant back in his chair. 'And will "Malcolm" be going to the capital too?'

'Not yet. But do you think you can arrange it, Sidney? After all, you're going to be an archdeacon. Doesn't that mean you're in charge of recruitment?'

'Only in the Ely diocese. Malcolm will have to stay in Grantchester to show my successor the ropes.'

'As long as he doesn't hang himself with them,' said Keating. 'I didn't realise you were seeing so much of the man.'

'Malcolm and I are *extremely close*.'

'Are you indeed?'

'It's not long on the train. And I'll come back at weekends if I'm not too busy. I know it will be difficult for Malcolm to come on a Sunday.'

'It certainly will,' said Sidney.

'So this isn't goodbye then?' Keating asked.

'I hope not. I'm relying on you two. I'm sure I got the job after I told them all about our escapades. I'll need you for tips.'

'Sources,' said Keating. 'Inside knowledge.'

'We have all helped each other, don't you see? And I am going to be a better journalist as a result.'

'That's good to hear.'

'Just as you, Sidney, are going to be a better detective because of me.'

'I am glad you think so. Although not a better priest.'

'I work in this world, Sidney. There is enough trouble in it without wondering what is going to happen in the next.'

'I have always thought that we should be prepared for any eventuality.'

'One world at a time, that's my motto.'

Keating looked down into his empty glass and was glum. 'So you're both leaving me. One's off to Ely; the other to London. What am I supposed to do? Who can I complain about when I get home?'

'You're going to have an easier life,' said Sidney.

'I suppose you want me to buy the next round?'

Helena patted his hand. 'Don't worry. Here's Malcolm. He'll pay.'

'Hello everyone.' The curate appeared slightly nervous.

'What could be nicer than all of us together?' Helena continued, breezily. 'Thank you so much, darling. The men always have pints. As I do when I'm with them.'

'I'll get them, sweetie.'

Helena smiled. 'You see how easy we make things for you, Geordie . . .'

The inspector could only manage one word in response. '*Sweetie?*'

In his head, Sidney tried to rationalise his investigations, and therefore his absence from home, as an opportunity for Hildegard to prepare for her concert. This attempt at justification was flawed, not least because Anna was not yet two and an au pair girl had so far failed to materialise.

'Where have you been?' his wife asked as soon as his first foot was in the doorway.

'Completing our inquiry.'

'But where?'

'I was with Geordie, and Helena and Malcolm.'

'You haven't answered my question. Where did this conversation take place?'

'In the Eagle.'

'The pub.'

'Yes, that's right.'

'So it wasn't really work at all, was it?'

'Well it was, in a manner of speaking, Hildegard.'

'Would you have been able to look after a child while you were in the pub?'

'Children aren't allowed in pubs.'

'Do you think you would be able to look after a child while you were practising for a concert?'

'Probably not.'

'And if you had to decide between looking after a child and going to the pub, which would it be?'

'It's not quite as simple as that.'

'I think it is, Sidney. Do you think your career is more important than mine?'

'No, of course not. That's not the issue.'

'Isn't it?'

'My hours are unpredictable . . .'

'But you *prefer* to be out investigating rather than at home with Anna and me.'

'That's not true.'

'Why do you go out then?'

'Because things happen, Hildegard.'

'Things that are more important than us?'

'Not "more important". No. Things that shout louder.'

'So if I shouted more loudly would you stay at home? Do you want a wife like that? Am I supposed to become one of those women who nag their husbands all the time? I don't want to have to do that. I don't want to become that kind of woman. Instead, I'd like you to *want* to come home. Is that too much to ask?'

'No, of course not.'

Hildegard turned on the oven, ready to heat up some supper. 'Anna's upstairs. I think she's asleep. She fell over today and cut her knee. There was a lot of blood. Although probably not enough to interest you.'

'That's unfair, Hildegard.'

'Don't "Hildegard" me. You could go and see that she is sleeping while I try and get some practice done. Not that it will be any good. I'm in such a bad mood I'm going to play very badly. You should avoid me until this concert is over.'

'I can't do that.'

'Leave me alone and let me get on with it – as you do when you pursue your investigations. Then you don't worry about anything at home. Now it's your turn to stay at home, and my turn to work. This family has to be your priority. If it isn't, I'll take Anna back to Germany with me and start again.'

'There's no need to be that dramatic.'

'How "dramatic" do I have to be, Sidney, to make you change your behaviour?'

'Really . . .'

'There's nothing more to say, Sidney. If you don't do what I say I'll leave you. It's very simple.'

'What?'

'I mean it.'

Bloody hell, Sidney thought to himself.

She's going to *leave me?*

He felt sick.

He hardly left the house for the next five days.

It drove them all crazy.

The concert was held on Saturday 5th September in the chapel of Corpus Christi and it was dedicated to the memory of Orlando Richards. Hildegard played the Bach fugues, with the final movement of Mozart's last sonata as an encore, linking the two great composers' final pieces, one in D minor, the other in D major.

As she played, Sidney could not quite believe that the performer was his wife. He thought he was watching a different person, in another world. Her fingers were confident, muscular and yet also capable of great delicacy. Her hands and forearms were stronger than he had ever realised, both commanding the music and, simultaneously, letting it come to her, so that there were moments when he wasn't sure if Hildegard was playing the music or it was playing her.

When it was over, Cecilia Richards's voice broke as she thanked her friend. The concert had been a blessing. The music was outside time.

'It has its own world,' Hildegard replied. 'It is secret and yet it is shared. It only asks for attention.'

'It's the first concert I've come to since my husband died. I hope he was watching.'

Hildegard took her hand. 'I'm sure he was.'

'I think you may just be saying that. But I can imagine him looking down on us all. That's what matters; and it has been easier than going to any choral music. That would be harder.'

Her son was leaning over the candles at the back of the chapel. He was wearing the false moustache again, and it seemed he was about to set it on fire.

'I must go and fetch Charlie before he does any damage. Please thank Sidney for what he has done. I can't see him.'

'He must be with the fellows.'

'I didn't want a fuss about Orlando's death. Knowing what has happened makes it worse. I will try not to hate the bursar who should have died in his place or the journalist who wrote that story. It's difficult, but the music makes it a little easier. It understands sorrow.'

'There is nothing I can say to comfort you,' Hildegard replied. 'But I played for him and for you.'

'And that is more than anyone else has done.'

Sidney rejoined his wife. 'I have been showing off about you,' he smiled. 'I'm proud.'

'I didn't let you down?'

'Never, Hildegard. You are the making of me. You played so beautifully. We must make sure you have even more time to practise.'

'Yes,' his wife agreed. '*We* must.'

When they arrived home, Sidney prepared a little salad which they had with cold ham, new potatoes, and a couple of bottles of beer. Hildegard was tired and asked for further reassurance. 'Did I do well? Really? All of it? I wasn't sure about the Mozart. I wanted to play at my best.'

'For Orlando.'

'Yes, for Orlando, for Cecilia, for everyone; but most of all for you.'

Sidney looked at his wife. 'I don't deserve you, my darling.'

Hildegard tilted her head to one side. 'No, sometimes you don't. But we have to make the best of things.' She picked up one of Sidney's new jazz recordings from the sideboard. 'What is this? Have you been saving it?'

'Chet Baker,' her husband answered. 'He's a very fine trumpeter. Part of the American West Coast "cool school".'

She read the record sleeve. 'Can you dance to it?'

'I think so.'

'Slowly?'

'Yes, there's one number that's rather fine: "Soultrane". I think it's the first on the album. I heard it on the wireless. Nice and mellow.'

Hildegard handed the record to her husband. 'There's a scrape of moon outside. The summer will be over soon. Play it, Sidney.'

'What do you have in mind?'

'Let's dance.'

They went into the sitting-room and opened the windows to let in the breeze. The sky was darkest blue. There were no stars. Sidney bent down, put the record on to the turntable, lifted the arm, lowered the needle on to the vinyl and checked the volume. Then, as the music began, he walked over to his wife's out-stretched arms.

A Following

THE FENS WERE AS uncertain as memory. Sidney could not fully trust this land that had been reclaimed from the sea. The silt built and eroded simultaneously, caught in an indecisive cycle of accumulation and decay. Tufts of solid ground rose above shallow water pools and mires that could flood at will. The remains of great trees from ancient forests that had fallen in long-forgotten storms had become semi-fossilised 'bog oaks' amid the alder thickets and reed beds. In the winter plain of day (not that there ever really was such a thing) a person should have been able to look out for miles but the fog made it hard to see beyond an outstretched arm. The locals spoke of strange apparitions, Jack-o'-lanterns, lost souls, untimely death and unsettling hauntings. Ely Cathedral, 'the Ship of the Fens', appeared to float over the flat landscape, attempting to provide solidity over the low-lying marshes, but sometimes it seemed that it, too, could have been a mirage.

Canonry House in Firmary Lane had become the Chambers family home. Having begun life in the twelfth century as the cellarer's hall for the monastery, it was a large, rackety old place, hard to furnish and impossible to heat, but it had a gracious drawing-room big enough for Hildegard's piano, a spacious study and an upper floor that could easily accommodate an au pair girl should they ever get one.

Felix Carpenter, the Dean of Ely, came for tea with his wife Cordelia. She brought a present for Anna: the beginnings of a model farm that she and Hildegard laid out on the green carpet of the girl's bedroom as the men talked shop.

The dean had already updated Sidney on many of his responsibilities and assigned his services on the rota. Nothing had been hidden, he was quick to point out, and the cathedral finances were in not too bad a shape. His only concern was the behaviour of another member of the Chapter, Canon Christopher Clough. There had been rumours about him, unsavoury gossip concerning the attention he had been paying to certain female members of the congregation; some vulnerable and new to the area, others recently widowed or heartbroken. The dean was not sure that anything could be proved, but he had a feeling that all was not as it might be. Their clerical colleague, it was alleged, may have been somewhat 'over-enthusiastic' in his attentions. If the new Archdeacon could keep a discreet eye on things then the dean would be grateful. 'That's one of the main attractions of your appointment, Sidney. You will be my eyes and ears.'

'I thought it was a condition of my employment that I was to cease all extra-curricular activity of that nature?'

'Oh, you don't need to worry about that. Besides, this is all directly relevant. We're relying on you to set us right when people stray.'

This was odd. Sidney had spent the last ten years playing down his investigative activities. Now the dean was asking him to make the most of whatever talent he had. 'As long as you don't bring in that inspector of yours,' he continued. 'We can sort things out for ourselves in the Church of England.'

'As they do in the University of Cambridge?'

'I am aware that you may have had the odd difficulty in the past, but clerical behaviour is a different matter.'

'Unfortunately, Felix, I have found that no matter the profession, there is no escaping the common flaws of humanity.'

'And Canon Clough is, perhaps, more prone to weakness than many. We don't want a scandal. It's best to nip these things in the bud.' The dean sighed. 'I find the winter very gloomy, don't you? And Lent hardly makes things better. I presume you will be abstaining from the troublesome grape?'

'Actually, I thought I might not this year. My wife tells me that every time I give up alcohol I become exceedingly grumpy.'

'Have you thought of an alternative? I hope you are not going to give up your investigations?'

'That has been suggested.'

'I myself am trying to give up anxiety. Only I'm worried about how to do it. A paradox . . .'

'That can only be answered by prayer.'

'You are more spiritual than people think, Sidney.'

'I am going to try very hard not to let you down, Felix.'

'Have you settled in all right?'

'I am suitably daunted,' Sidney replied. 'But that is better than being complacent.'

The two men left for evensong. Then Sidney had a quiet evening at home with his family, sorting through their possessions and, most importantly, his books. There were crates and boxes to be opened, but he was enthusiastic about the process, having the largest study he had ever known and plenty of spare shelving. In a few years' time, he hoped it would be the envy of many a Cambridge don.

The master bedroom was on the first floor. It too was large and draughty, with a new carpet, a beamed ceiling on which Sidney was sure that he would hit his head, and a second-hand brass bed acquired from an antique dealer whom Sidney had once saved from a murder charge. He had not yet told Hildegard that this same man had revealed their new home was haunted and that a barefoot angelic apparition had been seen in the upper rooms on moonlit nights.

Hildegard was sitting at a dressing table and applying cold cream to her face. 'The dean's wife was anxious that you two men should have some time alone together. She mentioned that there had been a bit of trouble.'

'Did she indeed?' Sidney took off the cufflinks Hildegard had given him at Christmas. He liked them very much.

'Yes, *mein Lieber*, she did. What did she mean?'

'Nothing for you to worry about.'

'I hope there are going to be no secrets between us in this new community?'

Sidney put on his pyjamas. 'Well, my darling, once again we are faced with the problem of intervention. A fellow cleric has been rather too "enthusiastic", shall we say, with certain lady members of the congregation. But is it any of our business? Canon Clough, for that is the man, is unmarried. These people are consenting adults.'

'Have I met him?'

'I don't think so. Tall, blond, ruddy and mustachioed.'

'Don Juan with whiskers! Has he been abusing his position?'

215

Sidney tucked himself into bed. 'I can see that he could be accused of preying on the vulnerable. Although some of the women with whom he has allegedly been involved are more than capable of looking after themselves.'

'I don't think people will like being questioned on these subjects. For example, I don't like it when people ask me about you.'

'Why has anyone got a reason to do that?' Sidney questioned.

'They want to know how I put up with it all.'

'And what do you say?'

'I tell them I cope with you very well.'

'Cope?'

'I think that's the correct word.'

'I don't know why people ask about other people's marriages. No one ever tells the whole truth, and we can't ever know what goes on behind the bedroom door. Relationships that seem loving in public may be dreadful in private, and those that are argumentative and fractious can be rather wonderful, like in Noël Coward's *Private Lives*. You remember? We went to see it at the Arts. I am reminded of the wife of our beloved archbishop who was once asked whether she had ever been tempted by the idea of adultery.'

'And had she?'

'"Never," she replied. "But murder, often."'

'I'll remember that,' said Hildegard, joining her husband in bed. 'It gives me comfort.'

'Comfort?'

'To know that I am not alone.'

*   *   *

The next day was cold, clear and unusually crisp. The lack of wintry dampness put Sidney in a cheerful mood that was further improved by the fact that Amanda was taking him out to lunch at the Lamb Hotel. She wanted to discuss the practicalities of her forthcoming wedding to Henry Richmond.

She arrived at the railway station looking stylish in a maroon coat and produced an envelope from her bag which she handed over at once 'before I forget'. It was a late birthday present, an opportunity that she was sure would change his life. Sidney was about to have his first pair of handmade shoes.

'I thought it appropriate, don't you see? This will help you keep your feet elegantly on the ground as you go up in the world.'

'That is exceptionally generous of you. I have been a bit down at heel lately.'

Amanda insisted on the indulgence of a taxi and positively cooed when they passed the cathedral. 'Every day you get a step closer to heaven, Sidney.'

'The place from which you came.'

Amanda cut short this easy flirtation. 'Although I think I'm unlikely to return. My place in the fiery pit was booked a long time ago.'

'Faith can always get you out again. How is Henry?'

'Well: but frightened. To continue with our pedestrian conversation, I think it's best to keep him on his toes.'

'So you've decided to accept him?'

'Since I can't marry you, Sidney, I've had to settle for second best.'

'Don't joke about these things.'

'You are secretly pleased to have escaped me.'

'I am very happy with my lot in life, it is true.'

'Then you need to be teased more often.'

The taxi pulled up at the hotel and they were shown to a discreet corner table in the dining-room. Amanda hoped that no one thought they were having an affair. 'I don't want to ruin your reputation before you've begun.'

'I think they will be giving me the benefit of the doubt. Besides, people have their own lives to lead. This is a town. It isn't like Grantchester. There is no Mrs Maguire to collect and disseminate information at will.'

'Oh, I think you'll find a new version. It won't be long before you'll have your usual collection of Pats and Margarets.'

'There's no need to be dismissive. It's not very Christian of you.'

'Well perhaps I am not in a "very Christian" mood, Sidney.'

The waitress arrived and Amanda scanned the menu. 'You probably aren't either, now that it's Lent,' she added.

'I'm taking this one off.'

'So you've left the wagon in Grantchester?'

'It makes me too grumpy.'

'You've noticed at last.'

'I thought I might try August instead.'

'When everyone's on holiday? That's not a bad idea. Anyway, I'm glad. Don't think I'll let up on the teasing, though. It's my job to stop you becoming a middle-aged bore. We don't want you turning into one of those complacent priests with a singsong voice. Are you going to have the lamb?'

'I don't have a singsong voice.'

'Touchy. I don't think I fancy the eel pie.'

'I think that's what you're supposed to have. Or the eel stew. You need to think of it as your initiation into the area.'

'I am not sure that I want that. I'm going for the chicken breast and some green beans. No potatoes.'

'You are cutting down?'

'I've gone off them. Someone told me they're poisonous when they're green beneath the skin.'

'Oh, Amanda. That can't be right.'

'One can't be too careful. You of all people should know that. Cherry seeds produce prussic acid. Bitter almonds are full of cyanide . . .'

'If you think in that way then most food leads to death. How do you know all this?'

'One of my admirers.'

'I thought you'd given them up?'

'Every girl needs insurance.'

Sidney looked at the menu. He could not remember what he was due to have at supper and knew Hildegard would ask what he had had at lunchtime. She didn't like him to have meat twice in one day so he avoided the lamb and plumped for the plaice.

Once they had settled they began to discuss the forthcoming nuptials. Henry had said that he would prefer a registry office wedding (he thought it best, having been married before, even though his wife was dead), but Amanda wanted a little bit of beauty, and since Sidney had Ely Cathedral at his disposal perhaps he could oblige with a service of blessing?

'It's not exactly "at my disposal", Amanda. I would have to

ask the dean. I presume you would want to have it in our Lady Chapel?'

'They are hardly going to turn down a request from the new boy, are they? Besides, you owe me a favour.'

'For what, may I ask?'

'For my life being in constant danger as a result of my association with you. Every time I see you I get into some kind of scrape.'

'It's not always my fault.'

'It is. You are a positive health hazard. Perhaps they should put a label on your cassock. "Warning: Deep Water."'

'I suppose you could have one too. "Danger: Acid."' Sidney wondered why his friend was being so prickly, so he took the bull by the horns: 'Tell me, Amanda. Is anything the matter?'

'Not exactly.'

'So there is something?'

'It's hard to talk about, but it is partly why I've come. I knew you would guess. This is not just about a service of blessing.'

'Is it Henry? Are you having doubts?'

'I don't want to complain.'

'No one said you were. And we are friends. We tell each other everything.'

'Not everything, Sidney. But most things.'

'The important things.'

Amanda helped herself to wine. 'It's other people. In Henry's past.'

'His former wife?'

'She's dead. You know that. He told you at that dreadful shooting party. But I think there's someone else.'

'Currently?'

'No. But recent.'

'And how do you know?'

Amanda reached for her purse. "This.' She handed Sidney a second envelope. 'Open it.'

Inside was a note, written in capitals in blood-red ink, spelling out four words. *I WILL RUIN YOU.*

Sidney looked at the letter. 'The Hon. Amanda Kendall' had been typed with her address in Hampstead. 'The writer knows where you live.'

'There are more.'

'Do you have them?'

'Of course.'

'Can I see them?'

Amanda fished out three more notes from her handbag.

He still loves another.

Imposter!

Marry him and die.

'I don't know what to do about it, Sidney. You won't tell Henry, will you?'

Sidney told Amanda not to open any more suspicious envelopes but to keep them for the police should the situation escalate. If there was anything other than a nasty letter she should let him know immediately and she should, perhaps, ask Henry a few more questions about his recent past. He would also raise the matter with Keating. In the meantime, he returned to his duties.

It was taking Sidney longer to get used to a cathedral environment than he had expected and he asked Canon Christopher

Clough for a more informal tour round the precincts: the tracery of the cloister walk, the old infirmary, Prior Crauden's chapel, the meadow and the great barn. It was both an architectural survey and a chance to meet some of the parishioners. It was also a way of doubling up on his workload since, if they came across any women, Sidney could begin his secret mission from the dean and assess whether his colleague's approach was inappropriately predatory.

The first person they met was a widow whose son had drowned in Whittlesea Mere while fishing for pike. Then, as they emerged into the high street, they bumped into an unsettling man who appeared to be still drunk from the previous night. He told Sidney to 'watch out for the monks' that still haunted the old monastery, sometimes popping up in the middle of evensong, and how the ghostly blue hand of the seventh-century St Etheldreda could still be seen gliding up the banister of Priory House. Sometimes people didn't so much walk round here, he said, they *floated*.

Emerging from the Sacrist's Gate was Virginia Newburn, an efficiently dressed woman from London in her mid-forties who told Sidney that she liked to walk on the Fens every day, whatever the weather. She offered to show him some of the wilder stretches of marshland, beyond Prickwillow and along the River Lark. One day, perhaps, she might even take him to hear the Singing Swans of Wash Fen Mere.

After she had moved on, Canon Clough confided that she was one of his 'vestal virgins'.

'Are there many?' Sidney asked.

'Legion.'

'That must keep you busy.'

'It does, I can tell you. They're like old cars that haven't been out much. You just need to give them a bit of oil and they soon get going. But it's quite harmless; most of them are barking. You have to be a little mad to spend much time with a priest, don't you think? Anyone who falls for the charms of a clergyman must have a screw loose somewhere.'

Two weeks later Amanda arrived with her fiancé for the first of their premarital 'chats'. Sidney had not seen Henry Richmond since the funeral of Sir Mark Kirby-Grey. He had not quite made up his mind about him, despite there being nothing obviously wrong with the man. In fact he had exercised considerable bravery in facing domestic violence. It might have been a small thing compared to the courage necessary in wartime, but sometimes, Sidney thought, the Englishman was more frightened of emotional than physical confrontation, preferring, for example, to attack an enemy gun position on a distant hillock than have it out with a friend.

Henry was dressed in a speckled mid-brown three-piece tweed suit with a plum windowpane overlay which so complemented his fiancée's maroon overcoat that Sidney wondered if Amanda might have ordered both of their outfits as a joint ensemble. The couple appeared to have emerged directly from the pages of *Country Life*, photogenic examples of the ease with which the British aristocracy still held itself, despite the loss of Empire and no clear understanding of what its future role might be.

It was the third time Amanda had been the recipient of one of Sidney's advisory sessions (previous conversations had concerned 'the brute' Guy Hopkins and 'the bigamist' Anthony Cartwright) and because her new fiancé had been married before she insisted that her friend did not treat them as children.

Henry told the story of his late wife's death over a whisky. Connie Richmond had been an Irish seamstress from County Down. 'I met her through my tailor. She was so very pretty; one of those women who need to be looked after. She had such innocent appeal and I couldn't resist her. But she was always frail and she had a weak heart.'

'It was a youthful *folie* with a wayward colleen,' Amanda explained, as if Henry had not spoken at all. 'I don't know if the Irish have a word for it?'

'When did you lose her?' Sidney asked. He hadn't liked to talk of this when they had been at Witchford Hall.

Henry Richmond spoke without emotion. His past life could almost have belonged to someone else. 'Five years ago. Long enough, I hope, to allow time for mourning and a return to love.'

Sidney did not like to comment on either the propriety or process of grief. As far as he was concerned, there were no rules other than the fact that attention had to be paid. This, in itself, was a form of prayer.

'So you feel that you are now ready for a second marriage?' he enquired.

Amanda gave a nervous laugh. 'Don't ask Henry in front of me, Sidney.'

'There's nothing I can't mention. There should be no secrets between you.'

'Really? I am not sure you practise what you preach.' Amanda leaned over and helped herself to a refill from the teapot.

'My wife knows everything I'm doing.'

'Hildegard? I am not so sure.'

'And do you know everything about her?' Henry checked.

'I hope we are honest about everything that matters.'

If Sidney had been a crueller friend he would have used this moment to divert the conversation on to the subject of the anonymous letters. They must surely be connected to Henry's past. But he did not do so because, as he had learned on many previous occasions, discussions about love require a tact that sometimes makes one less than honest.

'If you don't volunteer your secrets,' Amanda carried on, 'then you have no control over the moment of their revelation.'

Sidney was surprised by his friend's bravura. 'I suppose people hope they are never revealed at all.'

Henry Richmond joined in as tentatively as he could. 'Perhaps couples are discreet in order to avoid hurting one another. Not everything needs to be explained.'

'And women certainly like to keep a bit of mystery about them,' Amanda continued. 'We don't want to give the game away too soon.'

'Perhaps you have already said too much by admitting that,' her fiancé replied.

'I was joking. I was nervous,' Amanda flustered. 'I don't find these conversations easy.'

'Nobody does,' said Sidney. 'But I think one has to make a few ground rules. There must be nothing in either conversation or behaviour which involves anything that might hurt one another. There is a difference between tact and deceit; and, at the same time, between an act of kindness and a lie. Even if the truth is painful, there are times when it must be known.'

Henry cut in. 'I never want to do anything to upset Amanda. She is too precious.'

'I am sure that is the case,' Sidney responded. 'But when you are married you are no longer alone. It is not about "I" but "we". You should not have to worry so much about your own feelings. All are joint.'

'All of them?' Amanda asked.

Sidney leant forward to make his point. 'Marriage asks that you renounce your solitary life. It requires you to put the other person first, rather than yourself. It requires latitude, tolerance, understanding and forgiveness. These are difficult matters, not least because it means being less selfish.'

Amanda bristled. 'I don't think I'm that . . .'

'The idea being,' Sidney continued, 'that we become better people as a result. We improve each other.'

He was pleased that Hildegard was not on hand to overhear what she might consider the great chasm between what her husband preached and what he actually practised, but just as he was about to move on to the difference between a church blessing and a marriage, his wife entered the room and announced that Amanda was wanted on the telephone.

'But no one knows I am here. Who could it be?'

'The woman didn't say.'

Amanda went into the hall to receive the call while Hildegard reassured Henry that a second marriage could be much more – what was the word? She was about to say 'mature' but did not want to judge his previous experience – *aware*. She was struck by the fact that they had both previously been married to Irish people.

As the conversation in Sidney's study continued, Amanda heard a woman's voice on the telephone, low and threatening.

Marry him and your life will be over.

The line went dead. She returned to the room. Even Henry noticed that something was wrong. 'Are you all right, my darling? You look as if you've seen a ghost.'

The following afternoon, whilst walking Byron along Angel Drove, Sidney saw a woman a hundred yards ahead, dressed in the same maroon coat that Amanda had worn the previous day. Was it even her? Had she changed her mind and decided not to go back to London? Did she have other friends in the area of whom Sidney was unaware?

He began to walk after the woman, past Braham Farm and along Grunty Fen Catchwater, but made no ground. Byron barked and Sidney called: 'Amanda! I thought you'd left!'

The distant figure crossed the railway bridge at Chapel Hill. Sidney shouted out once more, sure he could be heard, but the figure did not turn round. Instead, she disappeared into the mist along the Ouse.

That is very odd, Sidney thought as Byron rejoined him. I must be wrong. But how could I mistake my best friend?

His Labrador began digging at a broad bank of silt by the river, pawing away at a stone, making what appeared to be a shallow grave out of the pebbles, his snout wet-black with gravel and peat.

It started to rain. Shortly after he had arrived back home, Amanda telephoned to tell Sidney more about the mysterious call the previous day. Before she could go into any detail, he asked where she was, if she had delayed her departure in any way or if she had left her coat behind.

'No, of course not,' Amanda replied. 'Why are you asking all these irrelevant questions?'

'Where did you buy your coat?' Sidney insisted. 'Is it common?'

'Of course it isn't. What do you take me for? I got it at Derry and Toms. I was thinking of fur but had a momentary economy drive.'

'Would it be easy to get another one like it?'

'I imagine so.'

'And have you worn it a lot?'

'Of course I have. It's new. Why are you asking? You've never taken much interest in my wardrobe before.'

'I always appreciate what you wear.'

'Never mind all that, Sidney. I have something more worrying to tell you.'

'More than the recent phone call?'

'I'm afraid so. It's getting worse.'

'You've had another letter?'

'I have.'

'And what does it say?'

'*You're not the victim, you're the crime!!!*'

'I told you not to open them.'

'There's another thing, Sidney. It is in a different handwriting from the other letters.'

'So you think there's more than one person sending the threats?'

'There has to be. What have I ever done to deserve this?'

Or what has Henry done? thought Sidney.

He went into the kitchen to make a pot of tea. Hildegard was teaching. She was nearing the end of a lesson because the music had stopped. Teacher and pupil were probably discussing plans for the following week. He would bring his wife a cup between

228

pupils and possibly a slice of cake, although their supply had been considerably depleted now that Malcolm was no longer with them.

The music resumed. 'Stronger in the left hand,' he heard Hildegard saying, 'now dance. Dance with the right. Let the music ripple. It's like a stream. Let it flow over the listener. Imagine it never ends.'

Sidney opened the cake tin. There was half a loaf of fruitcake left (not one of his favourites). He went in search of digestive biscuits. They would do perfectly well, but it was not the same as when Malcolm had returned from one of his forays round the parish.

He poured out the tea and heard Hildegard issuing her final instructions. He tried to imagine what it would be like to be her pupil. Frightening but rewarding, he thought. One would not want to let her down.

She was touched by the tea and began to talk about Adam Barnes, the pupil who had just left. 'He's the first student I've had who understands Bach. I think I'm going to put him in for Grade Eight.'

'Whatever you think best . . .'

'I don't want to push him. He's quite a shy boy; but he understands how to be elegant and light without being . . . what is the word?'

'Superficial?'

'I think that's it. It's what you have, *mein Lieber*. You are much more serious than people think.'

'I hope so.'

'You know there are home-made chocolate biscuits?'

'What?'

'I've hidden them.'

'Why? Malcolm doesn't live with us any more.'

'We need to finish the fruitcake first. If I produce the biscuits then the fruitcake will be abandoned.'

'So why are you telling me?'

'I don't know. I'm tired.'

'Perhaps Anna would like a chocolate biscuit. Where is she?'

'Playing with her farm. I thought you were keeping an eye on her.'

'I saw her a few minutes ago.'

'Minutes?'

'Half an hour.'

'Honestly, Sidney, you know that you are supposed to look after her when I'm teaching. Anna!'

'I'm sure she's all right.'

'I'll go and see.'

He took the tea upstairs with some juice for Anna and a chocolate biscuit. His daughter responded first with suspicion, then curiosity. After a first lick, a look of amazement and then hurt came across her features as she wondered how something so delicious had been denied her so long. Why had she not been introduced to this nectar before?

'You know she will never recover from this?' Hildegard warned from the doorway. 'She will ask for it all the time?'

'Chocklick,' said Anna. 'More.'

Sidney produced an extra biscuit. It disappeared immediately. 'Gone,' said Anna. 'More.'

Because there was no more, Hildegard sang her daughter a distracting song:

'Ringel, Ringel, Rosen,
schöne Aprikosen,
Veilchen und Vergissmeinnicht,
alle Kinder setzen sich.'

The three of them then began to play with the toy farm. Sidney crouched down and made animal noises, and together they made up a musical nonsense song about all the creatures waking up in the morning and how they greeted each other through the day.

It was a rare respite, broken only by the sound of the telephone. By the time they had heard, it was too late to answer.

Hildegard worried that it might have been Amanda.

Sidney tried to return to their game but the mood had been dispelled. He gathered up the tea things. 'I hope you are not going to get anxious about all this.'

'But who has taught me to be so?' his wife asked. 'This happens all the time. At least you can stop it before it gets worse.'

'We have to worry, I suppose, about precisely what is starting up.'

'Threats, secrecy, lies.'

'I don't think there have been lies, Hildegard, at least not as far as I can see . . .'

'And potential murder. Is that not enough? She should go to the police. You must tell Inspector Keating what is going on.'

The most important thing Sidney had to do, Geordie told him, was to find a decent pub in Ely; somewhere they could be discreet. People were beginning to cotton on to the fact that their meetings were no longer social. It had to be a place with proper beer, a warm ambience and not too many riff-raff. He didn't want to have to start breaking up fights or making arrests.

'I don't think you'll find too much of that in Ely,' Sidney replied.

'You find it everywhere if you know where to look. But at least the poor are honest about their crime. They slug it out. Not like your posh people.'

'They are not "my" posh people.'

'You know what I mean.'

'Alas, I do. But they are all my people. No one is excluded: the saint and the sinner, the entertainer and the bore. I must spend time with them all and show no favouritism.'

'I don't think you'll be so good at that. Even I can tell when you're fed up.'

They had chosen the Prince Albert pub in Silver Street. It was conveniently central, served good beer and the landlord promised to make sure they weren't disturbed. Sidney bought the first round, and settled down to receive his friend's initial enquiries.

'I suppose I should ask you how the new job's going?'

'You're not that interested, Geordie, are you?'

'Not really, but I'll hear you out if you make it snappy.'

Sidney explained that he was now one of the bishop's senior officers, with responsibility for the care of the clergy and church communities in his designated area. He was to oversee the induction of churchwardens. He had legal powers to give permission, via the Church's own planning system, for work on the repair and ordering of church buildings; he had to check parish records and church valuables . . .'

'Make sure they aren't stolen, you mean?'

'That kind of thing. I also have responsibility for the practical and legal issues relating to the appointment of clergy and work with others in pastoral reorganisation, clergy housing and occasionally with disciplinary matters.'

'Clergy who aren't up to the mark kind of thing? Those who stray?'

'Exactly.'

'That's why they must have appointed you. I can't imagine you're much good at any of the other stuff.'

'I am grateful for your encouragement, Geordie.'

'I was expecting to wait a lot longer before seeing you. I thought you might be busy.'

'I am.'

'But something must have come up.'

'It's all rather sensitive.'

'Out with it, man.'

Sidney explained Amanda's predicament and the need for secrecy and discretion. She was a resourceful woman who had been through a lot, but he didn't want to do anything to undermine her confidence. Her success rate with men was, it had to be said, appalling.

Inspector Keating defended her. 'We all know why that is . . .'

'My friendship with her has nothing to do with it.'

'I'll let that pass. But she'll have to make a statement if she's worried.'

'She won't do that, Geordie.'

'Then how am I supposed to do anything?'

'You are meant to help her as a friend.'

'She has to ask.'

'You know what she's like.'

Geordie emptied his pint and stood up to get another. 'I suppose you are suggesting that I do a bit of speculative investigation in a geographical area outside my jurisdiction, with no evidence as yet supplied to me, in the spare time that I don't have.'

'That's correct.'

'Let me get the pints and think about it.'

When he returned, Geordie cut to the chase. 'Tell me what you've got.'

Sidney talked about the letters and the phone call, and added that Amanda had told him that some of the messages were in a different script. Someone was either trying to disguise their hand, pretend there were more letter-writers than there were, or there really were several people all threatening Amanda at the same time.

'I can understand one man or woman but not several,' Keating replied. 'Can you get hold of any of them?'

'I should think so.'

'There's a lot we can do with graphology and forensic linguistics; if the person uses unusual words, that kind of thing. It's not an exact science but they can tell man or woman, left-handed or right-handed and things like whether the writer is a dog-lover or not . . .'

'Really?'

'I'm exaggerating but you get the idea. A friend of mine was on a case in 1958 where a woman got a month in prison for sending out this kind of thing. They are often mad fantasies but it's hard to tell when people get ideas into their head. That's what love does, I suppose. I've been married so long I can hardly remember.'

'I am sure you have had your fair share of passion . . .'

Geordie was not listening, but thinking. 'I also have to ask, Sidney, and I know this is hard, if Amanda could be making all this up?'

'You can't mean that, can you?'

'To get out of the match. Could it be an elaborate plan? Perhaps she doesn't *want* to get married.'

'I think she's perfectly capable of telling Henry to his face. She's a plain speaker. We both know that.'

'Fair point. I wouldn't suggest such a thing in her presence.'

Sidney thought about the possibility and dismissed it. 'Can you imagine her doing that? It's too much effort for a start. It would be ridiculous.'

'But is it any more absurd than what is happening already? Tell me about this future husband of hers.'

'I don't think he's behind it, if that's what you mean. He's a decent enough bloke.'

'So you think it's someone else? What about an ex-lover? A former wife?'

'She's dead.'

'Are you sure?'

'Well, I didn't see the body, Geordie.'

'And you like this Henry Richmond, you say?'

'I wouldn't put it as strongly as that.'

'But you approve?'

'She is my best friend. I'm not sure I'd approve of anyone.'

'But who would want to hurt her?'

'I think it's about him rather than her. Someone who is so in love with Henry that she wants to kill anyone who stands in her way.'

'A woman, then. Perhaps she did away with the first wife. How did she die?'

'Heart failure.'

'That covers a multitude of sins. Do you want me to take a look?'

'I think it happened when they were abroad.'

'That's no good. We could have used Jarvis. Your man would still have to register the death. At least I can check that.'

'Henry doesn't know about the threats.'

'What?'

'Amanda wants to keep him in the dark.'

'You've got to be bold about this kind of thing, Sidney.'

'Nothing has happened yet. There has been no crime.'

'Apart from harassment and what might be considered a practical joke. There's nothing we can do if Miss Kendall won't show us any evidence. But there is, of course, plenty that you can start to work on, discreetly, as you always do, pretending to be one thing when you are not . . .'

'Yes,' Sidney replied glumly, 'I was afraid you were going to say that.'

'I'll get the boys on to it as soon as you ask. You're not too worried, are you?'

'Of course I am.'

'I'm afraid I can't reassure you. These things have a nasty habit of getting out of control. But someone will know the person that's doing this. We just have to find out who.'

A few days later Amanda summoned Sidney to an early supper at Mon Plaisir in London. She told him that there had been further telephone calls and more notes, including references to various paintings in the National Gallery that featured harlots and adulterers who had met a fatal end. The perpetrator was therefore someone who knew where her victim worked and also her particular field of interest, since most of her references were to the sixteenth-century painters of the Northern Renaissance.

It was frightening, Amanda said when they met. Henry had gone away for a few days. She still hadn't told him.

'And it is impossible that he could be the one writing the letters?' Sidney asked over the pâté.

'The person who telephoned your home was a woman. If that suggestion had been made by anyone other than you then I might have slapped their face, but I have known you for so long that I have even started to think like you and so I have to tell you that *I have already thought of that.* But it can't be Henry or one of his friends, can it? Why would anyone be so cruel? What do they want? It's too horrible.'

'I suppose they're trying to make you break it off.'

'It makes me all the more determined to keep going. I think Henry knows that if he wanted to end it he'd just have to tell me. I *know him*, Sidney. I've spent such a lot of time with him because I am terrified of making a mistake. The only thing that's wrong with him is that he's a bit weak. So weak, I am sure he couldn't possibly do this. Oh, God. Now I am crying and we both hate that. I'm embarrassed. The waiter will think there's a scene. What are we going to do? How did we end up in a situation like this?'

After Sidney had given her his handkerchief and ordered further drinks, Amanda turned the conversation towards her childhood; how she wanted to run away back to the time when she was last happy, holidaying on the island of Skye, on a day with strong winds and dark skies, the barking of dogs, the bleating of sheep, the collapse of telephone wires – with no boat daring to go out to sea, and everyone stuck inside.

'No one thought we would ever go out again, but then the dark clouds moved and everything blew over the Cuillins and the sun came through the clouds and light fell across the tops. The wind was stilled and we could go out again and I felt such happiness that the darkness had passed. I often think that if I ever go back there then the same thing will happen, that the clouds will clear and the air will still be fresh, and the dogs will stop barking, and the light on the mountains will be sharp even if it's only for a short time. I will still have seen it. Do you understand, Sidney?'

'Like Noah after the flood.'

'We always need something to remember. A time when everything was possible. Do you think this too will pass?'

'Eventually. The compensation for losing happiness, for discovering that it never lasts, is that our troubles are transient too.'

'I don't think that's of much comfort to those who are in distress.'

'One cannot be trite about these things. But the ultimate end to suffering is death.'

'Then perhaps I could find the person behind all this and kill them myself?'

'I'll ignore that remark, Amanda. Have you received anything when you have been staying with Henry?'

'You mean when I have been at his parents' in the country?'

'Or visiting him in his flat?'

Amanda put down her knife and fork. 'He mustn't know

anything about this, Sidney. Underneath it all he's a great worrier. I don't want to put him off. You promised.'

'I can't remember making any such vow.'

'Please, Sidney, I'm begging you. I can't have another disaster . . .'

'But if he knew all this was happening then he might be able to help you. He will probably have to find out anyway, even if it's to save your life.'

'You think it's as bad as that?'

'I don't know.'

'Have you told Keating?'

Sidney wondered whether to lie. 'Yes.'

'I'm glad. What does he say?'

'He'd like to see the letters.'

'I've brought them for you. I can't stand having them in the house. I know that if I want it all to stop for good then all I have to do is to throw Henry over.'

'And do you want to do that?' Sidney checked.

'I have thought about it. When you lack confidence about these things . . .'

'You shouldn't . . .'

'You know I do. All this front's a bluster. I spend most of my life acting.'

'I think we all do that; we play different parts depending who we are with and the situation we are in.'

'But don't you ever want life to just stop, Sidney? Sometimes I want to just run away to somewhere like the Villa Cimbrone in Ravello. That's where Greta Garbo went. Did you know that? I could just stay there for ever and no one would ever trouble me again. It's very lovely. You should see it.'

'We can't let these threats beat you down, my darling.'

'Don't . . .'

'What . . .'

'It's nothing. Sorry. You should only call Hildegard by that name . . .'

'She won't mind.'

'She will, Sidney. Don't do it.'

'I'm sorry.'

'I like it. But don't.'

'I said I'm sorry. Do you love Henry?'

'He's kind but he's not strong enough to stand up to me like you do. And I think he likes the fact that I am rich. Rather too much. If part of his love for me is a love of my money, I don't mind. People often love each other for the wrong reasons. Physical beauty might be one of them too. We all know how that fades and disappears. At least if we go into all of this with our eyes open then we might end up with something a little more authentic.'

'Do you think you know everything that you need to know about him?'

'Don't tell me any more, Sidney.'

'But can you trust him?'

'I trust him enough to live with him. I like him – and perhaps what we have is enough. It may not be passion, or the height of romance, but it is an understanding. If we go into this with our eyes open then we won't let each other down.'

'It sounds like a compromise.'

'If you and I had married then things would have been different.'

'But we didn't, and it's too late.'

'I was stupid.'

'Perhaps we both were, Amanda, but we can't do anything about it now.'

'Maybe one day. When we're very, very old indeed and all our friends are dead.'

'Yes, well, perhaps, one day. But I love my wife and you love Henry.'

'Of course. I love Henry and you love your wife.'

Outside it was almost dark. Soft rain fell on hard pavements, forming shallow surface streams of water that gleamed under the streetlights and against the darkness. People moved at speed to be anywhere other than where they were, making for buses, taxis and the underground, seeking shelter from the wind that was against them, the rain and the world.

It was well after ten o'clock at night when Sidney caught the King's Lynn train back from Liverpool Street. He read the letters:

I watch your every step.
You have no hope. You are hope less.
Say goodbye to your frends.

Just as Sidney was wondering what to do next, Canon Christopher Clough joined his carriage. For one moment he thought that his colleague must have been following him. Perhaps he was being stalked as well?

His companion said that he had been spending the evening with one of his most intimate friends. They had been to see Marlene Dietrich at the Theatre Royal, Drury Lane. Perhaps Hildegard would have enjoyed it?

Sidney had not known anything about the performance but was sure that the tickets would have been too expensive. He tried not to feel resentful. Clough chattered on, saying how he was also planning to see Mary Martin in *Hello, Dolly!* and Brian Rix in *Chase Me, Comrade!* Theatre was his lifeblood, he said, and he was fortunate to know so many members of the theatrical profession.

'And how are your admirers?' Sidney asked. 'I saw Virginia Newburn in the cathedral on Sunday. She was asking after you.'

'I can't think why. She always knows where to find me. That's the problem with being a priest, Sidney. There is no possibility of secrecy. You have to live your life out in the open.'

'I thought that was the point. We are always on duty.'

'It's hard, though, isn't it? We all need to let our hair down at one time or another. Those of us who still *have* hair, of course.'

Sidney smiled but refused to join in. His wife had already warned him not to be too smug about his possession of a full head of hair while his colleagues had begun to lose theirs. Was Canon Clough vain enough to use a hairdryer?

'I imagine you have to be careful, Christopher. You wouldn't want any of your parishioners getting the wrong idea.'

'I think they enjoy a bit of flirtation.'

'You wouldn't want to lead them on.'

'There is no danger of that, Sidney. I tell them I am celibate.'

'And they believe you?'

'Sometimes they accept it at face value. At other times they take it as a challenge. I also tell them that I'm afraid of being touched.'

Sidney had never met a man so calculating. 'And what about Miss Newburn?'

'Oh, I don't think she's capable of much.'

'Tell me,' Sidney asked. 'Does she have a maroon coat?'

'Probably. She's always making things. She told me she could rustle anything up in a matter of days. She's said that if I ever become a bishop she'll make me a cope.'

'And do you think that's likely?'

'I very much doubt it. But there's no harm in humouring the woman, is there?'

'I don't know,' Sidney replied. 'You don't want things to get out of hand. How many more women are you stringing along?'

'That's not quite how I'd put it.'

'Are any of them married?'

'Of course not. Although I do see some, come to think of it. They all seem relatively happy; a little bored perhaps, lacking attention. Their husbands take them for granted. And I cannot always account for my effect on the fairer sex. Sometimes I don't even know I am doing it.'

There was strategy in this. All the women Canon Clough saw were vulnerable. If one of them ever complained then he could either say that the victim was making things up or that she was of unsound mind.

He had managed to cover his tracks in a way that Henry Richmond, perhaps, had not. Was Richmond a philanderer too? Sidney sighed as Canon Clough chattered on. He resolved to have it out with Henry.

In the pub the following night, Inspector Keating decided to have some fun by encouraging the landlord to tell a few stories:

the witches who turn into hares; the lucky charms made from the severed heads of executed criminals; and the legend of Tom Hickathrift who killed a giant whose ghost could still be seen hurling cartwheels at unseen foes on stormy nights.

'People believe all sorts round here.'

'I'm supposed to have no truck with that kind of thing,' Sidney replied as he picked up his beer and moved away to their regular table. Once he had sat down he told Geordie that he did, however, find the surrounding landscape all too eerie.

'Perhaps the Fens are getting to you.'

'The other day, when I was walking Byron, I saw a woman who looked exactly like Amanda. She was wearing the same coat.'

'You mistook your best friend?'

'I was convinced. But it was a coincidence.'

'It's unlike you to make a mistake like that, Sidney. It must have been the mist. It plays tricks on the eye. Figures appear and disappear so often that you can never be sure that they were there in the first place. The number of times I've been told about hauntings and apparitions when it's often just some harmless lost woman trying to get home. People read too many ghost stories, that's the trouble.'

Sidney confessed that he had been pushed to find a rational explanation for events. It was the first time he had not been able to trust his own eyes. 'I wondered if I was dreaming, or if I was suffering from the beginnings of a migraine. Then I thought that the woman I saw might have been one of the members of the congregation: Virginia Newburn. She appeared to be leading me somewhere. But then she vanished.'

'And does this Virginia Newburn know either Miss Kendall or her intended?'

'I haven't asked. I hardly know her.'

'You could make her acquaintance if you think it might help.'

'I might just do that.'

'You also need to talk to Henry Richmond. He may have other fish to fry. Stranger things have happened. I went to see a French film at the Arts Cinema the other night. Cathy wanted a treat. Turned out to be a busman's holiday. There's a murder in it that's very similar to the kind of cases in which we've been involved.'

'What happened?'

'There's a sign at the end telling you not to give it away. You should go and see if you can work it out before the finale.'

'I think I'm rather better in real life.'

'Then don't discount the husband-to-be. Henry Richmond could be up to his neck in the whole bloody thing.'

'I don't think he's got the brains.'

'Where is he now?'

'He's gone away for a few days.'

'There you are then. Even money he knows more than he's telling.'

A few days later Sidney took Byron out on a new walking route to the south of Ely along the Ouse and towards Little Thetford. He was keen to get to know all the surrounding area, much of which must have been unchanged since the land was first reclaimed. He passed a man who could have been from a hundred years ago, carrying a set of wicker traps. He said that he was out to cut back sedge and snare fowl. Sidney moved on to pass Holt Fen, keeping the cathedral still in view across the fields. And then it happened again.

Virginia Newburn was coming towards him. At first he mistook her for Amanda and couldn't help but say so.

'I thought you were my friend Miss Kendall only the other day. You seem to have the same coat. She got it at Derry and Toms. Did you?'

Virginia Newburn was unimpressed. 'Your friend may have acquired her coat from an expensive London clothier but I made my own. I used to be a seamstress in London. On the Row. After the war. Then I came back home to look after my mother.'

'Is she still with us? I'm sorry, I should know. I'm still relatively new.'

'Yes, I do the nursing. Then I walk. I like to get out.'

'And you are friends with Canon Clough?'

'I have many friends. Just because I am not married, it doesn't mean I don't have companions. They're all over the place. Not just here. I had a lot of them in London.'

'I am sure you did.'

'Many friends. Some living, some dead now.'

'Good. Well, I should be getting on, Miss Newburn.'

'Do you ever go to London?'

'Not as much as I'd like.'

'And who do you see when you go there? Do *you* have lots of friends?'

'I suppose I do.'

'Do you think you have more than me?'

'I wouldn't know.'

'I wouldn't think you did. I've got lots. I've seen that woman you are sometimes with. Not your wife. The other one. Is she your friend?'

'Miss Kendall? Yes, she is.'

'Is she your very good friend? Like Canon Clough and me?'

'I wouldn't know about that.'

'Do you tell her everything? All your secrets?'

'No, not really.'

'But does she tell you all of hers?'

'Sometimes. These are private matters, Miss Newburn.'

'You can call me Virginia. I don't mind. Not Ginny. Only Canon Clough calls me that. And my oldest friends. The ones I used to work with on the Row. Connie used to call me Ginny.'

'Connie?'

'She was married to your friend's friend.'

'Henry Richmond?'

'That's right. It was such a pity what happened.'

'Yes, I can imagine. Although it's never been quite clear to me . . .'

'And now he's marrying again. Five years gone. Like leaves off the trees. Everything bare. Do you think there were ever trees round here or has it always been flat? I don't like them very much. They get in the way of the view. Do you like trees?'

'Tell me, Miss Newburn, do you write a lot of letters?'

'And why would I do that?'

'To your many friends.'

'Do you want me to write one for you? Is that what you are asking?'

'No, I can do so myself.'

'Can Miss Kendall?'

'You know her name?'

'You just told me. Can she write? Can she read?'

'Yes, perfectly well.'

'Perhaps you can ask her to write a letter for you then?'

'No, I've said. I'm perfectly capable of writing my own.'

'Then what are you asking me for?'

'I was wondering if you had sent any letters to Miss Kendall?'

'Why would I do that? She's not one of my friends. I don't write to people who aren't my friends.'

'So you've never written to her at all?'

'No, I haven't.'

'Do you mean you know other people who have?'

'Everyone writes letters, Canon Chambers. That's why we have postmen. They know everything and everybody. Do you know many postmen? In your profession I expect you do. I bet you are always talking to postmen. Writing letters. Getting to know people. Finding out what's going on. What makes people tick. What they like and don't like. Who they love. What they do. When they die. All that. Then you probably write it down, don't you, Canon Chambers? Sometimes, I imagine, you might even write a letter yourself. Do people like getting letters from you? Perhaps you'd like to write me a letter one day? Then I could write one back. We could *correspond*. Would you like to do that? It would be like in church, "the responses", but we would do it by letter. What do you think? I could be your "co-respondent". That's a complicated word, isn't it, Canon Chambers? It means different things.'

'It depends if there's a hyphen.'

'It "depends" on quite a lot of things, Canon Chambers. The number of times you have the letter "r" is another thing. If you

248

were in a divorce suit, charged with adultery and proceeded against together with "the respondent" or "wife", you would have only one letter "r". But if you were writing a letter to someone like me, for example, you would have two. We would be in mutual agreement if we were "in correspondence"; do you know Swedenborg has a *Doctrine of Correspondence*?'

'The notion that every natural object symbolises or corresponds to some spiritual fact or principle . . .'

'The sun represents God, light is truth, the stars are faith, warmth is love. Canon Clough told me all about it. Don't you think it's rather chilly today? It's got colder since I've been speaking to you. That can't be very good, can it? Cold is not love. Perhaps we shouldn't correspond after all? One of the most important things about being a correspondent is how well people know one another. Some co-respondents don't know each other at all. It's just pretend. To save face. That's a bit silly, don't you think? Who's got a face to save? We all die, don't we?'

Sidney knew he had to get away from this woman but could sense that she was trying to tell him something important. 'Do you think you have to know someone well, Miss Newburn, in order to write them a letter?' he asked.

'Not at all. "Dear Sir or Madam". "Yours faithfully." Only "Yours sincerely" when you address them by name. Then there is "With regards". I'm not so partial to regards.'

'And sometimes you don't need to end a letter at all.'

'What do you mean, Canon Chambers?'

'People send notes. Sometimes they don't even say who they are from.'

'That would be very rude, though, wouldn't it, Canon

Chambers? Quite *aggressive*. You'd have to be quite annoyed with someone to write like that.'

'And are you ever very annoyed with people, Miss Newburn?'

'I can't be, Canon Chambers. I am a Christian.'

'There are angry Christians . . .'

'But they're not *my friends*, Canon Chambers. I only like to write to *my friends*.'

'Or on behalf of them perhaps?'

'No, I wouldn't necessarily say that. I wouldn't say that at all in fact. That wouldn't be right.'

'But might it be a possibility?'

'Everything's a possibility, Canon Chambers. There's a *possibility* that a man lives in the moon and that it's made of green cheese and that the Owl and the Pussycat jumped over it. There's a *possibility* that you might be late for your next appointment, whoever it's with, friend or even foe.'

'I don't think it's anything like that. But I must get on. The mist is rising. I think day might even be warming up.'

'Do you think there's a *possibility* that your friend Miss Kendall will come here again? Perhaps *it's possible* she'll be wearing the same coat, or even a different one? And then it might even be *possible* that I've chosen the same one. There's a *possibility* for everything when you think about it, don't you agree, Canon Chambers?' And then she was gone, lost in a swirl of mist. Byron stared after her, then turned for home.

Sidney was in one of those moods when all he wanted was an opportunity for silence, reflection, and probably some beautiful music. This was what his colleagues told him was the most important part of his job, and yet it was also the one that was easiest to overlook: time for God. There certainly wasn't too much of that available at present, even if Amanda had telephoned to say that Henry was back in London and the threatening letters appeared to have stopped. He did not need to concern himself any more.

Sidney found it more alarming when people told him *not* to worry than when they told him to do so, and he certainly wasn't going to let this case rest. When Amanda telephoned that evening he told her that he wanted to talk to Henry. The man should know what had been going on.

Amanda was having none of it. 'I don't see why we need to alarm him.'

Sidney was not so sure. 'I think he needs to know that you have been scared. In any case, this may be a temporary respite. Henry might even be able to help if any of the threatening behaviour resumes.'

'I don't want to worry him, Sidney. He is in a much better mood than when he left and we are the best of friends.'

Amanda's bright tone was unconvincing. 'That's good news,' Sidney replied, thinking that a couple about to be married perhaps needed to be a little more than 'the best of friends'. 'You'll be glad to have him back.'

'I had forgotten how much he looks after me.'

(Not, Sidney thought, 'how much he loves me' or 'how much I've missed him'.)

It was apparent that there was more to be said but neither he nor Amanda was prepared to come to the point. Yet Sidney could hardly pretend that nothing had happened. 'I met the strangest woman on the Fens,' he began.

His friend headed him off and her voice became brittle. 'That doesn't seem too out of the ordinary. Most of the people in your part of the world look like they still live underwater. They're so pale and bloated.'

'Not all of them, Amanda, but I'll let that pass. Miss Newburn seemed to think the person sending you all the notes and letters might have been the postman.'

There was a long pause. The purpose of the conversation had been lost. Amanda was normally so chatty on the telephone but now she was distant. After several awkward seconds she asked: 'Have you been discussing our affairs with strangers?'

'No. But I thought she might be a suspect. She knew Henry's first wife.'

'Thousands did, apparently. She was a much-loved woman. I hope she's not going to be a *Rebecca*-like act to follow. That film terrified me. Miss Newburn lives in Ely, you say? Have you told Keating?'

'I've only just got home.'

'What are you waiting for? She might be the one.'

'Why are you suddenly interested again? You told me that the letters had stopped.'

'Yes, I did. Of course.'

'So there's something else, Amanda.'

'Not exactly.'

'Please. Tell me.'

'It's silly really, but it's also horrible. I don't know how it's happened.'

Amanda explained that a series of expensive items 'on approval' had been delivered to her home from Peter Jones. She hadn't ordered any of them, but there was a dining table and eight chairs, a china service, a new canteen of cutlery, tablecloths, bed linen, and so many kitchen utensils she could have set up a restaurant.

'I didn't ask for any of it, Sidney.'

'Then who did?'

'That's the issue. The delivery boys said they had been told that the order was from me. If I had a complaint I should go to the shop. So I did.'

'And what did they say?'

'I spoke to a very nice woman who said that it must have been a misunderstanding. If all the goods came back there would be no charge. That is what "on approval" means, but I didn't care about that. I just wanted her to acknowledge that a different woman had made the order.'

'And did she do that?'

'She tried. She was polite. But I didn't believe her. So I pressed her . . .'

'You didn't need to do that, Amanda.'

'I asked her to tell me what she really thought. She said it didn't matter about that. She would say whatever I liked, provided the goods were returned and I left without causing a scene.'

'And are you sure,' Sidney interrupted, 'that you can't have been mistaken, that the woman making the order can't have been you?'

'For heaven's sake, Sidney! What do you take me for?'

'I was just asking. I saw a woman who I thought was you . . .'

'I am not going mad even if everyone is attempting to drive me round the bend. I have not been to Peter Jones for three weeks. I am almost scared to go out because someone always seems to know where I am; and I am frightened to stay at home in case more notes come, or there are even more horrible things that are about to happen . . .'

'I know it must be difficult.'

'Difficult? Is that all you can say?'

'Yes, well . . .'

'You don't know ANYTHING, Sidney Chambers. You have NO IDEA what this is LIKE. How dare you phone me up with your sympathy . . .'

'You telephoned me.'

'I DID NOT.'

'It doesn't matter, Amanda, really . . .'

'IT DOES MATTER. EVERYONE IS CONTRADICTING ME.'

Sidney had never known his friend to behave like this. He tried to pacify her. 'I am not . . .'

'YOU ARE. YOU JUST HAVE.'

'Calm down, Amanda, please.'

'HOW CAN I CALM DOWN? I JUST WANT ALL THIS TO STOP. I WANT TO BE ON MY OWN SO NO ONE CAN TROUBLE ME AND I WANT SOMEONE TO LOOK AFTER ME AT THE SAME TIME.'

'I am sure we can talk about this calmly. Do you want me to come to London?'

'NO.'

'I am sure there is a logical explanation.'

'THERE ISN'T. SOMEONE IS TRYING TO DRIVE ME MAD AND I DON'T KNOW WHO IT IS OR WHY THEY ARE DOING IT.'

'You should talk to Henry.'

'I CAN'T. HE'LL LEAVE ME IF I DO THAT. I DON'T

KNOW. I DON'T CARE. I DON'T KNOW WHAT I WANT. ALL I KNOW IS THAT I CAN'T GO ON LIKE THIS AND YOU'RE NOT HELPING.'

There was an abrupt break on the line and then the dialling tone. Sidney was shaking. He hated confrontation. It reminded him of being in trouble at school or being reprimanded by his parents. He felt his insides churn and had a desperate need for the lavatory. He had to talk to Hildegard, but she was reading with Anna. His daughter was eager to tell him about her progress as soon as he entered the room. 'Daddy! I've done a drawing!'

She held up a bit of paper that looked like an early Jackson Pollock. 'Very good, my darling.'

'What's wrong?' Hildegard asked.

'Amanda. She's angry.'

'She's never cross with you.'

'She is now.'

'Look, Daddy!'

'Perhaps it's about time,' Hildegard said.

'What do you mean?'

'Daddy, my drawing.'

'Are you going to have to go down to London?'

'Probably. But not just now.'

'Daddy, look now, Daddy. Look.'

'You will tell me, won't you?' Hildegard asked. 'I don't want you running off without me knowing where you are. People do ask, and we don't have Malcolm to cover for you any more.'

'He didn't cover for me.'

'He did. All the time. I think I miss him more than you do.'

Anna asked once more. 'Look *properly*, Daddy.'

Sidney refused to rise to his wife's challenge and left to see Canon Clough. He wanted to talk about Virginia Newburn. The letters had to be from her. But what had she got to do with Amanda?

He began by asking if Christopher had any notes from his admirer.

'Hundreds. Do you want to see them?'

'I am interested in her handwriting . . . and in her past.'

'Are you prepared to take her on then, Sidney? To be honest I could do with some respite. These things tend to get out of hand.'

'Only if you let them.'

'Then I'll leave it to you.' Canon Clough opened a desk drawer. 'How many of them do you want?'

'Four or five will do for now. What do they say?'

'Pretty much the same thing again and again: how lost she is, that I am one of the few people who understand her, how understanding is the key to knowledge and that knowledge is an act of love. I'm sure you've come across this kind of thing in Grantchester.'

'No, I haven't actually.'

'Then you must have led a very sheltered life.'

'I suppose one *could* say that,' Sidney answered, careful to keep his sleuthing skills discreet. He was surprised that Canon Clough was unaware of his reputation. Perhaps he was not as well known as he thought he was.

In the Prince Albert pub that night, Inspector Keating compared the letters written to Christopher Clough with one of the notes sent to Amanda. He said that he would have to show it to the experts, but even an amateur eye could tell that there was little that the two hands had in common. Virginia Newburn's style was small, delicate and slanting to the right, whereas the poison-pen letters were constructed in a much larger size, with straight, bold strokes, heavy pressure and angled to the left. Miss Newburn's prose was fluent and grammatically accurate, whereas the threatening documents contained spelling errors and erratic punctuation. Sidney wondered whether this could have been done deliberately, but Keating was fairly sure that it would have taken a good degree of skill to be the author of both hands.

'But if Virginia Newburn is not the author of the letters then who is?' Sidney asked.

'I think it's high time you had a word with the fiancé.'

'Amanda won't be pleased.'

'And she's happy now?'

'It would be taking quite a risk, Geordie.'

'And when have you been known to shirk a little thing like that?'

Sidney could not just drop everything to talk to Amanda but thought about his tactics as he made his way to visit a sick parishioner who lived near Chettisham Meadow. It was filled with the fineness of early summer, and he wondered whether he should gather some wild flowers for his wife. He thought fondly of Hildegard for a moment, missing her and quite forgetting that one of the reasons he had left was to escape the constant noise of piano lessons. She had been putting Adam Barnes through his paces and Sidney could only be relieved that he wasn't a pupil himself as he remembered Hildegard's running commentary through the music.

'Play with your body! Use more muscles – not just in your hands but in your arms, your shoulders, your back, and your stomach – conduct the piano – command it – your playing is too shallow, Adam, get down inside the ivory, play to the bottom of the keys. There's a whole orchestra inside there and you are the conductor.'

Lost in his reverie, Sidney looked up to see the same woman in the distance that he had seen before. It wasn't Amanda, but he wasn't sure that it was Virginia Newburn either. Byron began barking, something he never did, either with Amanda or with Miss Newburn. Who on earth could it be?

He made his way home and was stopped by the dean, who expressed surprise that he had not been recognised. 'I think you are in a world of your own, Sidney.'

'I must be. However, I don't quite know what that involves. I'm not sure that I'm secure about anything at the moment.'

'I thought you might have a few teething troubles. A priest can find it quite lonely sometimes.'

'Yes, I see . . .' (Although Sidney couldn't 'see' anything at all and was merely worried what on earth the dean was going to tell him next.)

'As priests we also have to be more careful than most in our selection of friends.'

'Yes, I have always found that to be the case.'

'One must not get too excited too soon. Or overenthusiastic.'

'I quite agree.'

'With women, particularly.'

'What on earth do you mean?'

'Miss Newburn. She is, I think you will have gathered, a dangerous combination of vulnerability and volatility. It's no surprise Canon Clough has dropped her.'

'I don't think he was ever holding her.'

The dean winced at Sidney's flippancy. 'These are serious matters, Canon Chambers. You will tell me if there is anything amiss?'

'I will inform you of anything I think you need to know. Otherwise I shall try not to trouble you.'

'I am not sure that I find that reassuring.'

Before Sidney could see Henry, Amanda telephoned again. It was almost midnight and there had been a new development. That night the doorbell had rung in her flat. When she had opened the door she had found no one outside, but a bouquet of a dozen dead roses had been left with a simple note:

As dead as your love will be.

She told Sidney that she was so upset she had gone to stay with her parents in Chelsea. She planned to take a few days off work and was effectively going into hiding. She did not know what to do about Henry. Could Sidney perhaps see him after all? He was staying at the Lansdowne Club.

'How much does he know?'

'Nothing.'

'And how much do you want him to know?'

'Tell him everything, Sidney. I only wish I'd listened to you before. Anything to make this stop.'

Sidney had once toyed with the idea of joining the

Lansdowne Club but it was too much of a luxury and it was simpler to enjoy the facilities as one of Henry and Amanda's guests. He assumed their marriage was still on the cards, but it could hardly be right for Amanda to be bullied into a situation where she was taking refuge at the house of her parents while pretending to her future husband that all was well. Clarification was necessary.

As they settled down to their gin and tonics, Sidney began to question Henry about his reluctance to get married in church. As a widower, there was nothing stopping him from doing so and Sidney suggested that it might be nice for Amanda to have a bit of a do.

His companion, however, was adamant. 'I'd rather not if you don't mind.'

'I suppose if you've had one church wedding already then it might feel strange. Was it a very big occasion?'

'On the contrary it was rather small. Connie didn't have much of a family and we didn't want anything too fancy.'

'How did you meet?'

'She worked for my tailor. My father had ordered half a dozen suits for me and Connie made the trousers. I don't think I was supposed to marry her. My parents certainly disapproved, but there you are, these things happen and, when they do, you can't do much about them.'

'I imagine she was very beautiful.'

'She was more distinctive than an obvious beauty. Dark-red hair, freckles, an elfish look, the kind of smile that turns a man's heart.'

'You must have been very much in love.'

'We felt we didn't need to know each other.'

'And you were happy?'

'It was passionate. She was frail. Perhaps it was always doomed. But I think we were happy. Certainly at the beginning . . .'

Sidney decided that he would return to the subject later but wanted to check on one thing before he forgot. 'Tell me, were you friendly with anyone else who worked with her at the time?'

'There was a whole team. Gerald Lowe is a reputable firm.'

'Indeed. Lowe of the Row,' Sidney continued. 'Did you ever meet a girl called Virginia Newburn?'

'She and Connie were friends . . .'

'She's one of my parishioners. She lives just outside Ely.'

'I wondered what happened to her. She was always quite religious. I thought she might even become a nun. But she was Roman Catholic, surely? I can't imagine her as one of your flock.'

'She is now. You haven't seen her recently?'

'Not at all. She and Connie fell out, I'm afraid.'

'Over you?'

Henry Richmond crossed his legs. 'It wouldn't be gentlemanly to say.'

'You mean that Virginia Newburn was keen on you?'

'I wouldn't quite put it like that.'

Sidney leaned forward. 'How would you put it?'

'I don't think it ever got that far. In any case, as soon as I saw Connie there wasn't any other outcome in my mind.'

'But Virginia Newburn held a candle for you?'

'If she ever did it went out long ago. I don't think it was that serious. In fact, you would probably have had a better chance than me. I seem to remember that she was always talking about her priest.'

'She seems predisposed towards clergy.'

'And are you on the receiving end?'

'No. I am fairly sure her current desire lies elsewhere.'

Henry Richmond summoned a waiter for a refill. He was keen to move to surer ground. 'I don't know why women become so attached to priests. They must know they are on a losing wicket.'

'Not all the time. Some priests string them along, I'm afraid. I try to play with a straight bat.'

'Unless you're knocked for six, I suppose?' Henry asked, exhausting the cricketing metaphor. 'I think you were once rather keen on Amanda yourself, weren't you?'

'A long time ago.'

'First love can be very deceptive. I think it's easier now that we are more mature.'

'And you are happy with everything?' Sidney asked, keeping his questions as open as possible.

'I think so. Amanda's nervous, I can tell. She's had her share of near misses. You can't get to our age without some history. The trick is to keep it in the background.'

'I agree,' said Sidney, 'although sometimes the past has a habit of springing back to life.'

'What do you mean?'

'Do you know anything about the anonymous letters Amanda has been receiving?'

'Not at all. What on earth are you referring to?'

Sidney explained.

Henry Richmond swore that he knew nothing. 'Why would anyone do such a thing?'

'It could be someone who is still in love with you.'

'Is this a long way round of telling me that you suspect Virginia Newburn of sending these letters?'

'It is. But they could also come from someone who is in love with Amanda. Whatever the case, someone wants to put her off your marriage. Can you think of anyone who would try to do that?'

'I'm not sure I can.'

'What do you mean you're not sure? Does this mean that there is a possibility?'

'I may have to think a little more.'

'If you do, can I suggest that you discuss this with Amanda?'

'Why has she not told me about all this herself?'

'I think she didn't want to alarm you. In any case . . .'

They stopped. The porter was at the table and had been waiting to interrupt for some time. Sidney was wanted on the telephone.

He was surprised. Only Amanda and Hildegard knew that he was at the Lansdowne Club.

'Indeed, sir. I think it is your wife.'

Sidney made his way to the office. Now he was frightened. Had something happened to Anna? She was perfectly well when he had left but perhaps there had been a ghastly accident. He thought of all the possibilities and his pace increased as he moved across the carpet. Why had he ever left home? What on earth was he doing when he could have been with his family?

His wife's tone was eerily calm. 'I am sorry to disturb you, my darling. Everything is good at home. No, there is nothing wrong with Anna. We are both well. No, not exactly. It is not all right. There is something I have to tell you. A woman has been found dead in the river. I think you know her.'

'Is it Virginia Newburn?' Sidney asked.

'Inspector Keating is here. He thought you were meeting tonight.'

'I forgot to tell him. Will you explain? Can you ask him what the woman was wearing?'

'That's what he wanted to tell you. She had a maroon-coloured coat, just like Amanda's. The one you mentioned. And he doesn't think it was an accident.'

Sidney did not tell Henry Richmond but made his excuses and left, pretending that he was returning to Cambridge. Then he went straight to Tite Street in Chelsea. On approaching the house of Amanda's parents he was amazed to see an under-taker's van waiting outside. He rang the bell in panic and was so relieved when Amanda answered the door that he kissed her full on the lips and held her tightly and for too long.

They were still holding each other when Amanda spoke. 'Oh Sidney, the most dreadful thing has happened.'

'Is it one of your parents?'

'No, it's the cruellest thing: a hoax. Someone telephoned the undertaker's and said that I was dead. The men just turned up. Who could have done such a thing? I can't trust anyone any more. I don't even know if I can rely on you.'

'Believe me, you can, Amanda.'

'But what if it is Henry?'

'He knows about the letters. Now we must tell him every-thing else that has happened, preferably in front of Inspector Keating. I want to see his face.'

'I don't know if I can do that. I have to see him alone.'

'I'm worried that's not safe.'

'It's as bad as that?'

'You are too precious to lose.'

'I can look after myself,' said Amanda.

I'm not so sure, Sidney thought, immediately planning to ask for police protection.

Gerald Lowe was practically dressed for a tailor, wearing two out of the three pieces of a grey flannel pinstriped suit, having abandoned his jacket in order to keep his arms as free as possible. These were used to make extravagant gestures as he explained the way in which he had built up his business in Savile Row, why his clients were extraordinarily important even though he could not possibly name them, and how he tried to be like a father to his staff. He could remember every one of them, and of course he could tell Sidney all about Virginia Newburn.

'She was with us just after the war. She had good little fingers; a fast worker but she was worried about losing her eyesight. They all do. You have to work so close you're never quite sure what you're going to see when you look up.'

He had heard about her death. 'Did she get lost, do you think? Perhaps she couldn't see where she was going. They have a lot of accidents on the Fens, don't they? Is that where you're from?'

Sidney explained the purpose of his visit. Although he did long to have a bespoke suit of his own one day, such a luxury was beyond his present means. However, he did have a friend who had offered to come with him after he had done some initial research into cut and fabric, and so perhaps they could look through a few ideas? His friend was called Amanda

Kendall and she was about to marry a man whose first wife, Connie, had worked for Gerald. Could the tailor remember her at all?

'Everyone loved Connie. She was from County Clare. We used to joke about it because it sounded like she had two Christian names or that her mother was called Clare. Connie from Clare. Beautiful hair and a little upturned nose. Wild green eyes. She was quite a dreamy girl but she had a temper on her, I'll say that. I didn't see her much after she got married. Have they got divorced then? I wouldn't be too surprised. She was always a wayward girl.'

'No.' Sidney stopped. 'She died.'

'Really?'

'She had a weak heart.'

'Connie from Clare? That doesn't sound right. She was a strong girl.'

'And there were no other people called Connie that you employed?'

'None at all.'

'And so are you saying that you think she might still be alive?'

'I think I'd have heard if she was dead.'

'When did you last see her?'

'A few years ago.'

'Less than five years ago?'

'Yes, I'm sure of it. She told me she was off to East Anglia. It must have been to see Virginia, I suppose.'

'Did she mention her husband at all?'

'She was always private about her admirers. She had a faraway look. I worried sometimes that she was a bit mad. But there was nothing wrong with her heart . . .'

'Might I use your telephone?' Sidney asked. 'I need to make a rather urgent call.'

After Inspector Keating had made the necessary checks with the public record office, Sidney was ready to proceed. It wasn't going to be easy and he hadn't quite planned how to deal with the situation but the important thing was to confront Amanda and Henry together. What made matters more complicated, however, was the fact that, shortly before Sidney arrived, Amanda had lashed out and accused Henry of killing Virginia Newburn.

'How could I?' her fiancé had responded. 'I hardly know her.'

'But you admit that you do know her?'

'She was a friend of my wife's.'

'You don't have a wife.'

Henry now began his confession. 'Amanda. There's something I haven't told you.'

'You've been lying to me?'

'Not lying exactly.'

'Withholding the truth would be more accurate,' Sidney explained. 'I am sure it has been with the best of intentions.'

'You mean you know something too? Have you *both* been deceiving me?'

'I have only just discovered your fiancé's secret.'

'I knew there was something,' Amanda shouted. 'Is there another woman? TELL ME. Was it Virginia Newburn? Has she been the one sending the letters and tormenting me? Did you kill her to protect me? How much have you told Sidney? Have you both been keeping things from me?'

'There's one thing . . .' Sidney began.

Amanda would not let him finish. 'My BEST FRIEND, and my fiancé, working together. I can't believe it.'

'That is not the case,' Sidney said quietly. 'But you should know that Connie Richmond is still alive.'

Amanda walked up to Henry and looked straight at him. 'You said she was dead.'

'She was to me.'

Sidney made it clear. 'They are divorced.'

Amanda refused to believe him. 'And she's behind all this?'

'She's not well, Amanda. She's in an institution,' Henry explained. 'I tried to behave as best I could but it's been impossible. Virginia Newburn kept an eye on her.'

'And your wife killed her?'

'We think it was an accident.'

'Was she going to kill me?'

'We're not sure. Connie doesn't have a very firm hold on reality. She is often disorientated.'

'Did she think the woman was me?'

'I don't think so.'

'How can you tell?'

Sidney tried to explain that the situation was under control. 'The police are with her.'

'She didn't mean you any harm,' said Henry.

'DIDN'T MEAN ANY HARM? WHAT DO YOU THINK SHE'S BEEN DOING? HOW CAN YOU EXCUSE THIS BEHAVIOUR?'

'She's not well.'

'NEITHER AM I.'

'Here,' said Sidney, handing Amanda a drink. 'Have some whisky.'

268

She looked at the floor but was speaking to Henry. 'It's obvious you are more sympathetic to your former wife than you are to me.'

'That's not true. You didn't tell me about the letters.'

'I was frightened. I told Sidney.'

'And he has only just told me. I would have stopped them, Amanda. You just had to tell me. I would have explained everything.'

'Would you?'

'You have both had secrets from each other,' Sidney interrupted. 'But let's try to be calm.'

'ME? CALM?' Amanda replied.

'If we could just establish the truth.' He turned to Henry. 'Virginia Newburn was a co-respondent in your divorce case, wasn't she? She had hoped to marry you.'

'I have tried to behave well,' said Henry. 'I only wanted to spare people's feelings.'

'You lied to us.'

'I did not think that either of you needed to know the truth. It was naive of me. And wrong. I know that now. But please believe me when I say that I have tried to be decent about this. Connie sent me letters too. Forgive me.'

'But it's even worse than if you had told me everything from the start,' Amanda said quietly, too shocked to shout. 'And, what's worse, it's clear that you still see your wife.'

'She's not my wife any more. We are divorced. She is, for want of a better word, mad. I was trying to stop her damaging our happiness. It was easier to say that she was dead.'

Amanda no longer made eye contact. 'Were you ever going to tell me?'

'I wasn't sure. I was afraid.'

'Of what?'

'This.'

'A couple shouldn't have such secrets,' Amanda said. 'What else have I still to find out? Perhaps I don't know you at all.'

'I didn't want to hurt you or let anything damage our relationship.'

'And this is why we can't be married in church? I see that now. It's nothing to do with faith. It's the law. I could tell Sidney was suspicious. He had that annoying look in his eye.'

'I was hoping that it wouldn't come out like this,' Henry went on, 'that everything would be gentler and more gradual. You know I don't like confrontations. They don't often help. I tried my best with your friend Elizabeth and we both saw what happened there. Mark killing himself . . .'

'You did the right thing.'

'With the wrong result. And this time, I didn't want to endanger our future together.'

'But it would have been built on a lie.'

'I thought that my punishment was to bear this alone. I only wanted to do what was best for you. If you knew you would have been anxions. You might not have wanted to marry me at all.'

'And how do you think I feel now?'

'I don't know.'

'I can't describe it. The feeling of stupidity. To be duped.'

'You weren't supposed to find out. I was trying to keep things from you.'

'Who else knows?'

'About Connie? Mark Kirby-Grey . . .'

'But not Elizabeth? She would have told me . . .'

'Mark was good at keeping secrets.'

'Anyone else?'

'Her family. No one you know.'

'But I know everybody.'

'Connie didn't move in your world, Amanda. She was a seamstress.'

'And not you, Sidney?'

'No.'

'You've got that shifty look . . .'

'Inspector Keating is aware of the situation.'

'I thought he might be.'

'But Henry has committed no crime. He didn't know about the letters or the threats.'

'Even though he says he received some himself.'

'They were nothing new. Did any refer to me?'

'They did.'

'I'm sorry about that.'

'And how did your wife know about me then?'

'She's not my wife. I told her.'

'What?'

'I thought she should know.'

'So you have been more honest with her than you were with me?'

'I wanted to protect you. I love you, Amanda.'

'You have a very odd way of showing it.'

'It's been a very difficult situation . . .'

'I could have helped you share it. We could have helped each other. You could have comforted me.'

'But you didn't tell me what was going on.'

'I couldn't . . .'

'And neither could I tell you. If you want to break this off and find someone else I will understand, but we have both kept things from each other. I will never love anyone other than you.'

'Did you once say that to her?'

Sidney issued a quiet 'Amanda . . .' but he was ignored. He knew he should leave the room but he couldn't find the right moment.

'I can't remember what I said to Connie. It doesn't matter now.'

'It does to me.'

'People can't be held to things they have said in the past.'

'I thought that was what marriage vows were all about.' Amanda looked to Sidney. 'You'll back me up on that at least.'

'Henry may have been deceived.'

'He probably deceived himself.'

Her fiancé tried to buy time. 'We don't have to decide anything now.'

'Am I going to have to meet this woman?'

'If you want to.'

'Do you think if I did then this might stop?'

'I don't know.'

'It's what we should have done in the first place . . .'

'I know. But . . .'

'You don't like confrontation. You keep saying. You're going to have to get used to it if you want to marry me. Am I supposed to forgive all this?'

'I don't know.'

'We could have made it clear from the beginning. We could

272

have gone to see your former wife as a couple. Started as we meant to go on.'

'We still could. Forgive me. I meant for the best.'

'I'll say one thing, Henry, and you may be able to draw some comfort from it. I am not going to be defeated by a madwoman.'

Two days later Sidney visited a mental hospital located in a converted orphanage outside Chettisham. Connie Richmond had been a patient for eight years after being caught shoplifting. She suffered from hallucinations, some of her actions were obsessive and compulsive, and although there had been hopes to return her to the community she had failed to thrive.

One of the most notable features of her condition was a sense of being persecuted and abandoned; emotions made more understandable given the fact that it was her own husband who had had her committed and who had divorced her after being 'unable to cope'. In order to make their divorce as straightforward as possible, he had concocted a story of adultery with Virginia Newburn, Connie's best friend. This had turned out disastrously, as the co-respondent had thought the 'affair' was rather more than a 'story'.

Despite confinement and divorce, Connie still loved her husband. She spoke to Sidney about the sanctity of marriage and promises made before God. What did the clergyman think? What was sanctity anyway? Was it in the home, in the kitchen and in the bedroom? Were there borders to it? Did it have a beginning and an end? Do children add to it or diminish it? And how much is sex a part of it?

Sidney could not imagine anyone other than a priest being asked such questions, and wondered what was abnormal about

Connie's interest in the answers. The conversation proved far more challenging than any he had recently had with a so-called 'normal' person.

Connie said she felt bad about Virginia's death. They had been walking and talking and laughing. Despite the mist and the cold they knew where they were going. They took the same route each time they met. Connie said that she had walked on without realising that her companion was no longer with her. 'I hardly heard the splash so I didn't know where she'd gone. It was unlike her to go and drown herself like that.'

'So you did not touch her?'

'I couldn't find her. I had a little panic, if truth be told. Then I came back here. Took off my coat and cleaned my shoes. It took an age to get the mud away. I didn't want anyone to think I'd done anything. I put a nice coat of polish on the shoes. They've never been cleaner.'

'And you were sending the letters?'

'I got other people to help. I told them I was writing a penny dreadful. I made up a whole story about a man who let down his wife. Some of the women here have been disappointed in love. I am not the only one. Ginny knew. She liked to join in. I said we could have real letters. I asked them all to think of what they would say to the men who had abandoned them and to the women they had taken up with. There was a flood, I tell you. The River Liffey would have burst its banks, such was the torrent. We sent some to him and some to her. We thought it was funny. *Die soon! Choke on your own vomit! Your car will explode if you drive it!* Some of them were too rude to send; the ones to my husband especially. *Cut your jangle off!* Your friend must have thought there were hundreds of us; and all of us hating her and her alone. But I wrote most of the ones we sent to Miss Kendall. I took an interest. Henry told me more than he thought; Ginny followed you and she also talked to Canon Clough. There's a revenge coming there one day, you mark my words. No Sherlock Holmes clergyman will be able to solve that one!'

Connie Richmond moved closer, challenging Sidney to meet her eye. 'I enjoyed it, pretending to be different people all the time, writing differently. I've always been good with my hands. I'm a bit ambidextrous. Sewing, stitching, mending, writing. Not so good with my heart. Only loved one man. That was the only thing I've done that's insanity. Finding the wrong man and loving him for ever.'

'I think sometimes it depends on *how* we love,' Sidney replied, edging away.

'And is my husband still going to marry that woman?'

'I'm not sure. She has to forgive him first.'

'Does she know what she's in for? Won't you tell her not to?'

'People can take or ignore advice, Mrs Richmond. I can't force my friends to do anything against their will. Sometimes you just have to watch them fall.'

'So you don't want her to marry him, then?'

'Probably not.' Sidney had never said this aloud or so baldly.

'And I could have saved her,' Connie Richmond answered. 'You should be grateful.'

'But you weren't acting in Miss Kendall's interests.'

'Were you?'

'I hope so. But these are private matters, Mrs Richmond.'

'Not as private as you think, Canon Chambers, just as I am not as lunatic as everyone takes me for.'

'I am not sure anyone says you are mad.'

'Then why am I here?'

'You may not be for much longer. Inspector Keating . . .'

'Oh, the police. Yes, I suppose they'll be back again soon enough. I'll have to make my escape by then.'

'I am sure there will be extra security now.'

'I mean from life, Canon Chambers.'

'Please. You wouldn't do anything as stupid.'

'I like it when no one knows what I'm going to do next. It makes everything more exciting.'

Sidney was exhausted when he returned home and Hildegard was in bed. She was reading *Wide Sargasso Sea* by Jean Rhys. 'You might like to have it after me, Sidney. It has many echoes. A former wife that's still alive . . .'

'I'm not sure I will, if you don't mind, my darling. I think I've had enough of that kind of thing.'

As he cleaned his teeth he thought about the past. He seldom asked Hildegard about her marriage to Stephen Staunton. That was private, he decided, just as, perhaps, Henry Richmond's past should be. But he should talk to Amanda if she wanted to proceed with the wedding, as he might be able to help. That was, in part, why he had gone to see Connie Richmond, so that he could brief Amanda about her prospective visit. He couldn't imagine how that was likely to turn out.

'Is the marriage going ahead?' Hildegard asked as she closed her book.

'Do you think it shouldn't?'

'I don't think it should be like Jane Eyre, when she nearly marries St John Rivers while she knows she's in love with someone else.'

'I don't think it's like that.'

'I still sometimes wonder why Amanda didn't marry *you*.'

'Like the clergyman in *Jane Eyre*, I was a vicar. It wouldn't have done. Amanda was after someone more glamorous.'

'And has she found him?'

'Perhaps she has changed her priorities. Henry's a good man. He means well. She could do worse.'

'That doesn't seem enough.'

'Friendship is better than loneliness.'

'Is that why you married me?'

'I could ask the same of you, Hildegard.'

'You haven't answered my question.'

'I think our marriage is a great deal more than friendship.'

'So much so that we can argue and forgive each other?'

'I hope so.'

Hildegard lightened the tone with a tease. 'And you have done much that needs forgiving.'

'While you, my darling, are clearly without fault.'

'I know I am bossy.'

'It doesn't matter.'

'You agree?'

'I think that is what I am supposed to do.'

'Not when I say that I am bossy.'

'Very well.'

'And I am getting fat.'

'You're not fat.'

'Would it matter if I was?'

'Of course it wouldn't.' Sidney hesitated. This was dangerous ground. 'You're not pregnant again, are you?'

'No, just fatter. Will you still love a fat, bossy wife?'

'I'll do my best.'

'As long as you don't become a fat, bossy husband.'

Sidney smiled. 'I can't guarantee it.'

He thought about Amanda and Henry. He had always hoped that a marriage could be based on a couple being unable to imagine that they could ever live without each other; but perhaps that romanticism had been the result of his own good fortune. He could not conceive having to settle for second best. That was his privilege and his luck in finding Hildegard.

This, at least, was one thing he *could* talk to Amanda about. Now they would both be committed to people who had been married before.

How, then, should one deal with a past in which the person who was loved had been passionately involved with someone else?

It involved acknowledgement and recognition. One could not pretend that a future partner had no hinterland, or that everything before could be ignored or forgotten. At the same time, was there really a need to go into the kind of detail that would renew the pain of failure and separation? Perhaps every couple needed its secrets. A person could not be so lost in love, like Connie Richmond, that infatuation led them to lose all sense of their identity.

What mattered was not so much the past but the idea that love could be built on a mutual desire for a better future. There had to be no resentment, no continuation of feeling from a time of hurt, even if the memory remained. This was where forgiveness might lie, and it was, as a result, the beginning of hope.

*　　*　　*

Ten days later, Amanda and Henry came for another of Sidney's 'chats'. They had thought a great deal, visited Connie Richmond together and decided, despite everything, to go ahead with their marriage.

'She's quite mad,' Amanda began. 'But then, most people are only a few steps away from the loony bin.'

'It's not a loony bin,' Henry added quietly.

'We had it out. I told Connie that if I got any more letters I was going to start writing back. I could out-threat her. And I had more friends. I said it as a joke of course.'

'I don't think Connie took it as that,' her fiancé replied.

'And I said I wouldn't be a regular visitor. In fact I was only coming this once and she couldn't expect me to allow Henry to visit in the future. That was going to have to stop and she was just going to have to accept it.'

'And what did she say to that?' said Sidney.

'Oh, some nonsense. I wasn't really listening. I was too busy speaking. I had to make my position clear.'

Henry filled in the details. 'She was very nice about it. Quite meek.'

'I felt sorry for her,' said Amanda. 'But I can't forgive her. She sent my parents a hearse, for God's sake.'

'Has she admitted to the murder of Virginia Newburn?' Sidney asked, not wanting to stir up his friend's animosity.

Henry jumped in with an answer. 'Connie is still saying that it was an accident. But there will be further questions; an inquest and a trial, I should imagine. I expect she will be taken to somewhere more secure.'

'A prison, you mean?'

'Eventually. Although Amanda's gracefully agreed not to press any charges.'

His fiancée checked her lipstick. 'I've behaved quite brilliantly, if you must know, Sidney.'

'I'm sure you've been magnificent.'

'You could preach about me at the wedding. How I was put on my mettle and came out shining.'

'I think I can write my own sermons. You'd like to proceed then?'

When Henry retired to the bathroom Amanda told Sidney that if she was going to marry anyone at her age, having given up on the idea of children, then she might as well have a bash with her fiancé. It was, perhaps, as good as she was ever going to get.

Sidney did not think that 'having a bash' was the best attitude to marriage, but he promised to help her if she still believed that she loved Henry. Amanda said she thought she did. He was, as her friend had already admitted, a good man at heart. He could be forgiven. And he could still, perhaps, be shaped and changed into the kind of husband she had always wanted. It wasn't perfect, but what marriage was?

And so, at the end of June, Sidney found himself taking a small service of blessing in the Lady Chapel of Ely Cathedral. It was one of the most beautiful spaces in England, built in the fourteenth century in the decorated style. Its sculpture, carvings and stained glass had been destroyed by Reformation zeal to leave an open space in bleached Weldon stone. The foliated arcading and the milky green light suggested a transcendent architectural garden: assured, contemplative, sacred.

He welcomed a small congregation of some fifty family and

friends. He joked that he thought this day would never arrive, but that good things came to those who knew how to wait; and although no one could ever call Amanda *patient*, perhaps this was a day in which they could celebrate the grace of God as well as their love for each other. The couple could even 'be an example to us all', demonstrating that the best relationships were not a matter of looking constantly into each other's eyes, but outwards, forwards, together.

It was a beautiful day, the air was still and warm and the smell of cut grass blew in from the lawn outside the North Transept. Amanda carried a bouquet of white roses and, to any onlooker, the ceremony would have been the perfect example of late-flowering love.

Sidney was, however, unusually nervous. It was more than the simple fact that he was presiding over a ceremony in which, ten years ago, he might have been the groom instead of the priest. He was happy with Hildegard, proud that Anna was a flower girl, and pleased that all their lives had come to such a harmony. But something was still not right, no matter how much he tried to give the proceedings an authoritative spirituality.

He felt he was having to force things to make the occasion more than it was. His hands trembled slightly and his voice was not as loud and clear as usual. It was almost a relief when the service was over, and he felt guilty as he raised his right hand in bidding with hope as much as faith.

'God the Father, God the Son, God the Holy Ghost, bless, preserve and keep you; the Lord mercifully with his favour look upon you, and so fill you with all spiritual benediction and grace that ye may so live together in this life, that in the world to come ye may have life everlasting. Amen.'

After the service, when Sidney had thanked everyone for coming and given his genial greetings, he left the Lady Chapel, crossed the Octagon and changed in the vestry. There he said a quiet prayer, asking for forgiveness for his thoughts. He wanted to be made more charitable, less suspicious, and more confident about the future of Amanda and Henry's love.

He took off his robes, checked his suit and dog-collar and left the cathedral by the Monk's Door. At least there would be some champagne at the reception, he told himself. Amanda was unlikely to stint on that.

He was just making his way into Firmary Lane when he caught sight of a woman in the distance. She was by the river, at the far end of Dean's Meadow, standing under an elm tree. Although the figure was partially obscured, she had made little effort to hide herself. In fact, she had been waiting to be seen. Sidney could not be certain but he had a good idea who the woman was. She was clothed in a wedding dress. It was exactly the same as the one Amanda was wearing.

Prize Day

I T WAS PRIZE DAY at Millingham School, a private establishment situated in a picturesque location by the River Ouse. Founded in the mid-nineteenth century, it lacked the history, tradition and scholarship of nearby King's Ely, and compensated for its lack of intellectual distinction by concentrating on its sporting prowess. Unkind rivals remarked that it was the kind of school where rich people sent their stupid children.

Millingham was currently without a chaplain (the previous incumbent having departed in circumstances that had been kept vague) and it was the Archdeacon of Ely's responsibility to find a replacement. At the same time, the school also had need of an umpire for the Prize Day cricket match.

While he very much enjoyed the game, Sidney had mixed feelings about the task. The last time he had officiated, Grantchester's finest spin bowler, Zafar Ali, had been fatally poisoned.

The prospect of a summer day at a minor public school was not, therefore, one of unconfined joy. It would, however, provide an opportunity to get to know the headmaster, some of the teachers and, more importantly, the pupils. Sidney was frustrated that he did not meet more young people and, now that he was undoubtedly middle-aged, he was less than certain about the pulse of the times in which he lived. It would be good, he told himself, to spend a while sharing the dreams and ambitions of adolescents who were deciding the kind of people they wanted to become.

A further consolation was that he would have Hildegard's company. One of her best piano pupils, Adam Barnes, had won the school music prize and was down to perform the first movement of Beethoven's *Pathétique* Sonata during the assembly.

After a ceremonial gun had been fired on the school green, the proceedings began with an assembly for parents and pupils in Memorial Hall. This was a Greek-style amphitheatre constructed in brick and stone soon after the Great War, a building that had once been generously situated but was now overshadowed by the addition of a modern science block to accommodate Prime Minister Harold Wilson's 'white heat' of technology.

The headmaster, Geraint Rogers (MA Oxon), was a stout, barrel-chested man in a navy suit that had begun to shine at knee and elbow. He was in his mid-fifties and possessed what must once have been a broad and welcoming face. Alas, time and chance had not been kind. Failure to control his weight had resulted in a box-like torso, double chin and pouchy cheeks. He had lost half his hair, and the dark slip of a toupee purchased to disguise the fact was too ill-fitting to convince anyone but the short-sighted, particularly on a hot and sweaty day. His silver-grey eyes, already appearing smaller due to the increased flesh on the face, were concealed behind half-moon spectacles that didn't quite achieve the donnish aura the wearer had intended. Put simply, this was not the look of a man who was going places.

It meant that Geraint Rogers had to make an extra effort

with his speech in order to persuade his audience that he was a serious man of achievement rather than the leading representative of a school that was never going to punch above its weight. He spoke as if it could almost have been a hundred years earlier when the boys were being prepared for Empire. It was his avowed intent to nurture young minds, he said, to help his pupils pursue learning, understand the rewards of discipline and discover passions they did not know they had. This was a school that believed you could be physically fit and intellectually agile, whether it was marathon running or mathematics. His mission was to produce men who were ready for anything.

The head boy reviewed the year. The rugby first XV had won four, drawn two and lost three of their matches, with the Colts unbeaten; the hockey XI had won more games than they had lost; and three members of the cricket team had been for trials with neighbouring counties. There had been expeditions to Snowdon, a kayaking trip to Scotland and the Combined Cadet Force had taken part in a series of exercises at Foulness.

A procession of some thirty boys walked up on to the stage to receive cups, certificates and awards for Sport, Classics, Modern Languages, History, Geography, Art and Science. Parents in old-school ties in yellow and burgundy designed, perhaps deliberately, to be easily confused with the 'egg and bacon' colours of the MCC, politely applauded other people's children while silently judging their own.

Some of the sixth-form pupils were already in blazers and whites ready for the cricket later that morning, but Sidney's task was simple: to give the leavers' prize for religious studies to an enthusiastic ginger-haired boy who had compensated for his lack of good looks by becoming the school jester.

Adam Barnes then walked on to the stage to play his Beethoven. He was a shy seventeen-year-old pupil in the lower sixth with dark-brown Beatle-cut hair, pale skin that had suffered its fair share of acne, and a thin mouth that had thought about smiling but decided not to. He was a boy who had grown too fast and was taller than he wanted to be, and he spent as much time as it was safe to do so looking down to his long fingers on the keyboard or his feet on the ground, minimising the embarrassment of direct eye contact.

He adjusted the piano stool, checked he was not sitting too close, and composed himself as Hildegard had asked him to do. ('Make them wait,' she had advised. 'Let them anticipate the drama. Then lean back, take a deep breath and command the opening chord. You are the master of the piano. You must not let it rule you! Tame it!')

After his bold introduction, Adam Barnes achieved a controlled and rhythmic tremolo in the left hand as his right picked out the melody 'con brio', as he had been instructed, 'playing to the bottom of the keys' in a performance that was remarkably mature even if it lacked dynamic range and emotional depth. On completion, after some eight or nine minutes, he received kind and full applause and looked to Hildegard when he took his bow. He smiled shyly. There was no sign of his parents.

After everyone had stood for the National Anthem there was a boisterous rendition of 'Men of Harlech', given for no reason, Sidney surmised, other than the fact that the headmaster happened to be Welsh.

A marquee had been erected next to the Great Lawn where the school band were playing a medley of military favourites, the CCF went about their exercises, and groups of parents roamed through the main quad to view work that was on display in the classrooms. Later that afternoon there was the promise of a visit to the Pearson Building, home to the new science labs. This was a two-storey brutalist construction in 'unfinished' concrete that had been built after several hefty donations from parents, a few of whose children had been on the verge of expulsion.

The cricket match began at midday and involved a tactful selection of Old Boys against pupils. Here, the promise of the young was pitched against the experienced but waning powers of fathers still keen to prove their virility before their retirement to that great pavilion in the sky.

Sidney was umpiring. Hildegard watched from a deckchair, with Anna and Byron by her side, while her star piano pupil fielded at midwicket. If those responsible for national tourism had wanted to show a perfect English midsummer day then this could have been it. Or rather, that would have been the case had not a mighty explosion ripped through the science block just before lunch, with the Old Boys on the verge of a hundred runs, creating a chaos of thunderous noise, shock, panic and debris.

The chemistry teacher, Trevor Paine, ran from the labs with his hands over his face and the back of his jacket in flames. He dropped to the ground and rolled over and over on the hard asphalt, desperately trying to put himself out as the roof of the building took fire. Boys ran towards him to help, buckets were summoned and one of the porters produced an extinguisher from the Memorial Hall. The school bell began to toll, the fire drill was activated, and the emergency services were called. Pupils and parents were ordered to assemble on the Great

Lawn as the building crackled and burned. A thunderstorm of smoke sprawled across a Cambridge-blue sky.

The cricket match was abandoned. Sidney ran over to see if he could help. The headmaster was shouting at teachers and prefects, establishing a line of command with buckets and hoses. Several of the boys, including Marcus Pearson, the star of the cricket team, were sent round to the back of the building to see if anyone was trapped inside.

Although Trevor Paine was badly burned it was clear that he would live. He was certainly well enough to issue a string of curses stating that the explosion had been no accident but a deliberate strategy to sabotage the day. He swore that he would find the pupil responsible and administer the most savage beating that had ever been known to man.

Sidney took a few steps forward so that he could hear precisely what the chemistry teacher was threatening to do but Hildegard pulled him back saying that it was none of his business, he was not a witness, and that he didn't have to become involved every time something dramatic or unexpected happened.

'I must stay. Besides, they may continue with the cricket.'

'You think so? After something like this?'

'The school will probably want to show that it can survive misfortune. The Dunkirk spirit.'

The headmaster approached. 'This is terrible, but we will not be defeated. Remember Dunkirk!'

'Indeed.'

'I am not sure what to do about the match, Canon Chambers. But let's review the situation over our delayed lunch. I trust you will stay.'

'I had no other plans for the afternoon.'

Hildegard gave her husband one of her 'looks' because she already knew that Inspector Keating was due to come over the following Thursday and that her husband would be unable to refrain from telling him that he had been present when someone had tried to blow up the science block with the possible intention of murdering the Head of Chemistry.

The drive back to Ely was moodily silent. Even Byron seemed full of foreboding.

It was the Chambers's first summer in their new home and they had not yet established a proper routine. Sidney had been better at keeping to a Tuesday 'day off' on which he looked after Anna and Hildegard packed in much of her teaching, but there were still many things left undone that ought to have been done. Anna wasn't getting the attention she deserved, the house was a mess, and there were regular piles of washed clothes in need of an iron that had been left in a basket on the kitchen sideboard. The solution to all this chaos was, Hildegard insisted, an au pair girl, and she had at last found an ideal candidate: Sabine Neuer.

Such was their domestic confusion, however, that Sabine arrived at the railway station a day earlier than they had been anticipating. Hildegard could not understand how they could have made such a mistake. It just showed, she told Sidney, how full their lives were and how impractical it would be if he decided to play a part in any investigation into the school explosion. Fortunately (or, perhaps not, Sidney conjectured silently) Canon Christopher Clough had shared the same train up from London, and had introduced himself to Sabine without, of course, revealing that he was well known as the local Lothario, a man whom one of the cathedral cleaners had recently dubbed 'the Casanova of the Cloisters'.

He staked his claim quickly, carrying Sabine's suitcase from the station, taking her over the meadows on the scenic route to the cathedral, and offering to help show her the ropes whenever she was ready. Sabine had replied that she had no interest in knots but she was grateful that Canon Clough had been so attentive.

'I'll bet he was,' Sidney murmured to himself.

Sabine was an athletic-looking girl with large blue eyes, a cheerful face, and shoulder-length blonde hair that was held in place by an Alice band. She was dressed in a printed rayon blouse and blue jeans that appeared a little tight for her, and she looked more like Hildegard's niece than an employee, sent to England to do a bit of growing up after disappointing exam results and a disastrous first love affair.

Anna had refused to come out of her room on the au pair girl's arrival. She was busy adding to the model farm that had already taken over all the floor space and could not be disturbed by anyone tidying or hoovering. Her recent request for a hamster was only likely to make things in the child's already overcrowded bedroom considerably worse.

Hildegard showed Sabine round the house and helped her unpack as Sidney made the tea and laid out a few biscuits. The cake that had been planned for tomorrow had not been started, and he knew that he would have to tread carefully with his wife and not even joke that this early arrival might in any way be her oversight.

He was just allowing himself to feel almost pleased with the way he had managed to keep the great ship of his family afloat, concentrating on his duties as a father and a priest, when the mood was broken by a visit from the Millingham headmaster.

'We don't know what caused the unfortunate incident,' Geraint Rogers began. 'The preliminary suggestion from the fire brigade is that someone left the gas on.'

'Deliberately or accidentally?'

'To cause that kind of explosion, every Bunsen burner in the room would have to have been fully open. That's more than an oversight. Our Head of Chemistry, Mr Paine, is a chain-smoker, everyone knows that, and the room is powered by electricity, so the light switch may have been tampered with. Anyone entering the room with a naked flame, such as a cigarette, or even simply turning on the lights could have triggered the explosion. The labs were, in effect, booby-trapped.'

'And was Paine the intended target?'

'We do not know, but on Prize Day he was likely to enter the complex first.'

Sidney poured boiling water into the teapot. 'Not the porter?'

'The doors were unlocked first thing . . .'

'And the explosion wasn't until just before lunch . . .'

'. . . which means that the perpetrator could have got into the building before the ceremony and left the gas on for three or four hours without anyone noticing. Then, when Paine arrived for Prize Day, the room was primed.'

'And either he was the intended victim or the whole thing was just a prank to blow the place up and create a bit of an impression on Prize Day. Would you like a biscuit?'

'I think I'll wait for the tea.'

'Would it have required any specialist knowledge?'

The headmaster was depressed. 'Not really. Our pupils study electrical circuits in their first year. And chemistry teachers are always blowing things up to get the pupils' attention in class.'

'But presumably the more dangerous substances are kept under lock and key? I would have thought the Bunsen burners would be too . . .'

'They will be from now on.'

'So,' Sidney continued, 'you think that this is more than mere carelessness?' He could hear that Hildegard was about to come downstairs and he didn't want to be caught in the act of sleuthing.

'I am afraid so, although we have told the emergency services that someone must have left the gas on by mistake.'

'And they are satisfied?'

'At the moment they are pretending to be, but I hope it will remain a school matter rather than anything that might involve an external investigation.'

'And your insurers will believe you?'

'We may have to pay for the refurbishment out of our reserves.'

Sidney was surprised. This conversation was going to take longer than he had hoped. 'You won't make a claim?'

'I think we can manage. As I say, we'd rather not have too much of an inquiry.'

'I see.' Sidney poured the tea into four mugs. 'And why are you telling me this?'

'You do have something of a reputation, Canon Chambers.'

'You are asking me to conduct some unofficial enquiries?'

'I'd like to know whether Trevor Paine was the intended victim.'

'You think the perpetrator was one of the boys or a group of boys? Milk?'

'Thank you. Everyone thinks it was Pearson. He has a grudge against Paine and he's already been in trouble this term for staging a mock knife fight in the town centre.'

'A free spirit, as it were?'

'Pearson is something of a rebel. But he was playing cricket at the time and he vehemently denies any wrongdoing. He even said that if he *had* been responsible he would have made a better job of it.'

'And you believe him? Sugar?'

'Two. He makes a valid point. One of his ancestors discovered nitroglycerin and his family ran the cordite factory at Gretna during the Great War. He's also owned up to anything he's done wrong in the past. In fact he's rather proud of his misdemeanours.'

'But you haven't expelled him?'

'He's going to be captain of the cricket team next year and we can't afford to lose him. Besides, he's done nothing that warrants automatic expulsion. He knows just how far to push us. There are other complications . . .'

'What do you mean?'

'His grandparents are on the board of the Pelouze Trust . . .'

'Yes?'

'. . . which gave a generous donation to the science block. Pearson's hardly likely to want to blow up a building his family helped fund.'

Sidney changed tack. 'Did the injured chemistry teacher have any other enemies?'

The headmaster tested his tea. He looked as if he didn't like the taste, but it was what he was about to say that concerned him more. 'There have been insinuations; complaints even.'

'What kind?' Sidney asked.

'Mr Paine has, in the past, been over-enthusiastic in disciplining boys . . .'

'Corporal punishment?'

'Indeed. "The cane of Paine".'

'And the accusation is, perhaps, that he enjoys punishing boys rather too much?'

'It's unfounded, I'm sure of it.'

'But it could be that a boy who had been at the receiving end was responsible for the explosion, or it could even have been a parent, eager to exact a kind of revenge?' Sidney began to recall a passage from St Paul's letter to the Thessalonians about 'fire taking vengeance on them that know not God'.

'It could be,' the headmaster answered doubtfully. 'But I am hoping the whole thing is just a prank. That's why I need your help, Canon Chambers. An inquiry conducted by a sympathetic outsider, a person who has guaranteed impartiality, who is not the police, but recognised by them if we run into difficulty.'

'I'm not sure . . .'

Hildegard called from upstairs. 'I HOPE THE TEA IS READY.'

Geraint Rogers could tell that it was time to conclude. 'I have already talked to the dean. I have his blessing.'

'You have been very thorough . . .'

'I don't want anything else to happen.' He took one last sip of tea and asked what to do with the cup.

'I'll wash that up,' said Sidney.

'All this has come at completely the wrong time. I was hoping for promotion. The Millfield job will come up fairly soon. "Boss" Meyer can't go on for ever. I thought I might have a rather good chance. His father was a clergyman, you know? But after this . . .'

'I will do my best, Headmaster.' Sidney could not offer much more, so flummoxed was he by his guest's delusional ambition.

Upstairs, Anna was teaching Sabine 'Old Macdonald Had a Farm'.

Geraint Rogers opened the front door. 'I can assure you of every assistance. I don't want this to get out of hand. We are both aware of how rumours can fly. Consequently I would rather we kept this between ourselves. I think I can deal with the police. We'll put it down as an accident.'

'Even though it wasn't?'

'I was going to let you decide. Then perhaps I, rather than anyone else, can take the appropriate action. Until that time, I hope I can rely on your discretion.'

'Of course,' Sidney replied, closing the door and wondering how on earth he was going to keep anything secret as soon as he started talking to the pupils.

Inspector Keating had been away in London, watching England beat Mexico 2–0 in the World Cup, so when the two friends met for drinks Geordie was more concerned with football than explosives. It was bound to be pyromaniac boys, he thought, and complained, as he had done so often before, about private schools being a law in their own right.

'It's just like the university,' he pronounced. 'They think their rules take precedence over the laws of the land. You can imagine the kind of pupils it turns out. They assume that they don't have to bother with the rest of us.'

'Not all of them are like that.'

'You are bound to be on their side, Sidney. You went to the same kind of place.'

'Marlborough is, I think you'll find, a superior establishment.'

'Well, it's the word "superior" that annoys me.'

Keating took a hefty swig from his pint and wiped the foam from his mouth with the back of his hand. 'Just because the parents can afford to give them a head start the boys start believing they are entitled to anything.'

Sidney finished his pint and pointed at Geordie's, offering replenishment. His friend nodded in assent. 'Now is not the time to discuss the British educational system.'

'Or its defects. No wonder someone wanted to blow the whole place up.'

When he returned with the drinks, Sidney asked if they could discuss the choice of the chemistry lab as the venue for the Prize Day sabotage. Clearly this had the advantage of available materials and the possibility of disguising crime as an accident, but an act of violence might just as easily have been arson in the cricket pavilion or food poisoning in the kitchens. Could there be a particular reason for an attack on the chemistry labs and was Trevor Paine the intended target?

Keating asked if the teacher had any obvious enemies.

'He has, apparently, already made an accusation. I am going to see him in hospital.'

'I'm not sure about you getting involved in all this, Sidney. That school has an unsavoury history with the clergy.'

'What do you mean?'

Keating had the appearance of a man who was reluctant to say what he had to say while simultaneously bursting to spill the beans. 'I made a telephone call before coming to see you. I guessed this subject might come up.'

'Please tell me what you know.'

'This case,' Keating began, 'if it is one, may not be entirely unconnected with Trevor Paine's friend, the Reverend Kevin Charles Warner, the former chaplain; or "Rev Kev" as he was called at Millingham . . .'

'They informed me that he left the school rather quickly. They implied he had been ill. Was it something different? Did he depart under a cloud?'

'You could say that.'

'Then where is he now?'

'Prison.'

Sidney was appalled. 'Why did nobody tell me?'

'I'm sure you can hazard a guess. There had been a great number of complaints about your colleague . . .'

'He's not my colleague . . .'

'Member of your profession, then.'

'To do with?'

'The usual. You don't need a teaching qualification in private education. It's jobs for the boys. Then they close ranks when it all goes to pot.'

'But not in this case.'

'Just about. There had been parental complaints about Rev Kev: interfering with young boys, bullying, and general buggering about. But it took a compromising situation in a public toilet to get him arrested. One of our men was an old boy. Relished the opportunity to see a former teacher get his comeuppance. Not as popular as he thought he was, Rev Kev.'

'Well, I can't imagine he'll be any more so in prison. But what has this to do with Trevor Paine?' Sidney asked.

'They were comrades-in-arms – and a lot more besides.'

'With each other?'

'I think they preferred young boys. Apparently the two men thought they were ancient Greeks. Born at the wrong time into the wrong civilisation . . .'

'I presume that defence was dismissed?'

'Absolutely.'

'Extraordinary how often the traditions of the classical world are misappropriated . . .'

'You say that you are planning a visit?'

'To Mr Paine, yes.'

'I'll be interested to hear how you get on. Normally these types of places try to keep things quiet. You can hardly hush up an explosion.'

'Do you think that was the point of it, then?'

'I don't know, Sidney. But you're the man to find out.'

There was a little domestic frostiness on Sidney's return from the pub. This was not, however, because he was later than he said he would be. (Hildegard was used to that.) Nor was it due to any anxiety that he was going to investigate the explosion. Instead, there was a cathedral matter his wife considered more pressing; namely the inappropriate attention Christopher Clough was paying their au pair girl.

Once they were alone in their bedroom, Hildegard went into

detail. The overeager priest was taking Sabine out for a drink the following evening. 'Perhaps she should have a chaperone? I would go myself but, of course, there is Anna.'

'I could stay at home, perhaps, or I could go for the drink too?'

'We can't have *two* clergymen eyeing her up. You're not judging Miss World.'

'I wouldn't be assessing her at all.'

'I thought I was getting *help*. Instead it seems I have a second child. Sabine is distracted by this man, Sidney. He is *nervensäge*: a nuisance.'

Hildegard added that the au pair was dreamy and walked about the house in a world of her own. All she liked doing was playing with Anna and her farm.

'That is good, is it not, if Anna likes her? They are becoming friends.'

It was not enough. Whenever her employer asked her to do anything Sabine said that she was too tired or too busy to concentrate on any domestic tasks. She also had lessons at 'the college' that meant she was often away at exactly the time she was needed.

'She hasn't even started on the ironing. Soon neither of us will have anything to wear.'

'I once heard a sermon about the nakedness of Adam and Eve,' Sidney mused in an effort to cheer his wife up as he joined her in bed.

'Don't.'

'The preacher was saying that it wouldn't take us long to get used to the idea.'

Hildegard shifted on to her side. 'If I had wanted to live in a nudist colony, Sidney, I would not have come to England. It's too cold and the people are ugly.'

She turned out the bedside light. Sidney decided neither to make any comparison with Germany nor to argue. 'Well, I only hope that doesn't apply to me.' He leaned over and kissed his wife on the mouth, hoping for more.

The next day he made a point of reassuring Hildegard before leaving to see the chemistry teacher in hospital. 'Cloughie can't do too much damage, can he? Sabine's only just arrived.'

'He's a very dangerous man.'

'Not in the criminal sense.'

'I don't know.'

'What do women see in him?'

'Confidence,' Hildegard answered. 'People say he is amusing and a little dangerous.'

'Is that it?'

'Women are aware he is naughty and they like it. They know there might be trouble but they are bored. They want excitement. And because he is a clergyman there is a safety net. They expect he will be decent in the end, even if he is not. That is his trick. It makes him even more devious.'

'It's very odd, isn't it, the people who find clergymen attractive?'

'Be very careful, Sidney . . .'

'I don't mean me.'

'Would you like me to tell you more?'

'No, I think it's best not to be too aware of these things. You just have to get on with life. I know you'll keep me right.'

'I will always inform you, *mein Lieber*, if there is something to worry about. Women know not to cause any trouble or they will have to answer to me. It is the one time when being German helps. People think I am fiercer than I am. In one flash, like the villain in the pantomime you once took me to, they are worried I will turn into a Nazi.'

'I am not sure people really think like that, Hildegard.'

'You don't notice. If you did then perhaps you would be more arrogant.'

'More?'

'So many women would fall in love with you. And I would have to stop it.'

'I don't think any women are likely to fall in love with *me*,' Sidney answered, half hoping for a denial.

'And what are you going to do,' Hildegard asked, 'when men are attracted to me?'

'I haven't really thought about that. I am not a jealous man.'

'Perhaps you should be?'

Sidney looked around for something to distract them both but his wife was looking straight at him, waiting for an answer.

'Is there something you want to tell me?' he asked. He was feeling decidedly shaky.

'I am teasing you, *mein Liebster.*'

'It doesn't feel very affectionate.'

'It is funny. Perhaps I am serious. Or not. You will have to spend more time with me in order to judge.'

'There is nothing I would like more.'

Hildegard smiled. 'I am always here. Why do you keep leaving me?'

'That's a very good question.'

'Then answer it, *Mein Lieber.*'

In the kitchen, Sabine was singing her own version of 'Pat-a-cake, pat-a-cake, baker's man' to Anna as they prepared to make gingerbread men. The house was becoming German once more.

> *Backe, backe Kuchen,*
> *Der Bäcker hat gerufen!*
> *Wer will gute Kuchen backen,*
> *Der muss haben sieben Sachen:*
> *Eier und Schmalz,*
> *Butter und Salz,*
> *Milch und Mehl,*
> *Safran macht den Kuchen gel'!*

Hildegard pushed back from her husband. 'You must go, I know. Visit your patient. Talk to Canon Clough. Then come home with your news. I will miss you.'

'And I you.'

'I'm teaching Adam Barnes later. He's going to make a start either on a piece of Chopin or Dvořák. I'm going to let him choose. You could ask him a few questions about Prize Day, perhaps?'

'I'm not sure how much he will know. Wasn't he with you for most of the morning in the music rooms?'

'He was. But he's a boy at the school and he likes me. He would make a good informant, don't you think?'

'You are ahead of me, Hildegard.'

'That is where I like to be.'

'Would you mind . . .'

'Keeping him until you return? Of course. Now you can leave. The price is one more kiss.'

There were times, as he bicycled through the streets of Ely with Byron running by his side, that Sidney wondered what on earth he had done to deserve such a wife. Was it a God-given gift, he thought, made as recompense for his endeavours in helping other people in war and peace? He did not believe that God behaved like that. Life, he thought, should be its own reward. But still, he decided, it would do no harm to be grateful.

The Tower Hospital was situated on the Cambridge Road and the authorities were as dubious about Sidney's visits as they had been at Addenbrooke's. The chaplain had already suggested that Sidney spent so much time there (and, by implication, so much less in the Cathedral Close) that it might be simpler if they swapped jobs.

Trevor Paine had just been for a cigarette and a cup of tea in the canteen. Despite the bandage round his face and on the right side of his body, the damage done would not be permanent and he was expected home in the next few days.

He was a small man with thick, bristly grey hair, a long dark toothbrush moustache and a ruddy face that looked as if its owner was no stranger to either drink or anger. He explained that he was sure that someone had come in after he had unlocked the building that morning. They must have opened up all the Bunsen burners, allowing methane gas to pour out into the room, mixing with oxygen and requiring only the tiniest spark from the electric light switch or the flame from a cigarette to set off the explosion.

'Didn't you smell it first?' Sidney asked.

'I was smoking as I entered the room. I reached for the light switch.'

'In broad daylight?'

'The blinds were down. We keep the room dark to preserve the chemicals.'

'I thought they were locked away.'

'They are. This is an additional precaution. But obviously no matter what safety measures we employ, it's not going to stop someone blowing up the labs if they feel like it.'

'Would it have to have been a sixth former?'

'It could have been any one of the little bastards. We teach them how to blow up empty biscuit tins and lemonade bottles all the time. It's part of the excitement of chemistry, moving copper wires through flames or seeing the different colours produced by things like copper sulphate, strontium chloride and boric acid. Sometimes the boys get out of hand, pouring methanol directly into a crucible rather than using a pipette . . .'

'What happens then?'

'The flame follows the vapour back into the bottle. Then there is a kind of flashover, and bang. Explosion. Fire. Drama. Panic. Most of the boys are pyromaniacs. Pearson especially. The headmaster will be on to him, I'm sure.'

'He was playing cricket when the explosion . . .'

'The timing is irrelevant. This was planned well in advance.'

'Targeting you? Or just the lab in particular?'

'I don't think it's necessarily to do with me. It may not be anything personal at all. I think it's one of the leavers showing off.'

'Pearson is not a leaver. He has another year at the school . . .'

'I don't think he was aware I might have been killed. I was just in the wrong place at the wrong time. But I wouldn't mind giving him a good caning.'

'There is still corporal punishment at Millingham? I know some schools have decided to do away with it.'

'More fool them.'

Sidney wondered if this was the right way of going about things. Just because the beating of boys had been passed down through the generations didn't make it acceptable. Tradition, he suggested, was no guarantee of morality.

Paine headed him off. 'I have no truck with those new-fangled educationalists who believe that their pupils should choose what they want to study. What is the point of one of those ridiculous schools where children are allowed to pick their own lessons? How can they know what they don't know?'

'I think the idea behind them is that the child lives his or her own life instead of one that anxious parents or traditional educators lay down for them.'

'Boys need to be guided and disciplined. It's as simple as that. They can decide what to do on their own when they're older.'

'Is that what your friend Rev Kev thought?' Sidney asked.

'I don't think he's got much to do with this inquiry.'

'How well did you know him?'

'What are you asking about him for?'

'It might be connected . . .'

'With the explosion? I don't think so.'

'The two of you were friends.'

'We weren't that close. And Kevin's in prison, as you probably know.'

Sidney leaned back in his chair. 'Could you tell me about the other boys that you have had to punish; and not just Pearson? Have there been some particular troublemakers who have kept coming back; any who have needed, for example, more and more discipline?'

'There are one or two of them every term.'

'I am thinking about the last three or four years; either a boy who is still in the school or one that left recently. Someone who might want a bit of revenge.'

'It's Pearson, I know it.'

'The other names would be helpful . . .'

Sidney made an unexpected stop on his way home at a riverside pub. Christopher Clough was having a drink with Sabine. Two things annoyed him about this. The first was that although his au pair girl appeared to be drinking an orange juice he couldn't be sure that vodka had not been added. Secondly, Hildegard was teaching. Anna would need supper, bathing and putting to bed and here was the person they had specifically employed for the task, dressed in little more than a T-shirt, which revealed an all-too-visible cleavage, out on a jolly.

Sabine said that they were just finishing and that she would soon be home. Christopher had been very kind, even, apparently, '*reizend*'.

'I am sure he has. There is something I wanted to ask you, Christopher. Am I mistaken, or didn't you once teach at Millingham School?'

'Like you, I helped out between vacancies. I was never an employee.'

'Was that just before Kevin Warner got the job?'

'Why do you ask?'

'You knew him?'

'Not well. I gave him some advice about teaching the young, that's all. A sorry end, of course. I presume you know all about it?'

'Not as much as I would like. This isn't the time, but perhaps I could come and talk to you about it? If you could find a moment in your diary.' Sidney looked at Sabine and could not resist a moment of tartness. 'I know you are very busy. You must have a lot on.'

'I will always have time for you, Canon Chambers. Even on a day off such as today.'

'Then I won't take up any more of your evening.'

It was unchristian to dislike a fellow priest but Sidney could not help it. Was it jealousy, he thought for a moment, before bicycling away? No, it was not, he told himself. It was fury.

Adam Barnes had stayed on at the Archdeacon's House but had been left to practise on his own while a disgruntled Hildegard mimicked cheerfulness and ran Anna's bath, angry that neither Sabine nor her husband had returned. Adam had opted for the haunting sonorities of Dvořák rather than the bravura theatricality of a Chopin étude and was slowly working through some of the more complex sections when Sidney arrived. He asked Hildegard's pupil how he was getting on.

'I'm all right,' the boy answered non-committally.

'That was quite a thing on Prize Day, wasn't it? I am only glad the explosion didn't happen in the middle of your performance. I very much enjoyed your playing, by the way. I hope your parents did too.'

'They weren't there. Only Mrs Chambers.'

'So you had no family watching?'

'Dad's away. Mum prefers to stay at home. She doesn't go out much. And I can play to her whenever she likes.'

'It would have been nice for her if she had heard the applause.'

'She's funny about coming to things like that. And what happened would have made it worse.'

'An extraordinary thing. I suppose it can't have been an accident.'

'I don't know.'

'The school seem very keen to blame a boy called Pearson. I think he's in your year.' Sidney knew he was pushing it.

'He wouldn't have done it.'

'Why not?'

Adam Barnes wasn't sure whether or not to go on. Sidney thought that he was working out if he was sneaking. 'It would be too obvious. He knows everyone would accuse him anyway. He's cleverer than that. He prefers to do things that get other people into trouble.'

Hildegard entered the room, expressed some pleasure that Sidney was back at last, and informed her husband that it was his turn to take over. His daughter had been asking for him.

Sidney tried one last question. 'Does he tell you then?'

'Not really.' Adam Barnes gathered up his music and put it in a case. 'He was a friend of my brother.'

'Was?'

'I have to go home now. Thank you for the lesson, Mrs Chambers.'

'I'll see you next week,' his teacher replied. 'Remember.

Take it slowly then build it up. Make it full of longing. Imagine a place you have always wanted to go to, or somewhere you once knew, where you were happy . . .'

'I'll think of somewhere.'

After he was safely out of sight, Sidney asked his wife why Adam was so evasive.

'He doesn't like to talk about his family.'

'Why not?'

'His father left. I'm not sure about his brother. His mother pays the bills. I've only met her once. She's a nice woman but she has very bad arthritis and she doesn't like to go out. I think Adam looks after her.'

'Is it just the two of them?'

'I think so. I don't like to ask too many questions. I am not you, Sidney.'

'I have to investigate. This could be attempted murder.'

'Well, that is what he is doing to his Dvořák at the moment. He was my best pupil before all this happened.'

'How long has he got before his exam?'

'It's next term. I don't want him distracted.'

'I think he already is.'

A few days later Sidney was back at Millingham to take prayers at the final assembly of the term. After a predictably disappointing lunch (spam, beetroot and boiled potatoes followed by a particularly revolting tapioca pudding served with a dollop of jam) he planned to interview as many pupils as possible before they disappeared on their summer holidays. The headmaster had organised what he called a 'rogues' gallery', starting with Marcus Pearson and followed by the more troublesome sixth formers who had been in Mr Paine's chemistry class: Fishwick, Swainson, Charkin and Newton.

Geraint Rogers was not confident. 'I can't promise that this is going to be easy, Canon Chambers. There is a great reluctance to sneak and the boys will be suspicious of a clergyman.'

'Is that to do with Rev Kev?'

'So you know about our other local difficulty.'

Sidney was not going to be hoodwinked. 'I think it was a bit more than that.'

'Some of the boys told their parents but they weren't believed. Now they are wary of saying anything at all. They don't trust the older generation.'

'None of them?'

'Some fathers might have believed their sons but didn't want to cause a fuss, or they were old boys who said that they had experienced it themselves and you just had to put up with it. Rev Kev had a good war record but he came out shell-shocked. His hands trembled and then they tended to wander, especially after a drink or two. He wasn't capable of very much. It was more a case of wishful thinking.'

'Still . . .'

'It wasn't assault or violence, just a bit of fumbling about. It's fairly common for teachers to fall in love with a pupil or two. As long as they don't *do* anything then it's fairly harmless.'

'That doesn't exactly excuse it.' Sidney knew he had to keep his temper in check in order to get the information he needed.

'I know. But there are degrees to these things . . .'

'I'm not so sure, Headmaster. You're telling me that some parents complained?'

'They did.'

'Some mothers?'

'Yes.'

'And was Mrs Barnes one of them?'

'I can't recall.'

'I think she might have been. What about Mrs Pearson?'

'Why do you want to know?'

'I am about to see her son.'

'Then you can ask him yourself. I don't think he's ever been on the receiving end of that kind of trouble. He's too busy getting into scrapes himself. Not everyone appreciates his exuberant personality.'

'Exuberant' was one of the last adjectives Sidney would have chosen to describe a sullen, good-looking sixteen-year-old boy who had loosened his tie and thrown off his school blazer for a conversation in an empty classroom.

Marcus Pearson came from London and had been to a good few schools before ending up at Millingham. His hair was defiantly long, he wore Chelsea boots and smelled of smoke. He denied everything, saying that not only did he have an alibi (he had been in the nets after breakfast, ready for the cricket, and had never been anywhere near the science labs) but there were more important misdemeanours that Sidney should be investigating. 'Crimes that cause more lasting damage.'

'What do you mean?'

'Doesn't your wife teach Adam Barnes?'

'She does.'

'Well, ask him.'

'I have. He told me that it couldn't have been you.'

'Is that all you asked?'

'He said that you were friends with his brother.'

'Did he tell you about Luke?'

'No. That was rather what I wanted to ask. Does it have any bearing on this case?'

'It might do.'

'Then what is it?'

'The teachers.'

'What do you mean?'

'Mr Paine. His mates.'

'Do you think the explosion was an act of revenge?'

The boy nodded. 'That's about right. It isn't very complicated once you know what you're after.'

'You are saying, I imagine . . .'

'What do you think? I can't do it all for you. The clergy haven't exactly helped us in the past. And only one of them has gone to prison. To think our parents pay money for this so-called education.'

'Then why do you stay here?'

'Nowhere else will have me.'

'I don't think that's true. You're good at cricket. Your family have been generous benefactors . . .'

'You mean they bought my place here . . .'

'I don't know the facts.'

'You should go and see Adam's mum, Canon Chambers. She'll tell you if she trusts you. Don't bother with Paine. Or with anyone else. They can talk as much as they like and you'll be no clearer.'

'Are you telling me everything you know?'

'I'm telling you as much as I think you need. That's different. Anything else might confuse you.'

Sidney was not going to rise to the boy's patronising provocation. 'I could be the judge of that.'

'I know. But this isn't to do with me. I've got nothing to do with your inquiry.'

'It's not an investigation.'

'What is it then?'

'A survey. A chat. Something like that.'

'I don't believe you. And I don't have to say anything. I've done nothing wrong.'

'I hope that's the case.'

'I don't need to lie. It's Mrs Barnes you want to talk to. Or Rev Kev. What a bastard that bloke is. They're all as bad as each other at this school. That's what's really *criminal*. Not us. *Them*.'

Geordie Keating said he was 'trying not to be optimistic' the next time the two men met in the Prince Albert. Sidney had hoped that he was talking about life and the solving of crime, but his friend had confined his hopes to the England football team after their World Cup quarter-final victory in a bad-tempered game against Argentina. 'I don't want to jinx things by complacency.'

Sidney carried the pints back to their table. 'There's no chance of that at Millingham School.'

'Are you still worrying away? Don't they want the problem contained? They must know you speak to me.'

'I have told them that I will keep matters to myself for the time being. However, I don't intend to remain silent if I discover any more unacceptable behaviour.'

'So you've lied?'

'I was careful with the truth. That is different.'

'And how's it all going?'

'Not well. There are probably two conspiracies of silence: one amongst the teachers and another amongst the boys. Everyone pretends they are helping but each person's point of view confuses the situation. The more people tell me, the less information I feel I am being given.'

'At least they are saying something.'

'And I am finding it hard to concentrate. Things keep *irritating* me, Geordie.'

'That's not like you.'

'I sometimes wonder if it's the job.'

'Do you mean being a detective or being a clergyman? It doesn't sound like you are doing much of the latter.'

'Do you think it's because I don't want to?'

'Perhaps it's because you are part of a team. In Grantchester you were running your own show. Now you are just any old clergyman.'

'I hadn't thought of it like that.'

'Don't you like your colleagues?'

'I do find some of them quite trying.'

'Anyone in particular?'

'*Yes*,' Sidney answered all too quickly.

'Blimey . . .'

'It could be serious but you might also find it entertaining. Talking about it will certainly take my mind off more pressing matters.'

'Tell me all.'

'It's about our new au pair girl.'

'She must be about the same age as my Jean. Are you having trouble? Once they reach sixteen they're nothing but a worry . . .'

Sidney explained the situation, adding that Canon Christopher Clough was not only old enough to be Sabine's father, but technically her grandfather too.

'And you are *in loco parentis*?'

'She is seventeen.'

'Then you have every excuse to attack with all guns blazing. I wouldn't dare do this with one of my own daughters, mind, but it's probably easier if she's no relation. You've got to go in hard and early, like Nobby Stiles making a tackle. You should have seen him against Argentina. He gave their captain such a run for his money he got sent off.'

'Nobby?'

'His real name's Norbert but he nobbles opponents early. Norman Hunter's the same. Leeds player. Hits the opposing forward before he knows what's happened.'

'And you're suggesting I "nobble" Cloughie?'

'Put the frighteners on him, Sidney. He's a "forward player" all right. You don't want your au pair girl going back to Germany for an early bath.'

'What?'

'Leaving the field of play . . . Up the duff . . .'

'I don't think it'll get to that stage, Geordie. We don't have to do anything drastic.'

'I'm not so sure.' Keating stood up to order another round at the bar. 'That's probably what they all thought at Millingham School. "Don't worry too much. It's nothing that serious." Then, before you know it, the chaplain's in prison, the science block explodes, and we're in all sorts of murky waters. If they'd behaved properly to begin with then we wouldn't have had any of this nonsense. That's what you've got to do with Clough. Go in hard and early. Take the moral high ground – even if it goes down badly.'

'It probably will.'

'But that's your job. Moral authority. What's the matter with the clergy? Why can't you lot practise what you preach?'

'It's not always easy.'

'Think about it, Sidney. You have to make a stand and compensate for the failings of your colleagues. You've got to be twice the man they are. Otherwise you might as well pack it in.'

Before Sidney could speak to Sabine or follow his friend's advice, he had visitors. Marcus Pearson's parents arrived to tell him that their son had been expelled. Could the new archdeacon do anything to intervene and rescind the decision? Perhaps he could speak to the Bishop of Ely, who was Chairman of the Governors, or even to the Archbishop of Canterbury who, they thought, was 'Visitor' to the school and therefore the final court of appeal?

Sidney was surprised by the turn of events. He had thought Marcus Pearson to be in an inviolable position.

'We can't do much if he confesses to the explosion,' Sir Joseph Pearson explained. 'I don't know what the bloody boy thought he was doing. He's claimed responsibility for everything.'

'They asked him to apologise to Mr Paine,' his wife, Lady Marjorie, continued. 'The headmaster called him into his study and said that if he owned up and said he was sorry then they would find a way to punish him but still keep him at the school. Marcus refused. Instead, he told them he was proud of what he had done and was unrepentant. We can't understand it. He swore to us on the day itself that he hadn't had anything to do with it.'

'And,' his father added, 'he was playing cricket at the time. I was hoping he might get a good fifty. He's due the runs.'

'So now we're going to have to take him back to London,' Lady Marjorie complained. 'Is there anything you can do? The headmaster implied that you were doing a bit of investigating. I think you've already spoken to Marcus.'

'Indeed I have.'

'And did he claim responsibility?'

'Not at all.'

'Then why has he done so now?'

'I have an idea, but I need to talk to a few more people before coming to any conclusion, and to one person in particular.'

'Can you tell the school?'

'That is the problem. I am not sure that I can. But I can ask them to reconsider your son's expulsion.'

'In the light of all we have done for them?'

'No. That would not be the reason. I would be asking, instead, because of what your son has done. I think it may be rather noble.'

'Noble? Marcus? You must have the wrong man. He's never done anything decent in his life.'

'Perhaps because no one has believed him capable,' Sidney replied. 'I am talking about Marcus Pearson. Your son.'

After the Pearsons had left, Hildegard refrained from asking too many questions. She did not want her husband to be any more distracted from what she considered to be the most pressing event in their lives, namely the potential ruination of their au pair girl. Had Sidney been to see Canon Clough and was he actually going to do anything? If not, then she was going to take matters into her own hands and complain to the dean.

'Don't do that, my darling.'

'Inspector Keating told me that we had to deal with the problem.'

'Since when did you speak to Geordie?'

'He telephoned. He wanted to change the time when he sees you next. There's a football match against Portugal. But that's not the important thing. Are you going to do something about this?'

'We have a meeting of the Chapter this morning. I will have a word afterwards.'

'It will need more than "a word", Sidney.'

Christopher Clough was in no mood for compromise when the two men met by the Sacrist's Gate. 'The fact is Sabine and I love each other,' he announced.

'Don't be ridiculous, Cloughie. You must be forty years older than her.'

'Thirty-five.'

Sidney was not prepared for this. 'You will look absurd.'

'I have never felt more alive. If you are a connoisseur of beauty, as I am, then the mind hankers after young flesh: perfectly formed, without the flaws of ageing . . .'

'Yes, yes,' said Sidney irritably.

'. . . clear in contour, firm to the touch . . .'

'I can imagine.'

'It's all very well for you. You are married and your wife hasn't lost her looks.'

'I think marriage should be about more than physical appearance.'

'Have you seen Sabine's mouth? It has an extraordinary sense of invitation . . .'

'These feelings are entirely inappropriate,' said Sidney. 'I hope you know that.'

'I can't do anything about it. Love walked in.'

'Well perhaps it's time it walked out again. I don't want you seeing her any more.'

'And what if she comes to me?'

'You must send her back to us. Immediately. Hildegard is talking to her too.'

'You speak as if I am some kind of criminal. I am not a danger. She likes seeing me. We have fun together.'

'It's not acceptable, Christopher. I don't care what you think of me. I'm not letting things go any further. That's final.'

Sidney walked away without waiting for an answer. He was fed up with virtually every situation in which he found himself. Keating was right. The time had come to show the people of Ely what he was made of.

Adam Barnes lived on the outskirts of Ely in a post-war new-build with a large garden and a view on to field and fen beyond. There was a dovecote in the garden and Sidney talked to Adam's mother as she fed the birds in her care. She told him that she did not go out much. Her son and her birds were her only company. Her legs ached. She told Sidney how bad arthritis could be.

'It's not so much the pain but the energy that it takes up. Everything is such an ordeal. You have to work out if it is worth crossing a room. You plan it as a trip, Canon Chambers, thinking of all the things you have to remember so you don't have to do it twice. I thought I was too young for all of this but it turns out I'm not. Would you like a cup of tea?'

'Perhaps I could make one for you?'

'That would be kind. Save me a few journeys.'

'Shall we go inside?'

'No, let's stay here. It's a good day. Not that I have many of them. The best I can say is that they are "less bad". I know I'm not supposed to grumble – my mother always used to say "no one likes a moaner" – but I do have an excuse. Not that it helps. People were sympathetic to my problems at first but they've gone back to their lives now. I'm sure you've seen all this before. Widows. Desolate mothers.'

'I have learned not to tell people that I can imagine how they feel.'

'I have my doves, Canon Chambers. They don't let me down. I know they will always come back. It's like the swifts at the beginning of summer. Even after everything that's happened, I could not imagine leaving here. I'd miss the return of the birds, the way the summer smells. There's a weight in the air. Can you feel it? Luke could.'

'Adam's elder brother?'

'I know he's here. He's with us in the silences. I just can't reach him. So I wait. It's another reason why I don't like to go out.'

'I don't want to cause you pain in talking about it. I can tell it's a difficult subject.'

'Anything that ruins your life probably is. Did they tell you he died?'

'No.'

'Did you guess?'

320

'I didn't want to presume. But I'd like you to tell me about it – if it isn't too much.'

'People think it was because he'd been bullied at school. That's what they say: the friends, the doctors, the people who try to tell us it was nothing to do with the way he had been brought up and it couldn't be our fault.'

'Blame, in these cases, is seldom useful.'

'You say "cases" and use the plural. There is only one case that matters to me.'

'Luke was unhappy at school, I take it?'

'From the start. It was odd because we thought it was all getting better. He had a new circle of friends, some of them younger than him. Marcus Pearson was one.'

'The boy who has been accused of the arson?'

'He wouldn't have done that.'

'Tell me, Mrs Barnes, did your son ever tell you why he was unhappy?'

'He didn't like to say. He thought it would get him into more trouble. His housemaster said it was nothing. I even went to the chaplain. He said Luke needed time to adjust; that adolescence was difficult and that my boy was a late developer. He was an August baby so he was always the youngest in his year; the smallest, too. His voice broke after everyone else's.'

'Was it when Rev Kev was chaplain?' Sidney asked.

'I didn't like that man very much but he was friendly with my husband and Donald said I was being silly.'

'I am not sure that you were. And who was Luke's housemaster? Was it Trevor Paine?'

'Yes. He was in Galahad. Adam is in Bedivere. You know the houses are all called after the Knights of the Round Table?

They advised us that it would be better to keep the boys apart. I'm not sure it was. They were less able to help each other. They almost had to pretend they weren't brothers because that would be sissy. I wish I'd never sent them there. There's a good state school that they could have gone to instead. Then they would have been with me. I could have kept them safe and none of this would have happened. But it was my husband's old school and it "never did him any harm". What a joke.'

'It "harmed" his eldest son.'

'It killed him. He killed himself. I can't normally say that out loud.'

'I am sorry.'

'Normally, I just tell people he died and they are too embarrassed to ask anything else. It's different with you. You must hear this kind of thing all the time.'

'No two things are ever the same, Mrs Barnes . . .'

'Alice . . .'

'*Alice*. You lost your son. That is a tragedy.'

'It is. It was. It always will be.'

'At least Adam is safe.'

'You think so? I'm frightened, Canon Chambers. I always think something terrible is going to happen to him too. Once the feeling starts there's no stopping it.'

'Nothing bad will happen to your son.'

'How do you know that?'

'Because I will prevent it,' Sidney replied, not knowing how he was going to honour such a promise.

Was Adam safe? Was any child, even his own dearest Anna, ever free from danger? As soon as a son or daughter was placed in the care of others a parent had made an act of trust. If that was misplaced or mistaken, it could soon come to be seen as carelessness or neglect. Perhaps being a parent was to live in a state of constant fear, where the cost of the freedom of youth lay in the anxiety of those who protected it?

Because the Barnes home was near the railway station, Sidney made an instinctive decision to get on a train and call on Inspector Keating. If everything went smoothly he could manage a round trip to Cambridge in just under two hours. It might have been easier and quicker to telephone, but a visit *in person* would ensure that his request would be met with urgency and seriousness. He could even wait while the information was retrieved.

It did mean missing a meeting of the cathedral finance sub-committee. This would probably cause trouble with the dean, but there were plenty of other people who were far better qualified than he was to make recommendations and Sidney decided, perhaps all too imperiously, that his own business was more pressing. Only when he had secured a window seat on a train that allowed a cooling breeze and a delightful view over summer wheat fields did he acknowledge that it was more a case of doing what he preferred to do. His choice of a visit to Cambridge was, of course, much more interesting than a tedious meeting, although it probably wasn't as important as spending more time with Anna, whom he had continued to neglect despite his determination to appreciate her growing up.

Why was he doing this then? Was it vanity or was it the idea that he could put his Christianity to practical use? He explained to Geordie Keating that he was just passing.

'Just passing, my arse,' his friend almost spat. 'Although,

given the context, I probably shouldn't be talking about that part of the anatomy.'

'There's no need to be crude, Geordie.'

'You enjoy it really. I'm your dose of the real world.'

'It is "too much with us; late and soon".'

'Never mind all that. What do you want?'

'I'd like your file on the suicide of Luke Barnes. I presume there was an investigation.'

'What do you want that for? It will probably be with your local boys.'

'But you could get it for me more easily . . .'

'I *could*. But what if I don't want to?'

'Is there something to hide?'

'No, of course not.'

'You say that, but why wasn't I informed in the first place?'

'Because, Sidney, this is not one of our inquiries, Adam Barnes is not a suspect unless you have just made him one, and I can't simply make our library of crimes and misdemeanours at your disposal whenever you fancy.'

'Then I'll explain why it's necessary.'

'You are not going to start questioning the coroner's verdict, are you?'

'I don't usually go against Jarvis, as you know . . .'

'Then what do you want it for?'

'I want to know where it happened and if the school did anything about it.'

'The family reported it. Death by misadventure, I seem to recall. There was nothing mysterious.'

'That may be, but I am interested in the psychology behind it. What drove a boy like that to take his own life?'

'I imagine he was being bullied.'

'That's right.'

'And I take it that you are going to show me that it was Mr Paine, the victim of the explosion, who was doing the bullying?'

'That's correct.'

'Are you then going to try and tell me that the boy did not kill himself after all and that Paine is either an accessory to murder or even a murderer himself?'

'I'm not sure I'm going to get that far. I don't know yet. I need the file.'

'And what are you going to do while we run around trying to find it in order to justify your little whim?'

'The job I am paid to do.'

'Which doesn't include this?'

'I don't know, Geordie. There are times when I think that my job includes every blessed thing in the entire universe.'

In the breezy back garden, as they took the dry washing off the line and folded the bed sheets, Hildegard tackled Sabine on the subject of her 'relationship' with Canon Clough.

The au pair girl did not seem to think there was much to worry about. In fact, she was almost amused by her employer's seriousness. 'He buys me Babycham. He shows me nice places.'

'But you have been to his house too?'

'I do his ironing.'

'I see. You have plenty of time to do *his* ironing while we have a Matterhorn piling up here.'

'He has no one to help him. So I do it. Chris gives me money.'

'Chris? You call him *Chris*?'

'He likes it. He says it makes him feel young again.'

'Don't we pay you enough?'

'It is good to have more. I would like to buy some more clothes. Some friends want to see the Rolling Stones in London. I hope I go.'

'We'd need to talk about that.'

'Chris says he can pay.'

'He's not thinking of coming too?'

Sabine giggled. 'No. He is too old. I know he is old. Do not worry.'

'And he hasn't made any suggestions or asked you to do anything you don't want to do?'

'No. He just watches me.'

'While you do the ironing?'

'Of course.'

'Really? Isn't that boring for him?'

'I make it interesting.'

'I'd like to know how ironing can become interesting.'

'I wear my underwear.'

'And nothing else?'

'It is hot. He likes it and I do not mind. I think it is funny.'

'And does Canon Clough do anything while you are ironing?'

'He tells me not to look. Then he goes to the bathroom. I finish my ironing. Then he pays me one pound. It's good.'

'No, Sabine, it is not good.'

'What is wrong? You think he should pay more?'

A redbrick building that looked not unlike a Victorian school, Bedford Prison was opened in 1801 by the penal reformer John Howard. Alfred Rouse, responsible for the famous blazing-car murder, had been an inmate before being hung there in 1931, as had the A6 killer James Hanratty. There was little likelihood that the Reverend Kevin Warner would meet the same fate, but his sullen features, unshaven appearance and prison uniform made any idea that he had once been a clerk in holy orders seem improbable.

Sidney sat with him in the visiting-room in the presence of a guard. He asked the prisoner how well he knew Trevor Paine, whether he had been at the school at the time of the suicide of Luke Barnes and if he remembered Marcus Pearson.

'Trevor certainly administered a good beating, but Luke Barnes encouraged him.'

'You are saying that the boy wanted to be punished?'

'He kept offending. He knew the consequences.'

'You don't think he was picked on?'

'Sometimes boys are complicit in these matters, Canon Chambers. Perhaps Barnes sought the attention?'

'I don't see how you can know that.'

'Most boys find ways to avoid it if they want.'

'I'm not sure that they should be expected to do so. Were you responsible for similar punishments?'

'I was asked to discipline the boys.'

'Asked? You didn't choose?'

'It was part of my job.'

'And did you enjoy it?'

'That's not the point.'

'But did you?'

'I don't see why I should answer that question. I was doing my duty. If there were what you might call ancillary benefits . . .'

'Such as pleasure . . .'

'Then that's all well and good.'

'I think it's neither,' Sidney replied.

After a moment of silence, Kevin Warner began to confess. 'I prefer something gentler if you must know.'

'And did you find that at Millingham?'

'It doesn't do that much harm.'

'It depends on who you talk to. What might be a passing moment in an evening, a day, a week or a month to a teacher can damage a boy for a lifetime.'

'It happened to me when I was at school.'

'And are you telling me that it hasn't affected you?'

'It can be quite loving.'

'Not if the boys are under the age of consent and it is against their will.'

'They knew what they were going along with, Canon Chambers.'

'I am not sure they had much choice. Perhaps they consented for fear of something worse.'

'I don't think that was ever the case. They weren't threatened.'

Sidney tried to contain his anger. This was a man who had made the erroneous and dangerous assumption that repetition normalised abuse. 'I find that hard to believe. Why did Luke Barnes kill himself?'

'I imagine someone found out.'

'Or perhaps he thought that no matter what he did or who he told no one would do anything about it.'

'Any father who had been to the school would have believed him.'

'Only they wouldn't have done anything about it. That's the problem. It "never did them any harm". Is that what you are saying?'

'It is not for me to say anything. I'm here. I'm enduring my punishment.'

'And you feel no remorse?'

'I am what I am, Canon Chambers.'

'What about Luke's younger brother: Adam?'

'I don't remember him.'

'Or Marcus Pearson?'

'The pretty one? Oh, we all remember him.' Kevin Warner smiled. 'He was a very naughty boy. Played right along . . .'

'Did he really?'

'Then he stopped. I think Matron had her eye on him. As soon as he hit puberty she was all over him. There are always some that are lost to us.'

Sidney was appalled. He did not know what to say. 'Don't you have any regrets?'

'I'm sorry I was caught.'

'Is that all?'

'As I have already said, what I did was loving . . .'

'It was exploitation.'

'That is not how I see it.'

Sidney persisted. 'Trevor Paine caned boys until they bled. There is evidence.'

'Pain can be a pleasure – for both parties.'

'These boys were abused. Can you not see that?'

'And can you not understand why these things happen, Canon Chambers? There is a history, a tradition even, in this behaviour.'

'Then it's one that should stop.'

'You didn't have it at your school?'

'I knew it went on.'

'Perhaps you weren't pretty enough . . .'

'I was lucky.'

'It depends what you mean by luck. Some boys enjoy it.'

'They are too young to know, and you should be too responsible to exploit them.'

'It's easy enough for you to preach about it.'

'And it should be morally obvious enough to observe. You have a duty of care to young people in your charge. People like Luke Barnes . . .'

'That boy had so many other problems.'

'So it can hardly have helped when you all made the situation worse.'

'You can't blame us.'

'I can, as a matter of fact, and I'm going to continue to do so until this matter is resolved.'

'Some things are best kept private.'

'This isn't one of them.'

'I can't understand why so many people today want everything out in the open.'

'Because they can't trust what is hidden.'

'There's no need to make such a fuss about it all.'

'There's every need,' said Sidney.

He had never felt such violence towards a man. What made it worse was that this was a man of the cloth. Kevin Warner had abandoned morality. What would it take to make him realise what he had done? Were some people beyond redemption?

No matter how understanding people thought he was,

Sidney was determined to show that forgiveness had its limits. Mercy had to be earned. If it was not, then only judgement remained.

On 27th July, Geordie Keating was in an exceptionally good mood, having watched England beat Portugal 2–1 the previous day to reach the World Cup final. He was looking forward, he said, to teasing Hildegard about the thrashing West Germany were going to receive. Sidney then reminded him that her family originally came from Leipzig, now in the GDR, and that his wife was likely to be neutral in the matter since she took very little interest in football.

He had come down to Cambridge to join his friend in the Eagle. Once the two men had settled in the RAF bar with their pints, Keating cut to the chase. 'Luke Barnes gassed himself,' he announced as he handed over the file. 'At home. In his mother's kitchen. Not very nice for her.'

'Or anyone else.' Sidney opened the manila folder. 'If his brother had anything to do with the explosion in the chemistry labs, caused by a surfeit of gas, it might be considered poetic justice.'

'Gives it a bit of symmetry. You are arguing that this was an act of revenge rather than an elaborate prank?'

'I suppose the death of Luke Barnes really was suicide?'

The inspector made one of his exasperated noises that Sidney always took to be theatrical rather than genuine. 'Don't start. He wasn't drugged beforehand, it wasn't staged, it happened at home, and there were no other marks on his body.'

'But it should be motive enough for the explosion.'

'And time for you to question the person responsible.'

'I had better go back to see the mother. I have had a sense of dread about this ever since Prize Day.'

'Adam Barnes was playing the piano at the time . . .'

'But we know that does not really matter. He could have set the gas going hours before, either with or without Pearson.'

'I'm sorry, Sidney.'

'What for?'

'I know he's Hildegard's protégé.'

'That gives him no protection.'

'Will you warn her?'

'I'll try to find a way of explaining it all.'

Sidney was delayed by his normal duties but found it hard to immerse himself in congregational concerns that were less than life-threatening. He tried not to intervene in a dispute between a mother and daughter and legislate over the length of the fifteen-year-old's mini-skirt; he extended his sympathy to a wife who had found a note in her husband's diary suggesting that he might be meeting another woman; and he felt sorry for some-one who was so lonely she said that she felt like a Christmas tree that had been left out in February: half dead and too late for anyone to do anything about it.

Sidney could hear Adam practising his Dvořák piece when he arrived. He spoke to the boy's mother by the dovecote. 'It must be hard for you, Mrs Barnes – to still be here, in this house where it all happened.'

'I've kept Luke's room as it was. I haven't changed anything. Just made the bed. Washed and ironed his clothes. Put them back. Sometimes I go to his room and sit at his desk. I try to imagine what it might be like to be him.'

'I wondered why your son Adam was still at the school?'

'He said it was what he knew. I don't know if he was being brave or not. I'm not sure how many friends he has. He doesn't go out much. He enjoys his music, though. And he likes your wife. She's been good to him. He needs someone other than me to stick up for him.'

'I think she would do anything for her pupils. Is Adam at home? I thought that might have been him playing the piano just now.'

'He'll be up in his room. I don't know what he's doing. Reading probably. He likes *The Lord of the Rings*.'

Sidney climbed the stairs. He felt anxious and thought of Anna. Was this what having a teenager was going to be like in ten years' time: the nervous confrontation with a closed door?

Adam Barnes was drawing a fossil and had a half-finished packet of Toffos on his desk to keep him going. The room looked out on to the dovecote. The boy could watch his mother from here, Sidney thought, and always see that she was safe. He was suddenly touched by how much the boy cared for and looked after her.

(He thought of little Anna; how she watched him as he drove the car, as he carved the Sunday roast, as he lifted her high above his head. '*Careful, Daddy.*')

There were a few photographs of past holidays, but none containing any images of Adam's father. Sidney asked again about the explosion at the school.

'It doesn't matter, does it? Anyone could have done it. We all hated Paine. That's what did for my brother Luke. He couldn't stand it any more.'

'Mr Paine was bullying him?'

'And Rev Kev. They took it in turns; found excuses to beat him.'

'Even when he was in the sixth form?'

'I think it was different then. Luke didn't like to talk about it. I knew something was wrong. He wasn't being hit. But they gave him money, I think, special privileges. They let him drink in their rooms. I know that much. Then things happened, although I don't like to imagine them.'

'You think the teachers did things with your brother that were against his will?'

'They said that if he told anyone anything then he'd die before he was thirty. Turns out they were right. But by the time he killed himself he didn't have much will left. They got him drunk. They made him feel bad about himself.'

'So how much did he tell you?'

'Only that I was lucky to be in a different house. And that if any teacher hit me or did anything I didn't like then I was to tell him and he could get it stopped.'

'So he had some level of power over his persecutors?'

'He would have hated to use it.'

'Did he leave you a note?'

'He didn't need to. I was the one that found him.' Adam Barnes would not meet Sidney's eye. 'I called my dad. He's the doctor. I knew I had to protect Mum. But in the end, she reached us first. I think she guessed what had happened. Somehow. I don't know.'

'Did anyone from the school say they were sorry?'

'Pearson. He showed me something Luke had carved into his desk. *Mors potius macula.*'

'Death rather than disgrace,' Sidney translated. 'Do you think that message was meant for everyone?'

334

'I don't know.'

'What were the last words your brother said to you?'

'"Have you got rugger this afternoon?" I think he wanted to check I wouldn't be home.'

'Apart from that . . .'

'"If anything happens to me, I want you to kill those bastards."'

'He assumed you would know who he meant?'

'Mr Paine, Rev Kev.'

'But Rev Kev's in prison. Did you therefore try and kill Mr Paine?'

Adam Barnes thought for a moment and then answered simply, 'What would happen if I said that I did? Is revenge forgivable?'

It was almost two hours later when Sidney began to wend his way home through the unhurried splendour of an English summer afternoon. The atmosphere was at odds with his feelings. He was going to have to persuade the school to let Marcus Pearson back after retracting a false confession. He would have to ensure that there was a police inquiry into Trevor Paine's behaviour (and any other members of staff who had abused their position of trust); and, at the same time, he would try to prevent the punishment of Adam Barnes. If the boy was to have any chance of securing a good reference for university then he would need an unblemished school record.

Sidney walked back into his home, longing to see his daughter and appreciate her uncomplicated innocence and unquestioning love. He called her name and Hildegard answered as she came from the kitchen.

'She's swimming.'

'Is that all right? Sabine can swim, can't she?'

'I decided they both needed to calm down. We all do.'

'Why? What has happened?'

Over a pot of tea, and after Sidney had told his wife all about Adam Barnes ('Are you sure? Adam?' before checking her pupil would be given a sympathetic hearing), Hildegard explained that Christopher Clough was in hospital. It was not serious, but he had been wounded in a domestic incident.

'Give me the details.'

'Sabine was doing the ironing.'

'Here?'

'No. At Canon Clough's. She was not fully dressed; she was only wearing her panties.'

'What? Or, perhaps more to the point, why?'

'He offered her more money if she took her top off. She was just finishing what she was doing when things went wrong. I don't think I need to explain . . .'

'You do.'

'Canon Clough found he could no longer control himself. He had promised that he didn't need to touch her, that looking was enough, but this was a lie. I could have told her it would end this way. Of course, the man wanted more. Luckily Sabine had just unplugged the iron when he made his move and she was able to defend herself.'

'With the iron?'

'Exactly. A very hot iron.'

'Is Cloughie all right?'

'Yes, but he is in hospital as I said. He has burns.'

'And where is Sabine now?'

'She said she was going to drop Anna off after swimming. Then she was meeting some friends for a drink.'

'To drown her sorrows?'

'I think she plans to celebrate. Her friends want to hear all about it. It's given everyone an idea of how to deal with their men when they misbehave. It's not just an iron that can be used in self-defence. Our homes are full of weapons: the carving knife, the meat cleaver, the axe for the wood, the rat poison, and that's before we move on to the bathroom, the electric fire, the sleeping pills, the medicine cabinet . . .'

'So are you telling me that the women of Ely are planning a series of outbreaks of domestic violence?'

'They might be. What are you going to do about it?'

'Be kinder to you.'

Millingham School had an elegiac feel when Sidney visited the next day. The empty cricket ground and abandoned swimming pool made it seem that summer had ended before its time. He looked out across the silent cricket pitch to the elms beyond and told the headmaster that Adam Barnes had left the Bunsen burners on in the science block as an act of revenge for his brother's suicide. Luke Barnes had been driven to his death after a sustained campaign of bullying, unnecessary punishment and sexual abuse suffered at the hands of the Reverend Kevin Warner and Trevor Paine. Other teachers may have been involved but further details of the case showed the school in an appalling light.

Sidney made his position clear. 'You do realise that reforms are essential? All this must be stamped out. There will be a police investigation.'

The headmaster tried to concentrate simply on the explosion. 'Barnes will admit to what he did?'

'I believe he will, but this is not really the issue.'

'It is to me. Prize Day was ruined.'

'Adam Barnes has suffered a very great deal. He may go on suffering. These events will stay with him for a long time,' Sidney continued. 'Forgiving him is the least we can do.'

'I am not sure about that. I don't want to show any weakness.'

'He is going to leave the school in any case. You can say that he has been expelled if you like. I only pray he will find a happier place to complete his studies.'

'We tried to do our best for him.'

'I am afraid that you did not. That is the point.'

After much forceful discussion the headmaster said that he would make amends. 'I will make sure that what Barnes has done doesn't count against him. Trevor Paine can take early retirement on health grounds.'

'That is not enough.'

'He will complain that it's the fault of "modern times".'

'It's considerably more significant than that and well you know it, Headmaster.'

'I do know. But it may be too late to change that particular sinner.'

'It's never too late to turn anyone away from a destructive path,' Sidney asserted, 'whether they are endangering their own life or the lives of others. Ethical positions exist outside time. I will talk to Trevor Paine again. So will the police. There is no excuse for his behaviour. He must understand what effect his actions have had even if he has to do so in prison. I owe that to all the boys who were placed in his care.'

'I'm sure that is the right thing to do.'

'It is the only thing to do.'

'We don't always know what's right at the time do we?' the headmaster said quietly. 'Sometimes you just have to hope for the best. One can't always rush to judgement.' He spoke like a man who had resigned but had forgotten to tell anyone. 'There are no absolutes.'

'I think there are,' said Sidney. 'Fairness, justice, toleration, support for the weak, care for those in need, truth and love. Surely those principles are no harder to follow in a school than anywhere else?'

'They shouldn't be. But the balance between discipline and freedom is often hard with the young.'

'And sometimes your staff let you down.'

'It's impossible to keep an eye on everything. You have to delegate responsibility. There are so many boys, all with differing needs. You have to help them find their own way without ruining them. It's different with one's own children. I try to keep mine at a tender distance. That way I do less damage.'

Sidney watched the headmaster's defeated face soften. His eyes travelled to the family photographs on his desk as the man went on. 'You never know whether you've got things right or not. By the time you've adjusted to one stage, they've moved on to another. In a school the first year is always the first year. They automatically renew themselves. You can give the same lessons every September and all the problems you have anticipated return. But in a family you have to keep adjusting as your children develop. They are always ahead of you.'

'You might be good at one stage and hopeless at the next.'

'You see some parents who are marvellous with the very

young and hopeless with teenagers. It can also be the other way round. It's easier with the children of other people. At a school they come and go. But your own sons and daughters are always with you. You worry constantly. The trick is to find out how much that concern is helpful and when to use it. So you keep re-evaluating the way you parent a child. You can never settle or be complacent. It's harder to do that in a school. Do you have children yourself?'

'A daughter. She's two and a half.'

'A lovely age. You should be all right until she's thirteen. Then it's hopeless. You have to let them reject you. Then you don't really get them back until they're married. But then they have children of their own and the whole process starts again.'

'Do you ever tire of all this?'

'Teaching? Children? Life? Which do you mean?' the head-master asked. 'I can't allow myself to tire. I've already run off the cliff. I just have to keep remembering not to look down.'

Inspector Keating decided to watch the World Cup final at Sidney's house. He needed peace away from a wife and three daughters who, he knew from past frustrating experience, would keep interrupting and ask daft questions about the game at all the wrong moments. He made it very clear on his arrival, carrying a brown carrier bag full of bottles of Newcastle Brown Ale, that he didn't want to talk about Millingham School if there was nothing that couldn't wait until Monday.

'All that money and privilege can't buy happiness, can it?' he asked, rhetorically, before holding up his hand and announcing: 'This afternoon is dedicated to football alone and that is all we shall discuss.'

His words were clearly directed to Hildegard and Sabine, who were busy folding the laundry. All hope of further uninterrupted viewing was, however, kiboshed by the fact that, with England 2–1 up and nearly home, the doorbell rang.

'Who on earth can that be?' Keating asked. 'It's the middle of the bloody game.'

It was Marcus Pearson. Sidney closed the door on the match and showed the boy into his study. 'You knew it was Adam Barnes all along, didn't you?' he asked. 'Did he tell you he was going to do it?'

'I guessed. But I don't snitch. I thought if I confessed then Adam would get away with it. I knew my parents could put the pressure on to get me back in if I wanted and then I decided I didn't want to do that anyway. So it didn't matter what I did. I just wanted Adam to get away with it after what happened to his brother.'

'So you took the blame for the explosion.'

'It was the right thing to do. Both for Adam and for his mum. You couldn't have her losing both children. He might have gone to prison or borstal or something. His dad left too. He doesn't have parents like mine. They can get me off anything.'

'I wouldn't rely on that.'

'Don't worry. I won't when I'm older. But at school . . .'

'Millingham have said that they will take you back? Your parents have complained.'

'I bet they have. But I don't want to return to a place that does those kinds of things.'

'Perhaps one day.'

'I don't think so, Canon Chambers. Some things can never be forgiven.'

'I despair that this may be true. Do you have any other plans?'

'My godfather's in London. He's thinking of making a film about a school like mine. What could happen if some of the pupils fight back. I told him I had an idea. He wants to talk to me. So we'll see. Then I might go to art college and study photography. Something like that.'

Marcus Pearson had just left when Germany scored. If there was no other goal then there would be extra time. They all settled down in front of the small grey screen. Keating asked everyone to maintain absolute silence until the game ended.

'You see, ladies, football is the only thing I'm really passionate about,' he explained as he opened another bottle of beer.

Sabine muttered that before she came to Ely she didn't think the English had any passions; now she was not so sure. It seemed that English men cared only about two things: football and sex. Hildegard told her that if she started with that assumption then she wouldn't go far wrong.

'Would anyone like another drink?' Sidney whispered and Keating waved a warning hand to silence him. Geoff Hurst broke clear.

'Goal! Bloody hell! Bar! No! Crossed the line! Linesman. Is it a goal or not? Sidney!'

'I don't think . . .'

'It is! Crossed the line! Goal! Three – two.'

'And that's the next thing to explain to you,' Hildegard smiled as she took Sabine into the kitchen to bring in the ham and pickle sandwiches. 'You have to understand all about

English men and their love of beer. It is a bit like German men but, in important ways, it is also very different.'

'And what are those ways?' Sabine asked. 'Perhaps we should watch the end of the football first?'

'There is no end to the football,' Hildegard answered. 'We might as well make a start on the ironing . . .'

Florence

I T WAS ONE OF those changeable London days when it was possible to experience all four seasons between dawn and dusk. It began cold and warmed slowly before a light rain fell on to leaves that were just beginning to take on their autumn hue. Sidney was walking through the National Gallery with Amanda. He liked seeing his friend at her place of work. She was at her most serious there, unembarrassed by the professional dedication that she sometimes had to disguise in social situations where the idea of a woman who worked full time was seen as both an anomaly and a threat.

The date was 7th September 1966, the first time they'd been alone together since Amanda's wedding in June. Sidney told her that he wanted to think more deeply about the relationship between art and religion and they stopped before the serene mathematical monumentality of Piero della Francesca's *Nativity*. Despite the studied calm, the scene was not intentionally beautiful. The five angels looked ordinary. The heads of the shepherds were worn away. The Christ child had outstretched arms and was calling to be picked up (rather than blissfully sleeping), while the bullock in the stable stared impassively out towards the viewer as if nothing unusual had happened. Sidney could preach about this, he decided; how the remarkable can exist beside the everyday; homely, unpretentious, accessible. One just had to seek it out.

'Why don't you come with me to Florence?' Amanda asked. 'I'm going in November.'

'That's a mad idea.'

'They are often the best, Sidney. I don't think you've ever visited, which is a black mark on your scorecard of culture. You will remember that Dr Johnson believed that "a man who has not been in Italy is always conscious of an inferiority, from his not having seen what it is expected a man should see".'

'But I have been there.'

'In wartime. I think that's different.'

'I certainly wouldn't want to repeat the experience.'

'You could bring Hildegard. And Anna. You know how the Italians love children.'

'She's a bit young.'

'Nonsense. I could show you all the sights. You could even give the Ely evangelicals a little anxiety by hinting that you might be going over to Rome.'

'It's true that Hildegard and I haven't had a proper holiday in a long time. I was a little distracted by local events over the summer.'

'At least in Italy there's less chance of the schoolboys blowing up their science block.'

'There still might be explosions, Amanda. I wouldn't want to get involved with the Mafia.'

'I would like to say that there's absolutely no chance of that. But knowing you . . .'

Sidney thought through the idea. 'I suppose that Hildegard

and I could stay with the English chaplain, Timothy Jeffers. We were at Westcott House together.'

'And I could take care of the flights; as a thank you for seeing me right with Henry.'

'I didn't do very much.'

'You kept the faith.'

'I just want what's best for you, Amanda.'

'Even if I don't know myself?'

'*Especially* when you don't know yourself.'

The trip was booked for two weeks in late October and early November. Amanda promised to organise a private tour of the Uffizi since she was due to talk to them about an exchange of loans with the National Gallery. A wealthy British collector, Sir William Etherington, together with his wife Victoria, would be joining them. They were, apparently, 'adorable': influential in the art world, charitable donors, and interested in meeting people unlike themselves. They might even come up with a bit of money if Ely ever launched an appeal for restoration.

'We're always needing repairs,' Sidney replied. 'It's an ancient building. Beauty is expensive to maintain.'

'Don't I know it?' said Amanda. 'You should see my hair-dressing bills. I hope you're looking forward to the trip. The weather may not be too good, that's the only thing.'

She advised the Chambers family to bring waterproofs and their autumn coats, and told Sidney that he could even wear his clerical cloak if he liked.

Her friend wasn't so sure. 'Do you think?'

'It makes you look almost medieval. And the Florentines like a bit of swagger. You'll fit in.'

'Is Henry coming?'

'No. He's never that keen to leave the estate. That's partly why I'm asking. I'll be lonely when I'm off duty and I'd like to be able to enjoy a little time off with the three of you. It will be good for my goddaughter to see some art. Get her started early. You will make sure she brings plenty of crayons and colouring paper? She could become the Artemisia Gentileschi of her generation.'

'She's still not three.'

'I've heard that some Japanese children start the violin at that age.'

'Well, we're not Japanese and I don't even know who Artemisia Gentileschi is.'

'She was one of the greatest Florentine painters of the seventeenth century and the first woman to be admitted into their Academy. Anna would be a worthy successor.'

'I think she's more interested in *The Magic Roundabout*. Will you be travelling with us?'

'I'll go ahead and get as much work as possible out of the way before you arrive. Then I'll be able to show you round. I only hope your chaplain's accommodation is comfortable. Are you sure you don't want me to sort out a hotel?'

'There's no need. Vicarage economy.'

'But you aren't a vicar any more, Sidney. You should travel in style.'

'I don't think that would create a good impression.'

'That depends upon who you are trying to impress.'

'I am fairly confident about my relationship with you, Amanda.'

'I wouldn't want you to take me for granted. And I don't

think you should spend too much time talking shop with a bound-to-be-tedious ex-pat clergyman who everyone in England has forgotten.'

'I imagine that, living in Florence, he might be glad if that is the case.'

'Perhaps so; but the city is small and even quite parochial when you get to know it. The Anglican Church isn't much cop in terms of architecture and English holidaymakers only get in contact if someone's died. If everything's going swimmingly they don't have any need for a priest and don't bother coming to church at all. Thinking about it, you need to be careful we don't end up like that in England.'

'I'll do my best.'

'I only hope you don't go looking for trouble as soon as you arrrive. I know what you're like.'

'I don't do it deliberately, Amanda. Sometimes trouble seeks me out.'

'Then I will protect you.'

'I hope the Lord will look after me.'

'Well, I'll be on hand if he's busy. I imagine he's got quite a lot on.'

'Yes, Amanda, I imagine he has.'

The Reverend Timothy Jeffers and his housekeeper, Francesca Tardelli, welcomed the Chambers family at Pisa airport. They were an odd couple: an extremely tall, thin and bespectacled English priest in his mid-thirties and a dark-haired girl in her early twenties with sunglasses, a sleeveless black dress, long gloves and a fur wrap. Tim made the necessary introductions and ushered everyone out of the airport and into the back seat of a battered cream-coloured Fiat 1500. He couldn't drive himself (hence the presence of Francesca) but still had to sit in the front as his legs were too long to be accommodated elsewhere, and he communicated with his housekeeper in a mixture of broken Italian and simplified English that gave the impression he couldn't speak either language properly.

It was quite a squash with the luggage, and they drove with the windows open as Francesca smoked Nazionali cigarettes throughout the journey. It was a muggy afternoon that threatened rain without ever producing any. Tim thought there would be a storm that night.

They passed women selling the last of the watermelons by the roadside and then, as they approached the town, a Communist rally with red flags flying and students handing out the newspaper *l'Unità*. Tim told them that the country, unlike Francesca's driving, was veering to the left, and that they should really have a quick stop at the Leaning Tower. Anna asked when it was going to fall over before announcing: 'I feel sick.'

Francesca assured the company that she would go very fast and they would be home in under an hour, but the speed of her driving did little to alleviate any of her passengers' fears. She used her horn aggressively at traffic lights, overtook on corners, and shouted '*stronzo*' at anyone who blocked her path.

Timothy Jeffers was serene throughout, explaining that there was no danger of his housekeeper being stopped or given a speeding ticket because her brother was a policeman. Francesca pointed to the rosary over the rear-view mirror and turned round to the back to explain that she was protected by the Virgin Mary in heaven and her brother on earth. She had

349

never been in trouble with the authorities, and could drive in any manner she liked.

Sidney spoke little, desperately hoping that the driver would spare their lives and return her concentration to the road ahead. He wondered if Geordie Keating's sister was given such a free rein as a policeman's sibling. He very much doubted it.

They approached the city from the west, passing Pontedera, San Miniato and Empoli. As they drove past the city walls and through the Porta San Frediano, Sidney tried to imagine how such a small medieval city had come into existence. What was it about Florence that made it such a cradle of power and beauty? And had its elegance come at a price?

On arrival at the vicarage in the Via Maggio, they were shown to their quarters. Hildegard had been hoping for a 'room with a view' over the Arno, or even a small but perfect court-yard, but there was only a narrow alleyway out at the back, populated by bicycles, rubbish bins and scavenging cats. Timothy apologised and said that everyone hoped they would be able to enjoy a perfect vista, but such a silhouette was only possible from the Piazzale Michelangelo. He would take them as soon as they had unpacked.

It was only when they finally did so, looking out over the city in the last of the light, that the Chamberses felt they had arrived. The view was a perfect golden mean, with the foreground, the river and buildings all in proportion against the darkening sky. The focus was the dome of the cathedral with its herringbone brickwork, marble lantern and octagonal drum emerging from the grey and golden façades along the Lungarno delle Grazie, now reflected in the waters of the Arno.

Sidney carried Anna on his shoulders as they walked back towards the Ponte Vecchio and into the Piazza della Signoria, where she was given her first Italian chocolate *gelato*. Here they were exposed to the evening *passeggiata* for long enough to realise that they would never be as well dressed as the Italians. The locals paraded past the Neptune fountain arm in arm, in fur coats and tailored suits, handsome hats and snappy shoes, their conversation animated by extravagant gestures, their faces more transparent with emotion than an Anglo-Saxon could ever be, filled with extremes of laughter, grief, bravura, surprise, joy and sorrow.

The travelling party returned to the vicarage shortly before seven and Francesca cooked simple spaghetti with *ragù* as a starter and left after producing a tray of veal cutlets. She had an important date with her boyfriend, Umberto Camilleri, who was set to go far in the state police. Padre Tim said that the family had a long tradition of working in law enforcement. Francesca's father Nico was Head of Security at the Uffizi, her brother Giovanni was an officer with the Municipal Police, and her mother worked as a cook for the *carabinieri*. They could hardly be in safer hands.

The guests retired to their room as soon as it was polite to do so. They were tired and Sidney wanted to review his sermon for the morning.

'Are you glad we've come?' Hildegard whispered, anxious not to disturb their sleeping daughter.

'I am only happy if you are,' her husband replied. 'It's quite a thing to be here.'

'You have not told me anything about your time in Italy during the war,' Hildegard said. 'You do not have to. Only, if you want . . .'

'I was at Monte Cassino in 1944, and then Trieste. This is my first time without violence.'

'Does it feel far away, like another country? Does it look as if there had been no war?'

'Not quite; not yet. But when I am with you, I don't have to think about these things.'

'Then I am glad. I hope the holiday will be beautiful. We need beauty, I think.'

It was a brisk Sunday morning with a light rain. Timothy Jeffers apologised for the weather as they walked to St Mark's English Church for the family communion. He said that it had been bad for the past few days but he hoped it would improve. At least it might remind his guests of England.

The congregation numbered around thirty and consisted of twelve to fifteen regulars together with the last of the English tourists. Hildegard and Anna shared a pew with a woman called Lydia Huxley from the British Institute and an Anglophile doctor, Luigi Cannavaro.

Amanda had sent a message to say that she was not able to attend but would meet the family for lunch. 'I go to church enough when I'm at home and, delightful as your preaching is, Sidney, I have heard you many times before. I've booked a lovely restaurant in Santa Croce.'

Sidney preached on the idea of travel, journey and pilgrimage. He wanted to explain how people are always on the move, whether it is from home to the workplace or out to see friends. Each one of these forays was a pilgrimage of sorts, and we should be mindful wherever we go, aware that our travels are all part of a larger journey towards death.

He quoted from *The Pilgrim's Progress*, conscious that it might be foolish to attempt a reading of Dante in the poet's home town, and then worried that he was being overserious. The congregation was elderly and probably needed cheering up rather than being given a grim reminder of their inescapable mortality. But Sidney could not think of any jokes to lighten his message. Had his new status as archdeacon begun to reduce his sense of humour? Was he becoming more pompous? It would be good to see Amanda.

They met at the Ristorante Boccadama, in the Piazza Santa Croce. It was just about warm enough to eat outside, although only foreigners did so. Timothy Jeffers explained about the tradition of Italian Sunday; how church was followed by lunch in a restaurant and then the children were told to play outside 'so that the parents can go back home and get down to their weekly hanky-panky. In a few hours this square will be full of children.'

They were joined by Sir William and Lady Victoria Etherington, who were keen to demonstrate that they were such old hands in Florence that they might just as well have a part in governing it. They spoke in a loud anglicised Italian in order to dismiss a group of Neapolitan singers trying to earn a few lire with their rendition of a Puccini aria. They were negotiating a loan of a couple of paintings from their family collection at Rushworth Hall, in Shropshire, and tried to visit Italy at least twice a year. They had just come down from Fiesole and were thinking of buying 'the most divine' little farmstead.

Sir William was a tall, lugubrious man, dressed in a battered raincoat draped over a two-piece grey flannel suit and a spotted red bow-tie. His wife was pale, distinctly English, and easily bored: a petite woman in a navy twin-set, with a white blouse and matching silver accessories that were worn as a uniform, even on a Sunday. She had short dark hair, suspicious eyes, economic lipstick and sensible flat shoes. Sidney guessed that no one would ever think of calling her 'Vicky'.

Her husband continued the conversation with what was clearly a well-rehearsed story claiming that Jesus was, in fact, Italian: 'because he believed his mother was a virgin, he stayed at home until he was thirty, and his mother thought he was God'.

It was the Etherington's second visit to Italy that year. Their first had been to the Palio in Siena. 'All too cruel,' Victoria complained. 'They had to put one of the poor horses down. No one was even surprised.'

'The Italians have a rather more stoic attitude to death,' her husband observed. 'It must be the centuries of violence and corruption.'

'Some people do say that the country's charms are fatal . . .' said Amanda.

'Unlike your charms, Miss Kendall, which are eternal.'

'I'm flattered.'

'I am sure you know the saying: "*Un momento senza lei sembra come un'eternità.*"'

His wife interrupted. 'That's enough now, William.'

Sidney did not think he had ever met a man who was so much less charming than he thought he was. Hildegard had avoided the general discussion by concentrating on her daughter, keeping Anna's hunger in check by introducing her to grissini, but these were now finished, and it was time to order their meal. The adults had fettuccine Alfredo and Anna was given her first small Margherita pizza. Two armed policemen passed by eating ice creams, amused by this English group dining outside in weather they would consider to be inclement. Sidney noticed the guns in their holsters and imagined Anna asking how those men could fire a weapon and enjoy an ice cream at the same time.

After lunch they walked into the cloisters of Santa Croce. They were perfect, Sidney thought to himself, so naturally rhythmic and clear; as healing as music. He would learn from this: the need for balance and proportion in a life, how equilibrium consisted of matching the opposing forces of duty and pleasure, public and private, expectation and reality.

He took his daughter's hand and Amanda continued the conversation. Could there be such a thing as objective beauty, she asked, and could comparisons be made, for example, between Brunelleschi's architecture, Piero's paintings and the music of Bach? Perhaps the spaces between architectural columns were like rests in music.

They walked through a delicate colonnaded porch into the minimalist interior of the Pazzi Chapel. Amanda explained how proportion, symmetry, circle and square combined to create a mathematically lucid space.

'Strange how such beauty also contains the echo of so much Renaissance brutality,' Victoria Etherington observed.

'What do you mean?' Hildegard asked.

Sir William told her about the Pazzi Conspiracy and how the peaceful chapel in which they were standing had been built for a family who had tried to assassinate Lorenzo and Giuliano de' Medici. 'Leonardo even drew one of the conspirators after he had been hung.'

355

'He probably drew the body after it had been cut up as well,' Amanda added.

'Please,' Hildegard intervened. 'Not in front of Anna . . .'

'But what is it about blood and beauty, art and murder?' Sidney asked.

Sir William thought for a moment. 'Does one compensate for the other, perhaps? Too much beauty must be destroyed because it is precious and impossible; and, conversely, a surfeit of violence requires some kind of compensation.'

'The consolation of art,' said Amanda.

'Sometimes everything exists in contradiction: good and evil, black and white, beauty and ugliness. Think of Ancient Rome. It was the greatest civilisation the world has known and yet it was supported by slavery and injustice. The Italians have always known that beauty is a counterweight to horror.'

'At least beauty lasts longer,' Sidney answered. 'It outstays the violence: in paint and stone if not in flesh.'

Sir William stopped to take in the sight of a beautiful girl crossing the square and he began to recite from Lorenzo de' Medici on the fleeting beauty of youth:

> *'Quant'è bella giovinezza*
> *che si fugge tuttavia!*
> *Chi vuol esser lieto, sia:*
> *del doman non c'è certezza.'*

*   *   *

The next few days saw heavy skies over the Arno, and the city was washed with a low grey light. No one in the streets appeared to look up and most Florentines dressed in black, darting into bars and cafés during the showers of rain either for a morning *ristretto* or for the odd sharpener to lighten the mood. Anna was wearing a bright-blue PVC raincoat and they bought her a matching pair of waterproof boots that allowed her to stamp and dance in the puddles, scattering both pigeons and passers-by. Sidney brought out his cloak, and his wife joked that he looked less like a vicar and more like a vampire. In fact he bore a strange similarity to Christopher Lee.

'I'd prefer being him to Bela Lugosi.'

'As long as you don't expect me to be one of the Brides of Dracula.'

Anna pulled at her mother's coat. 'Who's Dracula?'

'Your father will explain.'

Sidney improvised. 'He's a very frightening man who hides in cloaks and comes out when no one is expecting him. Would you like to try?'

They began a new game of Anna running into Sidney's cloak, hiding in it, and then coming out to surprise people with the word 'Boo!' This activity had little sign of ending and both Amanda and the Etheringtons were keen to move on and take in some more art.

The Uffizi was closed to the public and a private tour had been arranged. They stopped at Botticelli's *Birth of Venus*. Picking up on the conversation of the previous day, Amanda reminded them that this idealised woman was herself the product of violence; arising from the sea after Zeus had killed her father, torn off his testicles and thrown them into the foam.

'I don't think we need to know every detail,' Sidney commented, anxious that Anna might ask further questions.

They moved on, in chronological order, past works by Uccello, Leonardo, Raphael and Filippo Lippi, through the Quattrocento and the Cinquecento, until they reached a painting by Artemisia Gentileschi: *Judith Slaying Holofernes*.

Amanda touched Sidney's arm. 'This is the artist I was telling you about: an example for Anna to follow.'

Her friend made his inspection. 'I thought it was a Caravaggio.'

'Not a bad guess. The *chiaroscuro* is not as pronounced, the flesh tones could have greater modelling, but there is power and a sense of the dramatic, don't you think?'

'It seems rather matter-of-fact for a murder scene,' Sidney replied. 'She might as well be killing a pig.'

'Perhaps she thought she was,' said Amanda. 'Gentileschi had a cold eye. She was raped by her tutor, Agostino Tassi.'

'More brutality . . .'

'Inescapable, I'm afraid.'

'Do you know that in Webster's plays,' Sir William began, speaking to no one in particular but assuming that all might listen, 'the Italians are always poisoning people: by the leaves of a book, the lips of a portrait, the pommel of a saddle, and an anointed helmet. It's a country of traitors, cheats, pimps, spies and murderers.'

'Is there something simpler we can see?' Hildegard asked. 'Without horror?'

One of Amanda's favourite works, Piero della Francesca's double portrait of Federico da Montefeltro and his wife Battista Sforza, painted in 1472, was not on public display but was being restored and she took them down to the conservation workshop to inspect it.

'This tells you all you need to know about vanity and beauty in the Renaissance,' she said. 'At first sight, it's all about volume and detail, poise and majesty.'

She pointed out the miniaturistic description of Sforza's jewels; the wrinkles, moles and blemishes on Federico's olive-coloured skin. 'As in all portraits of the duke, the viewer only sees his left profile; a sword blow earlier in his life had cost him his right eye and the bridge of his nose.'

'So he is only ever seen from the one side?'

'In portraiture. Although, curiously, the duke was praised for his aquiline nose. Piero stresses this characteristic to give him an eagle-like appearance, because that's the classical symbol of authority.'

'That's one way of explaining away a big nose,' Sir William laughed.

Amanda ignored him. 'There's also something particularly moving about the portrait of his wife, Battista. It was painted after she died of pneumonia. If you look carefully, you can see that her blanched features and expressionless face are rather like a death mask. The strong flow of light almost diminishes her features. She is already absent.'

Sidney walked around the painting. 'Extraordinary. Once you know something it changes the way in which you look at a work of art.'

'And so these two paintings,' Hildegard asked, 'are a memorial to their marriage?'

'They are both idealised portraits. Battista Sforza had nine children but here the white pearls symbolise purity and chastity, the blonde hair nobility. This is meant to be a portrait of a woman at her most magnificent. She is made permanent in paint. Her beauty will not fade, while her husband lives to fight another day; and he certainly battled on.'

She explained that there was a theory that Federico da Montefeltro had been behind the Pazzi conspiracy. He had six hundred troops waiting outside the city to move in as soon as the Medici brothers were killed. But they only managed to get rid of one of them, the crowd turned on them, and they bungled their escape, unable to get out of a room with a hidden latch.

'The hidden latch!' Hildegard smiled. 'It makes me think of one of your escapades, Sidney.'

'I am glad that the Church of England is a rather more peaceful institution. We tend not to go round murdering each other.'

'That is not entirely true,' Amanda interrupted, remembering the Patrick Harland murders that had taken place only four years previously.

'These are double-sided portraits, I think?' Hildegard asked, changing the subject. On the reverse of each painting were two paintings showing the protagonists 'in triumph'.

'This is a rare example of husband and wife being seen as partners in a joint endeavour to bring authority, art and culture to their subjects,' Amanda explained.

'Even if it takes murder to do so?' Sir William asked.

'As I think we have discussed, in the Renaissance death was considered a necessary correlative to beauty.'

'Morality is often something of an afterthought,' Sidney observed.

Amanda smiled. 'Although sometimes the rich find it easier to afford than the poor.'

'Which is why they should be better at it,' Sidney snapped. He was puzzled by his mood. Despite the beauty of his surroundings, he found it curiously disconcerting. The art was almost too good to be true. What was it saying about humanity, and how much was the Renaissance culpable of creating the myth of individual rather than collective achievement? Was this the beginning of the desire for individual fame and recognition that contradicted Christian humility and shared responsibility; licensing the modern notion of ambition and selfish aspiration?

On the way out they met the small, and rather sweaty, Head of Security, Nico Tardelli. Francesca's father greeted them all warmly. Sidney could not imagine how a man who looked as he did had produced such a beautiful daughter. It made him wonder all the more what her mother was like.

'Do the family know everyone?' he asked Timothy Jeffers.

'I think they run their own little mafia. As a result, Francesca's a very useful housekeeper to have.'

'And beautiful too.'

'I try not to think too much about that.'

'That must be quite difficult.'

'It isn't easy, Sidney, but I have to acknowledge both that she's out of my league and that she's too young. Furthermore, she already has a boyfriend.'

'And she's keen on him?'

'Actually, I don't think so.'

'There you are then.'

'Her family will have to approve whoever she ends up with. In the meantime I will probably find a delightfully stout Englishwoman with an eccentric hobby. Something like beagling.'

'Really, Tim. You don't have to live up to expectations. You can always surprise people.'

'I suppose you did.'

'And I'm very happy. A foreign wife has its advantages.'

'Oh, Sidney, don't tempt me.'

Over the next few days the temperature dropped, the wind gusted in fits, the rain set about the city, and the waters of the Arno steadily began to rise. The tour party visited the Michelangelo sculptures in the Medici Chapel, the Fra Angelico murals in San Marco, and climbed the four hundred and sixty-three steps into Brunelleschi's great cathedral dome, holding on to the handrails as staircase after staircase, their treads worn down at the centre by the footsteps of visitors over the centuries, opened up before them.

'When will we get there?' Anna asked, even though Sidney was carrying her up through the narrow passageways. 'I'm frightened.'

They passed chambers full of old statuary, angels and medallions. They listened to the wind, looked out through the roundels in the drum that showed they were already higher than the rooftops, and finally emerged beneath the lantern to see the city stretch out before them: Giotto's bell tower, the church of San Lorenzo with its similar dome, the Bargello, the Badia Fiorentina, and Santa Croce.

It was midday. The rain and wind picked up as church bells rang throughout the city and the family sheltered inside before the descent. Sidney reflected on the fact that they had found protection so close to danger; that at one moment a man could be inside, shielded from the elements, with half an orb of heaven above him; and yet, within a few paces, he could be on the precipice of suicide or murder.

Once they were back in the nave, they sat down to rest. Sidney looked at Domenico di Michelino's painting of Dante with the *Divina Commedia* and lit a candle for his family and his parishioners, thinking particularly of all those who had died that year. Hildegard and Anna took out their colouring pencils and began to copy a fresco of the English *condottiere* Sir John Hawkwood on horseback. As they did so, a couple stopped and smiled to observe the blonde hair and pale skin of both mother and daughter, quoting Pope Gregory: *non angli sed angeli*.

They were sheltered and at ease. One day they would look back on this moment as the happiest time of their holiday.

The flood arrived at three thirty on the Saturday morning when most people were asleep. By seven o'clock the situation was critical. The rising water had submerged the supporting arches of the Ponte Vecchio, spurting through leaks and crevices in the parapets flanking the river. Now at the full, the Arno carried a deluge of water, mud, rubbish and uprooted trees, pouring into the quarters of Bellariva and Gavinana, San Niccolò and Santa Croce: every part of the city that was not on a hill.

Electricity, gas, water and telephone supplies broke off in turn. The river poured into basements and swept into heating plants, releasing tanks of fuel oil that merged with the water to leave greasy black lines on the walls of buildings. By eight thirty the flood had reached the historical centre, overturning parked cars, ripping through the canvas-covered stalls in the flea market, and tore into the basement and conservation areas of the Uffizi Gallery.

Sidney, Hildegard and Anna awoke to find that the flood had carried away rubbish bins, empty crates and sections of doorways. Cars that had been parked in the streets below turned three hundred and sixty degrees and swirled off downstream, pulling down traffic signs in their wake. Couples kept to the sides of the road, holding on to walls for support against the torrent as they made their way towards higher ground.

On the south side, in the Oltrarno, water rushed past San Jacopo sopr'Arno, Palazzo Guicciardini, the Palazzo Pitti, Santo Spirito and Borgo San Frediano. The city had become an immense lake. The bridges connecting the two sides were impassable. Police in hooded raincoats directed people away from the danger areas without being able to predict when the waters would abate. A twelve-year-old boy gave his grandmother a piggyback. A No Through Road sign (*Permanente*) was torn from its holdings. Thousands of people were stranded on rooftops, waiting, often in vain, for rescue from helicopters. One elderly woman lost her grip and fell to her death.

In time, the floodwaters reached up to fifteen feet, into the arches of the cloisters in Santa Croce. The statue of Dante was still visible, the poet looking like he might be contemplating a swim on a chilly day. Sidney remembered the lines from *Inferno*:

> Dost thou not hear the pity of his plaint?
> Dost thou not see the death that combats him
> Beside that flood, where ocean has no vaunt?

He went to help Timothy Jeffers protect the English Church, working with a queue of elderly volunteers, pumping out water, putting up new flood boards, and moving valuables into the organ loft.

Amanda had made her way to the Uffizi.

Hildegard and Anna spent the day in the top of the vicarage, unable to go out, hardly daring to look out of the window and down to the flooded streets below. They played *Topfschlagen* to pass the time, in which Anna was blindfolded and given a wooden spoon in order to find a cooking pot hidden in the room. Then they sang German folk songs and nursery rhymes:

> *Hoppe hoppe Reiter*
> *wenn er fällt, dann schreit er,*
> *fällt er in den Teich,*
> *find't ihn keiner gleich.*

It only stopped raining towards evening, the flood abating in the night. Rescue and repair would have to wait until the following day when there was a chance to assess the wreckage, the first grey light revealing upturned cars, shattered buildings, breached bridges and roads blocked by uprooted trees. Buses and cars had been abandoned. The streets alongside the river were as muddy as a wartime battlefield.

Hundreds of artworks were damaged or destroyed: Paolo Uccello's *Creation and Fall* at Santa Maria Novella, Sandro Botticelli's *Saint Augustine* and Domenico Ghirlandaio's *Saint Jerome* at the Church of Ognissanti. The greatest loss was the *Crucifixion* by Giovanni Cimabue in the Santa Croce Museum.

Once Sidney had helped with the clean-up of St Mark's he made his way to the Uffizi to join Amanda, ferrying paintings to the Limonaia in the Boboli Gardens where they could dry out. The Piero double portrait they had seen only a few days before was mercifully intact. Sidney was instructed to put the paintings to one side ready for the conservator's inspection.

Sir William and Lady Victoria Etherington were doing their bit too, with Lydia Huxley from the British Institute and a number of ex-patriates Sidney remembered from the church service he had taken the previous Sunday. The operation was methodical and surprisingly well organised given the scale of the calamity. It was similar to the preparations for a funeral, Sidney thought. As long as people were given something specific to do they were calm.

By the end of the day Sidney was exhausted. When he finally arrived home for supper he noticed Francesca helping Tim remove his wellington boots. They were laughing at how stuck they were, and if they would ever come off.

He could hear Hildegard singing once more to their daughter upstairs:

> *'Hoppe hoppe, Reiter,*
> *wenn er fällt, dann schreit er;*
> *fällt er in den Sumpf,*
> *dann macht der Reiter . . . Plumps!'*

He had never paid much attention to this bedtime ritual but now he tried to follow the words, translating them as his wife sang.

> Bumpety bump, rider,
> If he falls, then he cries out;
> If he falls in a swamp
> The rider goes plop!

Sidney was silently grateful that none of them had fallen in the swamp. How fragile everything was.

After an early-morning inspection of his church, and satisfied that there was no further damage, the Reverend Tim Jeffers settled down to breakfast with his guests. It consisted of cornflakes (which his sister brought over in batches twice a year; the English vicar could no more do without them than he could live without Marmite), toast with apricot jam, and coffee with hot milk.

He read his newspaper, *Il Giorno*, and observed how one writer, Carlo Coccioli, had lost his faith as a result of the flood.

'Amazing how such a comparatively minor thing can set a man off course.'

'Perhaps it's not so minor for those who experience it.'

Francesca interrupted their breakfast. She knew it was a bad time but her father was at the door with some of his colleagues. Nico Tardelli was shown into the room with Inspector Luigi del Pirlo and two *carabinieri*. They were dressed in their traditional dark-blue uniforms with a red stripe down the side of the trousers and white shoulder belts. Signor Tardelli looked at Hildegard and Anna before asking the vicar if there was somewhere private the men could talk.

Sidney had seen that type of look before and was sure that something was afoot; he only hoped that it wasn't anything drastic. He presumed that his presence would not be required but was surprised to find the exact opposite. Indeed, he was the very purpose of the visit.

Nico Tardelli explained in halting English that Piero della Francesca's painting of Battista Sforza, one half of a pair with the portrait of her husband, Duke Federico da Montefeltro, had gone missing. They had checked the conservation workshop in the Uffizi, and the temporary holding room in the Limonaia, and it was nowhere to be found. Could Sidney remember where he had put the painting when he was helping with the clear-up operation?

The request was oratorically complex and Sidney spent some time wondering if he had assessed the situation correctly. At first he had thought Francesca's father was talking about somebody else. The conversation had such a deferential tone, repeating what an honour it was that such a distinguished English clergyman had come all this way to their city, so that the final implied accusation that Sidney had stolen a painting was buried in a flurry of flattery.

Once he had understood what had been said, Sidney felt that he had to adopt the same flowery rhetoric in his response. He was sorry that there appeared to have been a misunderstanding. He had last seen the painting the previous day and had placed it on one of the trestle tables, well away from the windows and in the driest part of the room, against the wall by the wooden door leading back up to the gallery. The painting of the duke was already there. He had then handled a series of different paintings for the next hour. When he had left he had taken only his cloak. Yes, he was sure. No, he could not be mistaken. Yes, he had put it beside the portrait of Federico da Montefeltro so that the pair remained together. No, he couldn't explain why he remembered these paintings and not the ones that came before or after, apart from the fact that Amanda had pointed them out to him as being particularly impressive works of art. No, not so impressive that he wanted to take them back to England or look at them in his own home.

The inspector asked if Sidney had ever been absent-minded;

if he was, perhaps, sometimes distracted by 'higher things'. He knew that priests found it difficult to concentrate on the routine of everyday life when they spent so much time pondering the mysteries of eternity. Perhaps if he looked around the vicarage, even in his room, then the painting might turn up (possibly inside his cloak?) and they could be on their way and no one need say anything more about it.

Sidney explained that he was happy to show them his cloak and for them to look at his room but he was sure that they would not find the painting because he had never removed it in the first place. He was sorry for their wasted journey. While he did not have the painting himself he would be pleased to assist in any way he could in securing its safe return.

The inspector was grateful and asked Sidney if he was sure of his story. He would not want there to be any confusion.

No, there could be no misunderstanding. Sidney could remember precisely what he had been doing.

Perhaps not precisely? The inspector announced that it was with the greatest regret his men would indeed have to search the vicarage. While they did so, he would appreciate it very much if Sidney accompanied him to the station.

Would that really be necessary?

The inspector was full of a thousand apologies and stated that yes, it was necessary.

For one wild moment Sidney thought of asking Hildegard to watch the men search the house. He did not want the *carabinieri* planting evidence and framing him for a crime he had not committed, but he acknowledged that this was, perhaps (but only perhaps), taking suspicion too far. At least Amanda was in town. Would she know what was going on? Almost certainly not.

The inspector took Sidney into a car where two more police were waiting. He remembered a joke that Tim had told him. Why do the *carabinieri* go round in pairs? So that one could read and the other could write. It hadn't been amusing in the first place, and it certainly didn't seem funny now.

The clean-up operation after the flood continued as the streets were cleared of overturned and mud-spattered cars, wardrobes, mattresses, bicycles, cash boxes, tables and chairs, books, diaries, manuscripts and photograph albums. Through the window of the police car Sidney saw a shopkeeper putting back his wooden flood boards just in case the waters came again. Paintings, stepladders and picture frames were stacked against walls; a television crew was interviewing a woman who appeared to have packed her most precious family possessions in a cardboard box. Perhaps she had the Piero della Francesca painting inside it? Sidney thought. It could be anywhere.

Once they were at the police station he was taken to an interview room and asked if he wanted a cup of coffee or a glass of water. He was then told to wait while a translator was summoned.

Back at the vicarage, Timothy explained to Hildegard that there were three different police forces at any one time in Florence: the *carabinieri*, who were a special branch of the army, the state police and the local police. It was all to do with safeguarding liberty. They counterbalanced each other and it was, he smiled sadly, the Italian way to live with contradiction. 'In the grand scheme of things it is nothing to worry about. The police need to be seen to be doing something to satisfy any protest from the Uffizi about incompetence and inefficiency.'

'Even if they demonstrate both.'

'I am sure they will release Sidney later today or tomorrow.'

'They might keep him overnight? He is innocent. They can't believe that a clergyman would steal a painting.'

'I'm afraid that they no longer have the respect they once had for the Church. Some people think it is because the services are no longer in Latin. Everyone can now see how far priests fall short. But Francesca tells me that all will be well.'

'Her father did not seem so helpful.'

'He is different. He is in a position of authority.'

'I will ask Miss Kendall to talk to the director of the Uffizi. This has to stop.'

'I am not sure she will be of much help. You need to have a local on your side. That is why Francesca is such an advantage.'

Throughout the interchange Anna was confused, asking her mother, 'Where's Daddy? I want my daddy.' She went to look for his cloak in the bedroom wardrobe and followed the *carabinieri* round the house as they searched. One of them was kind enough to turn it into a game.

While she was preoccupied, Hildegard sought out Francesca in the kitchen, and asked if she could talk to her father.

'It is complicated. So many police.'

'But your brother is a policeman.'

'With the local force. They are different.'

'There are too many people; too many different organisations.'

'And none of them are good. People say it is because we have so much crime.'

'They are busy?'

'Perhaps if you make everyone a policeman then life is more

peaceful. But somehow we made a mistake. And now many of the policemen are criminals.'

'But not your family.'

'In my family we do nothing wrong. Your husband is a good man?'

'The best.'

'Then I will help him. I like Mr Chambers. He makes me smile.'

'I think you also have a boyfriend in the police force?'

'He is not so much. He takes me places. It is not serious.'

'And Padre Tim?' Hildegard asked, but before the housekeeper could divulge any further information about her employer they were interrupted by Anna running into the room in tears.

'Men won't let me play with Daddy's cloak. Where's Daddy?'

Once she had heard the news from Hildegard, Amanda telephoned the director of the Uffizi, convinced that Timothy Jeffers was hopeless, his housekeeper was corrupt, and that the situation was a fix. She would come over to see Alfredo Verga within an hour, and she didn't care if he had meetings, or that it was in the middle of a flood, or that he had a lot to do. The situation had to be resolved. There would be no deal on the exchange of paintings with the National Gallery and, indeed, no further relationship with them at all if necessary and she wasn't prepared to put up with her best friend's incarceration.

'Signora,' the director protested. 'I did not arrest him personally.'

'But you must have agreed to it.'

'It is not my business to agree or disagree. The *carabinieri* told me that your friend was acting suspiciously. He had a large cloak.'

'*They* have large cloaks too. And those stupid feathered hats.'

'You should not worry, Miss Kendall. No charges have been made. They only want to question your friend.'

'I don't trust them. They weren't even in the room at the time! You must have told them something.'

'It is not my job to go into details. Mr Tardelli assures me . . .'

'Mr Tardelli! Is there no escaping that family? I will be with you imminently and I will want answers.'

'I cannot promise to be available.'

'Don't you dare even presume that you can avoid me!' Amanda shouted, her voice breaking with anger. 'I will find you wherever you are.'

She picked up her handbag and was just about to leave her hotel when she was delayed by the Etheringtons. They wanted to know if there was anything they could do to help in this very unfortunate situation but asked in a tone that, although just the right side of sympathetic, suggested they would rather not be involved. Instead they seemed keen to extract any gossip and leave as soon as it could be considered polite.

'What evidence do they have against Sidney?' Sir William asked.

'None as far as I can see.' Amanda controlled her temper, but only just.

His wife wanted the details. 'He was in the room while we were conveying paintings to the Limonaia. Do you know if they said anything about his cloak?'

'Yes. They seem to have fixed on that very object. I've always hated it. It is the worst of Sidney's affectations. Sometimes I think he wears it just to annoy me.'

'I imagine they think that's where he hid the painting.'

'But he didn't.'

'Not even by mistake? He seems very absent-minded.'

Amanda adjusted her headscarf in the mirror and began to put on her gloves. 'He isn't at all. That too is one of his stupid mannerisms. At least this might all be a lesson to him.'

'He didn't strike us as an art-lover,' Lady Victoria continued before her husband added: 'One couldn't call him a connoisseur.'

'He isn't,' Amanda answered testily. 'That's the point. What would he do with the painting anyway? He wouldn't have a clue how to sell it.'

'But I suppose he might know someone who does. With his contacts – he must know quite a few people after all his investigations.'

'He does,' Sidney's best friend replied. 'Which is why he is so clear about the differences between right and wrong; good behaviour and bad.'

Hildegard tried to calm her anxiety by taking Anna to the antique carousel in Piazza della Repubblica and the children's museum in the Palazzo Vecchio. Francesca's mother had also offered to teach them how to make pasta. It was important to keep active, even if Anna found the excursions tiring and kept complaining that she was either too hot or feeling cold. The solution, her mother found, was to keep stopping either for ice cream or hot chocolate. It was an expensive way of going about things but it was preferable to being cooped up at the vicarage with nothing but worry.

Meanwhile Sidney was questioned by Inspector Luigi del Pirlo in the offices of the *carabinieri* in the Pitti Palace. Lydia Huxley from the British Institute acted as translator.

The inspector asked why Sidney was in Florence, how much he knew about painting, and why anyone would want to remove the portrait of Battista Sforza.

'I didn't take any painting.'

'You were seen with it.'

'That is true.'

'Do you know where it is?'

'Of course not.'

'Did you like it?'

Sidney was now distinctly bolshie. 'I admired it. But I don't need such a painting. I don't want one. Why would I steal it?'

'That is what we need to decide.'

'The whole situation is ridiculous.'

'Life is absurd. You were wearing a cloak.'

'I don't think that is a crime.'

'Are you a Communist?'

'No, of course not. Why do you ask?'

Before marrying Hildegard Sidney had been arrested and interviewed by the Stasi on suspicion of being a spy and so to be accused now of something as minor as theft was petty in comparison, but the humiliation rankled. He remembered Leonard Graham telling him that Tolstoy believed time and patience were the strongest of all warriors. Although he was not sure that he agreed with the sentiment, he did not have much choice.

'Communism is very popular in Italy,' the inspector continued. 'They believe everything should be shared. They are like Christians without faith in God.'

'You are not a Communist yourself?' Sidney replied, wishing that Keating was with him.

'I am apolitical. I only have opinions about crime.'

'And could they, like the politics of certain people, sometimes be mistaken?'

'I'm the man asking the questions.'

'And am I allowed to ask any myself, Inspector del Pirlo?'

'If they are interesting. If, for example, they are about the case, and who might be responsible for the theft.'

'I am not so sure about that.'

'Then please, Canon Chambers, desist while I get on with my job.'

That evening Hildegard begged Francesca to intervene. The housekeeper agreed to talk to her brother. 'He knows people.'

'You mean he can stop this?'

'He may need money.'

'We don't have any money.'

'But your friend has.'

'Amanda?'

Francesca nodded.

'Does everyone know that?'

'Some people. She dresses well. She has talked to the director of the Uffizi. She makes an impression. It is easy to see she is rich.'

Hildegard began to realise what was going on. 'You mean this is a trick to make money? That Sidney's been framed knowing that Amanda will bail him out?'

'I don't know. In my country some people want money all the time. It's not so nice.'

'It's never nice.'

Francesca lit a cigarette. 'You will need cash,' she said.

The director was busy. No one could say where he was. Amanda knew that this was nonsense. She walked up the main marble staircase, through the galleries, along the Vasari Corridor, down the far stairs, past the conservation workshop and into a small library. On her last visit Alfredo Verga had unwisely confided that this was where he retreated in times of difficulty. He had said so almost flirtatiously. Amanda had resisted the opportunity of making an inappropriate assignation while remembering the location.

Not that she was expecting any special treatment now.

She spoke in Italian and surprised the director by immediately suggesting that the theft was an inside job masterminded by Nico Tardelli, who was now being protected by the *carabinieri* and, most likely, the machinations of his daughter.

'But anyone who knows about art would have taken both paintings. They are a pair. Signor Tardelli would not be so incompetent.'

'Perhaps it was an act of opportunism.'

'Then how can they all be in it together? If one man suddenly decided . . .'

'I don't know.'

'You see why it is more likely to be your friend? Is he really a priest?'

'Of course he is.'

'It would be a good disguise. A priest can go anywhere. He has the key to many doors and no one notices his movements.'

'He's not like that at all.'

'Then why is Canon Chambers being so evasive?'

'How do you know that is the case?'

'I am kept informed. That is all.'

'Keeping quiet is unlike him, I must say. Sidney is not short on opinion.'

'Then perhaps a little imprisonment might do him some good.'

'I can't let you talk like this. What have you done with the companion portrait of Federico da Montefeltro?'

'It is locked away. I made sure that we did so as soon as we discovered that Battista Sforza had been taken.'

'Can I see it?'

'This is not a good time; with all the damage . . .'

'Please, Alfredo, for old times' sake.'

'I cannot remember any old times. Certainly not any good ones.'

'That is ungallant.'

'I will make it up to you.'

They retraced their steps back along the corridor, through the conservation workshop and into a temperature-controlled storage facility protected from all elements. Entering the room was like pulling back the steel gates of an enlarged prison cell.

'It is here,' the director announced. 'I think someone has wrapped it in paper for extra protection. That is unusual.'

'Do you mind opening it?'

'I do not have anything to cut the string.'

'Then let me.' Amanda reached into her handbag, produced a pair of nail scissors, and unwrapped a decorated Florentine tray.

The director was horrified. 'What is this? The painting was here. I left it safely. Someone must have moved it.'

'Or taken it.'

'I will fetch Nico. This is impossible.'

'It seems not,' Amanda replied. 'And it would be even more impossible for my friend Sidney Chambers to have taken it considering the fact that he is already in police custody. Will you please telephone the *carabinieri* and drop your ridiculous charges?'

Alfredo Verga was having difficulty concentrating. 'That is not the most important thing.'

'It is for me.'

'We must get help.'

'*I* will help you and,' Amanda added, 'if you are lucky, Sidney will too. He is something of a detective. But first you need to secure his release.'

'I will tell the *carabinieri* that the companion piece has been stolen. After I have given them the facts you may be able to persuade them to release your friend. It will not be easy.'

'Why not?'

'They will have to be made to think it is their idea. It will be hard if they have not made another arrest. They do not like to be in a situation where there is no one to blame. Especially now. You will need *garbo*.'

'And what is that?'

'It is our way of making things right; pretending nothing bad has happened, that all this was meant to be. It is the way we make our troubles disappear.'

'And how will I do that?'

'I believe 100,000 lire is the usual sum.'

'What?'

'To be sure. My word is not enough.'

'You should be ashamed.'

'Those men are very badly paid.'

'That's because they are always on strike.'

'I wouldn't advise you to make a fight, Signora Kendall. Be very gracious, be very beautiful and give them money. What is it? About sixty of your pounds? It's not so much.'

'It's the principle I object to.'

'Oh, principles,' the director answered quickly. 'Only the rich can afford to have them.'

As he waited for developments to take their course, Sidney wondered how much Christian patience he was expected to demonstrate. Would a loss of temper help or hinder the situation? It was not that he was uncomfortable, and the *carabinieri* were perfectly polite, even nonchalant about his captivity, but the plain fact was that this was not how he had intended to spend his holiday. He knew that Hildegard had been bold the last time he had found himself in such a situation, but that had been in East Germany when she was on home turf. Amanda too could be pretty forthright, but how would her English temperament go down with the Italians, and would the Etheringtons help? Had they, for example, managed to contact the British Embassy and would an ambassador be of any use?

He was mightily relieved to hear Amanda's voice in the reception area of the police station. He also thought he could hear Francesca, and presumed that Hildegard had stayed at home in order to protect Anna from what was being described as *il più grande malinteso*.

380

Inspector del Pirlo was hardly going to handle any dirty money himself and so the appeal and the bribe went through one of the *carabinieri*, Marco Rossi, who told Amanda that he was thankful because they were all too busy dealing with the after-effects of the flood to worry about a harmless English priest. Twenty thousand families had lost their homes, fifteen thousand cars had been destroyed, and nearly all the small traders hit by the disaster were unlikely to be able to resume business. This was a far greater tragedy than the loss of a painting.

The inspector was, however, reluctant to take any personal responsibility for Sidney's freedom and announced that the accused would first have to be handed over to the state police for questioning in their offices near the Botanical Gardens. It was an inevitable moment of bureaucracy and so, after a protracted negotiation, Sidney and Amanda, accompanied by yet another couple of *carabinieri*, were asked to make their way to a different part of Florence, one that had previously been something of a Garden of Eden but now looked as if the Four Horsemen of the Apocalypse had ridden all over it.

This further level of red tape was an inconvenience likely to require additional unofficial payment but at least Francesca's boyfriend, Umberto Camilleri, worked for the state police. He asked Francesca if the prisoner was likely to steal anything else.

'He hasn't done anything wrong. He is a good man. Like Padre Tim.'

'Padre Tim. Why do you always talk about him?'

'I want you to look after his friend.'

'He should be with the local police.'

'We were sent to you.'

'By del Pirlo? I understand. He wants nothing to do with this any more. His nose is so clean he wipes it more often than his arse.'

'There's no need to be crude. Signor Chambers is a priest.'

'He won't understand.'

'He is a clever man.'

'Normally this would be complicated, *bellissima* . . .'

Francesca smiled. 'Umberto, please. We can have dinner.'

'Tonight?'

'Why not?'

And so it was that Umberto Camilleri organised Sidney's parole with Giovanni Tardelli of the Municipal Police in the Palazzo Vecchio.

Francesca's brother was as handsome as his sister. Sidney guessed that he was the only son in the family, the eldest, and the most favoured, and almost certainly keen on a quiet life. He could tell, as Giovanni spoke to his sibling, that the policeman was already asking if she might share some of the workload so that he could spend time with his friends. It was clear that the curfew he had been instructed to impose would be lightly implemented.

Hildegard held her husband tightly when he returned to the vicarage, and confessed how worried she had been. Sidney tried to laugh it all off, saying that he had known far greater scrapes in the past, but it was clear that he had been rattled by events. It was also not over yet. He still had Francesca's brother in attendance.

And there were other concerns. Anna was listless, perhaps even feverish, clinging to her little rabbit as she lay, half-awake and half-asleep, on the couch. Hildegard was worried that their daughter was sickening for something. 'It must be the damp and the cold.'

'Will she be all right?' Sidney asked.

'I think so. She's tired. I have been creating a lot of distractions.'

'I am sorry. Has she enjoyed them, do you think?'

'She likes the ice cream and the hot chocolate. And the Italians do love children. But it's not been easy.'

'We always think of Italy as hot and romantic, but here we are: wet and miserable.'

Anna's cheeks were flushed. Hildegard looked to her husband. 'I should carry her up to bed. Could you ask Tim, or Francesca, to call a doctor? It's best to be on the safe side.'

Sidney stood up. 'Of course. I'll do it now.'

'Signore.' The policeman smiled.

'Ah yes, Giovanni, you will have to come with me. Let me find Tim. And your sister too. *La bellissima* Francesca. We need a doctor. And, while we are waiting, I think we might just go and see the Etheringtons at their hotel.'

'What for?' Hildegard asked.

'It's a little idea I have. It won't take a minute . . .'

'But, Sidney . . .'

'Don't worry, my darling. It's on the way to the doctor.'

'You've just got home.'

'I'll be less than an hour. And I'll be back before he arrives. I promise.'

He kissed his wife, blew another to the sleeping Anna, and then he was gone.

*　　　*　　　*

Giovanni Tardelli was amused by his prisoner's desire to risk further trouble. First he drove to Luigi Cannavaro's practice and made sure that the doctor would be able to make a house call. Then he went to pick up Amanda from her hotel and finally they made their way to the Villa Tolomei. It was, at the very least, an excuse to show off his new car on the hairpin bends of the Via di Santa Maria a Marignolle.

His driving was even more terrifying than his sister's. He honked his horn and joked as he saw a group of colleagues travelling in the opposite direction. 'There was this peasant who lived on a narrow road up in the mountains,' he told Amanda. 'One day, he saw a carload of *carabinieri* driving backwards up the mountain. "Why are you driving backwards?" he asked. The men replied: "Because we're not sure we'll be able to turn around up ahead." Later, the peasant saw the *carabinieri* driving backwards down the same mountain. "How come you're still driving backwards?" the peasant asked. "Well," the driver replied, "we found a place to turn around."'

'Yes, that's very amusing,' Amanda observed unconvincingly and Giovanni repeated the punchline just in case she had not understood. '"*We found a place to turn around.*"'

She had opted for the back seat, anticipating the fearsome nature of the journey. 'Sidney,' she announced, somehow hoping that a conversation with her friend would allow the driver to concentrate on the road, 'this is an inside job, I am sure of it.'

The response from her friend was in archaic English. 'Exercise vigilance, Amanda. The conveyor of this mode of perambulation comprehends something of the language in which we confabulate.'

'There is no need to sound like Henry James. I am not saying anything he has not heard already.'

'Although it would perhaps be something of a blunder, albeit a minor one, to allow our companion to hazard any estimation of our investigative procedures. "*Cum vulpibus vulpinandum.*"'

'Are you enjoying this?' Amanda asked.

'On the contrary, given the circumstances in which we find ourselves, it behoves us to exercise the kind of caution of which our chauffeur is perhaps . . .'

'ATTENZIONE!' Amanda shouted as Giovanni narrowly missed a farmer with his donkey and cart.

'*Si figuri,*' the driver replied before accelerating round the next corner.

After only eight minutes of this hair-raising drive they arrived at the Villa Tolomei and were shown into a large reception room which looked out on to a formal but storm-damaged garden. Sir William was seated at a desk and was using the hotel stationery to write a letter to his son. 'He's at Eton. Clever chap. Chip off the old block, I'm proud to say.'

His wife was reading that morning's edition of *La Nazione*. 'We were just discussing your plight, Sidney. Such an unfortunate misunderstanding.'

'It could have happened to any of us,' Amanda replied, looking round and wondering if they were going to be offered something to drink.

'Any of us who were actually there,' said Sidney. 'Anything interesting in the news?'

'It's all flood, flood, flood. Nothing much about the Uffizi. The library was hit the worst. We tried to help there too, but the destruction was terrible. Complete chaos.'

'Isn't there an English paper?'

'We sometimes read the *Herald Tribune* but it's far too American. This helps with my Italian. I try to look at it every day. I think I may have told you that before. Keep my hand in, you know?'

Sir William signed off his letter and turned from his chair. 'It's fortunate that we left earlier, otherwise we might have found ourselves in a similar pickle.'

'Have you been back to the gallery?' Amanda asked.

'There were plenty of people around; no need for us to chip in and confuse things. Any sign of the painting?'

'Which one?' Sidney asked.

'Battista Sforza, of course. You don't mean that someone's filched the other one too?'

'We thought you knew,' Amanda explained. 'That's why Sidney's a free man. He can't possibly have stolen the second painting when he was in police custody.'

'No, I suppose not.'

'And I couldn't possibly have taken the first,' her friend complained quickly.

Sir William folded his letter and put it in an envelope. 'No sign of either painting, then?'

'None.'

'And the police don't have any ideas, Canon Chambers?'

'The police don't, no.'

'Have they roped you in to help yet?'

'My Italian is not what it might be.'

'Sidney's had quite enough of the police as it is. He's got his own man waiting outside even as we speak,' said Amanda. 'When are you off?'

'Tomorrow,' Sir William replied. 'It's a long drive.'

386

'I thought you flew.'

'We prefer the car. It makes you feel that you are still on the Grand Tour. You can enjoy the Alps and stop off with friends in the south of France.'

'We like to spend a couple of days in Paris too,' his wife added.

Amanda began to talk of her discussions with the Uffizi and of the loans she was trying to arrange. Had Sir William had any success in his negotiations for an exchange of paintings for Rushworth Hall?

'Not bad. Although the flood's put the kibosh on everything. Now all the Italians want is money.'

'Which is the one thing we don't have!' Lady Victoria laughed.

Before they left, Sidney asked the Etheringtons if they could recommend a good place to buy souvenirs. They were rather surprised by his request. Surely Amanda could advise?

'I was just wondering what kind of things you like to take back to England?'

'Nothing of any significance. Sometimes we toddle up to San Gimignano and buy some pottery.'

'I love traditional crafts.'

Lady Etherington cut in. 'And, of course, William's bringing back a few books he found in a junk shop. Sometimes the Italians don't know what they have and you can pick up all manner of treasures for just a few lire. We don't spend much. We live quite a modest life, you know.'

As they drove back into town they could see that the clear-up operation from the flood was still in evidence. An elderly man with a knitted bobble hat picked up a muddied Italian flag that had fallen into the street, put it in the boot of his car, and tried to start the engine. A blonde-haired girl in a pale raincoat smoked a cigarette as her *amoroso* tried to start up his motorbike. A small boy walked past with a rescued kitten.

Amanda was dropped off at her hotel, and Giovanni accompanied Sidney to the vicarage. The doctor had not arrived but was on his way. Francesca asked if everyone would like coffee, and Sidney thought that, while he was waiting, he might like a word with her too. Having met her brother he was pretty sure that he could trust the Tardelli family and that they were unlikely to be part of an international art conspiracy. But was he right to be suspicious about the Etheringtons?

Francesca was studying a newspaper report of the flood in *l'Unità*. The headline read: *Salvare Firenze!* Sidney asked if that was her paper of choice.

'It is Communist. For the young. And the workers. It was founded by Antonio Gramsci. Have you heard of him? My father reads it.'

'But not, perhaps, his boss?'

'No. He would take *Corriere della Sera* or *La Stampa*. In Florence the people with money and position read *La Nazione*.'

'Not *l'Unità*? You wouldn't, for example, find *l'Unità* in a hotel for English people?'

Francesca smiled. 'No. Why do you ask?'

'Because when I was in the Uffizi, Lady Etherington picked up a copy of *l'Unità*. Why would she do that if she wouldn't normally read such a paper?'

'Maybe, in the basement of the gallery, where the guards and security staff work, that is the only paper they have.' She passed the newspaper across. 'Do you want to have a look? I could translate?'

'That is kind. I'll just try to get the idea. I don't think I need a full translation.' Sidney thought for a moment. 'Do you think I could speak to your father again?'

'Perhaps you have seen our family too much, Canon Chambers. What do you want to know?'

'It's just a thought I have . . .'

Sidney looked through the copy of *l'Unità*. He could hardly understand a word but could tell from the headlines and the photographs that this was a far cry from *The Times*. The authorities were being blamed for the flood and the prime minister, Aldo Moro, was accused of irresponsibility. America's President Johnson was 'escalating' the war in Vietnam and Mao Tse-tung had presided over a rally of the Red Guard in Peking.

At last, Doctor Cannavaro arrived. He was a kindly, well-dressed man who, it turned out, had fought at Monte Cassino in the war. He and Sidney had been on opposite sides.

'So,' he smiled, 'we might have killed each other. Such a tragedy. So many lives lost. Stupid. Now we must forgive the past and become friends.' On discovering that Hildegard was German he told her how keen he was to make amends. 'We must all lead better lives.'

He climbed the stairs and sat quietly by Anna as she slept. He let the back of his hand rest on her forehead and felt her pulse. Then he stepped away to allow Hildegard to wake her. He did not want the little girl to be frightened by the face of a stranger. He asked for Francesca and issued instructions.

After his patient had been given some juice and told not to worry (this was a doctor), Luigi Cannavaro brought a carved golden angel out of his suit pocket. He told Anna that it would protect her, and that she would soon be well. He showed her his torch and asked her to open her mouth wide; then he let her look in his mouth too. He said that he had brought a special medicine, but it was one that could only be used by English girls. Was Anna English? Was she a girl? The medicine was special because it was pink. It didn't taste very nice so it needed to be mixed with something else. Something cold and delicious that would stop her feeling so hot. Could Anna think what that might be? She couldn't. The doctor felt her forehead once more and asked for a damp towel. Francesca returned to the room with medicine, a bowl and a spoon.

'Aha!' the doctor exclaimed. '*Gelato alla fragola.* You see, Anna, this medicine is so special it can only be used with strawberry ice cream. It does not work if you do not have the ice cream. Do you think you can eat a little? I know it may be hard . . .'

Anna nodded. Then she took her medicine.

It was fifteen minutes before the doctor rejoined Sidney downstairs. 'It is a fever and a sore throat. It will pass.'

'Thank you for coming,' said Sidney. 'I know there must be so many calls on your time.'

'It is the same for you.'

'But I am on holiday.'

'I do not think a priest ever has a holiday.'

'It is easier in Italy.'

'When the English come here they are always excited. The beauty is too much.' The doctor opened the door. 'Lady Etherington, she faints . . .'

'When was this?' Sidney asked.

'After shopping. She carried many, many bags. After she helped at the Uffizi. It was too much. She fell like a child.'

'Was she all right?'

'It was nothing. She needed water. People helped her a lot.'

'What happened to her shopping?' Sidney asked.

The doctor looked surprised that this should be considered more important than the health of an acquaintance, 'Her husband took it. Everything wrapped up. No problem. It is normal. Italia. The English. Too much. But Lady Etherington, she was better in five minutes.'

I bet she was, thought Sidney.

He was going to have to act fast. He persuaded Giovanni Tardelli that they had to return to the Villa Tolomei immediately. He also assured the surprised policeman that this time he could drive as dangerously as he liked provided they got there, Francesca explained, *il più rapidamente possibile*.

He asked the housekeeper to make up a little story for Hildegard. He had gone with Giovanni to the police station. It was a bureaucratic matter. He also told her to get on to her father, her boyfriend, and Amanda Kendall. In fact she could tell whoever she liked.

'And what if you are wrong?' Francesca asked.

Sidney was about to say that he was hardly ever wrong when he realised that there was no actual evidence for this; certainly not in Italy. 'Trust me,' he said as he climbed into the front seat of Giovanni's car.

They arrived at the Villa Tolomei just as the Etheringtons' Rover P5, with British number plates, was disappearing down the drive. He and Giovanni stopped outside the hotel gates and looked at each other without saying anything. Sidney nodded. Giovanni smiled and put his foot down.

The Etheringtons were heading north, and after leaving the Via di Santa Maria a Marignolle they swerved on to the Via Romana, and drove in heavy traffic past the Boboli Gardens, hooting the horn repeatedly, before turning left along Lungarno Guicciardini and making their way over the Arno at the Ponte alla Carraia. They knew they were being followed. Once they had crossed the river they accelerated through narrow side streets, empty of people, but still wet and muddied by the flood. Here their speeding attracted the attention of the *carabinieri*, a squad car soon joining in the chase up the Via del Moro, the Via Panzani, and past the church of Santa Maria Novella with Alberti's famous façade.

As they raced by the railway station, another car full of *carabinieri* joined the chase. The Etheringtons turned on to the Via Bolognese Nuova and drove through the university. They were making for the motorway but, just before they reached it, and having noticed the cars in pursuit, they changed their minds, swerving off to the right and backtracking down towards Fiesole.

Sidney remembered them talking about 'a divine little farmstead' when he had first met the couple, and presumed that it was empty: a possible hideaway if they could get rid of the police.

Giovanni was gesturing to the *carabinieri*. It was unclear whether he was asking them to overtake or to back off, but lights were blaring and sirens flashing. The Etheringtons turned off their headlights, swerved up a track and vanished.

Sidney asked Giovanni to pull over. The squad cars braked

just in time and there followed a confusion of shouting and gesticulation, blame and explanation.

Sidney ran back and found the turning they had missed. He shouted at everyone to return to their cars and follow the new road. They found the surface increasingly uneven, until the track ran out in front of a remote villa encircled by a few olive trees.

Sir William and his wife were still inside their car when Giovanni and Sidney approached. The English aristocrat was complaining that they should have left earlier. His wife was telling him to shut up. 'Don't tell them anything.'

'What's the point? They are going to search the car anyway.'

The *carabinieri* asked them to get out. Giovanni told the couple that Sidney would explain everything.

'He doesn't need to,' Lady Victoria replied.

Her husband made one last attempt at friendship. 'I thought we English were supposed to stick together.'

'Not in a case like this.'

'If you hadn't interfered . . .'

'You would have been discovered anyway. What were you going to do with the paintings?'

'What makes you think we have them?'

'We'll find them soon enough. But I don't understand why you've done this. You could hardly put them on display, and they're too famous to sell.'

'They were going to be for our own use: in our bedroom, if you must know. We've given so much to this country we thought we deserved a reward.'

'A reward? That's something many of us only look for in heaven.'

'I suppose you would know all about that.'

'Not yet, Sir William.'

The *carabinieri* unwrapped a Florentine tray and a box of books to reveal the two paintings and a series of volumes that had been quietly removed from the National Library. They showed them to Sidney and Giovanni, transferred them to their cars and made the necessary arrests.

The Etheringtons were surprisingly unconcerned.

'We'll just say it's been a misunderstanding,' Victoria explained. 'No one wants anything as dreary as a court case. The director of the Uffizi is a friend of ours. I'm sure he'll find a way to forgive us.'

Sidney was aghast. 'You mean you think you can get away with it?'

'As we have with everything in this country. Some people are born lucky; some people aren't. You know the saying: *E meglio nascere fortunati che ricchi*? Well, we are both fortunate *and* rich. And what does it matter? These paintings weren't on display. Who would miss them? We're not bad people. We give enough money to charity. It's only fair we're treated properly in exchange.'

Sidney was horrified. 'Treated properly?'

He turned to Giovanni, who affirmed this was the truth. Often people did tend to get away with things. The paintings would be returned and, as long as they were safe, everything else would be considered a nuisance. Why waste time on justice when everything was back to what it was? *Non svegliare il can che dorme.*

Lady Etherington translated: 'Let sleeping dogs lie.'

'I am not sure I am prepared to accept that,' said Sidney.

'It is the way of the world,' Sir William answered.

'Yes, but the world extends beyond the Alps in the north and Sicily in the south.'

'What do you mean?'

'There is always the International Criminal Police Organisation at Saint-Cloud in Paris,' Sidney explained. 'The head of Interpol happens to be a friend of Amanda's father.'

'How do they know we are here?'

'They don't. Yet. But Rushworth Hall is very well known, is it not? I presume you were planning to return home. If not, and this is your hideaway, then we know where that is too. Giovanni has disabled your car. We have time. Everything else is in the lap of the gods. *Fortunae cetera mando*, as the saying goes. I prefer Latin to Italian, don't you?'

Sidney and Giovanni returned to the vicarage in the Via Maggio at a more stately pace. They arrived to discover that Doctor Cannavaro had come back to check on his juvenile patient. He was pleased to report that the flush had left Anna's cheeks and that she would soon be as pale as an English rose once more.

Sidney thanked him. The doctor said he had done very little. 'Like you. I try to take away worry. I give reassurance.'

'And ice cream. Anna has learned to say "*gelato alla fragola*".'

'I hope she will return many times. One day perhaps she will see Italy as another home.'

'That would be delightful. I am also grateful for something else.'

'Lady Etherington?' the doctor asked.

'You knew something was wrong.'

'I thought she was pretending when she fainted. But to accuse her would not be gallant. I knew that you would understand if I said enough.'

Timothy Jeffers had gone to bed. Francesca had left a saucepan of minestrone on the hob, and there was bread, butter and cheese on the kitchen table with half a bottle of Chianti.

Hildegard lit a candle, served up the soup, and told her husband that he had a lot of explaining to do. He should not expect to get off lightly. At least there was only one day left in Florence and Anna was better. She couldn't wait to get home.

Sidney was still exhilarated by his adventure and unable to relax as he told his story, standing up and walking about as he ate. He had been shocked by the attitude of the Etheringtons. What made them think they were entitled to take whatever they wanted? He wondered if they thought their experience in Italy gave them an excuse. Perhaps, Sidney began to extemporise, the origins of selfishness and unbridled capitalism lay in the Renaissance? Should the Medicis be blamed for their banking system as much as they were praised for their artistic patronage? Didn't Dante convey usurers to a deeper place in hell than blasphemers, murderers and violent suicides unable to ward off the whipping winds and flaming fire?

'You think the Etheringtons should go to hell?' Hildegard asked.

'I know that's not very Christian.'

'Some people might say that it was exactly Christian.'

'I am not so sure about hell.'

'Are you equally uncertain about heaven?'

396

'I don't know. I am concentrating on earth alone at the moment. I can't stomach the fact that the rich have a different morality. They think they can buy immunity from justice by donating to charity.'

'At least they are doing something.'

'But not at any cost or sacrifice. Their lifestyle remains intact.'

'You expect the wealthy to make themselves poor?'

Sidney thought out loud. 'What would it be like if everyone was paid the same? How would it work and how much would everyone have to live on? What kind of houses would people live in and how much geographical space could be shared?'

'Have you been reading that Communist newspaper?' Hildegard asked.

'No. I think I've always felt like this. But there is something about being away from home. It makes you re-evaluate your thoughts. I don't think the wealthy do enough.'

'Be careful what you say, Sidney. Amanda has been kind to us; she has helped pay for this holiday.'

'Amanda is different.'

'She is still rich. It does not cost her very much to be a good person.'

'You mean that we can only be good when we have made a sacrifice of some kind?'

'Perhaps. A poor person, looking at us now, would think that we too are rich. Look at the cathedral you work in, Sidney. Do you think Jesus would be happy seeing you there?'

'I am not sure he would.'

'It is difficult. The building is wealthy but the people who built it were poor. I know you will say it is all for the greater glory. *Soli Deo gloria.* As our lives should be.'

'Indeed, Hildegard,' Sidney replied. 'As our lives should be.'

The next morning, on their last full day in Florence, Amanda insisted that everyone came for lunch in one of her favourite restaurants. As the Chambers family set out, they could see that the city was returning to normal; a party of schoolchildren were being taken on a nature trail round the Boboli Gardens, a group of nuns were returning from Mass (one of them was even eating an orange), and a man in a large fur-collared coat waited outside the Pitti Palace for the arrival of a woman who could only be his mistress.

They crossed the river and found themselves in a small, dark trattoria hosted by a weighty proprietor who was happy to display charm to his diners and authoritarianism to his staff. It was not an expensive or pretentious meal, but it was comforting and it felt right: tortellini *in brodo*, chicken cacciatore, and zabaglione to follow.

Sidney started a mock grissini fight with his daughter, and Amanda suggested that next time they should all meet in Rome. She would make sure Henry joined them. They could make it a long weekend in the spring, when there was no danger of any flooding.

'Like this poor battered stick of grissini, we have survived,' Sidney said, 'in order to fight another day.'

'Let there be no more fighting,' Hildegard asked.

'And no more POLICEMEN!' Anna announced, striking down Sidney's breadstick.

The waiter was ready to take their order. '*Gelato alla fragola,*'

Anna called out before asking her mother: 'Can we paint the man on the horse again?'

Amanda leaned over to Sidney. 'We'll make an artist of her yet. Perhaps one day she'll come back and see those Piero portraits and she'll remember all this.'

'It would have been odd if the Etheringtons had only got away with one of them, don't you think?'

Amanda put down her menu. 'One is worth nothing without the other.'

Sidney turned to his wife but she was quick to prevent further speech. 'No sermon please, my darling.'

'I was about to be very nice to you.'

'You are always good to me.'

'We are our own double portrait.'

After the meal, Sidney and Hildegard walked back through the city arm in arm. Amanda showed Anna the shop windows and asked her goddaughter what she wanted for Christmas. They passed the *duomo* with its gracefully magisterial cupola, and Sidney said that it reminded him of the photograph of St Paul's Cathedral during the Blitz; when beauty stood out amid the surrounding devastation.

Less than two weeks ago they had sheltered inside that very same building when the rain had first come to Florence. He remembered how Anna had taken his hand and Hildegard had leant in to him, as if he, and he alone, could protect them from storm and thunder and all that might happen in the future. The members of the family were like pillars in a Renaissance cloister, he thought, individually contributing to the whole design. Together they formed something stronger and more beautiful than anything they could achieve on their own. Then, at the end of their lives, the least they might be able to say was that they had understood what it was to take part in something greater than themselves. They had known love. They would defend it against anything that came after it; taking risks in order to care for each other in the face of an indifferent world, working as hard as they could to nurture, preserve and protect what they had found and made. Such a love was too precious to put in jeopardy. It was life itself.

ALSO AVAILABLE BY JAMES RUNCIE

SIDNEY CHAMBERS AND THE PERILS OF THE NIGHT

Now a major, prime-time ITV series, *Grantchester*

1955. Canon Sidney Chambers, loveable priest and part-time detective, is back. Accompanied by his faithful Labrador, Dickens, and the increasingly exasperated Inspector Geordie Keating, Sidney is called to investigate the unexpected fall of a Cambridge don from the roof of King's College Chapel, a case of arson at a glamour photographer's studio and the poisoning of Zafar Ali, Grantchester's finest spin bowler.

Alongside his sleuthing, Sidney has other problems. Can he decide between his dear friend, the glamorous socialite Amanda Kendall and Hildegard Staunton, the beguiling German widow? To make up his mind Sidney takes a trip abroad, only to find himself trapped in a web of international espionage just as the Berlin Wall is going up.

'Runcie is emerging as Grantchester's answer to Alexander McCall Smith. The book brings a dollop of *Midsomer Murders* to the Church of England, together with a literate charm of its own' *Spectator*

'The series has a charming quaintness and deftly turning plot twists' *Independent*

'It takes a first-class writer to put together a convincing storyline for such unlikely circumstances . . . We should welcome him to the ranks of classic detectives' *Daily Mail*

ORDER YOUR COPY:

BY Phone: +44 (0) 1256 302 699; BY EMAIL: DIRECT@MACMILLAN.CO.UK

DELIVERY IS USUALLY 3–5 WORKING DAYS. FREE POSTAGE AND PACKAGING FOR ORDERS OVER £20.

ONLINE: WWW.BLOOMSBURY.COM/BOOKSHOP

PRICES AND AVAILABILITY SUBJECT TO CHANGE WITHOUT NOTICE.

B L O O M S B U R Y

ALSO AVAILABLE BY JAMES RUNCIE

SIDNEY CHAMBERS AND THE
PROBLEM OF EVIL

Now a major, prime-time ITV series, *Grantchester*

Canon Sidney Chambers is settling into married life with his German bride, but things in Grantchester rarely stay quiet for long. Our favourite clerical detective attempts to stop a serial killer; investigates the disappearance of a famous painting after a distracting display of nudity by a French girl in an art gallery; uncovers the fact that an 'accidental' drowning on a film shoot may not have been so accidental after all; and discovers the reasons behind the theft of a baby from a hospital in the run-up to Christmas, 1963. Meanwhile, Sidney wrestles with the problem of evil, attempts to fulfil the demands of Dickens, his faithful Labrador, and contemplates, as always, the nature of love.

'Chambers turns out to be a winning clergyman-sleuth . . . There is no denying the winning charm of these artfully fashioned mysteries' *Independent*

'Totally English, beautifully written, perfectly in period and wryly funny. More please!' *Country Life*

'Each tale is beautifully crafted and surprising. I hope for many more volumes' A. N. Wilson, *Spectator*

BLOOMSBURY